one

from

without

one

from

without

jack fuller

unbridled books

UNBRIDLED BOOKS

Copyright © 2016 by Jack Fuller

Library of Congress Cataloging-in-Publication Data
Fuller, Jack, author.
One from without / Jack Fuller
pages;cm
ISBN 9781609531300 (softcover)
PS3556.U44 O54 2016
813/.54—dc23
2015041595

1 3 5 7 9 10 8 6 4 2

Book Design by SH • CV

First Printing

for Debby

Two truths approach each other. One comes from within, one comes from without—and where they meet you have the chance to catch a look at yourself.

TOMAS TRANSTRÖMER

(translated by May Swenson)

THE

THREE-BODY

PROBLEM

1

On board mornings the Day and Domes senior staff gathered early. The unwritten rule was that the last one to arrive was late. Nothing broke the hush in the narrow, mahogany antechamber. Some looked over their scripts. Others checked and rechecked their BlackBerries. A few just stared at mirrors that weren't there. Eventually the corporate secretary opened the door to the boardroom, and the presenters filed through and took their places along the walls, always the same places, like members of a choir. This soothed Tom Rosten, the way the columns and rows of numbers on an Excel spreadsheet did.

Sam White had still been the CEO when Rosten attended his first meeting of the directors. It had been blowing that day too, and the brass chandelier hanging from the Tiffany dome above the long board table had swung as the building yielded to the wind, setting shadows to play over the sepia maps and lithographs that decorated the walls: Daniel Burnham's grand, unfinished plan for the city, the Marquette Building, the Rookery, and of course, the portrait of the company's Founder, his right hand resting on a stack of leather-bound ledgers, his left holding the lapel of his waistcoat.

Not long after that, a new man took over—Brian Joyce, the first CEO from outside the company. One of his early moves was to hire a lighting consultant who bathed the room in a uniform glow that eliminated shadows. The historic maps and lithographs were replaced by geometric paintings chosen by a committee chaired by the VP of Human Resources. The Founder's portrait moved to the hallway outside, where it gazed down from a distance greater than years. Though an element of charm was lost, Rosten was glad to have light in the corners.

Joyce called the meeting to order and moved briskly through the approval of the agenda and minutes, riding comfortably in his chair. Like so many people who care about appearances, he was both more than he seemed and less. If you had asked those closest to him what kind of man he was, they probably would have answered, "The kind he needs to be." Brian Brady Joyce: once the youngest commander of a destroyer in the Navy, now chairman, president, and chief executive officer of a publicly traded Fortune 1000 company. "Stars on my epaulets," he joked, as if he did not care about them.

Rosten rose from his chair when it was his turn to present. Open across his extended forearms rested a thick three-ring binder that contained the detail behind the financial summary it was his job as chief financial officer to discuss. Colleagues referred to the notebook as the Bible. Before he had gone back to school for a master's degree in business administration, Rosten had known nothing about accounting, let alone financial theory. He had been on the rebound from a short, dark career in government service, and escape into the numbers' clarifying light had been like being born again.

As he went to the front of the room, he noticed several directors' attention drifting upward to the hypnotic chandelier. He placed the Bible on the podium, adjusted the cant of the microphone, then clicked the remote to bring his first slide up on the enormous monitor over his left shoulder. Pausing a moment, he laid his right hand on the Bible. Let them gaze at the chandelier. Let them think about their upcoming week in Aspen. Have faith. Be not afraid.

When he finished presenting his routine report, he paused a beat to give the directors a chance at him, hoping they would not take it. Watch the chandelier. The wind is at our back. All is well. He saw Joyce twirling his fingers in a tiny barrel roll, which signaled him to move on.

Rosten touched the button on the remote. Behind him an animated slide was building.

"What page are you on?" said Lou Leavitt, the papers in his board book snicking back and forth like scythes.

"Just for fun, I had Tom prepare this technical analysis yesterday," said Joyce. "There wasn't time to get the presentation deck to you in advance."

"That's what e-mail is for," said Leavitt.

The corporate secretary was moving around the table serving a deck from each director's left, like a waiter with a side dish.

"Forgive me," said Joyce, "but I think you will like what you see."

At this point all eyes were on the screen. Rosten had warned Joyce that springing the long-term forecast on the board invited too much attention. The unexpected fixes the eye: A snake sliding from behind a rock. A lovely woman's face in a crowd, petal on a wet, black bough. No, that was from the other life.

Tempting as it was to turn to look at the screen, he kept his eyes on the directors, none of whom had eyes on him. Joyce had drilled this into all his senior managers: "Do not turn your back on the board." His point was respect, but Rosten's government service had taught him that behind respect was always the possibility of a snake.

The most quantitative directors were growing restless. He clicked the remote again. "You can see from this graph," he said, "that we have not even reached the first quartile on the upward growth trajectory." There was a strong correlation between Day and Domes's fortunes and the overall business cycle. Revenue growth tended to lag GDP by roughly six months both on the way up and coming down. Even though in building the graph Rosten had stuck to the conservative end of what economists were predicting for GDP, the picture on the screen of Day and Domes's future was so bright that he expected the board would feel the need to put on dark glasses. He braced for questions.

There were none. Even Sabad Chandrahary did not intervene. Rosten was not at all confident that the silence was assent, but at least it spared him from having to hide his concern that although history in general and the business cycle in particular tended to repeat, you could never be sure when circumstance would take you across a bridge with no return.

Joyce nodded. Rosten closed the Bible and carried it, spine down, under his arm to his place along the back wall.

"We should be able to get a little ahead of the agenda with the Audit Committee report, shouldn't we, Teddy?" said Joyce.

Teddy Diamond, committee chairman, was presenting out of order because he had to leave the meeting early. Trouble at home: a major embezzlement, which had caused a sell-off of the company's stock, a Moody's downgrade of its bonds, and today an emergency board meeting. Talk was that he was going to sacrifice a few sheep.

"I would hate for the brevity of my comments to leave my fellow directors yearning for more," Diamond said.

Audit's parched humor. Faint smiles all around.

Diamond's dark blue suit hardly stretched as he reached out for the pages Rosten had handed him at the boardroom door. His cuffs flashed in the light when he tapped the pages on the table. His suit fell on him as perfectly as if it were pinned to a mannequin. Not a vein stood out at his temples, not a single tremor passed through his fingers.

Rosten felt a tightening in the muscles of his own hands when Diamond began to speak, a lifting of his shoulders. Rosten's idea of the perfect report was 3D—direct, definitive, and done—because audit was a dark corner where you could not assume away the whiff of bad breath, the rumble of a troubled gut, the shifting eye, the lie-detector oscillations of the pulse. Rosten did everything in his power to make sure Day and Domes's financial controls were tight, locked with a cipher and double keys like a nuclear missile switch. But still . . .

He silently recited the words he had written as Diamond intoned them. "Clean audit . . . Unqualified opinion . . ." Diamond reported on the committee's meeting with auditors alone: no issues. The meeting with Internal Audit: no issues. No issues. No issues. No issues. Then came the motion, the vote to release the audited financial statements, the offhand ayes.

Diamond stood and gathered up his papers.

"Safe travels, Teddy," said Joyce.

Years before, when Rosten had interviewed for the position of treasurer at D&D, it had been like setting foot inside Old Campus for the first time. The lobby was a museum, the elevators designed to look original, the heavy porcelain pedestal sinks in the men's room mounted onto a granite floor with heavy brass fittings. This place had a history and wanted to show it.

Lately this had begun to change. When Sandra Harms came on board as vice president of Investor Relations, she persuaded Joyce to take the founding narrative out of the annual report and replace it with this: "Day and Domes is a global leader in the empowerment of businesses and individuals through comprehensive and reliable credit and associated data. It uses the most advanced technology to deliver information that drives sound customer acquisition decisioning, targeted messaging, and the management of accounts receivable and other risks."

Rosten did manage to preserve the history on the company's website:

Day and Domes was founded in 1906 by Thomas Woods Peterson. Son of a department store salesman, he parlayed his prodigious mathematical ability into admission to Harvard College. After graduating he traveled to England, where, to his father's dismay, he abandoned physics for a degree in history at Cambridge University.

Applying the methods of hard science to the study of the past, he immersed himself in the Domesday Book. This massive data set collected in the 11th Century for William the Conqueror eventually recorded the name and financial position of every landowner in most of England and parts of Wales. Peterson produced several published monographs based on it, but in academic circles his quantitative approach was seen as radical, and no faculty appointment that he considered adequate was forthcoming.

He turned away from the academy, returned home, and began applying his methods to contemporary needs like those of the department store where his father had worked. Success came quickly for the firm he named after its ancient inspiration. The building he built to house his creation he called the Dome.

In Peterson's time information was collected on paper and indexed in fat ledger books. Today, almost ten centuries after the Domesday Book and nearly a century after the company's founding, Day and Domes collects on its state-of-the-art computers more information every minute than William the Conqueror did during his entire reign.

Before joining D&D, Rosten had worked at one of the more go-go New York investment banks, which made its money by dancing along the brink of uncertainty. In contrast, Day and Domes was built on the solid ground of verified fact: John Doe lived at 2425 Ross Street and had a $175,000 mortgage on which he had always promptly paid the precise amount required. He had done this for seven years and five months. He had a MasterCard and Visa, on which he charged an aggregate average of $976 per month and had never had to pay a late fee or interest.

At the bank Rosten was an analyst. At D&D he got a title and a small staff, but making the move meant surrendering a lot of upside opportunity. In good times, even an analyst at the bank could bring in a bonus in the six figures. Making partner would add another digit to that. At Day and Domes, his salary was comfortable and steady, but the potential for windfall gain simply was not there.

"Why would you think of leaving your present position?" the interviewer from Human Resources had asked him.

"I like the risk profile here," Rosten had said.

"Good answer for a treasurer," said the interviewer.

It was still a good answer. Joyce was pushing for aggressive innovation, but he was no radical. He did not want to tear down the Dome, only to remodel it. He had a blueprint, which was why he'd had Rosten present the long-term growth forecast to the directors. The strategy Joyce had in mind was going to cost a lot of money to execute, and he needed the board to believe that, like John Doe, D&D could spend it and still be living within its means.

The discussion of Joyce's plan was the last item on the agenda, but before he could get to it, he needed to power through a fair amount of the routine business of business.

He asked the directors to turn to Tab 5, "Projects for Approval." First up was Sam Gunderman, standing in for the vice president and chief information officer, who was recovering from prostate surgery. Rosten thought well of this odd little man, who had more pure wattage than anyone else in the Dome. So why did he struggle so much with the simple things? Just get this done, Sam. Head down. No eye contact. And for God's sake, don't elaborate.

Gunderman stood, fumbling with his papers, and practically ran to the podium. Advance the slide, Sam. As if Gunderman had heard this, he touched the remote. No fumbling there. The device was like part of his body. In fact, he seemed surer of it than of his own mouth, which was so close to the microphone that the first words from his lips were gunshots. A couple of directors flinched.

"What page are you on?" Leavitt demanded. Gunderman did not answer. "It's a simple question."

"First page behind Tab 5," said Joyce, who had taken out a nail clipper, the sure sign that he was approaching the limit of his patience.

"Please . . . ," Gunderman said.

"Sam," said Joyce, "you can move a couple inches back from the microphone to good effect."

Joyce could not have spoken in a more self-controlled tone, but to Gunderman it seemed to carry the jolt of a six-pack of Red Bull. Words began running out of his mouth and skittering around the room for somewhere to hide. Unfortunately, Gunderman found his own refuge in technical jargon and digression, made worse by phrases like "I know you must be thinking . . ." or "Of course, it is not as simple as that." After several minutes of this, his first slide was still on the screen, untouched by explanation. Half the board was counting with the metronome of the chandelier.

The project Gunderman was supposed to be presenting should have sold itself. Reduced to its essentials, it was insurance. In old economy terms, Day and Domes wasn't much more than a landmark building and a lot of warehouses full of racks upon racks of digital equipment. This, however, was not what gave the company what the strategic planning consultants liked to call a distinctive competence that leads to a sustainable competitive advantage. Everyone had digital equipment, even kids in dorm rooms. What everyone did not have was unimpeachable data going back a long, long time, data that was righteous, purified with elaborate algorithms that spotted any foreign body and set in motion an elaborate immune response. Day and Domes not only knew its data; its data knew itself.

Still, it lived in a contaminated world. Ever-increasing amounts of information poured in each day, and the range was continuously widening: medical records, coupon redemptions, real-time purchase behavior from the Web. Customers deposited with Day and Domes the priceless information they collected because they trusted that it would be kept in sanitary conditions and protected from uninvited eyes. The more copious the data and the greater the multiplicity of sources, the more valuable it became to those to whom it did not belong. It was vital to D&D that it be able to secure the treasure. Terrorism, hacking, cyberwarfare—to Day and Domes these were cancer, stroke, and heart attack. Despite Gunderman's obscurities, the argument for the project was simple: Day and Domes needed to be a leader in digital security because trust was what it sold.

"I think the very complexity of what Sam is trying to lay out here," Joyce said, interrupting him, "is evidence of the critical challenge the project is designed to meet."

Gunderman clicked to the next slide, which bore the heading "Chaos and Cryptology." He began to speak of orbit diagrams, accumulation points, deterministic unknowables.

Bill Tobin closed his eyes.

"I get it that we have an issue," he said when he opened them again. "But frankly I can't follow a word you're saying."

"Small differences in initial conditions change everything in the encrypted space," Gunderman said. "The key is the nonasymptotic behavior of a nonlinear interactive process."

Sabby Chandrahary angled his index finger up from the surface of the table. Look his way, boss. Recognize him. He is the only one in the room who knows what Gunderman is trying to say.

A few board members weighed in with variations on the theme of discomfort. Finally, Joyce noticed the finger.

"It is a puzzlement," Chandrahary said. Coming from a man in a turban, this might in other circumstances have seemed funny. But there was a challenge to management on the table, and humor had fled the room. "It is ever thus in the field of cryptology. Puzzles within puzzles."

Nobody was looking at the chandelier now, except perhaps for Gunderman, who seemed to be using it to remind himself to take breaths.

"The advances in chaos theory have been thrilling," Chandrahary went on. "And yet chaos-based cryptology is unproven. I don't think it is safe for us to be on the bleeding edge when it comes to protecting our data."

Joyce looked at him without expression, which must have cost him a great deal of effort.

"I am glad that you have begun exploring this, Brian," Chandrahary said to Joyce as if no one else were in the room. "It is characteristic of your forward-leaning leadership. And yet I do think that in such an important area, it is crucial that the board be engaged. I would welcome the chance to have a more elaborate tutorial."

"Do you have a recommendation?" Joyce said.

"The proposal does not seem ripe for decision," said Chandrahary. Joyce scanned the directors.

"If everyone is all right with it," he said, "let's table this until next quarter." He put this as smoothly as if he thought it were a good idea.

Suddenly Gunderman's voice came from all directions on the speakers.

"Please don't delay," he said. When the initial p detonated, hands leaped to ears. "I'm sorry. I didn't explain the project well. But we have to begin testing this right away. The threats won't wait. They could be prying us open right now."

He was finally speaking English, but it was too late.

"Thank you for the note of caution," said Joyce.

"Installation for beta testing alone will take more than six months, best case," Gunderman said. "If anything should happen . . ."

"I want to assure the board," said Joyce, chin down, softly enunciating every word, "that we have complete confidence in the security measures already in place. This is an area in which we always cast very tight loops. Don't you agree, Sam?"

"Yes, sir," said Gunderman.

"Tight loops?" Bill Sebold whispered to Rosten. "Is that nautical?"

"Let's move on," said Joyce.

Gunderman stepped away from the podium, leaving his last, inscrutable slide on the screen.

"Before you go, could you get us to where we should be?" said Joyce, flicking his fingers toward the monitor.

Gunderman froze, then came to and turned to look. With remarkable speed he returned to the podium and raced through the slides he had not had a chance to show. Then the corporate logo appeared, haloed in silver.

Alexa Snow, vice president of Human Resources, was next up. As Gunderman slouched past her, she leaned back and turned her head away, like someone trying to avoid catching a cold. Her presentation of new software from a company called PeopleSoft

went without incident. Then it was Dick Chase's turn. He quickly won approval of $50 million and change for construction of
a new server farm. Sebold reported on the resolution of several lawsuits. Harms compared D&D's stock performance with
competitors' and quoted two glowing reports by analysts who
followed the industry. The last item before the executive session
went under the rubric "CEO's Comments."

"Thank you, everyone, for leaving us with a bit of time on the
clock," said Joyce, tall in his chair. "I want to use it to put some
context around our present situation and suggest some opportunities we want to explore.

"As our CFO's financial presentation indicated, we are at the
beginning of an extended upward cycle." As he spoke, he moved
his gaze down the long table, meeting every eye in turn. "In other
words, we have a lot of runway. Moreover, since our stock is out-
pacing a robust equities market, it is an appealing currency with
which to acquire what we need."

Several of the directors looked across at their colleagues; strong
currency can burn a hole in CEOs' pockets. But Joyce did not
go directly to the possibility of a major acquisition. Instead, he
turned to what the company might sell—the NumbersBank sub-
sidiary. It had built a good, though not leading, position in the
management of routine corporate archives, and it faced savage
price competition.

"Do we really want the cash?" said Chandrahary, because a
company with big reserves was as attractive to predators as a rich
widow.

"I believe we will be able to find uses for the proceeds," said
Joyce. "I'm sure I am not alone in this room in thinking that
we still don't have the scale or breadth to take advantage of the

growth opportunities in an increasingly data-driven world. Data is going to be very big. We cannot afford to be small."

"I'm not understanding why we need cash if we're confident of the strength of our stock," Chandrahary said.

There was a palpable gambler's rush in the room as directors began to sense the size of the bet they might be asked to make.

"If the opportunity is big enough, we might need both cash and stock," said Joyce, hands open upward. Then he brought them back to earth. "I want to assure you that we have not had any external conversations—beyond our bankers, of course—nor will we have any without a full airing in advance with you. That goes without saying."

"Good that you said it though," said Leavitt.

With that, Joyce nodded, and Rosten and his colleagues filed out into the Green Room.

The executive session went on for quite a while before Rosten heard a rustle inside the boardroom. He was on his feet by the time the corporate secretary opened the Green Room door and said, "They're done." Always first into the hallway, Rosten made himself available in case there were questions. Chandrahary approached him.

"Good initial effort," he said.

"I wondered why you weren't all over me," said Rosten.

"When it becomes important," said Chandrahary, lilting into the accent he usually suppressed, "you can be sure that I will be."

"I'll try to be ready," said Rosten.

Chandrahary gave a little bow, probably the same one his Sikh ancestors had given the British, knowing them to be unworthy of it.

The rest of the senior team had poured into the hallway and was making conversation with the directors as they climbed into their overcoats. Joyce went to the elevator hallway. He liked to see them all the way to the front door, to make sure they didn't return.

The long table in the boardroom belonged to management again, and Rosten went directly to his customary chair, the one where Leavitt had sat.

"Could you believe Gunderman?" said Snow, arranging the front of her jacket just so.

"I didn't think Human Resources would ever be surprised by something as human as a case of the nerves," said Rosten.

"Well, there's more for him to be nervous about now," said Sebold.

"He should have taken a lesson from Teddy Diamond and cast a tight loop," said Chase.

"Diamond's world is imploding," said Sebold, "and you did not even see a quiver."

"It was excruciating," said Rosten.

"It was Teddy's finest hour," said Chase.

"Teddy can fend for himself," said Rosten. "I was talking about Gunderman."

"I thought he was going to burst into tears," said Snow.

"At some point in your life you must have felt shame, Alexa," said Rosten.

"It has no place in a boardroom," she said.

"What doesn't?" said Joyce, who had come silently through the door.

"Tears," said Rosten.

"What is there to cry about?" said Joyce. "We won."

He sat, leaned forward, and bounced both hands on the board table like a boy with a ball.

2

Gunderman sat on the couch looking at the sand-colored rug through the top of the end table.

"Maybe it would have been better for all concerned if they had just fired me."

"Did you want that?"

"You mean a package."

"Package?"

"Severance. They call it a package. Guys laugh about it. 'Alexa Snow will handle your package.'"

"You weren't forced to accept the new position."

"I have a daughter in high school."

"And a wife."

"Yes, a daughter and a wife."

"Is it really only about providing?"

"Did the company ask you to push me toward the door?"

"I think you know the answer to that, Sam."

"They're paying for these sessions. Your Eames chair. The upholstered couch. The box of tissues. The clock that always faces away from me."

"I'm sure they don't need my help to let you go. In any case, I don't seek or accept guidance from the company on what we do here. Day and Domes is just another third-party payer, like an insurance company."

"There's a comfort."

"The only contact I have had was my initial conversation with your supervisor, which we have already discussed."

"His first idea was for me to take lessons in oral presentation. I should have done it. When I declined, he pushed me to come to you. Obviously I wasn't cutting it. Go see him, Lawton said. Try him out. An executive coach, he called you. He didn't say psychiatrist."

"Psychiatrists are MDs. I'm not."

"No pills."

"Doctor of philosophy."

"What kind of philosophy?"

"They call what I do self psychology. I help explore the person an individual has come to live inside."

"Sounds totally subjective."

"The subjective is who we are."

He arrived home early, not having called. Her Lexus wasn't out front, but he tarried in the garage in the old Toyota anyway. She was a presence, even when she wasn't there. He dreaded having to tell her. But he'd have more time for her now. He could put that out there. She would want to know about pay. There would be no cut in salary, but he wouldn't be getting the annual increases and bonuses that they were used to. You can't have everything, honey. Not as much money, but more of me. She wouldn't buy it. In the double-entry bookkeeping of their relationship, assets never equaled liabilities.

The only way to deal with his demotion wasn't pluses and minuses. Just say it is what it is. We'll be fine. Don't worry. It's all good. And so on.

So why was he sitting in a cold car behind an empty house?

"It isn't punishment, Sam," Dell Lawton had said as they had sat in his office, the glass wall exposing them to the whole IT Department. "Think of it as a fresh start."

"They didn't give me a chance to explain," Gunderman said. "They didn't cut me a millimeter of slack."

"They never do. They expect you to cast a tight loop every time."

Lawton had dropped a lot of weight since the operation. Too much. He looked the way Gunderman felt.

"I should have gone to charm school like you wanted me to," Gunderman said, unhooking the wire hangers of his glasses from behind his ears and rubbing at his eyes. "I lost everyone in the room."

"Not Tom Rosten," said Lawton.

Charlene buzzed. Lawton lifted his hands in apology and took the call. Gunderman put his glasses back on and looked toward the shelves above the credenza, resting his eyes on the portrait photos of Lawton's stunning wife and his children by her predecessor. No more babies now unless the current Mrs. Lawton had one started already. Gunderman had heard of couples who banked sperm before the surgery. He couldn't quite imagine the woman in the photo making a baby that way. In fact, he couldn't really imagine her at all or what it would be like to be with such a woman, let alone to be too damaged to make her happy in a world full of other men who would love to try.

Other than the photos, the only things on the shelves were the kind of corporate trophies that Gunderman shoved into boxes in the attic: awards encased in plastic, embossed pencil holders, group photographs taken at forgotten off-sites, little ovals and obelisks mounted on soft wood. Not a book in sight, not even *The Seven Habits of Highly Effective People*.

In contrast, in Rosten's office the shelves bore finance monographs, military histories, fat biographies of statesmen. Separate from these was a small group of volumes, most of them slim. He recognized only the sonnets of Shakespeare. One day Rosten had caught him turning his head horizontal to read the spines.

"A boss of mine once told me to ditch those," Rosten said. "He told me they made me seem unserious."

"Joyce?" said Gunderman.

"This was before D&D," Rosten said. "Once, even before that, I actually had a boss who hired me just because of books like those."

He swiveled, rose, and took down an old volume, which he handled as if it were blown glass.

"He gave me this," he said, opening it to the title page and handing it across the desk.

Personae of Ezra Pound. London. Elkin Mathews, Vigo Street. MCMIX. Signed by the author and dated September 15, 1909. Gunderman did not know anything about rare books, but he recognized the poet's name.

"Aren't you afraid it will be stolen?"

21

"Pound is out of favor," Rosten said.

Gunderman opened to a few pages at random then returned it, holding it out flat on his palms, an offering.

"Did you see the inscription?" said Rosten.

"It says 'Ezra Pound.'"

"The other one."

Rosten found the place and turned the book so Gunderman could read it. In the white space was this message, written in a small, shaky hand:

> *For an old bitch gone in the teeth,*
> *For a botched civilization.*
> *Ernest Fisherman*
> *Dec. 22, 1989*

"Who is he?" Gunderman asked.

"That's more than we have time for," said Rosten. "Anyway, he went out of favor too."

Then Rosten closed the book and replaced it on the shelf carefully but surely, the way a librarian might.

Lawton's call was dragging on. Gunderman stood. He was being traded away. There was really nothing more to say. As he turned to leave, Lawton held his finger out and made a show of struggling to push the call to a conclusion. Finally, he succeeded and put the telephone back into its cradle.

"It isn't that I don't see your value," he said to Gunderman.

"And Rosten went along," said Gunderman.

"The new regulations under Sarbanes-Oxley," said Lawton. "He needed someone with your skills."

"Which is a different thing than needing me."

"It was Joyce's idea, actually."

"Joyce," said Gunderman.

"He's not the man you think he is."

"I guess Rosten didn't have much choice then."

"This isn't passing bad cards to the left to improve your hand," said Lawton. "I believe Rosten is genuinely pleased."

"I wonder what made him think I could be an auditor."

"You'll mainly be checking up on me, actually," said Lawton. "I've always been good to you, haven't I, Sam?"

Gunderman went from Lawton's office to Rosten's, where his new boss could not have been more direct and businesslike in laying out the responsibilities of the job. Gunderman would be reporting to Max Poole, director of Internal Audit, but in the Finance Department they did not stand on ceremony.

On the shelf over the credenza, the Shakespeare and the other slim volumes were still there.

"Whatever happened to the boss who wanted you to get rid of the books?" Gunderman asked.

"He's the CEO of a Fortune 500 company," Rosten said. "I get a Christmas card from him every year with a picture of him with his wife and grandkids. Sometimes on skis."

"And the other boss, the one who gave you the signed book," Gunderman said. "He must not have liked you very much to write what he did."

"I don't think his mind categorized things by like and dislike."

"He called you an old bitch gone in the teeth."

"That wasn't me," said Rosten. "It was the cause we served."

The steering wheel had turned to ice. The windows had fogged and were becoming laced with frost. Gunderman wasn't going to find the right words for Maggie here in the garage. He took the key out of the ignition, climbed from the car, and locked it.

At first the house was silent around him, for which he was grateful. Then came a voice.

"Hi, Dad."

"Hi, sweetie," he said, turning toward the family room, where she sat among textbooks.

"I made you jump," she said.

"Not as big an accomplishment as you might think," he said, accepting a sidelong hug, which she had learned when she began to fill out.

After releasing him, she went toward the refrigerator.

"You want anything?" she said.

"I'm fine."

"Then stay a while."

She knew how to make him feel awkward. Women seemed to have an instinct for it.

"Might as well, right?" he said.

"Mom's not home," she said.

He removed his coat and put it on a hook by the back door.

"We wouldn't have hot chocolate, would we?" he said. "I'm a little chilled."

"Don't tell me the car heater's out again," she said. "You seriously should get a new one. A red convertible."

While she was warming the milk, he settled himself in the family room, where she gazed at him from every point of the compass—in person through the wide door to the kitchen, of course, but also from over there on the bookshelf snowshoeing in the woods, from next to the television posing in front of the net in pads and skates, from the end table at eighth grade graduation.

"Do you have a game tonight?" he said.

Silly question. Hockey was always. Games at Thanksgiving, at Christmas, at Easter. Games on Father's Day. In summer the local rink was available to the girls' team at reasonable hours, but boys had priority during the winter, so her team had to use a distant facility late.

"At 8:30," she said.

"May I drive you?"

"It would be better in a convertible."

"Maybe Mom will let us use her car," he said.

"She's going somewhere, I think."

"Well, then, you'll just have to scrunch down in the seat so nobody will see you."

She brought him a steaming Day and Domes mug. He warmed his hands on the list of the company's values: INNOVATION, INTEGRATION, INTENSITY, INSPIRATION, INTEGRITY. The five I's.

"Of course I feel I have integrity. They must think so too. They're making me an auditor."

"Not honesty. What I'm asking you is whether you feel you have surrendered too much of your self to the organization, your personhood. That kind of integrity."

"I honestly don't know what you mean."

"You certainly seem to be a unique individual."

"That's a new one. Usually they just say that I'm out of it."

"Who does?"

"The secretaries. We call them the Admin News Network."

"They say it to your face?"

"They might as well."

"Maybe what they are saying is that you are you, more than you know."

"Could you actually stay for the game?" Megan asked.

"I'm sorry," he said. "I was off somewhere."

"It would be great if you could."

"That's the idea, sweetie."

She sat down next to him.

"Are you saying you came home so you could watch me play?" she said.

"That's a pretty good reason, isn't it?"

Megan picked up a trig textbook and set it on her lap.

"That means you had other reasons," she said.

"I don't need others."

"I'm onto you," she said. "Oh, am I ever onto you."

She got into her trig, from time to time punching something into a calculator, fingers quick on the little keys. He wished his reason had been pure: just to be close beside her on the couch, with her totally onto him and yet staying there.

The front door opened. Footsteps.

"What are you doing here?" his wife said.

"Happy to see you too," he said.

"He's going to take me to the game," Megan said.

"Betty Cadwalader's set to give you a ride," said Maggie.

"I'll call her," said Megan.

"It isn't that simple," said Maggie.

Plans were important to Maggie, but it wasn't as if arranging for him to do the driving was trig.

"I can take Anna too," he said. "That way you'll both have the night off."

"I wish I'd had a little warning," said Maggie.

"It just takes a phone call," said Megan.

"All of a sudden everything is up in the air," said Maggie.

Megan had her new cell phone out, punching a single key and putting it to her ear. Her father's daughter, she had already figured out all the features.

"Hi. It's me. I'm going to the game with my dad. Yeah. Very nice. You can come with us if you want. OK. See you there then."

She snapped the phone shut.

"All set," she said.

"I wish we'd talked about it a little more," said Maggie.

Megan picked up her book and calculator and left the room.

"Sweetie?" he called to her. It did not even slow her down.

Maggie tossed her purse and keys on the coffee table and slumped in the chair across from the couch.

"If we had a son, I'd be the one butting heads," he said.

"I thought it was your head I ran into," she said, standing up and leaving him there to listen to her loud on the stairs.

Well, at least he would have some time with Megan on the long drive. He would get her talking about school, maybe even boys. She was easier with him about such things than he had ever been with his parents. At least she was when Maggie didn't add a third center of gravity to the equation, making the whole thing unsolvable.

Maybe they'd talk about college. It was still a ways off, but he knew she must be thinking about it. Perhaps he could sound her out about their next vacation. He didn't have many of those left with her. He wondered if she might want to see some of the national parks out west or maybe spend a week in New York City. He hoped she would not want to bring along a friend.

Maggie returned and sat down next to him where Megan had been. He leaned her way until they touched briefly.

"I'll go with you tonight," she said.

"You really don't have to," he said. "I don't want to ruin your plans."

"You already did," she said.

"We'll have a regular family outing," he said.

The north wind brought in dry snow that squeaked underfoot. After dinner Gunderman got the shovel from the back porch and cleaned the wood stairs, trying not to take a divot with the blade. Then he did the walk to the garage, the gangway between their house and the Fords', then on to the front. When he finished, he looked back at his work: sharp-edged, right up against the lawn so just a shadow of grass showed. The snow continued, and soon it would cover the pavement again.

He put the shovel at the top of the front steps, leaning it next to the wrought-iron mailbox. Maggie's car needed warming. He went to it and knocked his shoes against the rocker panel before getting in. The engine fired up beautifully. Maybe he would take this one and get her a new car. Not right away. They would have to see how the money worked out in the new position, get Megan going in college. Maybe then.

He turned on the radio and switched it from all-news to WFMT, which he had programmed on her last preset button.

The announcer was reading an ad for a play at the Steppenwolf Theater. After freshman year he had always driven himself to and from college. Crossing Pennsylvania, for long stretches he couldn't find anything but country stations. Then came Ohio and the sounds of Motown straight down from Detroit. There was a point as he approached the Indiana line where he could finally pick up WFMT. He would spin the dial and hear the soft voice of the announcer saying the names of the conductors and soloists of all nations, pronouncing them just right, and at least in one small sense, he felt at home.

Back on campus, he never did. His friends were not social, not really even quite friends. To women he was the invisible man as he walked with his stack of punch cards to the computer center. Then suddenly he crossed Maggie's trajectory. In chaos theory they talk about "strange attractors" that organize the welter into some kind of shape. Maggie used to do that for him.

Mother and daughter burst from the front door and marched down the sugar-sprinkled walk to the car. Maggie got in next to him, Megan in back.

"I told you he'd be waiting," said Megan.

"You tell me a lot of things," said Maggie.

"My fault," said Gunderman. "Do you want to drive?"

"I don't care one way or another," said Maggie.

The trip was as silent as dinner had been, except for the old-ies station that had replaced WFMT, a family compromise: "Up on the Roof," "Georgia on My Mind," "A Little Help from My Friends." The wind swirled the snow in the headlights like a flurry of zeros and ones.

He had first met Maggie in the university dispensary, where she did work-study.

"You look lost," she said as he inched toward the reception desk.

"It's that I'm, well, I've been having these . . . but not always. They kind of come and go," he said.

"Pains? Dizzy spells?"

"Yes," he said.

"Both?"

"No," he said. "I mean I'm just, well, just not right."

The way she gave a little laugh actually pulled him in instead of pushing him out to the edge of the universe.

"So what are you feeling right now?" she said.

He looked at the blouse tight around her, the eyes bright, the hair shining like a precious metal, and he was ashamed to say.

"Well, at least you're getting some color back," she said. "Why don't you take a seat? The doctor won't be long."

"Sam Gunderman," he said. "I mean, don't you need to take my name?"

"I know who you are," she said. "You're the one who always answers questions in Symbolic Logic. If p, then q. It isn't really fair. I mean, you're a math major, right? 'Mr. Gunderman, can you please deliver these humanists from their misery?' The old fart actually seems to like you."

"Why don't I recognize you?" he said.

"You're in your own world," she said. "Minding your p's and q's. Look, try to help the doctor. Answer his questions. Pretend you're in class."

"You'll be there?"

"I always sit way back," she said.

"I mean with the doctor."

"I'm not the one who's dizzy."

That was obvious. She always seemed to be at equilibrium, never swept away. Eventually, he felt that this was his fault.

The sports complex smelled of mildew and warm ice. Megan raced ahead to get suited up.

"Would you like something?" he asked Maggie. "A Coke?"

"Diet," she said and kept on moving when he stopped for it.

The high ceiling echoed with the carom of pucks and scrape of skates.

"Well, who have we here?" said a voice.

It was Bill Cadwalader.

"They let me out of my cage early," Gunderman said.

"You work too hard," said Cadwalader.

He was a stocky, talkative guy who looked like he did much of his work at home with free weights. Rinkside, he was never at a loss for advice, most of it directed at poor Anna. "Center it! Center it! Left foot! Shoot!" he would shout from his place in the bleachers just above the level of the Plexiglas. Sometimes Betty would shush him, but he was not a man who shushed easily.

"The job keeps me occupied," said Gunderman.

"You've got to learn to chill," said Cadwalader.

Anytime Anna wasn't on the ice, Cadwalader lounged back, his arms stretched across the bleacher bench behind him, as if the whole world were his TV.

"You must be talking to Maggie," Gunderman said.

"If she accuses me, I'll deny it," said Cadwalader, hale with delight. "You buying?"

"Sure," said Gunderman and went back into his pocket.

"Whatever you're having," said Cadwalader. "You know, Megan is really coming on. Her puck handling. Her shot."

"Her grades. Her piano playing," said Gunderman.

"Don't let her spread herself too thin."

"I wish I'd had a little more breadth when I was her age," Gunderman said. "Or now."

"She has a chance to play at a Division 1 college," said Cadwalader. "That'd save you a hell of a lot of money, old sport. But it takes focus."

"I'm not sure it's what she wants."

"At their age they don't know," said Cadwalader. "You've got to do the wanting for them."

Gunderman handed Cadwalader the drink and carried his two supersized cups to the bleachers, where he spotted Maggie.

"I'll have to swim home," she said.

She took a sip, and he put his hand in the small of her back. At one time, before they were married, she might have shaped herself to the touch. The important point now was that she still accepted it. That was what happened over time. Acceptance.

"I wish you could be at games more often," said Maggie

"I may be able to," he said.

On the weekend he would have to get Maggie off somewhere where he could talk logically to her about their new situation. If p, then q.

"I hope she shows you a good game tonight," Maggie said. "She's really coming on."

3

It had been a good table: the Stones, the Abbotts, the O'Connells, and Tom Rosten with a new friend, whose name Donna Joyce had already lost. The room, as always, had been too loud for conversation, and once the chairs of the ball had given their speeches, it had gotten even louder. Now the band was playing "Girl from Ipanema," which should have licked gently at the ear like a warm ocean kissing the beach. Amped through huge speakers, it was a tropical depression.

The O'Connells, who had flanked her throughout the meal, had gotten happy enough on the merlot to go to the dance floor. Tom and his date had sneaked off somewhere, perhaps to an early exit. The Stones and Abbotts were working the room, as was Brian, of course. This left Donna widowed, and OK with that.

The hospital's women's board had chosen a "Pirates of the Caribbean" theme. Every place setting had a little faux-leather sack full of Godiva chocolate doubloons wrapped in gold foil. Bird-of-paradise floral arrangements that must have cost a fortune screened one side of the table from the other. Remarkably realistic cutlasses held the flowers upright. Last night it had been something antebellum—in a careful, thoughtful sort of way, just Spanish moss and peach blossoms—and Monday night Harry Potter.

Brian had arrived uncharacteristically late. She hadn't worried, because Marcia had called to say he was running behind, which was always a personal defeat for Marcia, who would have fit in at the Royal Observatory at Greenwich. Donna had lingered near the main door of the ballroom, passing truncated moments with dear friends, interrupted by introductions of people she knew she would forget. When Brian finally appeared, he sailed right past her, as if into battle. When she caught up with him and touched his arm, he jumped.

"It's you," he said, as if she were the fleet come to the rescue.

He led her into a crowd that would not let them through without paying a bounty. As they crossed the room, late enough that people watched, Brian failed to notice when the Cardinal rose to his full red-draped height to greet them. She took Brian's arm, slowing and turning him, and said, "Your Eminence."

"Brian," the Cardinal said straight past her, "we missed you at Holy Name last Sunday."

"Early mass," Brian said, managing a wink as he took the hand the Cardinal presented him.

"You will be at our event in April, I hope," said the Cardinal.

"Three tables," said Brian. "Donna and I are bringing the kids."

"A fine example," said the Cardinal. "I would have expected nothing less."

Whether the example was for their children or in the number of tables went unclarified as the Cardinal declined into his chair to the fussing of the clerics around him. The whole ballroom was beginning to settle down. She could see the length of it under the chandeliers of crystal icicles that sparkled over the Caribbean. The master of ceremonies, with his famous voice, had begun to speak as they reached their table and made a once-around, bent over as they moved from guest to guest so as not to induce them to rise.

During the meal the O'Connells and the Stones had taken turns talking with Donna. Across the table Rosten had seemed easy with his latest date; whatever was distracting Brian tonight did not appear to involve him. Of all the senior executives, Brian seemed to trust him the most. At first Donna had not, since it was no secret that the man had once served in the Central Intelligence Agency. But over time she had warmed to him. He was polite but straightforward. She sensed that if she had some lettuce stuck between her teeth, he would simply tell her.

She really did not know much about the people Brian worked with. He protected her from office politics as much as he could so that she could focus on her own work. Of course, he couldn't come to every concert, let alone travel with her when the symphony toured. She did not like it that they spent so much time apart, which was why, even though she did not fish, she loved the trips they took together in search of the perfect river. Sometimes she sat on the bank watching him cast, the line unfurling from the rod like notes from a flute.

Because of Brian's job, she did not have to take on viola students to pay the bills, though she always liked to have one or two of special promise. There was enough live-in help that she had no chores and the children were always well looked after, not to mention the wing he had built for her to practice in and the new Steinway C for accompanists.

He loved her music with an intensity untempered by learning.

When they met, he was not yet forty and just home from the Navy. He had been at sea much of his adult life up to that point, with little access to the refinements found on land. And yet, from the beginning he had simply loved to hear her play. For her this was more than enough compensation for having to endure, from time to time, a dance band blaring Jobim.

"May I?"

She turned and there was Rosten, solo, bowing to be heard. She was not as accustomed to seeing him in a tuxedo as she was some of the others. She could not quite picture him in his past life. Even in evening dress, he was no James Bond. His bow tie bobbed like an oboist's.

"Thank you for having us," he said as he sat down in one of the O'Connells' chairs.

"I'm sure it was a command performance," she said. "But nice of you to pretend. I hope the band didn't drive your companion from the building. I never met her properly. I'm ashamed to say I don't even remember her name. She's new, isn't she?"

"Old, actually."

"Well, she certainly doesn't look it."

"We've known each other since college."

"Did you find her on the Internet and rekindle a spark, the way they say people do these days?"

"She's married," he said, "with bright children and a Manhattan apartment. In town on business. We would have gone to hear you play if there had been a concert."

"You'll have to let me know when you're going to bring someone to Symphony Center," she said.

"I've always wondered, do you sometimes get so full of the music that you keep playing after?"

She glanced at his eyes to be sure he was not making a joke.

"It's work," she said, "just like yours."

"A calling, I always thought," he said.

"I hope yours is too," she said.

He picked up the little sack of chocolate doubloons and weighed it in his hand.

"I was drawn to it," he said.

"Well, good," she said. "But I'm sure there are days and there are days."

"Lately, it's been nothing but blue skies."

He was different from the others Brian had close to him. Not like a spy, but not corporate either.

"Do you play?" she asked.

"My mother tried and tried, but I was hopeless."

"I know the feeling," she said. "With me it's balancing the checkbook."

He stood, and she saw that his companion was heading back to the table. The band was taking a break.

"Well, I'm glad it's blue skies at Day and Domes," Donna said. "From what Brian tells me, you're a big part of that."

"I just keep the checkbook balanced."

The woman was upon them now. Donna stood. Closer up, it was plausible that she was the same age as Rosten, also that they were simply friends. She had a ring, which didn't prove much, but she moved too easily to be a lover facing the boss's wife among cutlasses.

"We met earlier," the woman said.

"I'm sorry it was so perfunctory," said Donna.

"Grace Bondurant," Rosten said.

"Thank you," said Donna. "I can memorize a sonata, but a name goes through my head without stopping, I'm afraid."

"Tom told me you play viola in the symphony," Grace said.

"And you?" said Donna.

"Investment banking," Grace said.

"That must have been quite a school you two went to," said Donna.

"Who says English majors have no future?" said Grace.

Just then Brian finished his circuit of the room.

"Looks like a cabal," he said.

"Two recovering humanists and one who never took the cure," said Donna. "Have you met Grace Bondurant?"

"Yes," said Brian, not looking at any of them. "I hate to break this up."

"It's been a pleasure," said Donna, offering her cheek to Rosten and his companion.

"Likewise," said Grace. "Next time I hope we can hear you play."

"Make him bring you backstage," Donna said. Brian was already edging away from them. Donna followed and at a certain distance turned and waved.

"Are you all right?" she said to Brian.

"Robert will meet us at the curb on the south side of the building," he said. "The pickup circle is always so clogged." He looked at his watch.

"Something is off," she said. "Can you talk about it?"

The band was overdoing "Fly Me to the Moon" when they reached the exit.

"Do you have a coat?" Brian shouted.

"I took a chance," she said.

"Good," he said, and they escaped the room and rode the escalator single file to the ground level.

"Over there," he said, pointing to an empty corner with two chairs and a table with a lamp. She followed, and he looked about them as they sat down. He put his elbows on his black, creased knees and spoke softly.

"Why did you apply for a new credit card for us?" he said.

"Sorry?" she said.

"I'm not accusing you," he said. "I didn't want it to sound like that."

"What would we need another card for?"

He reached into his pocket and pulled out his nail clipper. He did not open it. He just turned it in his hand.

"Tell me," she said.

"You didn't send in an application?"

"Of course not."

"Well, we were turned down."

She laughed.

"Must have been quite a card," she said. "What comes after platinum?"

"I don't know what to think," he said.

"Some wires crossed."

He opened and closed the nail clipper until she said, "You're worried."

"It's very puzzling."

"Tom Rosten should be good at mysteries, shouldn't he?" she said.

4

When the CEO calls at noon and invites you to lunch, you put your Au Bon Pain sandwich away, let the Diet Coke go flat in its cup on your desk, and hustle to get down to the lobby before him. Eating was a continuation of work by other means. Of course, anybody else at Day and Domes would envy such access to the boss, but Rosten had been looking forward to the ham and Swiss that was now giving up its flavor to the blend of left-behinds in the office fridge.

"Let's go to the Berghoff," said Joyce as he came off the elevator. "How's that sound?"

With its squat waiters with coins in their aprons and menu that hadn't changed in decades, it wasn't the sort of place people would expect to find a CEO, which was probably what commended it to Joyce. He was the kind of rich man who did not mind being seen driving around Kenilworth in a rusty old Jeep.

"The Berghoff was my father's favorite," said Rosten.

"It never grows old," said Joyce, though it had.

When they got settled, he leaned directly into a story about his father taking him fishing on a river in Idaho. Apparently he hadn't brought Rosten to lunch for business. Rosten wanted to believe they were talking as friends, but there was something insistent about the way Joyce spoke, as if it was not simply to get away for a few moments but to flee.

"The fish weren't especially big," he said. "But the current, that was something else. It was so strong I had to lock arms with my dad to wade into position. I was scared of falling in and being swept away, but I stood there and cast into the rapids. The danger was a rush. Where you've been, you've got to know what I mean. The fear and the thrill together. In the end I got a reward for the risk. I wrestled it from the deep. Do you see what I mean? But you don't strike me as somebody who spent a lot of time in the woods as a kid."

Rosten's father had not had much taste for it, having been a Marine in Korea, where he had been decorated for courage in the face of the Chinese onslaught. His mother used to say that at Chosin Reservoir he had decided on an indoor life. But one summer, when Rosten was twelve, he announced that every American youngster needed to see the country's natural splendors.

"So we packed up the Chevy and lighted out for the territories," Rosten said over his Wiener schnitzel.

Toward the end of their trip, they stopped at Rocky Mountain National Park. By this time Rosten had had his fill of motels smelling of stale cigars and hand soap, let alone the bugs and long trails to nowhere. Then one morning his father woke him before dawn, gave him a package of sticky buns and a waxed carton of milk he had submerged overnight in ice water in the sink, and promised him a sight he would never forget.

They drove to a hillside, which looked like every other hillside they had seen in the states whose fresh decals decorated the Chevy's rear bumper. Along the dirt road Rosten noticed other unfortunate children in cars, all of which faced toward a hillside a ways away.

"There's going to be a burn," his father said.

"A fire?" Rosten said.

"To clear the understory so the forest can replenish itself," his father said.

"They control it, Tommy," his mother said. "There's nothing to be afraid of."

This made Rosten lose interest and start reading for the umpteenth time the Classic Comics he had bought for the trip. Soon, though, he put them down. Bright yellow fire trucks began swarming the hillside. Men his father called smoke jumpers hurried around, cutting fire breaks and spreading out hoses that they then attached to big tanker trucks. Even before Rosten saw the first flame, the activity appeared as intense as life and death.

Once ignited, the fire spread quickly, sending up a wall of smoke and flashing sparks. At first, miraculously, the trees themselves did not burn, but then at the crest of the hill they exploded, a line of torches against the sky. Then the wind shifted, and the smell of smoke grew thicker. The firefighters fell back and began cutting down trees and frantically digging a wider trench. Soon a yellow truck came careening down the dirt road where the observers were.

"You must evacuate the area!" a man shouted through a bullhorn, its metallic buzz a thing so outside of nature that it might have come from *The War of the Worlds*. "You must evacuate! Now!"

His father pulled into the line of retreating cars as calmly as if he were going to the grocery store. When they checked out of the motel that afternoon to head to the next park on their TripTik, Rosten could smell the smoke in the lobby.

"There's a lesson for you, son," his father said. "Sometimes it's best just to leave well enough alone."

"Is that what you're thinking?" Joyce said across the varnished oak table in the Berghoff.

"Don't you ever ask yourself whether we could be betting the company too soon?" said Rosten.

"Time is running ahead of us," said Joyce. "Time is the fire."

In the weeks after the Berghoff lunch, Joyce held Rosten at a distance. Maybe he had not liked the note of caution. Rosten was all right with that. His father used to say that you weren't earning your pay if you weren't willing to give your boss honest counsel and take your punishment.

It had been one of his more useful lessons, though at the time Rosten would not have guessed any of them would be. He used to dread the days when classes were suspended for teacher training, because his father always used the occasion to drag him downtown to the First National Bank to teach him "the way the world works" and praise the rhythm and ring of typewriters, the flutter of bills through fingers, the tap and scrape of adding machines.

"Someday you will appreciate the music of commerce," he said. "You can do a lot worse than getting yourself established at a bedrock company like this one. You may turn up your nose, but it's as safe as working for the federal government, and it pays better."

That was before First National merged into the National Bank of Detroit, which merged with Banc One Corporation, which disappeared into J. P. Morgan Chase, which made the acquisitive CEO the big man in New York that he had always yearned to be and left Chicago without its largest financial institution. As for the safety of government work, Rosten's father certainly had not been thinking about the Marines or the CIA.

There were never many cars on the executive level of the garage when Rosten arrived in the morning. Back in his father's day, everyone who wanted to have a future made sure they beat their boss in to work and stayed until he left. Many a night Rosten's mother muttered darkly, waiting for the late train to arrive as the dinner got dry on the stove. Now things were upside down. The only one who regularly beat Rosten to the office was Joyce, though today the car was missing, probably taken by his driver to be washed.

The parking structure had an elevator that connected to the lobby of the Dome. Rosten walked through Joyce's empty space and pushed the button. When the elevator opened, it released a disreputable odor. The little diode showed L as soon as the door closed, but the car barely seemed to be moving until it finally bumped to a stop. The back door opened. Maurice looked up from the security desk and tipped his finger to his brow. Rosten nodded past him. The brass-clad elevator that rose through the Dome smelled of polish from the overnight cleaning. He got off on his floor, dropped his coat and briefcase in his office, and took the stairs the rest of the way.

He needed to pass his ID in front of the scanner to open the doors of the stairwell. They joked that when the doors stopped opening, it was time to pay a visit to Snow's office and pick up your package. Rosten's ID got a green light and a click. The industrial carpet and heavy fire doors made the stairway so silent that it seemed to erase his presence.

Until now, Joyce had kept Investor and Public Relations out of the acquisition loop. "The less Sandra Harms knows," he said, "the more she can deny." The last thing they needed was for somebody to figure out that Day and Domes was planning to acquire a Silicon Valley darling. "You're the spook," Joyce said. If Fisherman had been there, he would have quoted Benjamin Franklin to the effect that three may keep a secret, if two of them were dead. But, of course, Fisherman himself was one of the casualties.

Eventually, Rosten persuaded Joyce that they were better off with Harms being in the loop: She couldn't very well spin people away from the truth if she didn't know exactly where it was. So Rosten was going to brief her this morning, and he thought that it would be a nice touch if Joyce joined them. Maybe it would even close some of the distance between his boss and him. But there was no light under Joyce's door.

The elevator played Mozart on the way down. They had Donna Joyce to thank for this. Rosten held the door open when he reached his floor, just to let a phrase play out, then he stepped out into a silent corridor. No light came through the masked windows of the conference room. His key was a little stiff in the big, new dead-bolt lock. Inside, he flipped on the overhead fluorescents, which hesitated a moment before illuminating the conference table scattered with legal pads and the walls hung with large pages torn from the two large easels in the corners. Written on them were lists, calculations, skeletal spreadsheets in black and red marker pen: corporate wallpaper.

They had been careful to keep some things obscure—A Co., B Co., C Co., and of course New Co. Fisherman would have found this pathetic, but Rosten was a long way from that world, where everything could become its opposite in the blink of an eye like one of those optical tricks in which a cube turned itself inside out or a rabbit became a duck. Here two plus two always equaled four. If it quacked like a duck, you did not have to worry that it was a hunter.

An interloper might not have guessed, if he had stumbled into the jumble of code names, numbers, and bullet points on the walls of the war room, but behind it all was a perfect clarity of purpose: maximizing the total value that Day and Domes provided its shareholders. The definition of this value was the increase in share price plus dividends. The constant dollar was the meter stick, like the distance light travels in 1/299,792,458th of a second, absolute.

Until now, Day and Domes's promise to the market had always been steadiness and predictability, with no big spikes, no big drops, a straight line with a gently positive slope. But when Joyce came aboard, he realized that if the company stuck with credit reporting alone, it would decline. Basic credit information was old economy. Already, despite Day and Domes's dominance, some analysts were saying that with the Internet revolution, the company's core business could become a commodity, like wheat.

Nobody wanted to be a farmer. Joyce reasoned that as companies captured more and more information about their customers through loyalty cards, Internet sales, online ratings and surveys, and the like, Day and Domes should not only house the data but should also apply advanced analytics that would allow clients to sell to each customer as if he or she were an intimate. Firms could entrust the precious asset of their customer data to Day and Domes because its name was a synonym for rectitude. This was essential because eventually D&D would know more about their customers than its clients did. But you needed more than trust. You needed to innovate, and you needed scale.

Joyce's first acquisition target was a Silicon Valley firm called Gnomon Co. A big commitment of capital carried a risk, but there were models that could quantify it, which was why Rosten's team was working overtime.

Rosten had recognized the models' power in business school, and at the investment bank he had used them to predict the price a complex derivative security would sell for on the first day of trading. He nailed it within a penny and got a promotion. In certain moods, though, he brooded that behind the models' success was the fact that everyone used them. He had gotten the price right because all over the world brilliant young men and women had gone through the same analysis he had. They spotted the same hidden options, calculated their Black-Scholes values. They used the same equations, made the same simplifying assumptions, and when they rolled it all up into a single number, it reflected the way it was derived. The model might not mirror reality. Perhaps what the model modeled, in a profound sense, was itself.

Rosten had asked Sandra Harms to arrive early. She had a lot of catching up to do before the work teams arrived. He respected her wattage and drive, though it gave her the reputation of being unapproachable. This, of course, beckoned attention, but it was not the only thing about her that did. She defined any space she stepped into, unless Joyce was in it, too. Then they defined it together. She had the figure of Degas's woman after the bath and met you with bright blue, unaverted eyes. Her long, black hair was pinned up in a swirl that made men want her to let it down. But there was gossip about an incident in which a Day and Domes manager came on to her and ended up gone, with a package that could only have been described as limp. So when men in the company talked about her among themselves, they often intoned a warning: "First do no Harms."

Rosten did not generally warm to people like her, but he had no trouble working with them. Help them execute on their long-term career plan and they would do what you asked them to. The door opened.

"Why didn't you just lock your team in a safe?" she said. "Did you actually intend to get everyone in the Dome talking?"

"What are they saying?" he said. "Welcome, by the way."

"They expect a layoff."

"That works."

"What a nice thought," she said with a rumor of a smile. "So who are we buying?"

He pointed her to a chair at the table.

"Not absolutely sure yet," he said. "I'll go through the state of the bidding."

"You mean A Co. and B Co.," she said, pointing to the easel. "Sounds like an infantry battalion." That was not a simile he would have expected from her. "My father was in the Army," she said. "You did service yourself."

"Not in the military."

"You're not at liberty to disclose, I suppose."

"Have you heard any talk on the Street?" he said.

"About your time in a le Carré novel?" she said.

He fumbled with a folder on the table and eventually came up with the one-pager he had prepared. As he handed it to her, she said, "Are you afraid of me too?" Her face added nothing, not aggression or challenge, not sport. She remained so silent and blank that he felt an intense desire to answer. He used to know how to deal with this.

"We have to get to work," he said.

"Yes, let's do," she said. "Let's get down to the data."

"It is our business, after all," he said.

"Data is everything that is the case," she said.

It surprised him that she made the allusion, but more that she made it ironically. This was a woman of parts.

He handed her the one-pager and started taking her through the bullet points. It was big, big picture stuff, not the valuation model that he would be going into detail about in the larger group. She interrupted him.

"I know the strategic arguments," she said.

"Sorry," he said. "I'm a plodding sort of a guy. I like to put down footings and a foundation before putting up the walls."

"And here I thought that behind closed doors you would be dark and daring," she said.

Yes, maybe a little afraid of her.

"Your reading of the Street and how to make this public when the time comes will be vital," he said.

Clearly, hearing that was something she needed, because she opened up.

"I'm worried about Brian," she said.

"He knows how to pace himself," Rosten said.

"Not that way," she said. "I've seen it happen before. Enough time in the saddle and a CEO begins to think he's eight feet tall, when it's only the horse. Ordinary management issues start to bore him. He doesn't want to listen to cautionary voices, puts off the people who could help him most."

"Have you told him this?" he said.

"Have you?" she said.

"He's been in some other place lately," he said, "but he's OK."

"CEO is a progressive disease," she said.

He turned toward the easel then back to her.

"He's always been willing to keep really smart people close," he said. "Look at the way he protected Gunderman."

"I thought that was your doing."

"I certainly didn't object," he said. "Gunderman sees things nobody else does."

"Like Fisherman did?" she said.

"Who?" he said.

"Please," she said. "I do my homework."

"Nothing about this is similar," he said. "Not Gunderman, of all people. Not anybody."

"If it all goes the wrong way . . . ," she said.

"We won't let it," he said.

"We'll have to throw very tight loops," she said.

"Do you know what that means?" he said.

"Control," she said.

"Casting a feather into the wind," he said.

5

Before he'd had the surgery, it had taken only ten minutes for Dell Lawton to walk from the urologist's office to the Dome, but now he needed to figure on at least twice that. It had all begun when his PSA had started to rise. Then came the biopsies. He was told to strip below the waist, lie down on his side on a table slick with white paper, knees to his chest, his rectum a bull's-eye. The probe entered and the spring gun fired darts into him, one after another after another. The procedure left him bleeding for days when he peed, months when he came. In all, he had a half-dozen biopsies, seventy-two darts, before one of them found a cancer cell.

As Lawton left the medical building today, the sun shone in a bright blue winter sky. A little snow remained in shady areas, but the air was so still that the temperature actually felt comfortable, although since going under the knife he couldn't be sure of such things; it was as if someone with a sense of whimsy had hacked into his internal thermometer and taken control. To questions about this and everything else, Dr. Dick always said that everything was proceeding nicely and then told Lawton he could pull his absorbent underpants back up. In fact, Lawton had to admit that nothing seemed disastrously wrong down there. The pain was all but gone, except when he coughed. He had almost forgotten what the catheter felt like. There was no blood in his urine. The point was that, though nothing was wrong, nothing was right either. He could not remember what it felt like to become stiff. And sometimes he leaked, which left him clammy and so deflated that even a short, parkside walk on a beautiful day could not raise his spirits.

He should have been hustling to give himself some cushion before the meeting with Joyce that he had only learned about when he'd gotten a call while sitting in Dr. Dick's waiting room. But instead of hurrying, he had to tarry on the sidewalk, trying to catch a second wind and blend in with the tourists. Lawton stood looking up at the mosaic half-sphere atop D&D's headquarters a block and a half away. The Dome was part of a wall of landmark buildings that stood along Michigan Avenue, the tallest in the city when they were built, a rock face that looked as if it had been made not by man but time.

He had heard several versions of why Thomas Woods Peterson had decided on the peculiar design of his building. One very businesslike variation attributed it to branding, an architectural play on the company's name. Another had Peterson taking a trip to Turkey and being moved by the grandeur of Byzantium. The version Lawton liked best identified Peterson as a secret Mason with an inclination toward the Ancient Arabic Order of the Nobles of the Mystic Shrine, which had built its Medinah Temple some years before Peterson had built his tabernacle to data.

What Lawton liked about the Masonic version of the story was the symbolism—the square and the compass caliper—and the stonemason's slow, precise craftsmanship. Anyone schooled as an engineer would have felt an affinity. The Dome was a temple to measurement. Building a cathedral and building a great database were similar: stone by stone, bit by bit, each needing to be perfect so that the whole would be steady and durable; the way the work stretched over years, even centuries, with men born and dying to it, believing they were building for eternity. Maintaining the great dome and its thousands of mosaic pieces needed constant effort, just as the computer network did. Before Sam White had retired, he had put millions into restoration. He had spent well beyond safety, and just in time, because Lawton doubted that Joyce was a man to spend a penny on heritage.

What was so urgent that he would have Marcia interrupt some-body at a doctor's appointment? He probably didn't even think about it. Your time is his. That's what being CEO means.

Lawton pressed ahead. When he reached the Dome, he pushed the antique brass crossbar of the revolving door and entered the heat of the grand old lobby. It had its own mosaics high on the walls: French missionaries paddling a canoe down the Chicago River, Abe Lincoln being nominated at the Wigwam convention hall, the Fire, Daniel Burnham at White City. Off in the corner, easy to overlook, was one last image—Thomas Woods Peterson himself, standing in this very lobby, surrounded by these very mosaics, including the one of him standing in the lobby.

Sweat began to roll down Lawton's back and be absorbed by his underpants. He nodded to Maurice.

"Somebody should dial down the heat," Lawton said.

"Seems a little cool to me, Mr. Lawton."

He opened his coat and went to the elevators, his calipers and square all out of whack. They couldn't fire him for losing his prostate, could they? Not without paying him a bundle. Lose a package, gain a package. What would he say to Barbara Jean? And if she left him, what would he do? An old man in diapers watching CNN all day. But what if Joyce wanted to talk to him about a promotion? He had seen stranger things happen, and there had been rumors that Joyce was thinking of appointing a chief operating officer. With the possibility of a big acquisition and the challenge of integrating two companies, Joyce must be feeling the need to hand off some direct reports. There were no plausible internal candidates for the job except Tom Rosten and himself, though Sandra Harms would certainly see herself in contention, maybe Dick Chase, too, which was preposterous. Any more preposterous than Lawton? Who would pass the baton to a man just out from under the knife?

The elevator came. As the door closed, Lawton took the handkerchief from his back pocket to swab his face. He did not want to be COO. Homeostasis was all he wanted. Steady state, nothing more. As the car rose, his body grew heavy. Then the weight lifted and the door opened. As he started to step out, he almost bumped into Joyce stepping in. The CEO had a youthful face, but today his metal-rimmed glasses, tight against his barbered temples, looked as though they were keeping his skull from exploding.

"Let's go to your office," he said. "She said you were at the doctor's."

"I wasn't in a compromising position."

Joyce clearly did not want a picture. He pushed the button for Lawton's floor.

"You're OK though," he said.

"Right on schedule, he says," said Lawton.

When the elevator door opened again, Joyce gestured him out first, as he might a senior citizen. At Charlene's desk, Lawton draped his coat on the counter for her to hang up.

"Hold the calls," Joyce told her.

He closed the door behind him and went to the round table and blue upholstered chairs that came with the offices of all executives of Lawton's rank. Lawton waited for him to choose a place then eased himself down on the opposite side.

"We have a problem," Joyce said, putting his hands flat. His fingernails were trimmed to the quick. "I believe our database has been compromised."

"I would have been notified," said Lawton.

"Well I am notifying you now," said Joyce.

"Who told you?"

"Citibank."

"Good God, is it out on the Street?" said Lawton. He had completely lost his square and caliper. It was as if everything, even the walls, were suddenly askew.

"Fortunately, I don't think Citibank realizes what it knows," said Joyce. "They sent a boilerplate e-mail."

"What were they thinking, for God's sake?"

"It notified me that I had been turned down for an elite Visa card."

"That's absurd," said Lawton. Then he breathed out. "A mix-up in names. I'll have someone talk to our contacts there and straighten it out."

"That could be disastrous," said Joyce.

"It has to be their error."

"It's ours," said Joyce. "When I checked the database, it put my

55

credit score south of destitute. And it isn't just the score. There are mortgage payments I supposedly missed, credit cards revoked for nonpayment."

"You're sure you were looking at the right file?"

"It was like seeing my head on a street beggar's body," said Joyce.

Lawton stood, listing. He put a hand on the table edge. He hoped Joyce didn't notice.

"Let's check the competition," he said.

"I already did," said Joyce. "They were all 100 percent accurate, down to the address of the first home Donna and I bought, and every payment on time."

"May I look?" Lawton said, moving toward his computer.

"Be my guest."

Lawton signed on as System Administrator. He glanced over at Joyce, who was staring out the windows at the park or something beyond the park. He was not clipping his nails, not glaring at Lawton to get a move on. He was just standing there. This did not fit the man Lawton knew, any more than the credit score did.

"Your Social Security number would expedite things," Lawton said.

Joyce gave it.

"Could someone have gotten my password?" Joyce said.

"What do you use?"

"Shannon3. My grandmother's maiden name."

"We'll need to strengthen that," said Lawton. "Hackers start with common names. But having your password wouldn't let someone alter the database. Even you don't have the authority."

Joyce turned and looked at him.

"No offense," said Lawton. "Specific need is the protocol."

The file came up, and Lawton saw that it had been thoroughly trashed.

"I don't have any idea how they did it," he said. "It's one thing to sneak a piece of bad data through. But even if a hacker was able to pose as one of our customers, he would only be able to put in data going back three months. The mess in your file goes back decades. Somebody got all the way in. Did anything unusual happen before the Citibank e-mail?"

"Who would do a thing like this?"

"We'll need to figure out when the intrusion occurred."

"The e-mail came on Monday," Joyce said. "Until then I didn't have the slightest inkling."

"The first thing we have to do is to determine how much of the database has been corrupted," said Lawton. "I should know by close of business. We'll blitz this thing."

"A blitz might be just what they want," said Joyce.

"He'd have to be able to monitor in real time," said Lawton. "I really can't believe he could do that."

"Just how certain are you, Dell?" said Joyce. "As certain as you were that an intrusion was impossible because you would have been notified?"

"If someone is in that deep," said Lawton, "he could destroy us."

"In which case running off in a panic will accomplish nothing," said Joyce, looking out the window again. "Is there any way for you to see when this thing with my file began?"

Joyce seemed impossibly calm, as though danger were Xanax. For Lawton it was a stimulant. He was alive again. If he did not know better, he would have thought that what he felt was desire.

"We can go back step by step," he said.

"Not we," said Joyce. "You. No consultants. Just you."

"And Gunderman," said Lawton.

"Yes. And Gunderman."

"I can't believe this is widespread," said Lawton. "If it were, people all over the world would be having trouble getting a loan. There would be a spike in error reports."

"I think it is best," said Joyce, "to fix our minds on the idea that right now we can believe in absolutely nothing."

Joyce turned back away from the window, and Lawton saw that what had seemed like calm might have been what believing nothing actually looked like in a man.

"Have you told anyone else?" Lawton said.

"Not even my priest."

He stood and came around the table. As Lawton started to rise, Joyce put a hand lightly on his shoulder.

"I know this is not coming at a good time for you," he said.

"Don't worry about me," said Lawton as Joyce turned toward the door.

Lawton heard Joyce's big voice greeting the secretaries. As it faded down the corridor, Charlene appeared in the doorway.

"Are you here for Sara Simons?" she said.

"I'm not here for anybody."

"Did you want the door closed?"

"Closed door, empty office," said Lawton. "I'm among the missing."

"Got it," she said.

He signed in again as System Administrator, this time using the fob that gave him the synchronized numbers that would permit him to do anything he wanted. First he went to his own file. Credit score right where it should have been. As he scrolled

through the data fields, he saw every timely payment of a credit-card bill and mortgage payment, every old address, all perfect.
When he reached the field that displayed inquiries by Day and
Domes customers, he found the usual array of the banks that
filled his mailbox with credit-card offers, insurance companies,
brokers, advisory firms. Nothing out of the ordinary, though it
did irritate him that the hospital where he'd had his surgery had
taken his financial temperature first. There had been no call for
that. He was on the hospital's board. His annual donation was
more than the damned surgery cost.

He closed his eyes and tried to center himself. It took several
steps to get in a position to page back into the database's history
on Joyce's account. He would need to be prepared with some explanation for why he was doing this, since it would show up on
the logs, which even he did not have the authority to revise. He
would not be able to put it the way he felt it—that someone had
come between him and a thing he cared for, that when he looked
at the screen now, the screen was looking back.

6

Sara Simons had a light day, no sales call, just the lunch. It was not something she looked forward to, but she did not like the slush or the salt on the sidewalk either. Still she walked. She always did. Along the way she passed the Standard Club, which stood at the intersection of her father's anxiety and pride.

It had been founded in the late 19th Century by Jewish immigrants, most from Germany, who had gone on to prosper as the city rebuilt after the Great Fire. Such importance did the club place on the great tradition of giving that it had taken her father a month to put together the financial information he was required to disclose in the vetting process. By then, he was a wreck.

"I should have done better than 10 percent," he said, dropping his pen to the desk upon signing the application. "Even the goyim tithe."

"It'll be all right, Daddy," she said. "You are a very generous man."

"If they look at last year, it's better," he said. "But they ask for five years for a reason."

"They'll look at everything," she said. "They'll look at Mommy's death and Grandpa's hospital bills. You did tell them, didn't you?"

"The men in the club," he said, "their families have all been here forever. They'll think I'm a schnorrer just off the boat."

"You weren't on the boat, Daddy," she said. "They'll see that you're natural born."

"What kind of thing is that?" he said. "My parents were unnatural?"

The immigration clerk had turned Simonowicz to Simons. In the records on Ellis Island, Simons had found the book and seen that an anonymous agent of the United States government had added a little grace note to almost every name he had Anglicized. An "s" here, a "son" there. Simons thought she would like a man who would do a thing like that. She wished she knew his name.

"They'll understand, Daddy," she said. "There were no Jews on the *Mayflower*."

"Their families came in the next ship," he said. "And I bet it wasn't steerage."

"What I mean is that you won't be the first peddler's son to dine at the Standard Club," she said.

"Look at me," he said. He had long since shed the more distancing garb of orthodoxy but still stuck to black and white. He assimilated no further than to join a very conservative congregation. "I am neither this nor that," he said.

"You will look to them the way you look to me," she said. "You will look like who you are."

"I'm sunk," he said.

When the letter welcoming him to membership came, he made her read it out loud slowly, just to make sure. His acceptance became his arrival, but whether he had ever felt that he really belonged, Simons was not sure.

"It's a curse to be a pioneer," he said as she stood before him in her mortarboard and robe outside the football stadium in Evanston the day she got her MBA. "Nobody shows the way."

"You were there for me," she said. "And now I have an advanced degree in peddling."

Not long after graduation she dropped the *h* from her first name for the same reason the immigration officer had added the *s*. For her father's sake she fasted and ate as expected, when he was there to see. She married holy, though that did not last. Her father would have liked her to have been with him more often, of course. She pleaded distance; he was by then in Highland Park, and she lived downtown near the Dome. At the point in her career when Day and Domes granted her the perk of a club membership, he all but ordered her to follow him into the Standard. She joined the Union League instead.

"It's for the WASPs," he said, with a face that made her fear for his heart. "They would not have us, even for lunch."

"It wasn't long ago that they wouldn't have women either," she said. "You and I are pioneers, remember? It's who I am."

"And being who you are means forgetting who you were?" he said.

Not forgetting so much as coming into her own. At Day and Domes she thrived: better offices, promotions, bonuses, the club membership, the vice presidency. She believed it was because she had an instinct for what her customers needed. That you gave me, Daddy. That I kept.

After passing the Standard Club, she looked into the lobby of the high-modernist, glass-and-steel Federal Building and wondered what she would have become had she grown in that greenhouse. The places where we spend our working lives shape us the way our traditions once did. It would have felt like being filed alphabetically in a drawer.

The old wood and brass of the Union League Club could not have been more different. She could imagine Mark Twain holding forth in the lobby, the most redolent cigar in the box. The foyer murmured with judges and lawyers, echoing conversations that had been going for a hundred and thirty years. She checked her coat at the long counter, where tips were not allowed, then took her newspaper to the sitting room, where she had a view of the lobby so she could see Dick Chase when he made it in from his meeting out beyond O'Hare. She could have given him directions to the library upstairs with its leather-stuffed chairs and polished tables, which was a better place for reading a newspaper, but she preferred reading people, imagining how she would approach them.

Those two men near the stairway had obviously known each other for a very long time and would be delighted to tell stories to anyone who hadn't heard them before. That young man greeting the woman in spike heels might like to have a wingman. Those three men by the cigar stand seemed not to trust one another, or perhaps anyone else. They might accept her as a sucker at their poker table.

She eased back into a chair that was too big for her and folded the paper the way her father had taught her when they rode together on the El. This allowed her to hide her attention whenever the object of it looked her way. A young woman coming through the revolving door slowed down so much that Simons thought she might stop inside and flutter there, a butterfly in a jar. Ever since becoming Day and Domes's vice president for Sales and Marketing, Simons had not hesitated at any entrance. The young woman took one step into the lobby and saw someone Simons couldn't see. Her expression was recognition, but not relief. The man stepped into the frame. He certainly knew that he belonged, probably born to it. The woman's date? Her potential boss? The man took her by the elbow. More than an interview, less than a date. Or worse, a little of both.

At least she was beyond all that. Her lunch engagement was at the same level of intimacy as all her dates these days—Dick Chase, of whom someone had once said, "He's like a first husband who never got the word." This was not quite right. He behaved just as badly to men.

Chase had a big, pudgy face on which he cultivated a mustache and pointy goatee, which made him look like a hypnotist you would never allow to put you in a trance. But, then again, she could not imagine allowing herself to be entranced by any man. She'd had relationships after divorcing Noah, and early on, some of them had been quite intense. The trouble was that the thing always turned out to be like business, the get and the give. Now all she wanted of her men was that they be presentable. She took them to the charity balls. Occasionally she would go with one to a play. A few she even took home. They did not stay. Tom Rosten seemed to live the same kind of life. She would see him with some lovely woman a couple of times. Then nobody. Then another.

"You're early," said Chase, who suddenly loomed. She stood, rising in her shoes to almost his height.

"You're looking particularly dapper today," she said. No harm in trying, even though what he really looked like was a plumber dressed for church.

"Traffic on the Kennedy," he said.

She looked at her watch, a Movado, nice enough but never better than what her customers had on their wrists.

"Actually I've been enjoying myself," she said. "Don't you like being invisible so you can watch people without them knowing?"

"I thought Rosten was the spy," he said.

"Let's take the elevator," she said, moving him toward the lobby. "The stairs are grand, but they weren't made for heels."

Thank goodness he wasn't quicker or he would have heard both meanings.

"What union is it that this club was named for?" he said.

"Abe Lincoln's," she said. "But that was before my people's time."

"Mine were on the other side."

"That explains a lot," she said. This he seemed to take as flattery. "But I don't hear an accent."

"I grew up in Beverly," he said. "It was my grandfather who had the twang. He wouldn't have been welcomed in this club."

"Mine either," she said, "and yet here we are."

The dining room always made her think of the stateliness of the Walnut Room at Marshall Field's. She had once begged her parents to take her there before the tree came down after Christmas. "It's a Hanukkah bush," she said, following her Reformed friends. "There is no such botany," her father said, and made quick work of his lunch.

Simons and Chase had to wait a few minutes before the maître d' seated them at a table along the inside wall.

"You don't rate a window?" said the Chase she knew.

"A woman wants to be a little private when out with a gentleman," she said.

They sat, and he fell to straightening the alignment of the silver and china before him.

"I know what I want," she said.

He picked up his menu and went over it line by line. When he finally looked up, she took his order and filled out the card for the waiter. Chase put his forearms on the table and leaned toward her, the way she sometimes saw lawyers leaning toward judges.

"What is it you want?" he said.

"I was hoping you could help me understand what's going on with our CEO," she said. It wasn't her real purpose, but it was the kind of thing that would loosen Chase up.

He sat back.

"He trusts me to be discreet," he said.

She nodded.

"The thing is, sometimes it's like he isn't there," she said. "I go to his office to brief him on an important contract negotiation, and he interrupts to ask whether I think he should redo the boardroom again."

"The woman's touch," said Chase.

"I haven't heard of any problem with the acquisition," she said. "Have you?"

He turned and looked behind him.

Chase's representative on the working group was Rob Greener, the one Lawton had traded to him when they were shuffling people around to place Gunderman. Everybody was surprised that Chase had given him the working group assignment, because Greener had been all over D&D and never done much.

Sara leaned forward and put her hands down halfway across the table.

"You've been noticing something about Joyce, too," she said.

"I didn't say that," he said.

"But you've poked around."

"Who said I have?"

She took a sip of breath, then of her iced tea.

"Mind reading is in my job description," she said. He stared at his perfectly centered plate as if it were a mirror. "Look," she said. "Everyone has the same question. I figured that if anyone had an answer . . ."

"And here I thought I was going to work you for information," he said. "Why do you think I've been so pleasant?"

"I imagined it was me," she said.

The waiter brought their meals, in which they took refuge for a time.

"So you don't know any more than I do," she said.

"I don't know how much you know."

"I hear Dell Lawton has been holed up in his office with the door closed," she said. "You don't think it's the COO job."

He put down his fork. His eyes moved back and forth over her face as if he were trying to read something printed on the skin.

"You mean he's been told it isn't him," said Chase.

"Isn't it?"

"He's lucky still to have a job at all after losing his manhood," he said.

"That's vivid."

It was funny what people saw and what fell into a blind spot. Everyone but Chase knew that he had even less of a shot at the COO job than Lawton did.

He took a bite of Cobb salad and a sip of cranberry juice.

"You don't imagine that you'll get it," he said.

"I'm not quite ready," she said. "But look, this lunch really isn't about the COO job."

He took another bite of greens.

"Maybe he's heard a death sentence," he said. "That would make a man close his office door."

Sara had let the conversation wander a long way from what she wanted of it, which was to smooth the way for a visit by a potential customer to the largest data-storage facility. It was important that he not feel like he was entering Guantanamo. She was about to bring things around to this when suddenly it came to her.

"Joyce is in trouble," she said.

There was a slight hardening at the corners of Chase's mouth. This was the only tell.

"A fight with his wife?" he said. "A brother with a nose for drugs?"

What she could not decide was whether he was trying not to show what he knew or what he didn't.

"Something involving Lawton," she said.

Chase met her eyes as if he were checking her for glaucoma.

"What kind of trouble?" he finally said.

"I was hoping you would be able to help me with that."

His eyes were not examining hers anymore. They were warning.

"This conversation never happened," he said.

7

When the war room door scraped an arc in the carpet, all conversation ceased. Rosten was the only one who could see that it was only Sandra Harms.

"Did I penetrate a secret?" she said.

"You know we would keep nothing from you," he said. "I was just summing up."

"So sum away," she said.

One of the bankers stood and offered her his chair. She waved him off.

"I'd like to have the financial modeling wrapped up by close of business Friday," Rosten said.

"That's aggressive," said Grace Bondurant.

"That's Tom," said one of Rosten's young analysts.

"Next week will be for kicking the tires," Rosten said.

"To see if they need inflating," said Harms.

Rosten felt himself tighten. His role had been to let excess air out of the numbers, not to pump it in.

"Stop that metaphor," he said. "Let's put it this way: Next week we'll look for weaknesses and fix any we find. Now, go straight home, everybody. We meet again at dawn."

This met with the standard stage groans as folks began to stand and gather up their papers. Rosten turned to erase the white-board. He felt a hand on his shoulder.

"You've put all this together remarkably well, Tom," Harms said, leaving her hand there for a beat past business. "So often I've seen the bankers take control."

Grace stood off from them, but close enough to hear.

"They've been great contributors to the process," he said.

"Bankers are always for the bank," she said.

He put down the eraser.

"I'm the one pushing, not the bankers," he said.

"And I concur," she said. "The sooner we green- or red-light this thing, the better."

She touched his hand and left. The door scraped slowly closed.

"You were making yourself quite a challenge for her," said Grace.

"I wasn't impolite, was I?" he said. He put his papers into the file jacket he carried around now in place of the Bible. People had started calling it the Book of Common Prayer. "She was just trying to get a rise out of me."

"I've been there," she said.

"That was different."

"I remember."

He was sorry for the memories he had left her with.

"When Harms looks at me," he said, "she sees an H-P financial calculator and a sheaf of spreadsheets."

"I'm pretty sure she sees more," said Grace.

He put the folder under his arm and pushed in his chair.

"Maybe you'd better warn her," he said. He regretted saying that. The memories weren't her responsibility.

"Do you have plans for dinner?" she said.

"People may get the wrong idea," he said. "It's one thing to be seen at an obligatory charity event. Half the people there are partners of convenience."

"Then choose an out-of-the-way place."

An hour later, they met outside a bar a few blocks from the Dome. It was drizzling.

"Better not," he said, looking down at her hand as she placed it in the crook of his arm.

"Slick pavement," she said.

"Here's a cab," he said, freeing himself to open the door for her. When she got inside, she slid over to give him room, but not enough. They touched at the shoulders and hips.

In New Haven he had been the bold one. Now he hugged the taxi's door. He did not know her anymore, and he had not let her know him. She could not possibly want him to fail her again.

They had been a couple for almost three years, he a class ahead of her. They were both outsiders in the East, he a Chicago Pole and she part Sioux and straight off the North Dakota plains. They went everywhere together. Even if they did not belong to the place, the two of them made it belong to them. Then, as his graduation approached, he was recruited by the CIA.

During the long, black time that followed, Rosten had no contact with her. But then, when it got so black that he finally realized he had to walk away, he went straight to her. While he was gone, she had married a man from her class named Jim Bernsten and had a new baby. He had no right to intrude on them. At that point Rosten wasn't sure what, if anything, he had the right to do.

But despite everything, she helped him. He did not know why. When she looked at him, he no longer knew what man she saw.

The taxi pulled up at the place he had chosen for dinner. He paid the fare and did not flinch when she took his hand to make the long step across the puddled gutter to the curb.

"We've eluded surveillance?" she said.

"Let's not go there," he said.

There were eyes on them in the hotel lobby and restaurant, smiles and nods.

"Do we look happy?" she said.

"Are we?"

"Yes, actually."

They had a good table, lush with flowers, the sepia light sparkling off the crystal like sunset.

After they ordered drinks, she took out her BlackBerry. He took out his, too, but then he felt her looking at him, head aslant, and realized she had turned her device off.

"How did you manage to get this assignment?" he said.

"When I heard about the D&D project, I offered and let nature take its course," she said. "I'm not much of a schemer."

"Which is why you chose investment banking for a career."

"The analytic side."

"Funny that we both ended up hiding under spreadsheets," he said.

The wine came.

"Is Jim all right with your working with me?" he said.

"I didn't ask."

Her eyes were examining her fingertips, which were tasting the condensation on the water glass.

"I was never anyone for him to worry about," he said. "I was just a cloud passing."

She ordered fish. He had a cut of pork trimmed with things on the menu whose names he did not recognize as food. As they ate, he got her talking about herself. Some of it he already knew, some he didn't. She told of following Jim to New York, where his math major had gotten him an entry-level position at McKinsey. Her education up to that point had been almost perfectly nonquantitative, so she had to settle for proofreading at a midtown law firm whose senior partner wrote essays on Wallace Stevens and Dickens on the side. He liked to lend her books from his office. She had a lot of time to read at home, with Jim gone so much. Usually novels, at first new ones that got attention in the *New York Review of Books* and *TLS*, but eventually the self-absorption of formal invention became tiresome, and she turned to novels of life. She loved her boss and did not mind the work, which was as orderly as justified lines, but some of the firm's lawyers were a trial.

"Of course they were," Rosten said. "You were so much smarter than them."

She thought about getting a teaching certificate, but dragging tenth graders through *Julius Caesar* did not hold much appeal, so when Jim announced that he was going to apply to Harvard Business School, she decided that she would, too. She was accepted and he wasn't, so they ended up at Wharton. "Good investment," his father said, "like long-term care insurance."

Both of them got jobs easily. They received promotions, had a child. They moved to a better apartment, had another child. By all appearances, the investment had panned out. Then the marriage faltered. His parents saw that something was wrong.

At Thanksgiving dinner with the kids at the table, Jim's father turned to him and told him to think carefully about what he was doing. "Run the numbers," he said.

It was funny, really, she said, because Jim had ended up in marketing, so if anyone were going to run numbers, it would have been her.

Her eyes went to her lap and she plucked the napkin.

"Excuse me," she said.

As she moved away from the table, he caught the waiter's attention. When she returned, she was fresh and he had paid. He walked her toward her hotel but stopped about two blocks out.

"What a pleasure," he said. "Catching up."

"Except it was all about me," she said. "You could come up, you know. There's a minibar. Do they still call it a nightcap?"

"That'll have to be a road not taken, I'm afraid," he said. She deserved better than that worn old line. "I have nobody to blame but myself," he said. "It's my fault you're spoken for."

"Hardly spoken to," she said. "Jim's out of the picture. I suppose it was when he found another woman to add to the other woman. He ran the numbers and four's a crowd."

"Do you want to talk about it?" he said.

She did not answer.

"It can't be at your hotel," he said.

"Nobody would be shocked," she said. "They're road warriors. It happens all the time."

"To you?" he said.

"No. That's Jim, not me."

He stepped to the curb and lifted his arm. A taxi pulled over on the opposite side of the street. He took her elbow and crossed over. He may only have imagined it, but when she slid in, she seemed to place herself a little farther from him than before.

"Your husband is a fool," he said as the taxi pulled away.

The driver lurched onto Michigan Avenue, throwing Grace awkwardly into him. She recovered quickly. This, she thought, must be what it felt like to go home with someone you just met in a bar.

They passed the Dome and eventually pulled up at a town-house—three stories, with a fence, a little lawn, and a flower box. Lights were on inside.

"Should we have called ahead?" she said.

"I have the cleaning lady leave them on."

It was foolish to assume anything about him, as it had always been.

"The lived-in look," she said. "Two kids and a dog."

"One man rattling around in too much space," he said. "I don't know what I was thinking. A good investment, I guess."

"It's lovely," she said.

A pair of topsiders sat just inside the door, lined up in the center of a small throw rug. The stairway bore no trace of him. The off-white walls were bare. The carpet smelled as if it had just been shampooed. It was clear that two people did not live here. In fact, it was hard to believe that one did.

When they stepped through the door at the top of the second flight of stairs, she found herself outside on a deck, looking across some railroad tracks and Lake Shore Drive into the empty darkness of the lake.

"I wish there were a moon," he said.

The east wind smelled of water. She dared to lean into him for a moment, just barely, then pulled back before he could. Mistake on mistake on mistake. She did not know him, and yet she felt that he knew everything about her, what she wanted—him beside her, the smell of water, a moon.

His idea of a house tour was to open doors and let her peek in. She tried to find something in the few pieces that hung on the walls, but there was no person behind them. Even the master bedroom, which he barely let her glimpse, looked like a room your secretary would book for you in a first-rate business hotel. When they got to the living room, he asked if he could get her a drink. The wine from dinner had grown heavy on her. She said Scotch.

"Really," he said.

"A little splash in a big glass, with soda and ice."

He disappeared into the kitchen, leaving her to look for photos of smiling women standing with him on the ski slope or with the Mediterranean at their backs. She found only a group portrait, the logo behind them, at the bell-ringing on the opening day of trading in Day and Domes shares. The sole woman was the one from Investor Relations who had flirted with him this morning. But the most remarkable thing about the room was that it had no bookshelves, not a single volume anywhere, not even something oversized with pictures lying on the coffee-table glass.

"Can I see your office?" she said when he returned.

It was off to the left. He let her walk in ahead of him, and in the darkness she saw the car lights running white and red on Lake Shore Drive. Then the overhead fixture came on, and she realized that he had placed his desk so that his back was to the lake. She turned. No shelves here either.

"OK," she said. "Where's the library?"

He stepped aside to cue her exit. She stayed put.

"I have some books at the Dome," he said. "My little act of corporate rebellion. I don't really have time anymore. I think we'll be more comfortable in the living room."

She hesitated, but he was already switching off the light.

"I have to admit that I don't go in for anything very heavy myself these days," she said, sitting down on the couch. "I even pick up a thriller once in a while when I run out of reading matter at an airport. They usually disappoint, starting at the level of sentences." She did not say spy novels, which disappointed differently because she went to them for explanations they never provided.

He put down his glass, whisky neat from the look of it, and lowered himself into an armchair on the other side of the coffee table. He did not seem comfortable in it. It did not seem possible he had ever been comfortable in it.

"I'm not doing very well by you, am I," he said.

"We were just going to talk," she said.

"What is the use of talking," he said, "and there's no end of talking, there is no end of things in the heart."

She put down the drink, then picked it up quickly and wiped the tabletop with her hand.

"I'm sorry. I should have thought this through," she said.

"It's Pound," he said. "No end of things of the heart. I read it to you once. When I came back."

"The timing was horrible," she said. "We were both lost."

She was on maternity leave from the bank when he appeared.

She welcomed his presence. They tended to baby Jonathan together and talked when he slept. When he woke up, they read aloud the Brothers Grimm, Robert Louis Stevenson, Shel Silverstein, which to the infant could not have been anything but sound. They would take different speaking parts, making up odd voices and laughing. One day she turned the conversation to *Lord Jim*, which was a favorite of his. He started to give an interpretation of what had gone wrong inside the man with ability in the abstract, but then he stopped. There was a boundary, his Iron Curtain, keeping her out and holding him in.

Not long afterward he told her he was leaving New York.

"To Boston," he said. "For an MBA."

She wanted to warn him that business school was not a place to find yourself. It was a place to put yourself on ice. It did not dawn on her until seeing his apartment that this was exactly what he had wanted.

He leaned across the empty coffee table. She was afraid that he could see her feelings welling.

"It must be hard, losing him," he said.

She wiped her eyes.

"It's better now than it was when we were putting up a front," she said. "I thought it could not get worse than that. Then we told the kids."

She had never seen Luisa cry the way she had that evening. Before Jim had gotten out all the words, their daughter began breathing in spasms, as if she had pulled something hard and sharp down into her lungs. Jonathan said that he was sorry for everyone but not to worry about him because he was grown, having reached his sophomore year in college. With that he began to leave. Jim said that it wasn't either his or his sister's fault. Jonathan turned and said, "Obviously." Jim went on like an actor delivering his lines as a scene fell apart. Grace could only whisper, "I'm sorry, I'm sorry, I'm so sorry."

"You were strong not to put them in the middle," he said, "but I'm sure they knew what had happened."

"I don't know what anybody knows or doesn't know anymore," she said. "When Jim said he wanted a divorce, our past was like a jewel box lying open on the carpet, everything precious in it gone."

"Do you have the kids' pictures?" he said.

She was determined not to cry.

"Always," she said, touching her purse. Sometimes their photos were the only things that kept her from disappearing.

Tom came around the coffee table and sat down close to her on the couch.

"Can I see them?" he said.

She fumbled with her purse, which suddenly seemed large and hollow. She managed the latch. Her hand mercifully encountered the wallet, which she withdrew. The pictures came out from behind her driver's license, clinging together.

"Jonathan has become a man," he said. "Corn-fed and healthy, like you."

"It's wheat, Tom," she said. "You always wanted it to be corn. But in North Dakota it's wheat."

He put Jonathan's picture behind Luisa's in his hand and shook his head.

"I thought you and Jim had it all figured out," he said.

She took the photos back, which brought his eyes to her.

"I've heard that a lot," she said. "But obviously I hadn't figured out a single thing."

She was not sure she could stop the tears now. She turned her head and drew air against them.

"It's OK," he said. She felt his arm around her shoulders, holding her up. She pulled against it. "I've cried with you."

This was a password that unlocked an image of New York on a rainy afternoon together. It wasn't the past that had been stolen. It was the present, what was real and who.

8

On his way in, Rosten stopped at his secretary's desk for messages.

"Why the short face?" Gail said.

"Meaning?"

"Mona Lisa," she said.

"My little mystery."

Gail had come with the treasurer's office. From his first day, she had not taken him entirely seriously. This, she later explained, was because the men she had worked for before Rosten were like bran: "They just kept moving through." He surprised her by moving upward and bringing her along.

"If it's meds you're on," she said, "I'd like to ask my doctor for some."

"Don't even try to guess," he said and tapped his knuckles on her countertop.

"You know you're on in five minutes in the war room," said Gail. "And don't for a minute think you've stumped me."

"Save your energy."

"You're smitten, aren't you."

"The folders," he said.

"On the table"

"You're coming with me."

"I'm right, aren't I," she said.

"Two minutes," he said.

He retreated to his table and checked the top file. Gail did not make mistakes. At his desk he booted up then opened his personal AOL account, which Gail could not access. At the top of the queue was a message from Grace:

—Who would think I could get so excited about a meeting?

He hit reply:

—The Joy of Decks.

Before he could sign off, another message popped up:

—Soon!!!! :)

He returned to the table and counted the folders. Each jacket carried a large label with a number in red, and each page inside bore the same number. When his team saw this, there would be jokes about CIA Rules.

"It's only a question of who," said Gail, leaning against the door frame.

"You might as well just give up," he said.

The crowd in the war room was restless and Grace an eye of calm at the heart of it. He opened the meeting, briskly explaining the security procedures. Gail began calling names.

"Taking attendance," said one of the analysts.

"It'll be the time clock next," said Chase's man, Rob Greener. Rosten would have understood an even sharper edge. Everyone knew it had hurt him when Lawton had traded him away.

When they had finished the preliminaries, Rosten launched into his presentation. This would be the only time he would run through the deck before going to Joyce. Some practiced so much that you would think they were performing Lear, but fundamentally it was just numbers, and they made a robust case for acquiring Gnomon at a substantial premium to the public market price.

"We believe we can make a preemptive bid that Gnomon's management will find attractive," he said as he reached the final slide.

The room was silent. Grace was nodding.

"Comments?" he said.

Greener raised his hand. He always wore a suit and kept the jacket on, its sleeves riding a bit above the cuffs of his white shirt, which was always in need of a little bleach. His tie was thin, no matter what the fashion. It was not so much that he seemed uncomfortable in his clothes, rather that his clothes did not seem quite his own. Before working for Lawton, Greener had been in the Finance Department, starting at the same time that Rosten did. He was one of those people who seem to know how to do everyone's else's job but could never figure out how to put things together himself.

"Rob," said Rosten.

"Page 14 of the supporting document," Greener said, and the room fluttered, a flock of pigeons rising and settling back to the sidewalk. "You include a figure for system security upgrades for the combined company. I question that. We should be doing those whether we do the deal or not. The incremental cost for the merged enterprise will be minimal. I mean, is the number really material?"

Rosten nodded, but of course no number was material. Numbers were Platonic. In an acquisition exercise, numbers weren't even resolute. Rosten had seen them jump to meet expectation and retreat from criticism. Yell at them loudly enough and you could stampede them right off a cliff.

"Thank you, Rob," he said. "I'll rethink that."

"For the record," said Greener, "the Operations Department is willing to commit to keeping all costs low."

A snicker went through the room. Where exactly was this record that Chase's people were always saying things for?

Now other hands were up.

"This may be a little granular," said another one of Rosten's financial analysts, "but on page 11," more pigeons fluttering, "shouldn't we footnote our assumption about the weighted average cost of capital going forward?"

"Maybe in the leave-behind," said Rosten.

The questions went on, none of them the big ones like what if the wind changes and there's a recession? Or another terrorist attack? What if interest rates spike? What if all the data-mining business goes to some kid in a dorm room who stumbles on a piece of code?

From the back of the room, Margery Strand raised her hand. Rosten barely knew her, but in the annual leadership review Sara Simons always listed Strand as the leading candidate to succeed her as vice president for Sales and Marketing. Some people said it was only because Strand was African American, though they were careful about being overheard.

"Why don't we just get on with it?" Strand said. "It's way too late to abort this puppy. I mean, everybody knows the boss wants this. We're here to show him that he's right. But what I see is top-line growth that is, shall we say, aspirational. And it will be my ass if I can't make the numbers you all have been putting up on the whiteboard."

"I wouldn't assume anything about Joyce's preconceptions," Rosten said. "He will look with a fresh eye at what we've done here and feel free, I assure you, to disagree. By the way, do you?"

"Pardon?" she said.

"Disagree," he said.

"I just know sales will be on the hook," she said.

"There'll be plenty of hook to go around," he said.

A few others said they didn't want to get down into the weeds, then took out their gardening implements. While they were rooting around, the door opened and Gail appeared. She came straight to the front of the room and handed Rosten a folded pink message slip.

The words were printed on the blank side.

"The Man needs to see you in the boardroom," it said.

Rosten read this and picked up his explanation where he had left off. Another pink slip appeared.

"NOW!" it said.

"I'm so sorry," Rosten said to the room. "I've been summoned."

Rosten looked at Grace and then away. As he started toward the door, Gail whispered, "He was in a state."

"Angry?" he said.

"Something else," she said.

"What?" he said.

"After you see him, you can tell me," she said.

Rosten was called to see the CEO so often that he did not usually tense up the way some did. But why the boardroom? Was there a directors' meeting? Rosten would have had to handle the preparations. Some awful impropriety then. Fraud. Sexual harassment. Was it about Grace? A chill went into his belly. Wait, breathe. He'd had nothing to do with deciding which bankers to use. That had been Joyce's call. Technically, she wasn't even on the D&D payroll. He took hold of the brass knob, pushed open the door, and entered.

Joyce sat alone in his chair at the end of the table, the light from the windows behind him making him dark.

"We've got trouble," he said.

Rosten took the chair at Joyce's right hand where Sabby Chandrahary usually sat. Odd how different a room can look from an unfamiliar spot at the table.

"With the deal?" Rosten said.

"This can kill the deal," said Joyce. "Somebody has penetrated the database."

Rosten turned to the door out of a strange impulse to see if he had been followed.

"How?" he said.

"We don't even know what damage he's done," said Joyce. "Or she. Or they. Or it. A phantom. Anyone and no one. He comes and goes and leaves no tracks."

Rosten looked to the door again.

"That can't be true," he said. "There's always a way to trace."

"Anything can be true, I'm afraid," said Joyce. "That is the sum total of our knowledge—that this could be absolutely anything."

Rosten closed his eyes.

"It doesn't go away," said Joyce.

Rosten looked upward. The chandelier had begun to move.

"You've informed the Audit Committee?" he said.

"We don't know enough," said Joyce.

9

The waiting room was empty—its walls blank. The only color was a bouquet of magazines on a low rack, and they had wilted. Gunderman could not get comfortable in the chair. He looked at his watch. In two minutes he would be losing time from his session. Not such a terrible thing, since he was not sure what was safe to talk about.

When Lawton and Gunderman had gone to give Rosten a lack of progress report, Gunderman had wanted to include Joyce. "Let's leave the CEO clear of this, OK?" Rosten had said. No dispute there. As far as Gunderman was concerned, the responsibility was all on him. Until he changed jobs, system security had been at the top of his position description. The Wise Man probably would remind him that even if he had gotten board approval to test the new encryption system, it could not possibly have prevented the disaster. Gunderman knew this was logically correct, but sometimes his brain drove past the accumulation point into the tumult where all failures swirled together—the disaster at the

board, Maggie's growing list of his faults, the hacking. No wonder Lawton had traded him away to the only man at Day and
Domes who would have him.

Suddenly a large head appeared in the doorway to the inner
hall. Gunderman jumped up from the chair as if he had been
found out. He followed the Wise Man to his office.

"So, Sam. Where to begin?"

Gunderman was only sure where not to.

"Have you ever heard of the three-body problem?" he said.

"Most of my patients find that having one body is problem
enough."

"When Isaac Newton used differential equations to explain the
movement of the heavenly spheres, he only considered them two
by two. Earth and sun, for example. The pull of the mass of the
moon was too small to have an effect anyone could imagine measuring at that time, so he simply disregarded it."

"This has something to do with your feelings?"

"The trouble was that over the years measurements became
more and more precise, and the problem of the effect of the third
body became unavoidable. When scientists attempted to use
Newton's calculus to compute it, the equations became unsolvable. This became one of the great mathematical mysteries of the
19th Century, so intractable that the King of Sweden offered a
prize for its solution. The French mathematician Poincaré won,
and in the process of writing up his proof for publication, he got
the first glimpse of what mathematicians now call chaos."

"It's an old story. Things fall apart, make a mess."

"Chaos isn't random. It is deterministic—fully governed by the
laws of physics—but not predictable the way the arc of a parabola
is. Think of the weather."

"That's a comfort."

"When you model a three-body system, you get a fuzzy-looking orbit diagram. You see, you cannot say precisely where each of the three bodies will be in relation to one another at any given moment in the future. There are laws, but they're not linear."

"Have you been feeling unsteady?"

"I guess what I'm feeling is perturbed."

"That's a word from physics, Sam. Try another."

"Something is happening at home. My wife. I can't solve her anymore."

"You see her as a mathematical problem?"

"The thing is, biological systems themselves are nonlinear, given to chaos."

"Often we intellectualize in order to avoid our feelings. How does chaos feel to you? See if you can tell me in common language."

"Her mood has been oscillating."

"A story. Tell me a story, Sam."

"Sometimes at dinner, when I'm talking about my day, she just gets up and leaves the table. Not just the table. Sometimes she leaves the house altogether."

"Do you ever ask about her day?"

"When I do, it always seems to be that she has been caught in the middle between women she thought were friends. The three-body problem."

"You were doing well up till the end."

"Even if I take her side, she says that I don't really mean it, that I'm only humoring her, that I treat her as though I think she's being too sensitive."

"Do you think that?"

"Sometimes."

"Well then."

"She keeps an iterative map."

"Try again."

"It's like keeping score. Each of my failures sets off a strobe and stops that moment in time, preserves it forever. Pop! A data point. She never forgets even one of them. Pop! What is it that you call it, like when the twin towers fell?"

"Flash memory."

"And when the strobe goes off again, she flashes back on all the earlier data points."

"Do you ever connect the dots?"

"Imagine them spreading to the right from the y axis. The x axis is time, the y is intensity of resentment. As time passes, the dots rise and become more concentrated. Little things: an unsympathetic word. Big things: leaving the hospital room during delivery because I was beginning to feel faint. More and more of them accumulate until the map is so heavily populated that when you connect the dots, it looks like a piece of woven cloth. That's what I mean when I say I can't solve her anymore."

Gunderman stopped and looked over at the Kleenex box.

"Do you want to take a moment?"

Gunderman did not answer. Nor did he take a tissue.

"Can you try to describe the feeling another way?"

"The score isn't right. Some of her data points are moments when I actually stood by her, when it was a sacrifice to do so, when I felt what she felt, moments when I really loved her. As far as she was concerned, even then I failed the test. If you look at a distorting mirror long enough, you'll see the reflection as real."

"Do the strobe lights ever make you cry?"

"I don't cry."

"You got close a little bit ago."

"Frustration."

"Or was it anger? You are allowed to be angry when you are wronged. A great scientist once said that."

"I'm getting annoyed now."

"Or is it fear?"

"I'm afraid of what exactly?"

"I want you to think more about that third body. The one that perturbs you. Can you come in twice next week?"

"I'm going to be very busy. I may have to cancel the sessions we already have on the calendar."

"Well, we'll need to think about the why of that, too."

Grace had worked in a lot of temporary offices over the years: sans music, sans art, sans view, sometimes even sans window. Just a Steelcase desk, a phone with a single line and no voice mail, an Aeron knockoff to sit on, and perhaps a tiny, round table with two uncomfortable chairs. She always brought along a family photo in an Office Depot frame. Until recently it was Jim and kids at the beach, cross-country skiing, hiking in the mountains at Banff. She and Jim took turns with the camera, so each photo was a member of a pair, one with him in it for her and one with her in it for him. Now the one she brought along had just the kids, and soon the older photos would be divided, the family as a matter of law being two overlapping sets, like a Venn diagram.

She looked at her BlackBerry for the nth time since returning from the war room but still found nothing but RSS feeds about the companies she followed, the usual traffic from the bank, and some more ads for something called Viagra for women. She had never been in less need of pharmaceutical aid. OK, except for the pill. She had restarted that when she made the bid to be on the Day and Domes engagement. She felt foolish when she took the first one, but she did not fail to take the second. By the time the bank had put her on the team, she was toggling between thrill and shame. Tom hadn't even known she was working on the project until he'd walked into the war room to do the first overview. His expression when he saw her pushed her deep into the shame quadrant. He left as soon as he finished his presentation, giving scarcely a look in her direction. She didn't see him again for days. Once, after hours, when she knew he was out of town, she looked into his office. She could have used some pharmaceuticals then—a Xanax-SSRI cocktail—because she had gone beyond shame into mortification.

Now she could scarcely believe there was a straight line between that time and this. The first night, she came close to the fear quadrant, but then they were touching, and she flew all the way out beyond time and the best corner of the graph.

"I am so sorry for leaving you," he said.

She reached out and touched his hand.

"Now is not the time for talking," she said.

They fell asleep without turning off the lights, and by the time she woke up, he had already gone to the Dome. Later that morning, they were together in the war room. He was called away, then in the afternoon he came to her temporary office. He kept the desk between them as he put a key next to her BlackBerry.

"To let you in tonight," he said.

"You won't be there?"

"I don't know when."

"Did he hate the presentation?"

"It isn't that," he said.

"I'll get something we can warm up."

"Maybe you'd rather stay at the hotel," he said, "so I don't wake you."

"Wake me," she said and came around the desk. He turned toward the door before she was ready.

"I'd feel better if I knew you would let yourself fall asleep," he said.

"Whatever it is, good luck," she said.

The rest of the day there were no meetings in the war room, no bustle in the hall, no hint of what was going on. At one point she took the elevator to the boardroom floor, prepared to describe her purpose as architectural if she were caught. She saw no one and felt no hint of his presence.

When she let herself into his townhouse that evening, everywhere she looked she sensed diminishment: the colorless walls; the way the furniture kept a distance; the picked-up pieces that lay on flat surfaces—a lake-polished stone, a large feather of brown and white, an empty picture frame. Whatever it was that had happened to him had taken away most of what he was.

She ordered pizza with a lot on it. Waiting for the delivery, she turned on CNN. The news passed through her without snagging. When her BlackBerry rang with "What a Feeling" and it wasn't him, she didn't answer. After eating, she put the rest of the pizza in plastic containers, wrapped herself in a sweater, and disposed of the cardboard box in a Dumpster outside. Back in front of the TV, she soon caught herself nodding. She checked her BlackBerry again, but there was nothing from him. She did not want to get into bed, but what was wrong with curling up on the couch? It must have been much later when the door opened, because at first it was a dream.

"Tom?" she said, raising herself on an elbow.

The only light came from the television. He turned it off. She started to sit up.

"Stay," he said, slipping out of his coat and pulling off his tie. He sat down, put his hand on her head, and eased it onto his lap.

"Is everything OK?" she said.

"Sleep," he said.

"What about you?" she said. "There's pizza."

"This is what I need," he said.

She rolled her head for a kiss, but he was looking straight out into the darkness. She touched his cheek and he leaned down to meet her. Then he began gently stroking her upper arm, and she relaxed into him.

When she woke up again, it was still dark. Four thirty by the LED next to the TV, and he was gone.

two

THE

MAN ON A

BRIDGE

1

Rosten left her a note saying he was sorry to have gotten back so late and gone so early: "Crisis at the Dome. Nothing to do with what you're working on. We'll talk tonight."

She did not see him all day and ended up getting back to his apartment before him in the evening. She had no idea what he had steeled himself to do, so she just chatted away as she warmed the pizza and put it out on the coffee table with some vegetables and dip. He had no taste for any of it.

"I need to tell you what happened," he said.

"You were tied up," she said. "I understand."

"I mean in New Haven and after," he said.

"Let's just enjoy our time together," she said. "Now is now."

"Now came of then," he said.

Her plate went down onto the glass tabletop with such precision that it made no sound.

"It started at the Lizzie," he said.

"That was a whole other life," she said.

"Professor Hawthorne had invited me to meet him there," he said. "I can't say I wasn't flattered. Whenever he spoke to you, it made you feel like you were something."

"Actually, he only spoke to you," said Grace.

"It was one of those late-February days that seem like spring," he said. "It got me thinking about graduation—starting to write, getting some kind of job, reading difficult verse at the Elizabethan Club."

"And being with me," she said.

She put it out there as if to get the worst on the table, which saddened him, because she had no idea how much worse it was going to get.

"I was early, so I waited outside in the garden near the statue of Shakespeare," he said. "When it was time and I went inside, Hawthorne was at the table, directly under the portrait of the Virgin Queen, his hair as electrostatic as hers. He was wearing that Army field jacket of his with the upside-down American flag on the back, the janitor pants with a hammer sling on the leg, and, of course, the awful black Keds. He was immersed in *Critical Inquiry*. I started to pull out a chair, but he stopped me and said we had to go into the vault. You remember it."

"It was like the basement of a bank."

"Why didn't you let me get you into the Lizzie?" he said. "The Elizabethan was your period. Marlowe. Kyd. Jonson. They were all in the vault."

"I would have still been your guest," she said.

"Everybody gets in through somebody," he said. "Hawthorne got me in."

"That was different," she said. "It meant something."

"Not what I thought," he said.

The vault had stood wide open. It had always made Rosten think of "The Cask of Amontillado," so when Hawthorne began pulling the door closed behind them, he stepped forward and put out his hand.

"Don't worry," Hawthorne said, dropping his eyes to where a brick prevented the door from closing all the way.

Deprived of the light from the outside room, the shelves of ancient volumes under the bare incandescent bulb went amber. Hawthorne looked like some extinct creature preserved in it.

"I asked you here," he said, "because we need to discuss something that cannot go beyond the two of us."

For a moment Rosten thought he was being tapped.

"Is there a secret society?" he said.

"A secret society," Hawthorne said. "Very good. I had never considered it that way."

Rosten felt worse than a Fool; there was always some wisdom in a Fool.

"Actually," Hawthorne said, "I'm acting on behalf of Ernest Fisherman. I don't imagine you know the name."

"It seems familiar," Rosten said. He saw his lameness reflected in Hawthorne's expression.

"From time to time I encounter a young man who strikes me as having the qualities that suit him to help in Fisherman's work," Hawthorne said.

"He's a scholar?"

"A very unconventional one." Hawthorne's face took on a sudden intensity that Rosten had not seen even in the pictures from the years of rage. "I'm not talking theory," he said. "This is real life and real death. Fisherman is with the CIA."

Grace pulled back at the head and shoulders.

"It was Hawthorne who recruited you?" she said.

"He had gone to work for the Agency straight out of the College," Rosten said, "brought into it by a man named James Jesus Angleton. Angleton had grown up in Italy, had known Ezra Pound there. He had come to Yale as an undergraduate and soon was editing a literary journal, *Furioso*. Very avant-garde for its day. You'd be surprised at the names he published. As Angleton rose in the intelligence world, he kept his contacts in the English Department. Fisherman was his first recruit. The two of them pulled in Hawthorne, who had already managed to publish a dazzling paper on the *Pisan Cantos*."

"He did like to dazzle," said Grace.

"They had a lot to talk about. Angleton thrived on the *Cantos'* opacity," said Rosten. "In his line of worked, he lived it."

"So the spy novels are right," she said.

"Understated," said Rosten. "The best were by Beckett."

Grace darkened as the opacity began to descend on her.

"There's that famous picture of Hawthorne leading a huge antiwar rally on the Green," she said. "You're telling me that was all an act?"

"He said he turned against the war when he realized that the Soviets couldn't have been happier, seeing us bleed in Vietnam for nothing," said Rosten.

"And yet he continued to lure students into the CIA."

"He recruited only for Fisherman," said Rosten. "It seems that, much as he hated communism, Fisherman saw the war the same way Hawthorne did."

"Unbelievable," she said.

"That day in the vault I was informed that I was a young man of adequate intellect who knew how to do an assignment. Hawthorne assured me that Fisherman valued these qualities, which he associated with the Heartland."

"Hawthorne barely knew you," said Grace.

"He knew more than you would imagine," said Rosten. "He told me there had been an extensive investigation. 'By the way, we looked into that young woman of yours, too,' he said. 'Everything suggests that you are both cut from the same cloth.'"

"This is making me really uncomfortable," Grace said. "Can we stop?"

"We've only started, I'm afraid."

"Did he listen to us in the bed?" she said.

Rosten had never thought to find out.

"I told him that the CIA wasn't the life I imagined," he said. "He told me that it was the life I could have. 'You might even find the thing you are meant to write about,' he said. 'You know, the right subject covers a lot of inadequacies.'"

"You must have been devastated. Why didn't you say something to me?"

Rosten had not been allowed to. All he could tell her was that he had taken a position in Washington, D.C. Immediately after his graduation they drove there together to look for a place to live. She was ready to stay the summer, but as soon as they arrived, he said he didn't think that would be a good idea. He was going to be gone a lot. It wouldn't be fair for her to be stranded alone in an unfamiliar place.

The flat they found wasn't much—one large room with a closet of a kitchen that had a long venetian blind in lieu of a door. She found ways of brightening the place, a batik to hang on the wall for a flash of color, fabric to cover the horsehair mattress of the bed that doubled as a couch. She helped him put up shelves of cinder blocks and two-by-tens and then watched him arrange the books.

When he had them all in place, he stepped back and said, "What do you think?"

"It's you," she said.

Then Sunday came and he drove her to National Airport for her trip to North Dakota. She wrote him every day from her father's farm. He sent her only two letters in return. The second said that he would be going into intensive training and had to break off contact. Those were the words he used. How cold they must have seemed to her.

Sometimes at night in bed, the pain that his silence was surely causing her came over him, pulling him back to the Tom Rosten she had known. They had taken away all the other touch points by which he had formerly located himself—clothes, family, the long hair Grace had liked to stroke. In place of these were compartments, secret boxes, in one of which, he was given to understand, he would one day come to find exactly what his country needed of him.

When the cloistered phase of training concluded, he finally wrote her again. She was back in New Haven, and he was careful to have his letters posted from somewhere he was not. She must have sensed that he was lost to her, but they settled on getting together in Washington on a date certain in early fall.

He met her at Union Station, carrying a travel bag himself, and took her to a big, anonymous hotel off Scott Circle that smelled of cigarettes and disinfectant. She wanted to know why they didn't stay at the apartment. He said he it was to be a vacation, and they did behave like tourists: the White House, the Capitol Building, the I. M. Pei East Wing on Pennsylvania Avenue. She wanted to take the FBI tour, but the Bureau was in one compartment and he was in another. He told her he had heard that the tour was too boring for words. Because of the location of the hotel he chose, every day they ended on 16th Street, where they passed the shuttered, haunted house of the Soviet Embassy.

When they returned to Union Station, she talked of a next visit. He said he would need to clear a date. But their time together had made him realize that he needed to break it off, this time for good. Being with her, he felt himself sliding back into what he had been, imagining they could be like the other couples on the tours—heedless, happy, of little use.

After Thanksgiving she wrote him to say that she had gone down to Washington and found his apartment vacant. The manager had told her he had moved out after only a couple of months, walking away from the deposit. Rosten had the Agency reseal the letter and send it back Addressee Unknown. By then he had been given his assignment. All that was left of what he and Grace had thought they'd had together was collateral damage.

Now, all these many years later, he touched the back of her hand with his fingers.

"I went down the wrong path, Grace," he told her. His mouth was dry, but at least he had begun.

2

For weeks, Gunderman struggled with the fact that he could see what the hacker had done inside the database but could not figure out how he had gotten there. Then suddenly his overnight processor served up an algorithm. How anything so clear could come from the jumbled, unpredictable mush of dreams, he never knew. For weeks he had been stuck, then this came, not words or numbers but an object in three dimensions, sharp-edged and obvious, like a building by Mies. When applied to the database, the algorithm would grind away, repeating the same steps over and over again as it crawled along, feeling with its digits until it found the wormhole where the intruder had entered.

Maggie's breath fluttered through her lips in an unsteady cadence as Gunderman snuck out of bed as carefully as a cheating man might sneak into it. In the warmth of the car, speeding down the expressway, he could not believe the solution was as simple as it was. All he could remember of his dream was "The Sorcerer's

Apprentice" music from *Fantasia*, which he had not seen since he was a child. He did not have to go his Wise Man to figure out the meaning of that. It was a warning. If they did not deal with the problem properly, it would split into two problems, then four, then eight, sixteen. He needed to go to Rosten.

"'The Sorcerer's Apprentice'!" Rosten said.

His rage shocked Gunderman. He heard himself speaking faster, louder.

"Stop!" said Rosten. "Control-alt-delete."

Gunderman took a breath and tried to slow down.

"I have an algorithm," he said. "We can go to the audit chairman with both the problem and a plan. Otherwise trouble will increase geometrically, like Mickey Mouse's brooms."

"Grow up," said Rosten.

"I'm not saying tell the public," Gunderman said. "Just the Audit Committee chairman."

"Teddy Diamond is in trouble at his own company."

"Unless we do something, this will metastasize," said Gunderman.

"So it's not brooms," said Rosten. "It's cancer."

Metaphors were Gunderman's enemies. Code was his only friend.

"Teddy Diamond is a professional," he said.

"I'll tell you what he would do," said Rosten. "Run for cover, just like you're doing. He'd demand an independent investigation. By the time he got done, everybody in the fucking world would know that our system is a sieve."

"Actually, it let something in, not let something out," said Gunderman. Warm air whispered in the ducts under the ceiling tile. The hush was unbearable. He finally broke it. "Every system made by man has bugs," he said. "You just have to deal with them. That's all I'm trying to say."

"You think this algorithm of yours will show us something?" said Rosten.

"It will find the breach in the firewall."

"That might lead somewhere, I guess," said Rosten. "Bring it to Lawton. See what he thinks. But leave Teddy Diamond the hell out of it."

At least it was a start. One logical step at a time, just like writing code. Gunderman found Lawton deep in his terminal.

"I've checked the accounts of the senior executives and a few others," Lawton said. "You're past due on an electric bill, by the way."

"I guess I've been distracted," Gunderman said.

"Then I looked at the top people at our bigger clients," said Lawton. As he spoke, his mouth barely opened. Gunderman had to move closer to hear. "Not a single data set out of whack. An overdraft here, a missed payment there, but by the next cycle everything squared up again."

Lawton was wearing a sweater, even though warm air blew down on them. Suddenly a shiver went through him.

"You want to believe it was a transient event," Lawton said. "You want to think you'll wake up in the morning and feel foolish for having been afraid."

"I woke up with an answer," said Gunderman.

"But the thing is still there. You can feel it," said Lawton.

The chill came on again, and Gunderman felt something go through his own body, too. You wanted to believe that you were basically all right. You wanted to believe that those close to you were all right, too. You weren't looking for two standard deviations to the positive. Just something a little to the right of the mean.

Lawton held his arms tight across his chest.

"Maybe you should go to the doctor," Gunderman said.

"Tell me what you've got," said Lawton.

Gunderman walked him through it. "I still have to write the code," he said.

"Do it," said Lawton.

Making sure the algorithm captured what Gunderman was searching for meant that it kicked out a lot of false positives. These he had to deal with one by one. If it had been an ordinary situation, he would have taken time to automate the part being played now by the processor in his skull. But it was all right. If he didn't keep his brain occupied, it might take him to places he did not want to go.

The algorithm ground away 24/7, popping lines of suspicious computer language onto Gunderman's screen, but more than a week into it, nothing had turned up but odd bits of foreign matter that the security programs had disabled—unsuccessful viruses, worms, Trojan horses, and scraps of executable code that had probably come in on a zip drive somebody had picked up as a tchotchke at a conference. Sticking one of those into your laptop was like putting into your mouth a piece of gum you had scraped off the bottom of your shoe.

The sun had been down for hours. The office was quiet, and yet Gunderman could not focus. There was nothing to do but to go home and hope that in the morning there would be light.

Maggie was in the kitchen when he came in the back door.

"Hi," he said.

She said something that sounded like a word.

"How was your day?" he said.

"She's not speaking to me," Maggie said.

"Not speaking about anything in particular?" he said.

"Not speaking as in mute," she said.

"Should I attempt to make contact?" he said.

"We'll work it out," she said.

Megan remained upstairs while he and Maggie ate dinner. Their only conversation concerned the passing of the salt. When the TV came on for whatever Thursday's programs were, he went up to change. Along the way he knocked on Megan's door. Hearing no complaint, he turned the knob and poked in his head.

"Hi," he said.

"Hi," she said.

"You OK?" he said.

"Ask her," she said.

"Love you," he said.

"I know," she said.

He fell asleep even before the news. Maggie had to shake him awake to go to bed. As they went through their ablutions, he was deep into the problem again. Maggie did not seem to care where he was.

The next morning his overnight processor had done it again. The algorithm hadn't missed the answer. It had found it: There was no breach in the fire wall. He popped out of bed. Maggie stirred but did not wake. He hurried his toast and cereal and sped downtown. Lawton was already in his office. He had a little color in his face and was no longer shivering like one of the homeless. When Gunderman revealed what had come to him, he did not need to provide his reasoning. Lawton grasped it immediately. Now the question was how to put it to Rosten.

"We've defined the set," Gunderman said as they stood before him.

"I don't want a set," said Rosten. "I want the hacker."

"The set of those who could have done it," said Gunderman. "See, now we have something to tell Teddy Diamond. The hacker is one of us."

"Somebody who is very bitter," said Lawton, looking as though he could actually taste it.

"Are you bitter, Dell?" said Rosten. "If you are, you know what you can do."

Lawton said nothing. He simply walked out.

"What got into him?" Rosten said.

Gunderman wanted to believe it was the pressure that was turning Rosten hard.

"Let's stick to the evidence, OK?" Rosten said. "Has there been any change in the pattern of complaints about inaccurate data in individual credit reports?"

"That's a silence I don't think we should put much faith in," said Gunderman. "Somebody has tampered, and he can probably do it again."

Rosten looked past him.

"Tell Dell I'm sorry," he said.

"He's just been trying to view things objectively," Gunderman said. "It isn't easy."

"The fear," Rosten said.

"It is affecting all of us," said Gunderman.

Rosten smoothed the neatly piled papers on his desk with both palms as if somebody had crumpled them.

"Do you think he'd be willing to have lunch with me?" he said.

"I think you should ask him."

He wasn't sure Rosten heard.

"You do agree that at the moment we have nothing to report," Rosten said.

You wanted to be able to read people, but they lived beyond the point where the system goes chaotic. They flipped from one orbit to another.

"I'm not going to be writing a memo to file," said Gunderman, "if that's what you mean."

"Of course not," said Rosten, going at those papers again. The conversation was over.

There was supposed to be a big snow coming in, but Gunderman went out anyway, heading east to the other side of Lake Shore Drive. He walked past the empty boat slips, across the bridge over the frozen river, then to Navy Pier, which was crowded with children. He watched a marionette show. He walked under the lowering sky to the end of the pier, where he stared out over the ice toward Michigan. Eventually he made his way back to the Dome in time to beat the leading edge of the storm.

With the holiday weekend starting the next day and the commute threatened by weather, the secretaries' desks were already empty, leaving him unobserved and unjudged. No phones buzzed. No BlackBerry ringtones revealed the musical tastes of their owners. Suddenly a form loomed up. They collided.

"Sorry about that," said the young number cruncher, half into his topcoat and as big as a linebacker. "Didn't think anybody else was still here. I was finishing the final deck for the board presentation. At least I hope it's final. What's your excuse?"

The young ones were heedless of seniority. They never called you mister or sir. But the fact was, the kid was in the loop, and Gunderman clearly wasn't.

"Board presentation?" Gunderman said.

"To me, it's just another deadline," said the young man.

"This is a deck laying out the deal?" said Gunderman.

"What else is there these days?" said the young man, slipping the rest of the way into his sleeve. "I've got to catch a train. You should bail, too. Nobody's taking names."

When Gunderman reached his desk, the lines of symbols on the screen had not changed since he'd left. He dialed Lawton.

"He's sorry," Gunderman said. "He was out of line, and he knows it. Maybe he's said that to you himself already."

"He hasn't," said Lawton.

"He asked me to tell you," said Gunderman. "He said he was going to invite you to lunch."

"I should have told him off," said Lawton.

"Don't do it," said Gunderman. "Take the weekend. I mean, think about your medical insurance."

"A few minutes ago I learned that somebody has altered my account, too." Lawton said.

3

As Rosten went through his training, he did not hear a word from or about Ernest Fisherman. He began to doubt Hawthorne's story about the great man handpicking him. Clearly, to the trainers there was nothing chosen about him. This only made him work harder, just as he had done in college among the prep schoolers. In the war games the Agency trainees played against veteran FBI agents, whom his trainers called "the Sisters," Rosten eluded tails, passed messages unseen, and with impressive accuracy identified photos of the Sisters who had been on him. He came to imagine that he might have a gift that would get him posted somewhere behind the Wall, but when assignment time arrived, the lead instructor told him his first station would be London.

"What's in London?" he said.

"For you the most remarkable individual you will ever meet," said the lead instructor. "Frankly, I don't understand why he chose you. I suggested several others. But you were the one he wanted. We need men like Ernest Fisherman. Correction. We need one man like him. And for some reason he needs you."

Rosten's orders directed him to report to the Embassy on Grosvenor Square. His passport was unmarked when he arrived at Heathrow; he had never been abroad. Coming out of the airport, he got into a taxi. Rosten knew its steering wheel would be on the right, but once they got into traffic, he felt as though he had stepped into a mirror.

The next morning, armed with a cartoonish map from the front desk, he walked. At every corner he checked the sidewalk for the sign that said, "Look Left" or "Look Right." Eventually he found the modern concrete box of the Embassy, which did not fit with the old opulence around it. On the way in he passed a statue of Eisenhower in military uniform, hands on hips, watched over by a huge American eagle on the roof. A young Marine guard checked his orders and credentials and directed him to the security office, where a dour lady checked them again. Eventually she satisfied herself and sent him to an office upstairs. He supposed there would be papers to sign, an ID photo to be taken, perhaps a briefing on local customs.

When he got there, he found himself in an antechamber where, at the secretary's desk, sat a small man in a shabby jacket and ancient tie who did not look up. Nothing indicated what kind of person the office belonged to. Rosten laid his orders in front of the old fellow and asked if he could be announced.

"This isn't Buckingham Palace," said the man, who went on rooting around in the desk drawers. He found what he was looking for and held it up for Rosten's inspection: a box of government-issue paper clips.

The man's manner, though in no way impressive, did suggest

that he had not spent his whole career behind a receptionist's desk. Physically, he was nearly featureless, a guy in line for a teller to whom you would never give a second look, even if he looked at you, which this man seemed determined not to do.

"Mr. Fisherman is expecting me," said Rosten. "At London Station, I imagine."

"You will learn not to imagine you know what he is thinking," said the man, finally looking up, his gray eyes large in the lenses.

"You are Mr. Fisherman, aren't you," said Rosten.

The eyes behind the heavy black frames of his glasses revealed nothing.

"This is not a test," said Fisherman. "When they come, they're much harder."

He stood and went to the inner door, which had a keypad lock. The way he positioned himself blocked Rosten from seeing. The apparatus clicked and Fisherman turned the knob.

"Come in," he said without looking back. "And bring your orders. It would not do to have them lying around a place that is fit only for secreting paper clips."

Rosten stood at the chair across the desk from where Fisherman had lowered himself. Just as this man's eyes got their power by being without expression, his voice drew force from not rising above a whisper.

"Sit," he said, and Rosten obeyed in silence as Fisherman busied himself clipping papers together and laying them out evenly before him like a hand of solitaire.

The inner office was as nondescript as the outer, though it did have a window with a bright view framed by trees. The walls were blank, without even the standard photo of the President. Magnetic signs on the front of two formidable, combination-locked filing cabinets read, "Closed." A walk-in safe in the wall was open.

"I'm told you have an interest in poetry," said Rosten.

"Perhaps at some point we will have time for that," said Fisherman.

He slid each collection of papers into a separate folder. When he finished, he slipped them all into a large, red-striped manila envelope marked HUMINT for human intelligence. He pushed it across the desk.

"Go ahead," said Fisherman. "It only looks radioactive."

The envelope was much heavier than Rosten expected, as if sheathed in lead.

"I want you to tell me who the men in these files really are," said Fisherman. He turned his back and looked out the window. "Your office is just down the hall. You will find in the envelope the key along with the combination for the filing safe. Do not place the combination in the burn bag. Burn it yourself as soon as you have memorized it. At Yale they still teach one to memorize, don't they? You will find matches in the envelope. There is an ashtray on the desk. Be sure to stir the ashes then put them in the bag. Do not take any materials out of the office. Lock them in the filing safe each time you leave, even to go to the bathroom. Tell me tomorrow what you have learned."

Rosten found the right door and dug out the key, which let him into a windowless room. At first he thought it was for a secretary, but when the fluorescents in the ceiling came on, he realized that this was his office. The walls were bare and needed paint. Under the light his skin had a sick, bluish cast. On the standard gray desk stood a reading lamp with an incandescent bulb. He switched it on and went back to extinguish the morbid overheads. This obscured the walls. The warm glow went only as far as the edge of the desk.

He hung his coat on the back of the chair and opened the envelope. Inside were dossiers on nine potential informants. The documents were typed on a manual typewriter, single-spaced, and promiscuous with fact. There seemed to be no organizing principle or criterion of selection. Reading them reminded him of confronting one of those experimental poems with words scattered across the page like litter.

By pulling an all-nighter, he was able the next day to bring Fisherman concise, handwritten summaries. Gone were the repetitive ins and outs recorded by Agency spotters around the world. These Rosten turned into neat timelines. References to family members and associates he made into a single paragraph. What Rosten found most difficult was the portion of his summary that he assigned the rubric "C.V.," under which he reconstructed the subject's job history. Most dossiers had gaps, sometimes of several years' duration, representing the blank time between one report from a confidential source and the next. The nature of the sources was never given, but Rosten knew from his training that they could range from newspaper and magazine articles to moles, defectors, and electronic surveillance. In some instances the reports contradicted one another; Rosten noted every discrepancy.

When Fisherman read what Rosten gave him, he said, "You have a nice, clear hand. Is there anything of a more discursive nature that you did not feel comfortable committing to paper?"

"Should there be?" said Rosten.

"Disappointing, but unsurprising," said Fisherman. "Information of the sort you found in these dossiers is often more important for what it hides than for what it reveals. The times unaccounted for, the conflicting reports. Remember that whatever we see could have been fabricated precisely to be seen. Go back and prepare a report for me of what the dossiers do not say."

"I think I've indicated all the holes," said Rosten.

"Fill them," said Fisherman.

Not even during his freshman year, a Midwestern son of public education, a nobody from nowhere, had Rosten felt so inadequate. Fisherman wanted him to doubt everything that was written, and doubt ate its own tail. Doubt the fact, doubt the doubt. This was worse than the sophistry he had gotten used to in critical theory. It was about real beings. He was being asked to divine from without what was within, which for all he knew could be Schrödinger's cat in its closed box, quantum strange, both alive and dead, only one or the other if someone opened the lid.

He reread a dossier and put it aside. Then, in his careful hand, he wrote a story. He repeated this process over and over until he had done them all. A few depicted the subject as just another man afraid of the future, afraid of his boss, afraid of his wife. The majority of his stories, however, portrayed a deceiver, compromising everyone with whom he came into contact. Story became Rosten's way of dealing with the closed box. He simply invented the cat.

"Good," said Fisherman when he had finished reading Rosten's work, "though with a few of these men, you may have been a bit credulous."

"Which ones?" said Rosten.

"We shall see," said Fisherman, handing him another large, sealed, red-striped manila envelope. "Now work on these."

In the windowless office, day and night were indistinguishable.

He knew no one in London, so he worked long hours, only occasionally taking a break in the afternoon to hunt for a permanent place to live. It wasn't long before looking the proper direction at intersections became habit.

Eventually, he visited London Station and made the acquaintance of some analysts not too much older than himself. They hung out at a club called Bigsby's, which was far enough from the Station that they had to take the Tube. The first time he went with them, the man at the door challenged him.

"Show him your Agency ID," said the analyst who called himself Brick.

Rosten balked.

"He's ours," said Brick.

It soon became clear to Rosten that everyone else in the place was, too. The décor did not say American. In fact, it tried just a little too hard not to. On one wall hung a dartboard that had not been struck by many darts and on another a very recent portrait of the Queen. The bar stretched along the back wall. A red-faced guy behind it could have come from Chaucer, until he spoke and you realized he came from Texas.

"We call this our safe house," said Brick.

"It's swept," said his pal, Travers.

"So you don't have to worry," said Brick. "You can tell us all about your boss."

"He's a man apart," Rosten said, nothing more.

The long hours Rosten spent in the office took on a rhythm. He read. He imagined. He wrote:

"It was the good fortune of Arkady Pavelovich Simkov to join the Red Army in time to march unimpeded through Poland and take over from the Americans in Leipzig after the German surrender. There his name became associated with victory and Soviet orthodoxy, drawing the attention of the GRU, which had a weakness for men of unearned promise. Simkov did not disappoint. He contented himself with making and moving documents, took on a good, solid, Soviet wife. He was an inside man without a hint that he heard the call of the wild until a year ago, when he found himself posted to France. There, his duties from time to time took him to Nice, accompanying delegations from the film collectives. One day he was seen catching a train to Monaco.

"When he returned, he bought many rounds of drinks for the filmmakers in a bar overlooking the Mediterranean, after which he entered an elevator with an actress, Agrafina Ivana Rogozin, who had many men buying her things.

"The wheel of fortune did not continue to treat Simkov well, which is what eventually brought him to our attention. He has the requisite weaknesses and needs but is too frightened to do what would be worth our keeping the wheel spinning."

These narratives seemed to satisfy Fisherman, as did the increasing skepticism Rosten demonstrated in them, but Rosten was becoming dissatisfied.

"I'm tossing my judgments random on the wind," he said.

"So you know your Euripides," said Fisherman. "Too bad it's such ancient knowledge. We are creatures of darkness. We see by our own light. That's Gide. He's more current."

When Rosten got together with Brick and Travers now, he sometimes allowed conversations about Fisherman to develop, hoping to learn any little bit of gossip that might enhance the story he was writing in his mind. He had already picked up certain things during training, beginning with the miracle of Fisherman's survival of the post-Watergate purges. Few who had worked counterintelligence for James Jesus Angleton had come through undamaged, and none who did had been as close to Angleton as Fisherman.

Often when men fall who have built empires on fear, their ideas fall with them. So it was with Angleton. Close to two decades later, Rosten's trainers still used his relentless mole hunt of the 1960s as a case study of the damage that can be done when skepticism tips into paranoia. When Rosten pressed them to say why Fisherman hadn't been destroyed, each had his own explanation, one more improbable than the next. Only one retired Agency veteran, now on contract to teach recruits the art of escape and evasion, dared to say a thing that had the sting of truth: Fisherman's split with his former boss could have been a deception. "I wouldn't put it past Angleton," he said, "to have frozen some of his semen."

As Angleton weakened, the Director of Central Intelligence apparently came to fear that the whole counterintelligence function could collapse with him, so he pulled Fisherman in to be his Plan B. Fisherman must have chosen his moves well, because even after Langley rebuilt a regular counterintelligence unit under another man, the DCI found it convenient to keep Fisherman on his own payroll along with a staff of meaningful size and skill. It was here that the two reasonably detailed stories that Rosten's trainers told came in, both involving successful encounters with one of the Soviets' most accomplished agents, Anton Ignatyeff Kerzhentseff. It was said that Fisherman, in triumph, claimed to have given him this name, but it was just his little joke. The nom de guerre he almost certainly did give the man was Zapadnya, the Trap.

In the first case, Fisherman had managed to trick Kerzhentseff into thinking the system used to communicate with Soviet deep-cover agents had been unriddled, though in fact the code breakers at NSA could not read a syllable. Deceiving the master deceiver had cost the life of one young American soldier, a suicide.

Later, as Fisherman approached retirement age, a new DCI reattached him to the regular counterintelligence unit, which eliminated his autonomy. Just when it looked as if the old man would not get to serve past sixty-five, Fisherman delivered a figure from the National Security Council so high-ranking that some years later the trainers did not dare speak his name. Fisherman got his waivers. In fact, he went back on the DCI's payroll, with more freedom than ever, which was what had brought him not long ago to his garden-view office in the Embassy in London, from which he said he could smell the continent all the way to the Urals without actually having to get it on his shoes.

With evidence mounting that the Soviets had someone well placed within the Agency, Fisherman's position was secure. As the Agency's eyes closed in the Soviet Union and Eastern Europe, most of them ending with pennies on them, Fisherman did not spin up elaborate conspiracy theories the way his mentor had. He built dossiers, challenged assumptions. When he made a case, he made something happen, or stopped it before it did. When he took the top off the box, he was ready to deal with the cat, dead or alive.

As the months wore on, Rosten began to detest the hermetic nature of the tasks he was given. He had been trained for the outside. That had been the purpose of the games on the Washington streets with the Sisters, and he had a gift for it, a gift unopened as he sat in his windowless room.

Finally he reached his limit.

"I trained for the real world," he told Fisherman.

"And where is that, exactly?" said Fisherman.

That was the whole conversation.

Rosten continued on as before, feeling as if he were writing for an obscure scholarly journal that nobody read but those who wrote for it. He tried to relieve his boredom by going to the theater. At the bar between acts one night, he struck up a conversation with an attractive woman. They went out several times, but then she said he was just too distant, even by English standards. After that experience he asked out a few young American women from the Embassy. One became interested, even eager, but when she did, he backed away. Apparently word got around. So he frequently found himself at Bigsby's with Brick and Travers. There he sometimes encountered veterans of what they called the Holy War, who often came from Central Asia to London for a kind of R&R. Rosten would see them drinking as if it were the last alcohol that would ever pass their lips.

Late one evening Rosten returned to his office after a siege at Bigsby's and nodded off at his desk. The telephone shouted him awake. He gathered his files; there were enough of them that he had to cradle them on his forearms. When he reached Fisherman's office, he balanced the stack of folders carefully as he pushed into the anteroom. He let the door ease against his back until he felt it latch. But for a sliver of light under Fisherman's inner door, the room was black. He felt for the unused secretary's desk. When his knee found it, he put the stack down and knocked. No answer. He knocked again, louder this time. He put his ear against the door. Silence. Then, without so much as a scuff of warning, the feel of the wood vanished in a burst of light.

"There are better ways to eavesdrop," Fisherman said.

"You didn't answer," said Rosten. "I'm sorry."

"That is something one so rarely hears in our line," said Fisherman, "and even more rarely believes."

"The dossiers," Rosten said, stepping back out of the trapezoid of light.

"Bring them in, but you won't need them," said Fisherman. "I have another for you."

Rosten sat down in the hard chair that he had come to think of as the Rack. Fisherman handed the file across the desk.

"You will need to read it here, I'm afraid," said Fisherman. "And you may not take notes."

The envelope bore no warning stripes, no notation on the tab, no markings of any kind.

"Now?" Rosten said.

"You are booked on an early flight to Barcelona."

"I don't even know Barcelona."

"That way you may actually be able to see it," said Fisherman.

On the first page Rosten saw that he was to participate in the interrogation of a potential defector, a KGB officer of particular promise, if he could be believed. The principal examiner would be Peter Nederlander, Langley's chief of Soviet and Soviet-bloc counterintelligence.

"Heavy company," said Rosten.

The Russian was Leonid Shchusev.

"Shall you and I call him Khlestakov?" said Fisherman. "One never knows who has an ear to the door."

"From Gogol," said Rosten.

"You get a gold star."

"I assume you want me to come back with an opinion whether he really is an inspector general or an impostor," said Rosten.

"Do you actually know the play," said Fisherman, "or did you just see the Danny Kaye movie?"

"The movie."

"You see," said Fisherman, "there is an impostor in every man. But it is not Khlestakov I am interested in. Focus on Peter Nederlander."

4

isherman booked Rosten into a hotel that was a favorite of tourists, saying that even a novice could avoid being noticed there. As the taxi from the airport worked its way deep into the city, Rosten began to see the extraordinary specificity of this place. In the United States you might not be able to look out the car window and know whether you were in Cleveland or Kansas City. In Barcelona the buildings were not just unique; they were from an alternate universe. This one had chimneys that looked like a procession of hooded gremlins. That one was a stack of enchanted grottos. There were Moorish harems, miniature castles, buildings that seemed to have sprouted from spores in the night.

But none of this prepared him for what he saw when the taxi turned into a narrow side street. Up ahead rose a cluster of spires like nothing he had ever imagined existing under the eyes of God. If it had not been for the scaffolding, he might have mistaken them for stalks of strange, petrified plants. He rolled down the window and leaned out to see better.

"Sagrada Familia," said the driver.

"Do you speak English?" said Rosten.

"Yes," said the driver. *"Estamos cerca del hotel."*

When he got to his room, Rosten was disappointed to discover that his windows faced the wrong way. Fisherman's orders were that he immediately call a local number and leave a prearranged message then wait by the phone. But he had to see more of the cathedral first.

Up close, it was something you awoke from. A great stone column stood atop a tortoise. Sprouting from a vertical element of a buttress was the boll of something like cotton. Form did not follow function. It did not even appear to abide by the ordinary formulas of balance and load. Not a single corner seemed square. This wasn't architecture; it was evolution.

After about an hour he returned to his room, dialed the phone, and spoke the word. Then, for more than a day, he was frozen in place, waiting for the return call that would set him in motion. He chose his meals from the bland room-service menu. He spoke English to the waiters, not even attempting *gracias* with a lisp. He had not brought enough to read. Except for the same things over and over on CNN, the television was unintelligible. Finally the phone rang, and a man said it was time.

He took a taxi, alighting some distance from his destination, which was in a working-class neighborhood. Soon he was crossing an empty expanse of brown grass littered with discarded plastic and shards of glass, a haze flattening the gray faces of housing projects that bordered the open space. Rosten found the right building, its number painted by an unskilled hand on the concrete wall next to the door. The uric smell as he entered had no nationality. He pushed the elevator button.

"Tiene que subir las escaleras," said a voice behind him. He turned and saw a man in a torn Chicago Bulls T-shirt with the number 23 on the back. He was pointing to a doorway with a sign whose pane and lightbulb had been broken a long time. Rosten made his way up three flights in darkness, and only when he emerged into the corridor did he realize that he was one story too low. The floor numbers started at zero, not one. He went back to the stairwell and felt his way upward again.

Derelict as the building was, each door had a metal plate with the apartment number. When Rosten found the right one, he gave a simple knock. The peephole darkened. Somebody worried the dead bolt. The door swung open. Nederlander was taller than Rosten had imagined from the photograph, but the long, oval face and wavy hair were a match.

"So you are Ernest Fisherman's new boy toy," said Nederlander.

An uncovered metal table and four chairs held the center of the room. A thin piece of fabric, which could have been the remains of a curtain, covered a couch pushed up against the side wall. Above it hung a print of the Virgin Mary wracked with mourning and another of Jesus bloody on the cross. Mother and Son gazed across at a kitchen sink marked by black melanomas where pieces of the porcelain had chipped off. Next to the sink stood an old refrigerator dirty enough on the outside that you did not want to think about what might be within.

"Very authentic," said Rosten.

"How would you know?" said Nederlander.

"I am nobody's anything," Rosten said.

Nederlander showed a bit of pleasure at this and sat down at the table. Rosten remained standing.

"You will be the last to realize what you are," said Nederlander.

His speech seemed a little off. Rosten was not sure whether this was because he'd had too much to drink, but his face and hands had a bluish color that Rosten associated with someone who, over the years, had had too much of something.

"There are better patrons than Fisherman," said Nederlander.

"My bad luck," said Rosten.

"He always likes to keep a young man close," said Nederlander, "and make him think he has singled him out for glory."

Nederlander dressed blandly enough to avoid notice, except for the little bow tie. His hair curled at the collar and over his ears. The razor had missed a patch of pinfeathers on his neck. The pulpiness of his nose told an old story.

"You speaking from experience?" said Rosten.

Nederlander gave a sniff.

"How much do you know about our Russian?" he said.

"I read the dossier," said Rosten.

"They're losing focus," said Nederlander, "starting to slip. Some fall down on the simplest things. Forget to clear dead drops. Garble their countersignals. Go sightseeing rather than do what they've been told."

"I behaved like the tourist I'm supposed to be," said Rosten.

"They don't know who to be afraid of anymore," said Nederlander. "Every time Gorbachev turns his head West, a dozen of these guys come running to us."

He pulled out a pack of cigarettes from his shirt pocket.

They were French. Tapping the pack against his finger made a few cigarettes poke out. He waved them in Rosten's direction.

Rosten shook his head.

"I forgot," said Nederlander. "You children have no vices."

"If the Russians are coming to us because it's the endgame, why should we cut deals with them?" Rosten said.

Nederlander let his chair down onto all fours.

"Isn't the question what do we lose?" he said.

"Dealing with the enemy is always a risk," Rosten said.

"Ah, the moles," Nederlander said.

"More than one?" said Rosten.

"Now there's a question for your boss," said Nederlander. "And if you think of it, ask who."

A knock on the door made Rosten flinch.

"Easy, boy," said Nederlander.

The case agent was first in, having used a key. The Russian who followed could have been mistaken for a government bureaucrat from any country in the world. His skin had taken on the color of fluorescent light. He carried more weight than the tolerances to which he was built. He fidgeted with his ring, looked around the room with distaste, did not meet anyone's eyes.

Nederlander put Shchusev between himself and Rosten so that the Russian could not see them both at once. The case agent sat on the couch directly behind him. The Russian sloughed off his leather jacket and placed his hands flat on the table. Whenever he lifted one of them from the surface, a trace of moisture stayed behind.

Rosten wanted to try the interrogation techniques he had learned in training, but Nederlander was in charge, and clearly his technique was to let the samovar steep. Name? Birthplace? Mother and father's name? The questions droned on. Draw the organization chart of the Directorate in which you served. Who is in this box? What are his particular duties? Weaknesses? Shchusev replied as if from a script.

Eventually Nederlander hauled out a folder of photographs, the usual kind, taken with a long lens that eliminated depth on high-speed film that increased contrast, which made everything either black or a chalky white. He placed each photo before Shchusev in turn and asked for the identity. Rosten recognized some of them from the dossiers. These were men who had already been compromised or were offering themselves.

The process dragged on. It was an effort for Rosten to concentrate. Shchusev answered in a heavy monotone: "Yiez. Nau. Iz Dimitri Tsvilyenyev. Iz naubodye."

As the interrogation wound down, Shchusev's hands left no prints anymore. Nederlander began putting the photos back into the proper order in the file. Shchusev leaned back in his chair.

"May I ask something?" said Rosten.

"If you feel compelled," said Nederlander.

Rosten had only one question. It was a name. When he spoke it, the Russian's little finger became palsied just above the tabletop. He looked at Nederlander. He said nothing.

The case agent touched his shoulder and pointed to the door with his chin. There were no *do svidaniyas*, no next steps established. Whatever the encounter had been, it was over. The Russian fumbled with his jacket and left. When he was out the door, Rosten stood.

"He didn't answer," he said.

"No recognition," said Nederlander.

"He seemed afraid," said Rosten.

"Point in his favor," said Nederlander. "I always like to see fear in a man who is playing for his life.""

The Marine guard at the Embassy door when Rosten returned was a Polish kid from Connecticut named Ray Kowalczyk. Rosten had told him he was Polish, too, and they had gone out for an off-duty pint. Usually when Kowalczyk was on duty, he was all starch, but this day he leaned forward and whispered, "He's already called three times looking for you. You'd better move."

"Patience isn't one of his virtues," Rosten said.

"Hey," said the Marine, "don't say I didn't warn you. Wait one. Don't say I did either."

Fisherman was waiting for him in the doorway of his inner office.

"Elevator broken?" he said.

"I stopped at my office."

They assumed their positions opposite one another across the desk. Fisherman seemed to be in no hurry now. At first he busied himself with some papers as if he were alone. Rosten tried to find a comfortable position on the Rack.

"I think Nederlander is a drinker," he said.

Fisherman looked up, flashing impatience. He controlled his signals like a cuttlefish.

"Many men drink," he said.

"He clearly did not like having me there."

"Interesting that he did not feel the need to hide this."

A cloud must have passed, because the sun through the window behind him grew as bright as a Regency doorway, turning him into a shadow in the water.

"He called me your boy toy," said Rosten.

"He worked for me once," said Fisherman.

"Do they call all of your assistants boy toys?"

"They have used different words at different times but all to the same effect," said Fisherman. "It started with the Dutchman, not because he was effeminate, but because he was a lickspittle. I couldn't abide it. He never got over that."

Rosten stood and laid out on the desk the photographs he had pulled out of the dossiers in the safe in his office.

"Nederlander showed all these men to Shchusev—excuse me, Khlestakov," he said. "Would he have known that you had opened cases on them?"

"I don't see how," said Fisherman.

"But he surely would have known that they are ours or want to be."

"Surely."

"What better way to pass to Moscow the identities of its traitors?" Rosten said.

"Don't you think he knew we would see this possibility?" said Fisherman. "If you had asked him, he would have said he was checking into bona fides."

Rosten should have anticipated. Doubt the man. Doubt the doubt.

"With a man he wasn't sure of?" said Rosten. "What was he really thinking?"

"If we knew that," said Fisherman, "we would know whom we are dealing with."

"And if we knew who we were dealing with," said Rosten, "we would know what he was thinking."

"So you remember how to construct a chiasmus," said Fisherman. "You get an A in rhetoric. And so far an F in the assignment I gave you."

Rosten retreated to the safety of surfaces, reciting the exact words he had heard. Fisherman's silhouette was so motionless that he could have been listening or he could have been asleep.

"I left out one thing," Rosten finally said. "I asked about one name myself—Anton Kerzhentseff."

Fisherman's head moved just enough to eclipse the sun.

"Khlestakov missed a beat," Rosten said.

"I imagine he did," said Fisherman.

"Something seemed to pass between Nederlander and him."

"You know nothing of Kerzhentseff," said Fisherman, "only what was told to you by someone else who also knows nothing. Don't flatter yourself to think that you have read the minds of the Dutchman and the Russian. Our brains trick us into believing that we can. Does she really love me? Can I get his price down by 10 percent? Is my wife cheating? For trivial purposes our mind-reading ability serves us well enough, which is why it was selected for on the African savanna. But in the work you and I do, we do not deal with *Homo sapiens sapiens*. We are not natural human beings. We all have been remade for sovereign purposes. We are selected not by nature but by men."

"I saw what I saw," said Rosten.

"Seeing what we did not see and recognizing it," said Fisherman, "this is what is required."

As Rosten left the office, he heard what he had not heard. Fisherman had not asked how the Russian had answered the question about Kerzhentseff, had not asked why Rosten had thought to ask the question at all.

The next day on his desk he found a single dossier: "Anton Ignatyeff Kerzhentseff, aka Zapadnya, born Leningrad, April 10, 1920." He was almost exactly Fisherman's age. Rosten read through the file, which was unusual in many ways, but one stood out. The only weakness indicated was his lack of the use of his right arm, which had been wounded during his service in the Red Army during the long Hitler winter. Rosten wished there had been a photo in the file.

5

The Agency trainers provided many techniques to use in order to avoid being broken by torture. But nobody says that sometimes when a man confesses his whole truth, the torturer can be him.

"I imagined Kerzhentseff's face as being as triangular as a balalaika," he told Grace the night of revelation, "eyes like Ahab's, traces of shrapnel scars still visible on his neck. Zapadnya's traps had snared us many times over the years, probably more often than we realized. He was credited with rolling up our best deep-cover networks in Eastern Europe in the 1960s. Nobody knew how many people had ended up with bullets in the backs of their heads because of him. Fisherman had outsmarted him twice, but I came to think Kerzhentseff had been the one who was now destroying our networks—Prague, Bucharest, Warsaw—one by one. When Nederlander and Shchusev reacted to his name, it was complicity. It had to be."

At some point he took Grace's hand. He wished he could communicate through it, nerve end to nerve end, so she would experience the very intensity he had felt. But even touching, there was a vastness between them.

"Fisherman warned me that I was mistaken about Kerzhentseff," he said. "'I know him,' he told me. 'We are both men with no lives save when swords crash.' That was Pound, but it wasn't from the *Cantos*. It took me hours to track it down. The man was incredible."

He felt her hand turn against his thumb. Maybe without realizing it, he had been putting too much pressure on her fingers.

"He was a fascist," she said. "He was insane."

"I mean Fisherman," he said. "He was capable of anything."

"Maybe we should stop now," she said.

But Rosten did not stop. And much later, after he put her into the cab, he did not sleep. He went to work at 3:30. He had always been able to escape into the numbers, but now everything—the poetry shelf in his office, the music in the elevators, the silence of the corridors—was alive with her. And she was lost.

It was the Friday of a long weekend, and all morning Rosten sat useless at his desk. Then came his encounter with Gunderman and Lawton, who wanted him to go to Teddy Diamond about the security breach. He lost it and snapped at poor Dell.

Early in the afternoon, Alexa Snow put out a note freeing people to go home because of the threat of a big winter storm. This left the Dome in silence. Rosten got up, went to the window, the hall, did not see Grace, closed his door. He checked his e-mail. There was nothing from her. He looked at the phone. The screen again. He looked at his hands, touched one to the other, fingers to a mirror.

Someone knocked on the door. Rosten closed the PowerPoint board presentation he was supposed to be reviewing.

"Sorry to disturb you," Gunderman said. Lawton stepped in behind him.

"Maybe we all ought to go home and give everything a rest," Rosten said.

Lawton leaned so close that Rosten thought he could smell the sickness.

"Somebody has gotten into my account," he said.

"When?" Rosten said.

"Sometime between the day my surgery was scheduled and the day Joyce told me what he had discovered," said Lawton.

The first time Lawton had checked his data, he had been annoyed to find that Northwestern Memorial had made a credit inquiry. He had not followed up on it at the time. Then he had run into the hospital CEO at a luncheon and complained, and today the CEO had called him to plead not guilty. The hospital had never gone to Day and Domes or any other agency about him. This sent Lawton back to the database. The record of the inquiry was there, including the date it was supposedly made, a week before his surgery. Lawton closed his door and did a scan of every inquiry that had come into the system through the customer interface on that date. Nothing. He checked the ten days before and after. Still nothing. He searched on Northwestern, his doctor's name, the firm that did physician billing.

"The algorithm would have found any intrusion," said Gunderman. "There was none. And yet there's a tiny turd on the counter. It's someone inside."

But Rosten knew how logic can lead you down a path a cunning man has set out for you, with arrows that took you into the dark wood.

"Maybe the hacker is smarter than you and your algorithm," he said.

"Joyce is determined to go ahead with the deal, isn't he," said Gunderman.

"We don't even know whether the attacks were separate incidents," said Rosten. "We don't know how long ago they occurred. We don't know whether anything has happened since. What do you expect me to tell Joyce?"

"The truth," said Gunderman.

"Which is?" said Rosten.

Joyce was seated at his conference table, the PowerPoint deck squared away in front of him.

"We're a tweak or two away," he said.

Rosten sat but did not open his deck.

"Take a look at the fourth slide," said Joyce.

"There's a problem we need to discuss," said Rosten.

"Is it before the fourth slide?"

"This isn't a tweak."

Joyce kept his eyes on his deck.

"Let's do this in order, shall we?" he said.

"I think you pay me to be straight with you," said Rosten. "The board presentation is moot. There's been another breach of the database."

Joyce pulled out his nail clipper as Rosten took him through the things Lawton and Gunderman had told him. His nails were already at the quick.

"Did you tell them you would come to me with this?" Joyce said. His voice had nothing in it. Did you check with my secretary? Did you try the new pastry at Au Bon Pain?

"Containment isn't a viable strategy at this point," Rosten said.

"Are you threatening?" said Joyce as he took a snip that must have drawn blood.

"The security problem is real," Rosten said. "It will grow. Then it will burst."

"This is nothing," said Joyce, putting down the clipper. "There was a prank. Weeks, maybe months ago. Nothing since. It is immaterial."

"You'd better get Sebold's opinion about that," said Rosten.

"So he's in on this, too," said Joyce. He stood up so abruptly that it knocked the pages of the decks askew.

"I've spoken to no one but Lawton and Gunderman. For God's sake, Brian," Rosten said, rising from the table himself.

"Sit down," said Joyce. "Please sit. You make me nervous. You know, when I commanded a destroyer, threat conditions were not uncommon along hostile coasts. The other guy's ships playing chicken. Dire public warnings from a communist dictator thumping his chest. Then, out there alone, hundreds of miles from the nearest support, something would show up. A sonar ping or something incoming on the radar.

"Do you know what the man on the bridge had to do? He had to wait. Take no action. If he reacts and is wrong, he can start a war. Ask the commander of the *Turner Joy*."

Joyce was over him now, leaning in.

"If he fails to react," Rosten said, "he can lose his ship."

"It's called having balls."

"All right," said Rosten, "let's look at the intelligence. We know somebody is attacking us. The radar signal isn't a ghost. There's no reason to believe he can't do it again. Think about the Gnomon negotiations getting to the short strokes. Then comes another intrusion, a big one this time. Big and public, maximum malice. Now everyone knows what we have hidden. The Audit Committee. The board. The Gnomon shareholders. The Securities and Exchange Commission."

"The Congress," said Joyce. "The President. God."

He had begun to pace.

"You think this will just go away?" said Rosten. "Let's put a probability on that. What? Seventy-five percent? Are you ready to take a one-in-four chance of exploding the company and maybe going to jail?"

"Steady," said Joyce.

Rosten picked up the deck and let the pages flutter down to the table.

"All these representations to the board?" he said. "Complete bullshit so long as you leave this out of it."

"This," said Joyce. "This what? This fear? Jesus, Mary, and Joseph. The CEO has a dark spot on his hand and we need to disclose that it could be cancer? You know why I'm CEO, Rosten? Because I don't panic."

"You need a second opinion," said Rosten. "Sometimes the mole really is malignant."

6

It wasn't clear which was unraveling faster, the Soviet empire or the CIA's deep-cover operations inside it. A half-dozen men whose dossiers Rosten had analyzed disappeared, including one whose photo Nederlander had pushed across the table to Shchusev.

Rosten studied Kerzhentseff's dossier more intensely than he had ever studied any poem for Professor Hawthorne. Then he wrote the man's story. Fisherman read it and shortly afterward laid out a secure way to make contact in case either of them had to go dark. It involved a book code based on a volume of criticism called *Seven Types of Ambiguity* and a classified advertisement in the *Telegraph*. Still Fisherman refused to acknowledge the possibility that Nederlander had become Kerzhentseff's asset.

One night Brick and Travers arrived at Bigsby's with an older man in tow. Rosten thought at first that he was another of the hot warriors back from Central Asia, where a bunch of bearded zealots with surface-to-air missiles were taking the Soviets down.

But then Brick introduced him as Reg Schneider from London Station. He had an air of weary confidence to which Rosten was drawn. The two of them stayed on when the others left.

"You come in as a kid and they have you sorting paper," said Schneider. "Eventually they send you out. If you survive, you get old. They bring you back in and have you sort paper again."

He told stories of ancient times, just as Rosten's trainers had. This was pleasant enough after all of Fisherman's elusions, but at some point Rosten said he had to go. Early-morning wakeup, he said.

"Ernest likes the dark before dawn," Schneider said.

"You know him?" said Rosten.

"One of the men who trained you is an old pal," said Schneider. "He asked me to take you under my wing, but my wing is kind of small."

The next day Rosten reported the conversation to Fisherman.

"He's OK. Indulge him, Tom," said Fisherman. "You may learn something."

Fisherman had never called him by his first name before.

Schneider was large in the shoulders and chest, more muscular than might be expected in a man his age, which Rosten could estimate pretty accurately from the lines in his face.

"The secret is Indian clubs," Schneider said. "Five pounds apiece. Every morning. Found them in an outdoor market. Somebody's grandfather must have brought them home from the colonies. You look like you could use a little exercise yourself, laddie."

They got together from time to time for a lunch-hour run in Kensington Gardens. Schneider talked about the headiest days of the Cold War, when nuclear bombs were going off in the atmosphere and people were digging shelters. One day Rosten was able to bring the conversation around to the purges.

By the time of the Watergate break-in, Schneider said, he was safely on ice on the analytic side, but at one point he had worked in New York in Angleton's mail-opening program. A criminal investigation was opened. Luckily for Schneider, the statute of limitations had run.

The more the two of them worked out together, the more Schneider opened up. Chopping along the Serpentine one sunny day, avoiding the children and ducks, he talked about his first tour in London.

"Most of the wreckage from the Blitz was gone," he said, "so you could easily feel like London was safer than a lot of other postings. Well, we know what that got Ben Wheeler."

"Sorry," said Rosten, "am I supposed to recognize the name?"

"An outside man's outside man," said Schneider. "How he could listen. Didn't matter how green a laddie was, Ben would open his ears. That's how he and Ike McWade got so close. You've heard of him, I hope."

"I read the papers," said Rosten.

"Now he's got an office in the West Wing," said Schneider. "Ben saw his potential right off. Funny. They were as different as Scotch and scones."

Schneider kept the pace at a steady shuffle, easy enough for Rosten since he didn't have to spend much breath talking. At the Hyde Park end of the Serpentine, they cut through a carnival, passing a merry-go-round and a Ferris wheel. There were lots of kids in line, and Schneider went mute. When they broke out of the crowd, he spoke again.

"A terrible death," he said, his fists punching the air. "He didn't see it coming. How could he? Not the kind of thing you expect in the Charing Cross Tube station. It was a pellet filled with ricin delivered by a spring-loaded device in the tip of an umbrella. Very bad shit, laddie. It takes days to kill. Stuff they use now gets you in a heartbeat. Not that they're the Humane Society. It's just that after Wheeler, they realized they had given us time to spin things our way. Poor old Benny. By the time he finally passed, we had managed to get the whole thing so far under wraps that you would have thought it had been his heart."

"I remember something about it," said Rosten.

"You're thinking of the guy on Waterloo Bridge who worked for Radio Free Europe," said Schneider. "When he got it, we didn't have anything to lose by raising holy hell."

"Romanians, was it?" said Rosten.

"Bulgarians," said Schneider. "With Wheeler it was the Russians themselves."

"Was Fisherman in London then?" Rosten said.

"McWade drew the assignment to investigate," said Schneider, "and somewhere along the way he got it into his head to blame Fisherman. It didn't make any sense, but McWade was in a rage. Blamed everyone. Probably blamed me. He loved Benny like kin."

They had reached the stoplight at the street corner but were keeping their legs moving.

"Did Kerzhentseff have anything to do with it?" Rosten said.

"You're smarter than you look, laddie," said Schneider.

"What's become of him?" said Rosten.

"Ask Ernest," said Schneider.

"He has me trying to guess," said Rosten.

"Interesting exercise," said Schneider. "I don't suppose you've come up with anything."

"He seems to have gone to ground," said Rosten.

"He's like Ernest," said Schneider. "It's when you don't see him that you need to sweat. Hell, you're sweating like a pig, laddie. Give Ernest my best. Next week then?"

They set a time, but as it turned out, a call came from Langley a few days later summoning Rosten to Washington for a series of unspecified meetings. In the meantime Fisherman had disappeared. Rosten wasn't comfortable leaving without getting instructions, but he had to assume that Fisherman had been consulted, so he packed and took the first available flight.

The Old Executive Office Building had never looked American to Rosten, more like the pictures he had seen of old Berlin. He could imagine Bismarck there, balancing nations like an apothecary balanced powders and poisons. They checked Rosten's ID at the door and told him to wait. Eventually a secretary came to show him the way through the long, high-ceilinged halls. He was not prepared for the room she took him to.

"It's where President Eisenhower held the first televised press conference," she said.

"What am I doing here?" he said.

"You'll be trying to stay awake," she said.

The Indian Treaty Room rose two stories with a fancy cast-iron balcony one floor up. In the metalwork Rosten made out molded sea horses and dolphins, creatures heaved upward by deep forces. The ceiling was covered with stars. From a skylight in the center hung a chandelier. Under it eight tables had been set up in a rectangle around a compass pattern in the ornate tile floor.

"You'll be sitting along this wall," said the secretary. "Go ahead and get comfortable. The others should be drifting in soon."

"Do you know the agenda?" he said.

"That's somebody else," she said.

Nederlander was one of the first to take a seat at the table. He did not seem to notice the splendid ceiling or the extraordinary mosaic underfoot, and he certainly did not notice Rosten. Soon a healthier-looking man entered and placed himself at the head of the table. Rosten recognized him from the photographs in the papers. It was Isaac McWade.

A large number of younger men and women, each armed with a yellow legal pad and several pens, arrayed themselves along the walls. The sun slanted down through the balcony windows, making everything almost too brilliant. Within a quarter of an hour, and only two minutes after the appointed time, the doors were closed by the security men and McWade began to speak.

"We are at a pivotal moment," he said. "I believe we all sense this. But there is no consensus. Perhaps the Soviet leadership is falling apart. Perhaps Gorbachev has a master plan and the support to execute it. Everyone and every agency has a perspective. We are not here to come to a single point of view. We are here to take the conversation out of the shadows."

McWade's CIA background gave him a reputation as a risk-taker, but he showed none of that here. He was so measured that quite a number at the table diverted themselves by catching up on their correspondence. Not the people along the wall, however. They were not principals. Not deputies. They were factotums like Rosten, and they leaned in to McWade's every word.

Rosten leaned toward Nederlander. He had to assume that this was where Fisherman wanted him to focus. As McWade delivered his remarks, Nederlander read the Pentagon's Early Bird collection of the day's newspaper clippings. He was better groomed than he had been in Barcelona, and the fussy little bow tie seemed more appropriate.

As waiters passed along the conference table offering the conferees coffee and tea in china cups, Rosten turned to the woman next to him and asked if he could bring her anything from the table of urns and soft drinks in the hallway. He did not know what to call it but the bar.

"It's the White House," she said. "It's morning."

"I was thinking coffee," he said.

"Oh, well then," she said.

"How do you take it?" he said.

"Shaken, not stirred," she said.

As he stood, he caught a whiff of her sweetness. It wasn't perfume. Perhaps soap from a much better hotel than the one he had checked into. When he returned, he held two cups in steady hands. As he sat down, she slid over to give him space then slid back. Someone from Defense was droning on about symmetrical and asymmetrical threats.

"He's got a shopping list," the woman whispered.

He pretended to have trouble hearing, which gave him a reason to turn and get a good look at her.

"You aren't very subtle for a spy," she said.

"I think you have mistaken me for someone else," he said.

"Please," she said. "I work for Ike McWade."

"I'd better be careful what I say," he said.

"You people usually are," she said.

The gentleman from Defense had finally completed his sales pitch with an obligatory reminder that the Soviet Union was still ready to launch a devastating attack at any moment. Several at the table nodded.

"If I may take advantage of my prerogative as chair," said McWade, "I would like to make a change in the agenda that will bring us back closer to the foundational issue. I think all of you know Peter Nederlander. I have asked him to give a perspective that ranges as broadly as possible and, Peter, as deeply as you deem prudent."

Rosten had been careful not to stare, but now that the man was the center of attention, he bore in on his eyes and pulpy nose, the tar-and-nicotine smile. Nederlander's manner was not arrogant, the way it had been in Barcelona, but his voice was confident, even when he was acknowledging that he could not say with any certainty what was going on inside the Kremlin.

"All we hear," he said, "are voices arguing in another room. There are divisions within the leadership, but that does not tell us much. This stately room in which we meet today has echoed with raised voices from time to time over the years. It may happen again before our sessions end."

He waited for more laughter than came. Then he went on. It was best to assume, in the absence of evidence to the contrary, he said, that Gorbachev had the cards. "Make no mistake about him. He is determined to prevail not only against his domestic rivals but also against the United States."

Nederlander recited the evidence that the Soviet Union had not been tamed. Though he managed to make it seem revelatory, it had all been out already in one form or another. Of course, he did not mention the success Soviet intelligence was having in eliminating our eyes and ears. The closest he came was when he lapsed into the ursine cliché and said that Afghanistan was not the only place where the Soviets did their work with claws bared.

"Still," he said, "Gorbachev is as much a realist as he is a communist. He sees that the United States has been willing and able to spend heavily on strategic forces, including missile defense. The Soviet economy is bending to the breaking point under the weight of its need to respond in kind. Money is for us what the winter has always been for Russia."

The gentleman from Defense seemed about to lead a round of applause.

"Did everyone but me get a list of the attendees?" Rosten whispered.

"I'm Ellen Bradley, by the way," she said, handing him her card. "You were already en route when the list went out."

She was clearly more than McWade's girl toy, though on looks she would have fit the part, with an athlete's cut of strawberry-blonde hair and a barely detectable wash of freckles. She would have made a fine picture jumping a horse or stroking easily in the pool. Though you noticed many things about her, it was the unexpected blue of her eyes that called to you.

"I'll fill you in when we break," she whispered so close to his ear that he felt the warmth. He had to be the most junior man in the room, and yet she seemed to be attending to him. He glanced at the card. It had both a mobile and a home number written on it in pen.

Nederlander had begun to discuss intelligence that had not yet leaked. From the middle level of detail he presented, Rosten inferred that everyone in the room had at least Top Secret clearance. Some must not have had access to code-word matters, because Nederlander was careful to stay away from communications intelligence. "He's walking the line like a Wallenda," Bradley whispered. "Look how relaxed the guy from the National Security Agency looks."

"Clearly one area of debate has been Afghanistan," Nederlander said. He held up the Early Bird digest. "Even reports in the press have suggested that the growing success of the mujahideen has led a substantial faction close to Gorbachev to favor complete and expeditious withdrawal."

"Do give the Director our compliments," said McWade.

"Their tanks are still in Kabul, of course," said Nederlander.

"Meaning, don't cut our budget yet," Bradley whispered.

"But looking long term," Nederlander said, "we have to think about the aftermath. If the Soviets withdraw, what will be left behind?"

"Our worthy allies," said McWade.

"Yes," said Nederlander. "They need us now. We have trained and armed them. But we haven't converted them. They are believers, and it is certainly not the West they believe in."

The men at the table who were nodding now were probably from State. Post-Soviet risks were their talking points, not the Agency's.

"We will have to be eternally vigilant," said McWade. "Which is, of course, the writ of the agency you serve."

This cued Nederlander back into place.

"Vigilance is the note I wanted to conclude on," he said.

"A skillful, provocative performance, Peter," said McWade. "We are a bit ahead of schedule, so I suggest that we break now for lunch and return at a quarter to one."

The room extended its limbs, mumbling. Bradley was in motion. Rosten stayed seated, trying to process what he had just heard. She turned, saw he wasn't following, and showed her displeasure.

"Come with me," she said.

Rosten caught up at the door.

"Could you tell what your boss thought of that last business?" he said.

"He thinks you guys just love to issue warnings," she said. "That way, if something turns to shit, you pull out the memo. But you should ask him yourself."

The people who had sat with them along the wall all turned toward a buffet table that had been set up in the corridor. Bradley took his arm and steered him in the opposite direction.

"I'd be delighted to have lunch with you," he said.

"Yes, that might be pleasant," she said, giving him the slightest little squeeze. "But actually you'll be sitting with Ike."

"My God," he said.

"He used to work for your boss," she said. "Did you know that? Here we are."

The room was not nearly as fancy as the one they had been meeting in, but it had portraits on the wall and tables sparkling with silver and crystal on fine linen. Each table was set for six.

"I'm supposed to know which fork?" he said.

"Use your education," she said, taking him to a table at the center of the room. "Here's you. Here's Ike." Side by side.

"Where is Nederlander?" he said.

"I put him at a table in the corner," she said. "Do you two have a history?"

"I don't know if you've got the clearances," he said.

"You would be surprised what I have," she said.

At this point he did not think he would be surprised by much.

"Where is your place?" he said.

"At the buffet," she said. "I don't work for Ernest Fisherman. When lunch is over, I'll pick you up at the door."

He was the first at the table, having no urgent telephone calls to answer, Early Bird to read, or important documents to review. He was left looking at the portraits of men he did not recognize, each of whom had obviously once been a commanding presence here and then was not anymore. Washington had ways of reminding you of tradition and impermanence at the same time.

Other conferees began to fill the room. Each person who arrived at Rosten's table asked him his job. He said deputy cultural attaché, London. Even if they read that as Agency, they figured it was very low level and looked at him as if to say the buffet is down the hall. When McWade arrived and greeted him by name, there was no more of that.

"I'll never forget hearing the Messiah at the Royal Albert Hall," said the man on his right. "A thousand voices, I think it was."

"That's probably enough," said Rosten.

"Yes," said the man.

The rolls were passed.

"So you work for Ernest," said McWade. "How is he these days?"

His hair had faded from copper. Beneath his diplomatic manner, Rosten sensed a Viking rage, red beneath the gray. A man stepped up and said something into his ear.

"Tell him to go ahead," he told the man, "carefully."

The man showed McWade a piece of paper, which McWade took in at a glance before returning it.

"Ernest is a piece of work," McWade said to Rosten. The table paused to listen.

"Did you read the Will column this morning?" said the woman on McWade's left.

"Yes," said McWade then immediately showed her the back of his collar again.

"I heard that you worked for Fisherman once," Rosten said.

"Everyone should," said McWade, "and then should get over it."

They talked throughout lunch, the woman on the left occasionally trying to bring George Will into it again and the man on the right trying to insert his thoughts about the plans for the new Tate. McWade never allowed Rosten to be trapped for long. His curiosity about Fisherman—his health, his work habits, his demeanor, his views—seemed insatiable. Rosten tried to be responsive but careful.

"I think it is fair to say that Fisherman is concerned about the Soviets' continued ability to compromise us," he said.

McWade put down his fork and stared across the table at a man who did not seem to know what to do with the attention. Before he decided, McWade looked away.

"I have never known a moment when Ernest was not concerned," he said.

"He isn't specific," said Rosten.

"Which is why I've never had a moment when I wasn't more concerned than he."

As soon as McWade finished his main course, everyone's plate was removed.

"You worked for him when?" said Rosten.

"A long time ago," said McWade. "Many of us find that we seem to have been working for him all along."

"I was interested in the point Mr. Nederlander made," Rosten said.

"What did you think of it?" said McWade.

"I was intrigued."

"I'm sure Ernest will be, too."

"Did you understand him to be raising doubts about the muja-hideen?" Rosten said.

"I'm sorry," said McWade. "I must be impolite and leave you. There are some things I need to take care of before the afternoon session. It has been good to meet you. Ellen will look after you and give you my coordinates, including the direct line in case you ever need to get in touch urgently."

"It must be quite a secret society, Fisherman's alumni," said Rosten.

"The chosen," said McWade. "Eventually each of us comes to understand what he was chosen for."

As he left, the table rose and put themselves in his path to shake his hand. He managed to touch most of them. Those too poorly positioned he simply disregarded. Then the waiters brought berries.

"You two were deep into it," said the man next to him.

"Friends in common," said Rosten.

The lunch had barely begun to break up when Bradley reappeared and led him out ahead of the crowd. He noticed people noticing him. One of them was Nederlander.

"Here," she said as they reached the corridor. She handed him a piece of paper with three numbers. "The last is only when it is very urgent."

"Mr. McWade used that word, too," said Rosten. "What is urgent?"

"You'll know it when you see it," she said, bringing them to a stop in front of the grand room, which was still largely empty. "I have a few things to do, so you'll need to fend for yourself."

"I'll navigate by the compass in the floor and the stars on the ceiling," he said.

"You really were an English major," she said.

He did not know what to do but to put out his hand. She touched the back of it then turned. The click of her heels faded down the corridor.

Back in the grand room, he took the same chair as in the morning and had to tell several people that the one next to him was taken. The meeting eventually resumed and quickly began to drone. Rosten started to make notes, not of what the gentleman from State was saying, but instead as much as he could remember of what McWade had said at lunch, the exact words. Fisherman would expect that. When he finished, he moved to Nederlander's presentation. This caused him to miss a lot of what was now being said, but he could not imagine that Fisherman would care. Throughout the afternoon the chair next to Rosten remained empty. He found himself looking toward the door frequently. Meanwhile, McWade, too, seemed distracted. When he adjourned the session, he was first out the door. Rosten stayed where he was and reviewed his notes.

"An unexpected pleasure," said a voice.

Rosten looked up. Nederlander was standing over him. Rosten did not rise.

"It isn't like Fisherman to concern himself with these little charades," Nederlander said.

"I haven't heard anything more about our friend in Spain," Rosten said. "Have you?"

"He survives."

"That's a relief," said Rosten. "So many have not."

"As I said in my presentation, the bear has not become a lapdog."

"Though it seems to have one," said Rosten. "But I'm sure you know that better than anyone."

"Interesting that you still think you are sure," said Nederlander. "Say hello to Ernest for me."

He moved off before Rosten had a chance to answer back. The room was almost empty now. Rosten turned toward the door just as Bradley came through it.

"Good," she said. "You didn't get away."

"Wasn't trying," said Rosten.

"You're having dinner with me," she said. "McWade's orders."

"Maybe I have other plans."

"You don't," she said.

"And how is it that you know?" he said.

"Look at you trying to figure out my sources and methods," she said. "Don't you think a girl can tell when a boy wants to be with her?"

The place she chose was in Georgetown, naturally. Young was how she described it, young and well positioned. They got a good table, away from the window, secluded from the rest of the room. She ordered a wine miles beyond him, and they relaxed into it until the waiter brought the entrées. The food was so perfectly arranged on the plate that it felt like vandalism to touch it. It turned out that Ellen had not been to this restaurant since graduating from Georgetown's foreign service program.

As he had guessed, she had grown up in the East. He had passed through her hometown whenever he had taken the New Haven Railroad to the city. She had gone to boarding school through twelfth grade and could not quite fathom the idea of actually spending a childhood with parents.

"You must have known lots like me at Yale," she said, "probably slept with some of them."

"I had a different kind of friends," he said.

"You had to sleep with somebody," she said.

He had the sense that, although he may have come to Washington to observe, he had also come to be observed.

"Tell me, why do I have McWade's numbers?" he said well into their second bottle. "And yours."

"Networking," she said.

"Does he want something?"

"Something," she said. "If I were you, I'd keep my eyes open."

"For what?" he said.

The check came and she took it.

"It's on the government, I hope," he said.

"I imagine you'd like to come back to my place," she said. "It isn't far."

"For what you call networking?" he said.

"Forget it," she said. "Bad idea."

"We could stop for a drink somewhere," he said. "Keep our eyes open."

"You're too young for me."

"A gentleman never asks."

"And anyway, it wouldn't be good if I actually got to like you."

"Perish the thought," he said.

Things would have been so much better if it had.

7

Lawton pushed through the revolving door, stirring icy air into the lobby, which smelled of fresh, warm bread from Au Bon Pain.

"Morning," said Maurice from behind the security desk.

"Brutal," said Lawton.

"They say more snow," said Maurice.

In the elevator the music was a piano solo. One of the Germans. His wife would have been able to come up with the composer and name of the piece, just like that. Most people only knew her to look at her. They saw the surface, how she became her clothes, like a model in high gloss. They noticed that she did not speak much, but they had no idea how deeply she was able to hear. Lawton had known from the very beginning how much more she was, and she had known that he did, because she heard him deeply, too.

The doctor gave him an even chance of being whole for her again one day. We'll just have to wait and see. We. It was a matter of Bayesian probability. Every day things did not get worse actually improved the odds of things getting better.

These days Joyce seemed to be living the same way. Ever since Lawton had discovered that his file had been tampered with, the Gnomon acquisition had gone on hold. But the more time passed without another security breach, the more you could see the desire rising in Joyce. How much lack of evidence of something was evidence enough of nothing? Gunderman had come up with Bayesian numbers and taken them to Rosten. He called them lipstick on a guess. Only Joyce knew when he would be confident enough to make his move.

"I need help."

"That's why we do this."

"It's Megan. Somebody has been impersonating her on AOL."

"This is not a problem I know how to deal with, I'm afraid. I can't find the on switch. They have code words or something, don't they?"

"Passwords. Great name. The girls all pass them around."

"These cannot be changed?"

"She doesn't know who's doing it."

"Not change the friends. Change the password."

"I did that first thing. But the harm's already done."

"Being betrayed is painful at any age, but particularly in adolescence. They don't expect it yet."

"Someone sent a message in her name to all her friends saying that her mother is having an affair with one of her friends' fathers. Do you want the details?"

"They are always pretty much the same. We will want to deal with the cruelty of those messages first."

"Megan was in shock. I told her everything would be all right, which actually used to work. She wanted me to say that I didn't believe it."

"Did you?"

"Of course I said it."

"Of course."

"She had called me at work. She never does that. I came home as soon as I could, but she had already gone to practice. Maggie was in the kitchen. I asked about her day. She said this and that."

"It does no good to let your imagination play X-rated videotapes."

"When we went to bed that night, I couldn't sleep. I could tell that Maggie wasn't asleep either. We lay there, not touching, facing outward in the dark. It's been a long time since we really touched."

"We were talking about your daughter."

"I got ahead of myself, I guess."

"It is hard not to in this kind of situation."

"When Megan came home from practice that evening, Maggie and I were still at the table. Megan couldn't look at either of us. Maggie acted no differently than she did any other evening. It was as if Megan and I were the only ones feeling shame."

"You don't know what your wife was feeling."

"This morning I was out of the house before either of them got up. I don't know whether I should even go home tonight."

"Do you think she believes her mother really is having an affair?"

"Not a chance."

"We can't hide from our children as well as we can from each other. Our children are actually paying attention."

"I'm sorry."

"Please. If you need a tissue."

"I mean, her knowing but not being able to tell me."

"She did tell you. Go ahead. Take a minute."

"I'm so sorry."

"I am finally seeing a whole person across from me. That is what the tissue is for. For whole people. Do you realize that you haven't used a single mathematical metaphor today?"

"What am I supposed to do? I've never doubted Maggie."

"Ask her."

"She'll deny it. I know her."

"Sounds like your trust was already showing some cracks."

Simons's lunch meeting had been easy. It was a huge account but a long relationship. She knew his kids. He had known her father. There was always business along with coffee, some glitch that had to be worked out, a revision of policy on one side that needed to be accommodated by the other. Someone had told her once that give-and-take in a marriage was a 60-40 proposition, with both sides being the 60. Good business partnerships were like that, though she doubted that marriages ever could be.

As she walked back to her office, the wind rasped her face and got through the buttons on her coat. She wished she could wear fur again. She kept hers in storage, just in case. They said you could get a Patagonia that would keep you just as warm as mink, but those things made a woman look like the Michelin Man.

She had just entered the Dome lobby and was waiting to tell

Maurice to let her appointment from Sears go right up when the door hissed behind her on a very low note, sounding like someone was having trouble pushing. She turned and there was Sam Gunderman. He slowed to a full stop inside the door. When he saw her taking a step toward him, he got the thing moving again.

"Sam?" she said, touching his arm.

"The wind," he said. He fumbled to open his baggy old parka. "Sorry. I've got a handkerchief." The zipper stuck. He wiped his eyes on his sleeve.

Sara reached into her pocket and pulled out a cocktail napkin she always kept there just in case.

"Thank you," he said.

"Let me buy you a cup of coffee," she said.

If she let him go upstairs like this, the talk on the Admin News Network would be merciless.

"No, really," he said.

"You look like you need a drink," she said, controlling his arm now. "Come on. The lunch crowd's gone. We'll have Au Bon Pain all to ourselves."

He let himself be led, not willingly, not unwillingly. She steered him to a table in the corner.

"What in the world has happened to you, Sam Gunderman?"

He offered his nose to the napkin again.

"Coffee black?" she said.

She took his silence as assent and brought him a cup. This wasn't like looking at a stranger and playing the game of what does he need. She had known Sam forever, all his techie quirks.

"OK," she said, sloughing off her coat. "What is it?"

He sat up straighter.

"Nothing," he said.

"Well, it wasn't the wind."

"I've been driving around aimlessly," he said. "I went south. I went north. When I got here, I walked to the lake."

"Nice day for it."

"I blew off a meeting," he said. "I never do that."

The gossip on the Admin News Network was that somebody had seen his wife with another man. He wasn't going to talk to her about that. No man would.

"I've got no taste for coffee," he said. "I'm sorry."

"When I'm in a state, I always go shopping."

"No, really," he said. "I have things I have to do."

"We'd better get a move on then," she said.

Her confidence was enough to propel him out the door. Brooks Brothers was several blocks into the wind. She would have liked to take him to a custom tailor. She thought of bespoke blouses as a continuous massage for the spirit, just the knowledge that something in the world had been cut for you alone. But he required help right this minute, ready-made.

She marched him in the bitter cold with a determination that warmed her. He began to lag behind. She stopped to let him catch up and then took his arm. He pulled back, and she said, "So I don't blow away." He seemed to accept that, even to carry his head a little higher.

The store was busy with a sale. She did not know the people in menswear, but she had no trouble attracting someone. Then the salesman saw Sam and hesitated.

"Right here," said Sara.

"Are you looking for something in particular?" the salesman said to her.

Sara did not warm to men who shot their cuffs.

"A good dress shirt, maybe two," she said. "And a sweater."

"I never wear—" Sam said.

"You do have cashmere," she said.

"Of course," said the salesman. "Blue or white in the shirts."

"One of each," she said. "Oxford cloth."

"Collar?" said the salesman.

Sam seemed at a loss.

"Button-down," she said. "Moderate collar-point length."

"Size?" said the salesman.

She turned to Sam.

"Medium," he said.

"At the neck and sleeve," said the salesman.

"Measure him top to bottom. Who knows what we'll want him to try on before we're done," she said.

She touched the zipper of Sam's parka and went behind him to lift the heavy thing from his shoulders. She did this with such skill that the salesman raised his eyebrows and tilted his chin in recognition. Her first real job had been at Carson, Pirie, Scott during a Christmas break. She was in charge of rehanging men's jackets and slacks, but occasionally, when everyone else was engaged, she minded a customer. It turned out she had a flair for it. She knew when a man wanted to be told what to try on and when he had control issues. She knew how to settle a jacket on his shoulders so that it felt like a caress. They asked her to stay on full time as a real salesperson, and she was tempted. But at school she could outperform the men, not just serve them.

"There," she said, handing the parka to the salesman, who took it with one finger and draped it over the counter.

After he recorded Sam's numbers, he went to a vast wall of shirts.

"It would be great for you to wear one of them back to the Dome," she said.

"The dressing rooms are right over there," said the salesman.

Sam went to change, and Sara looked through the sweaters, holding one after another up against the salesman's chest.

"They're classics," he said.

"I want them to feel downright Italian," she said.

"This is Brooks Brothers, ma'am," said the salesman.

Sam returned from the rear of the store.

"A huge improvement," she said. "How does it feel?"

"A little scratchy."

"Think of the smell of a new car," she said. "You'll miss it when it goes away. Now pick one of these."

He took the sweaters and looked at the price tags.

"Way too much," he said.

"You're good for it," she said. "If you're not, I am."

"I couldn't."

"Then get out your credit card," she said. "You'll thank me later."

Sam balked.

"Let me pick up the check," she said. "How many times have I called you with a mess?" She answered the salesman's look. "Computers," she said.

"Ah," said the salesman.

"I couldn't," said Sam.

"Damsel in distress," she said. "You've been a regular Galahad. You didn't send me some kid. You patched me up yourself. You don't think that's worth the price of a sweater and two lousy shirts?" She turned to the salesman. "No offense."

Sam pulled out his wallet and put a Visa on the counter next to the parka.

"Try the sweater on while the nice man starts ringing you up," she said.

Sam picked one up and headed for the dressing room.

"You can slip it on right here," said the salesman.

Sam raised the sweater overhead and pulled it down over his hair, tousling it. The transformation was remarkable.

"Can I interest you in a topcoat?" Sara said.

A piano organized a room. A viola usually gave it depth, but this young man's tone had an edge that cut right through. Only a conductor with a special ear would warm to it. Solti would have. Barenboim maybe not.

But that was rushing. This was the young man's first big moment, and it was a long way from Symphony Center, though as he kept reminding her, the audience would actually be paying.

"The caesura," she said when he failed to pause. "The silence must be total. The listener must have time to wonder whether it is the end. Why don't you try it again."

The young man looked to her for the downbeat. She gave it with a drop of her head, feeling for an instant some small sense of what Solti must have felt.

They could have rehearsed with a recording of the piano part. This was how the young man practiced. But Donna wanted to do her very best by him, so she had hired at her own expense the finest accompanist she could find. She lost track of how many times the young man had thanked her.

"You are going to make my name," she said.

Of course, she already had her husband's.

The piece suited the young man, Arnold Bax's "Legend," with

lots of double stops and great, emerging crescendos. It was no wonder he let his forward motion barrel straight through the caesura. Momentum was the very thing that made the silence speak. She liked the jazz musicians' word. They called it a break. Done right, it split time as if it were a gem.

He began again.

"Good," she said to herself in the perfect caesura he made. When the piece ended, she said aloud, "You are ready."

"I sure hope so, Mrs. Joyce," he said.

She took the pianist into the hallway to give him his fee. When she returned, she no longer saw a violist. It was a high school boy in a varsity jacket. She touched the letter.

"For God's sake, don't break a finger," she said.

"I'm off-season," he said. "Here. I almost forgot."

He pulled his mother's folded check from his pocket. As she reached for it, her cell phone vibrated. She never muted it all the way, because when she did, she often forgot to unmute it. Brian hated that.

The young man left as she brought the phone to her ear.

"Hi," she said.

"Ten minutes out," Brian said.

"You're early."

"See you soon."

She found Mrs. Yu in her room watching the Travel Channel.

"He's early," she said.

Mrs. Yu sprang off the bed.

"What time dinner?" she said.

"You don't need to get started yet," said Donna. "I just wanted to give you a heads-up."

Mrs. Yu followed her into the large kitchen and began pulling pans out of the inlaid cherry cabinets and opening and closing the doors of the two refrigerators as if she were taking inventory.

"Really," said Donna. "You can watch your show. I'll let you know the plan when there is one."

But Mrs. Yu was as busy as she would have been preparing to feed a wedding reception, which the kitchen could handle, with its stove that was good enough for a star in Michelin, its three ovens, and in the middle a stainless counter the size of Île Saint-Louis. Donna rarely cooked anything more than a cup of soup in the microwave. She was a Suzuki student playing a Guarneri.

She passed through the living room, which Mrs. Yu once said could house a village. One wall was entirely windows opening out on the lake. All you saw was water and sky, some days with absolutely no line in between. If you didn't know better when you came into the living room, you might have thought they were on a high bluff. In fact, it was only a few steps down to a small beach and a removable pier the groundskeeper put in every spring so they could launch kayaks or their Sunfish, if they ever found the time.

Whatever Mrs. Yu was doing, the house was silent. Donna rarely had music on during the day unless she was ready to listen, but it was playing inside her head every waking hour, and probably many of her sleeping ones, too. Only in high school had she realized that her classmates were not immersed this way. That was how she had decided to make music her life. But she had never imagined then that it would be this life. Musically she had worked hard to get where she wanted to go. But the lake and sky, the extraordinary sound system, the concert grand in a room designed for her fiddle, these were all Brian.

She dropped the morning papers in the recycle bin on the way to the bedroom. There she checked her face, which was all right, and went to the bathroom to brush her teeth. When she came out, she heard the car turning into the long drive and hurried to the door. Brian was on the phone in the backseat, so he didn't see her come down the walk. The driver's window hummed down.

"I have a huge favor to ask of you, Robert," she said.

"The kids," he said.

"I hate to slow you down when you have a chance to get home early for a change."

"It's still light out," he said. "I'm way ahead of the game."

"What game is that?" said Brian as he hit the button on the phone. Robert knew not to answer idle questions. Brian sat looking through the messages on his BlackBerry before finally opening the door. "Have you been waiting long?"

She gave him a hug, and he pecked her cheek.

"You must be frozen," he said.

Inside, they took off their coats and hung them on the rack. There was a time when Brian would have immediately taken off his suit jacket, too, pulled down his tie, and opened his collar. That was a job ago.

"How was your day?" she said.

"You first," he said.

"My child star is nervous because people will be paying two dollars apiece to hear him," she said, "one for students and seniors."

"Are we going?" Brian said.

"I didn't want to bother you."

"Maybe we should try," he said. "I haven't been here for you enough lately."

"Busy time."

"I wish I knew how to lead two separate lives," he said, "one entirely for the family."

"The deal you've been working on," she said, "is it going well?"

His eyes turned toward the darkening lake.

"Hasn't gone at all," he said. "It hit a reef."

"A caesura," she said.

"English?" he said.

"A silence that lets the passion speak," she said. "Then the music begins again."

"Get two of those two-dollar tickets," he said, pulling down his tie and unbuttoning his collar. "And after this is all done, we'll really reward ourselves."

She did believe he wanted that.

"Shall I tell Mrs. Yu to start dinner?" she said.

He stood in the temporary office Grace had used. The picture frame had vanished, so had her yellow plastic mechanical pencils. Everything had gone back home with her. He had never thought to get her address in New York. It had been so abrupt. Gail could get her coordinates from the bank, but what would he use them for? To say that he didn't blame her for leaving? That he had tried to break free of Fisherman, but that you never can? Even if you throw yourself into hard numbers, the ambiguities are always inside you.

I told you too much, Grace. I told you too late.

8

His plane landed in a dirty fog, and he went directly from immigration down into the Heathrow Tube station. When he came up again at Euston, the fog had burned off, and he was disoriented by the intensity of the light. It was as if being underground had lagged him back into the Washington night, suspending him between one unreal city and another.

His flat was a studio as close to Bloomsbury as he could afford, a half-step above London University student digs, with what passed for a kitchen on one wall, a mush of a bed on the other, and one window high up under the eaves. He had to stand on a chair to see out of it, which wasn't worth the effort, since nothing was there except an expanse of tarpaper, litter, and chimney pipes.

He threw down his bag, reset his watch, and decided it was time for lunch, which he picked up at a shop down the street. Fully intending to stay awake through dinner to get himself synced for work the next morning, he picked up a book Fisherman had given him about Russia's history in the Caucasus and beyond and sat down on the sofa.

He woke up in darkness, lying half atop the book. Without hope of sleep until the sun caught up, he rose and showered behind the mildewed curtain. The bus to Marble Arch did not run often at this hour, which gave him plenty of time to review his circumstances. There was Fisherman. There was Nederlander. There was McWade. There was Bradley. There used to be Grace. And he was alone. When the bus finally came, both decks were vacant. Along the way, a sad, old drunk stumbled on, then a few others.

Rosten's windowless office seemed to exist in a time zone all its own. He switched on the autopsy fluorescents. On the desk was a note in Fisherman's hand telling him to check his safe. He hung his trench coat on the steel rack, turned on the warm desk lamp, extinguished the overheads, and took the coffee pot down to the gents to fill. When he returned, his hands were so unsteady he had trouble measuring out the grind.

He had hung a rendering of Sterling Library on the wall opposite the desk. It seemed askew, so he went to level it. When he did, it seemed tilted in the opposite direction. After several attempts, he gave up. It wasn't the watercolor; it was his eyes.

He opened the safe and found three sets of folders, held together by heavy rubber bands, lying unfiled in the top drawer. The first set contained the usual Slavic and Eastern European names. But the individuals in the second set were different: Farzin Ibrhimi, Hamal Nabiev, Botir Ghazanfar. The material inside their files read like translated verse.

Even when he was just starting to work for Fisherman, the lives of the Russians and Czechs and East Germans had been reasonably familiar. They rose through the ranks of the classless society, ranks not all that different from the ones in which Rosten found himself. Yes, the guideposts along the way were different (Look Left), but that was just a matter of convention.

In contrast, this man from Kyrgyzstan might as well have been a Canto in Chinese characters. None of the others were any less opaque. The men—they were all men—came from the southern Soviet Republics or Afghanistan. Many had Russified names, but from their histories it was clear that they were nothing like the usual Ivans.

The doorknob rattled before Rosten got to the third set.

"So the prodigal has returned," said Fisherman, more chipper than morning. "You look spent. Perhaps you partied."

"My trip was entirely work-related," said Rosten.

"Yes, work."

"If you don't think it was, why did you send me?"

"You really should have become more wary of assumptions by now," said Fisherman. He sat down across the desk in the penumbra of the reading light. "So you met Isaac McWade."

"I didn't expect contact at that level," said Rosten.

"And what was your assessment?"

They weren't talking about Ivan. Or Nederlander. This was someone close to the President.

"Efficient in the meeting," said Rosten. "Cordial but guarded at lunch."

"You broke bread with him," said Fisherman.

"He seated me next to him," said Rosten. "I learned that he once had worked for you, too."

The cuttlefish flashed nothing.

"The others must have taken notice," he said.

"The only one I recognized was Nederlander," said Rosten.

"Other than him and McWade's assistant, nobody knew who I was."

"I understand she is efficient at what she does, too," Fisherman said.

"Seemed to be," said Rosten.

"Bradley, isn't it?" said Fisherman. "I knew her father. It must have been intriguing, you and McWade and the Dutchman watching each other watching each other."

Perhaps it was jet lag, but Fisherman's voice grated.

"Nederlander approached me," Rosten said.

"Waiting until everyone was out of the room, I imagine," said Fisherman, "so he would not become known for knowing you."

"Comrade Nederlander had nothing much to say," said Rosten. "But during the meeting he alluded to the danger our mujahideen allies could become for us in the event of a Soviet pullout. It was subtle, but it was there."

"Brave of him," Fisherman said.

"When I raised it with McWade, he flicked the subject away."

"He has always known the line and usually hewn to it."

"Frankly, I don't know what to make of these," said Rosten, laying his palm on the three sets of dossiers.

Fisherman leaned back in the chair, putting himself entirely into the shadows.

"Frankness is always the unanswered question, isn't it," he said. "You might want to think of those as part of a little experiment in frankness." He reached across the desk and picked up the first set. "These will seem more like your usual fare. The difference is that the individuals have already revealed their truth. Some have defected with distinction. Others have proven to be doubled against us. The files you have do not indicate the outcomes. I want you to predict them."

"You're treating me like a schoolboy," said Rosten.

"I have only described Part One of the little experiment," said Fisherman, picking up the second set. "These are dossiers on men from the southern Soviet Republics who have assimilated. Imagine how uncomfortable they must feel now that the ground is shifting. If a veteran intelligence officer in the GRU worries what will happen to him as Moscow falters, think of the anxiety of a closet Muslim serving as a functionary in Tashkent, let alone Kabul. The question for you is which of the men in this second group is most likely to accept a Christian offer."

"You already know," said Rosten.

"I only have a view," said Fisherman. "I want yours."

He picked up the third set and held them suspended over the desk.

"Now we come to the most interesting collection," he said. "You will notice that these documents are not classified. That is because they do not officially exist. I have used my own devices to have them prepared. These are men we are supporting against the Soviets. You will find quite a range. Tribal warlords, mullahs, dealers in drugs. I want you to write me the story of what each will do after the fall."

"I'm ignorant of their culture," said Rosten. "Anything I write will be Scheherazade."

"I'll be away for ten days or more," said Fisherman. "You will give your report when I return. Please deliver it orally."

"And if I pass your exam?" said Rosten.

"Don't let what you imagine Isaac McWade sees in you distort your vision," said Fisherman. Then he stood and left. No wonder people who had worked for Fisherman hated him.

Rosten put away the South Asian files in order to work on the apparatchiks; at least this was the part of the exam that he had studied for. These men had recognizable needs: intoxicants, sex, a way to hide the truth from the wife and children. Vodka was cheap, but women were dear. Drugs and gambling made non-negotiable demands. What these subjects required, only a market economy could readily supply. The Volograd GRU man whose experience in the German siege might explain his attraction to rough sex. The bureaucrat from Minsk, who could have been an accountant in the West but in Moscow specialized in valuing human assets. The second-generation son of the secret police whose time in the KGB office in Dresden was marked by vanity, drunkenness, and a fondness for fondling women who said no.

The next day his brain felt a little clearer. He turned to the Central Asian Soviet functionaries. Many of their names had been transliterated twice—once from their native language into the Cyrillic alphabet and then from the Russian into English. Quite often the file contained a religious history, the name of a madrasa, the date of the negotiation of the *nikah*, which binds a marriage under Allah. In a few cases there was a *takfir*, when a subject renounced Islam in favor of official state atheism. Rosten made a list of these. Come the collapse, life for them among the believers would be brief.

Fisherman had disappeared again, so Rosten felt free to spend time in libraries and the British Museum in order to get some sense of the world with which he was dealing. Material was plentiful, much of it dating from the era of the Great Game, when it was the British against the Russians and yet somehow the Afghans prevailed. The people in the dossiers had predecessors in those times, dark men who wore British woolens, drank British tea, and accepted British condescension in return for the power to condescend to their own. Perhaps some of their lineal descendants drank at the samovar today.

Very different were the mujahideen. Mohammad Shaur. Abdul Qadir. Nek Muhammad. Their dossiers contained much less biographical detail than those of the Soviet collaborators, but they were rich with tales of fighting prowess and implacable will. The documents appeared to have been compiled by a single individual with an Agency background. The style of presentation made an effort to depart from Langley standard, but there was a telltale accent. This one fell out with that one over a girl. This one accused that one of being a Paki shill. The back-fence gossip of the trade.

At first Rosten thought he might be able to put things together to make at least a partial organization chart of the mujahideen command structure and the subjects' places in it, but soon he realized that there was no structure. Affiliations were opportunistic and provisional. Tribal leaders from the ungovernable mountain hinterland between Pakistan and Afghanistan learned their martial skills fighting each other, though for the moment, the miracle of a common enemy kept them from killing one another most of the time. As Fisherman had promised, there were figures from the opium trade fighting alongside monarchists bent on a restoration, bespectacled Islamic intellectuals next to rugged tribesmen who were only able to read through a gun sight.

In the sandstone and gravel of the alluvial wash from the Hindu Kush, the mullahs were granite. Many had years of formal education in religious schools, the Koran their only textbook. They may not have been the most accomplished fighters, but their hatred of communism and its godless promise was total.

Then there were the Arabs. Though they were not all Saudis, they seemed to share the experience of having been converted from the modern ennui to an ancient clarity through contact with Wahhabism. Not that they had abandoned all of the advantages of the world against which they rebelled. Some even seemed to find opportunity in it, such as the Saudi rich man's son who recognized how much money the Agency was pouring into the region and showed up along the Afghan-Pakistani border to build concrete fortifications and soak some of it up.

Fisherman's absence had gone past ten days when Nederlander appeared at the Embassy. No rumor of his arrival preceded him, not even a call from the Marine guard. Rosten was at his desk when the dead bolt began to rattle, followed by a fist pounding on the wood and something that sounded like a curse. Before opening the door Rosten put the files that did not exist in the safe, locked it, and put up the Closed sign.

"What are you doing in there, boy?" said Nederlander. "Pulling your pud?"

When Rosten cracked the door, Nederlander pushed past him into the windowless room.

"Where is he?" he said.

"Wherever he wants to be," said Rosten.

"Are you still his plaything, or are you McWade's now?" said Nederlander, so loudly that Rosten heard doors opening all along the polite, diplomatic corridor.

"Fisherman doesn't run his itinerary past me," said Rosten. "But when I see him, I'll give him your best."

"You're a cocky little shit," said Nederlander. "You think you've got both Fisherman and McWade in your pocket. But here's some advice: They aren't good at sharing. They're going to tear you apart."

That was an exit line, delivered as if he had rehearsed it. Rosten stood for a moment, then grabbed his coat and went to the stairs. As he reached the bottom, he saw Comrade Nederlander pass

Lance Corporal Kowalczyk. Rosten waited until he was well out the door before following.

Nederlander moved at an easy pace. This man had decades of experience in evasion; Rosten had to rely on what he had learned playing games with the FBI on the streets of Washington. He turned into Grosvenor Square Garden, where he could follow at an oblique angle, partly screened by hedges. Nederlander went straight down Brook past Hanover Square. The man seemed all about where he was going. He never turned his head. When he started down Regent, Rosten left a large interval. Jostling through the crowds at Piccadilly put him at the limits of his training. Fortunately, Nederlander was wearing a scarlet scarf. At Leicester Square he abruptly turned into a doorway. It was, of all things, a tourist pub.

Rosten was able to slip into a mob of kids and cutpurses on the green. It was easy to find a place where he could see the entrance of the Merrie Olde England unseen. Could this really have been the destination Nederlander had been so intent upon? Time passed, too much time. A back door. What a rookie mistake. Rosten went to the corner and looked down the street. Fortunately, there did not seem to be an alley behind.

Quite a few of the kids and buskers on the square were doing their thing near a statue of Shakespeare. Given what Elizabethan London was like, the Bard would probably not have felt out of place. Suddenly, Rosten realized that his attention had drifted. He could not have said whether anyone had entered or left the pub door. He pulled focus, and as he did, he saw an apparition. A small, stooped figure in a black raincoat and gray Homburg was going inside. It was Fisherman.

"Fink you could spare me a square?"

Rosten had no choice but to look to the voice. It belonged to a

Cockney girl in leather boots, a long, threadbare blue suede coat, and luminescent short shorts that peeked out where the coat fell open.

"Sorry," he said.

"Gimme a nicker," she said.

"I'm busy," he said, looking back to the doorway. He felt something and grabbed her hand before it got into his pocket. She cried out. He let go. He wanted the police less than she did.

"Wanker," she said.

He kept glancing her way as she headed toward the statue. There she approached another man who looked as out of place as Rosten. He was much older, shortish, thin, and carefully dressed in a charcoal gray suit. When she spoke to him, he reached into his pocket and in one movement pulled out a pack of cigarettes and shook a single one toward her. When she took it, he put the pack back and pulled out a matchbook, folded a match over, and snapped it alight.

Rosten moved a little closer to the tourist pub to see if he could get a glimpse through the window, but he could not. The situation was utterly beyond him. He was operating in Fisherman's world now, just as he had always wanted to, and he was lost. He had been able to follow Nederlander only because Nederlander was leading him. At any moment the old man would come out the door and see him, the way he saw everything. Get out! Get out now!

He cut a diagonal across the square, accelerating to a jog. He passed the Cockney girl, who gave him the finger. At the corner he felt eyes on his back. He kept himself from looking.

When he reached the Embassy, he was winded and pouring sweat.

"Forget your running gear?" said Kowalczyk.

There was only so much repair work Rosten could do in the restroom. If Fisherman had taken a taxi and was waiting for him,

Rosten would say that he had taken a walk at lunch, lost track of time, and raced back to continue working on the little experiment. Fisherman would enjoy the performance.

He opened his door and felt his way to his desk, where he switched on the reading lamp. Then he opened his safe and took out the dossiers, arranging them next to a government-issue legal pad. An hour passed. Two. The burn bag began to fill with crumpled yellow sheets. Fisherman did not appear.

Eventually Rosten left his office and counted the twenty-five paces down the hall to Fisherman's. He could see no light under the outer door. He let himself in. The door to the inner office was locked. He knocked. No sound.

"Are you there?" he called.

Nothing.

He returned to his office to stare some more at the dossiers and the blank legal pad. The phone rang. It was Schneider inviting him for a drink.

"Rumor has it that Peter Nederlander is in town," Rosten said.

"First I heard of it, laddie," said Schneider. "But I did hear that you met Isaac McWade."

"Did Fisherman tell you?"

"You knew that McWade tried to do Ernest in at one point, didn't you?" said Schneider. "A couple of DCIs tried, too. They're gone. Only McWade and Ernest are still standing."

"McWade seems to be standing pretty tall," said Rosten.

The pub Schneider chose was on a side street south of the river near Tower Bridge. He ordered Scotch for both of them, and after another he became talkative. The changes he had seen in the Agency over the years. So many ex–special ops guys with tightly cropped hair and steel-rimmed glasses.

"Is that the future?" said Rosten.

"Langley obviously thinks so," said Schneider. "That and national technical means of intelligence. Satellites. NSA's monitoring arrays, which are nothing but glorified vacuum cleaners. All they get you is a lot of dust. No computer will ever be able to think the way Fisherman does."

Rosten let him go on and on, but what Rosten wanted to talk about required an empty street. Eventually he asked Schneider how he intended to get home.

"I'm sober," said Schneider.

"Mind walking a bit?" said Rosten.

"Next best thing to a jog," said Schneider.

When they were out of range of unwanted ears, Rosten said, "I think Fisherman is in contact with Peter Nederlander."

"Why wouldn't he be?" said Schneider.

"Black contact."

"Does Ernest know any other kind?"

Rosten slowed to a stop.

"I don't trust Nederlander," he said.

"Good policy as a rule."

"I've told Fisherman."

"There's another," said Schneider.

"I think Nederlander is playing both sides," said Rosten. "I told Fisherman that Kerzhentseff might be involved."

"Be careful with that one," said Schneider. "Leave him to Fisherman. Nederlander, too, for that matter. If there is something deep, you can be sure that Fisherman understands it a whole lot better than you ever will. We going to run tomorrow?"

The next morning Rosten was in no particular hurry to get to the Embassy. Kowalczyk stopped him at the guard booth.

"Your boss has been on my ass for an hour about you," he said.

"It's because we're Polish," said Rosten.

"No shit," said the Marine.

Rosten did not hurry but did not stop in his office either.

"You become a man of leisure when I'm away," said Fisherman. "Go get your files. We don't have much time."

When Rosten returned, the light from the window behind Fisherman made it impossible to see his face. Others would have wanted this office for the view; Fisherman probably wanted it for the cover.

Rosten began with the cases in which Fisherman already knew whether the subject was a deceiver or not. In the windowless room he had sorted these individuals into three categories: the bona fides, the doubles, and the don't knows. He started to speak but only got as far as explaining this taxonomy before Fisherman interrupted.

"Don't knows?" said Fisherman. "I know. I assume they do, too."

"As well as you or I know ourselves, I suppose," said Rosten.

"Go on," said Fisherman.

Rosten began to discuss the first individual.

"No need to continue," said Fisherman after a minute or two. "Just leave me the list you're reading from."

"Are you going to tell me how I scored?" Rosten said.

"Please move to the Central Asians," said Fisherman. "We are wasting time."

Rosten pulled out the next set of files.

"The collaborators," he said, "can best be categorized by the nature of their fear."

Fisherman opened and closed a small pocket knife, sometimes pausing in the process to use the point of it to clean a nail.

"Am I boring you?" Rosten said.

"They all know they can be killed by either side," said Fisherman. "Everyone is afraid. This is a dry hole. I wanted a story."

"I'm trying," said Rosten.

"Just tell me this: Do any of these men believe in the cause they serve?" said Fisherman.

"I can't imagine even Lenin would anymore," said Rosten.

"What about Mohammed Omar?"

Rosten fanned out the third set of file jackets until he found the right one.

"Pashtun," he said. "Born around 1960. Fights under Nek Muhammad. Very intense about his religion."

"Tell me," said Fisherman, "does he believe in what he's fighting for?"

"Absolutely."

"Good word," said Fisherman.

He put down the little knife and leaned forward.

"Whom do you fear most?" he said. "The men in the first two groups or Mohammed Omar?"

He stood up before giving Rosten a chance to answer.

"We need to get to Paddington Station," he said. "We'll leave your material in my vault. Did I ever tell you about my year at Oxford?"

The taxi they hailed just outside the Embassy gate was no place to talk about the encounter at Leicester Square. Neither was the train. During the Oxonian walk Rosten was given no chance as Fisherman kept up a monologue on the history, architecture, and landscape. Along the way, he revealed little bits of personal information, which he had never done before.

On the train ride it had been raining, and though the rain had stopped, the Cotswold stone and old brick of Oxford were still shadowed with moisture. Fisherman in his Homburg led across greens, along the narrow Thames, under the arches to the sound of the rehearsal of madrigals.

"I wish I had met William Empson," said Fisherman, "but he was banished to China by the Cambridge dons for having the temerity to like sex with women. The lecture we'll be hearing today is on his view of Shakespeare's Sonnet 94. You remember it, don't you? 'They that have power to hurt . . .'"

Rosten could not summon up so much as a single line.

"I assume you have actually read *Seven Types of Ambiguity*," said Fisherman.

"Your friend Hawthorne challenged me to come up with seven more," said Rosten.

"The lecturer we will be hearing today is from Princeton," said Fisherman. "She's Hawthorne's younger competition for the American crown."

"You keep up with all that?"

"This is the great Christopher Wren's Sheldonian Theater," said Fisherman. "They say he was a Freemason, but it is still a matter of debate."

"They knew how to keep secrets back then," said Rosten.

Fisherman seemed pleased. Or perhaps the cuttlefish was flashing a pretty color in order to get Rosten to come close. They had never spoken of art or friendship or the irrelevant past. They were not natural men. Neither of them.

A surprising number of people had already gathered at the lecture hall by the time they arrived. Fisherman led the way to two wooden folding chairs in front of a row of women about Fisherman's age, all in dowdy dresses. Up front stood a lectern without a microphone and behind it a fireplace clad in wood darkened at the edges by centuries of smoke. Gray light came in through tall, leaded windows.

As they sat down, Rosten picked up a sheet of paper that lay centered on the seat.

"At least they didn't expect us to have it memorized," he said.

Fisherman glanced at the paper, folded it lengthwise, and put it into his inside breast pocket.

> *But if that flower with base infection meet,*
> *The basest weed outbraves his dignity:*
> *For sweetest things turn sourest by their deeds;*
> *Lilies that fester smell far worse than weeds.*

When Rosten looked up, a courtly man and a tiny woman had moved to the lectern. The reading lamp illuminated the man from below, making him into a wizard. She stood off to the side, looking at the audience without a hint of self-consciousness as he introduced her.

"As you know," she began, "William Empson read mathematics before turning to literature. Perhaps it is no surprise, then, that he began his explication of Sonnet 94 the way he did. There were, he wrote, four thousand ninety-six possible 'movements of thought' as to the meaning of the poem. That may be good mathematics, but it is very poor hermeneutics."

She went on to explicate the poem with great precision and even greater confidence, drawing particular attention to Shakespeare's comparison of the cold, self-controlled aristocrat of the beginning of the poem with the sweet flower at the end.

"Only when it suffers base infection," she said, "does it begin to reek. One has to strain mightily not to read this as a clear warning to the aristocrat: 'Behave yourself, or you'll end up stinking worse than I do.'"

"Leave it to the Americans," whispered one of the women in the row behind.

Had Rosten been in class, he would have enjoyed offering other plausible interpretations. It had been too long since he'd had the opportunity to exercise his mind on something of so little consequence. He looked over at Fisherman. Chin on the knot of his tie, he was asleep.

As she drew the lecture to a close, the professor said, "Empson believed stability of meaning could be found even in utterly contradictory readings. He wanted to prove that, with such a great poem, all four thousand ninety-six possibilities could be embraced, that perhaps this was the very thing that made a poem great. But, sadly, the math does not work. It turns out that the possibilities are in the thousands only if we insist on being obtuse. I conclude with a plea: Let us not dwell on statistics but rather on the beauty of the expressive, intelligible human voice."

With the generous applause Fisherman awakened. The man who had introduced the lecturer stepped to the podium and called for questions. Fisherman stood and, half bent over, slid down the row of seats into the aisle. Rosten followed

They went directly toward the train station. The street was empty.

"I saw you meeting Nederlander yesterday," Rosten said.

Fisherman did not lose a step. "He told me you had followed him," he said.

"This outing of ours today is somehow connected to my having seen you?"

"He thought it was hilarious that you took the hook so deeply."

"You planned this together?" said Rosten. "The scene he made at the Embassy? To make sure I followed him."

"He did not consult me in advance," said Fisherman. "When he told me, I told him he was a fool. He had something to prove to you; such people always prove too much."

"What is it that I'm supposed to think?"

"He thought you were trouble, and he wanted to show you that you were actually in trouble," said Fisherman.

"Somebody is."

"I don't think so," said Fisherman. "You see, I had business with him."

"At a tourist pub," said Rosten.

"I had hoped that you might have recognized by now that I have adequate reasons," said Fisherman. "I don't entirely disagree with your reservations about Peter."

So now it wasn't the Dutchman. It was Peter. Peter and Ernest.

"Do you agree that he could be working for Kerzhentseff?" said Rosten.

"I am certain that he is not," said Fisherman.

They had reached the outskirts of the university. Midway across a bridge over one of the city's many streams, Fisherman stopped.

"Do you remember Empson's seventh type of ambiguity?" he said.

"Can we talk about reality?"

"It is when a word or a phrase has two directly opposite meanings," said Fisherman. "Interesting that a mathematician focused on cases in which p equals *not p*. No excluded middle."

Fisherman leaned on the rail, looking out at where the stream disappeared into the trees that lined it.

"A person is always the seventh ambiguity," he said. "Nederlander. Kerzhentseff. You cannot sum a man any more than you can count on him. There aren't only four thousand ninety-six possibilities. When p equals *not p*, the possibilities never end."

He let go the railing. Rosten had been trying to look where Fisherman looked. He had seen nothing in the trees, not even a rustle of branches. Then he looked down at the water moving beneath him. It drew him so strongly that he felt dizzy. He stepped back.

Their pace picked up as they neared the station, and they reached the platform only a couple of minutes before the train arrived. The car was quiet, some riders reading the *Evening Standard* and not looking up, others dozing. The station began to move backward. Benches and pillars accelerated and then were gone.

"I hope you found something of interest this afternoon," Fisherman said, rubbing his fingers on the glass. "Fogged windows that show the streaks. That's what draws us to poetry, isn't it."

"Is it?" said Rosten.

"Some like to understand life by the numbers," said Fisherman. "But that's not the life we live." He spoke so softly that what he was saying might have been classified. "P equaling *not p* is what makes people so useful."

9

Gunderman was a burglar in his own house, where he had stripped and stained the woodwork, discovered old gaslight pipes behind the cracked plaster wall, trapped the mice, and bombed the roaches. Everywhere he looked, he recalled broken glass he had cleaned up, an earring he had found, a lost toy recovered to stanch a child's tears, yet it was no longer his home; he was casing it.

Maggie had left Friday afternoon on what she called a girls' escape. Girls without names.

"You wouldn't know them," she had said. "They're from before."

"And the resort?"

"If you have to call me, use my cell."

"So it's another mobile mystery spa."

"Don't even start with me."

But start anywhere, and Gunderman ended up in the same place. The cell phone, for example. They both used to be on the same account, which he paid each month. At some point, he noticed that all the minutes were his, and he asked her about it.

"Oh," she said, "I fell in love with a flashy new number and signed up. Different company. You can cancel me from yours." He did and never once saw bill for her new service.

"I need to be sure."

"I think you are."

"It isn't only that I don't know her anymore. I don't know me."

"You don't like the reflection you see in her eyes. Do you think she likes the reflection she sees in yours? She blames the mirror. This is normal."

"I'm not interested in normal. It's not about medians and means."

"Of course not. When the pain is yours, it is unique."

"I've tried to be a good provider. A faithful husband. But apparently it's not enough anymore."

"At some point nothing is."

"I've never once strayed. Not a millimeter."

"Do you ever think about how? Did you make yourself unattractive? Invite mockery? Did you use your algorithms as shields? Perhaps you are just now realizing that in doing these things, you may have withheld something from your wife that she needed. Could it be complicity that haunts you, makes you so desperate to know?"

A single branch of the maple scraping the roof made the empty house into a drum. He opened drawer after drawer in the bedroom, lifting up her sweaters, slips, bras, panties, doing it carefully so that they would go right back into place. No cell-phone or credit-card bills were hidden beneath, no incriminating letters. But they wouldn't have communicated that way. She had taken an interest in the computer, which she had always before treated as a rival. All of a sudden she wanted him to show her how to boot it up, how to get onto AOL, how to use the password to keep your e-mail safe.

There was no password on the mailbox outside their front door. There had to have been bills, and yet not once had he found one there, even when she was on one of her trips to a spa on wheels with girls who had no names. A bill would have pointed to the man. She must have taken a postal box.

He stepped very quietly into the little office he had set up for Megan and her. State of the art. They could have started an Internet company in here. He had put in a secure local area network based in his office downstairs, which hooked into as high-speed a connection as he could get. He sat down on the Aeron chair, the casters making an incriminating clatter on the wooden floor as he pulled it close to the desk. When he booted up the machine, he saw that someone had changed the wallpaper on the front screen. It was now a scene of snow and pines. This probably reminded Megan of Canada, where all her ice idols seemed to come from. He clicked on the AOL icon. He had wanted them to switch to Gmail's beta site. Megan was game, but Maggie wasn't having it. She said she wasn't anybody's lab rat. Google really knew what it was doing, he said. "What kind of name is Google?" she said. "From googolplex," he said, but it hadn't been a question.

When the log-in appeared, he pulled down the list of screen names and selected Maggie27. He had them set up with strong passwords based on simple phrases so that they could remember them. Hers was tMo1$fMI: the Matriarch of 1 $trong family aM I. He typed in the first three characters and then stopped. This was worse than rifling her drawers. His fingers slumped on the keys, and "aaaaaaaaaaaaaaa" appeared on the screen. He deleted it and started over. When he hit enter, "Invalid password" appeared. He tried again. Same thing. Somehow she'd figured out how to change passwords. Or Bill Cadwalader had.

"Don't visualize," the Wise Man had told him. He never said how not to.

Gunderman picked up the phone and dialed the Cadwaladers' number. Maybe the oaf was there. Maybe this weekend Maggie was escaping from him, too. That was a picture he could live with. The phone rang four times then went to the recording. Gunderman hung up.

The night before, Megan had sat with him as he ate the frozen ziti he had nuked. He had gotten home late, and she had already grazed her dinner, but she'd joined him at the table, placing herself in the chair where Maggie usually sat. She had the smile that her mother used to have, but lovelier. How did such beauty come from Maggie and him? Especially him. Her ash-blonde hair came from Maggie's side. Her sister had it. Megan's large eyes reminded him of the photos of his aunt as a girl. It was as if family traits had assembled themselves into a puzzle picture finer than any of its pieces.

"So what did you do today?" she said.

"Day like all days," he said.

"That bad?"

Smart girl. He had to be careful.

"You have your name back?" he said. He had changed her screen name and given her a new, very strong password: nBm-wmB1M0t,hp$, nobody Better mess with me Because I aM 0ne tough, hockey playing $ister.

"Megan Gunderman," she said.

"Everyone will get hacked eventually," he said.

And now, if he wanted to look at Maggie's mail, he would have to become a hacker himself. There was a heavy shade on the window of the office. Maggie had put it there. She said it was to keep the sun off the screen, but he was sure that she had done it so the neighbors would not see how much time she was spending. As he sat in the dark, the house dead around him, he began to weep. He looked for a tissue box but found none. She had obviously not felt the need. He slid out the printer's tray and took a sheet. The paper was hard against the skin around his eyes and absorbed nothing. He blew his nose, crumpled the paper, and threw the wad into the empty Blackhawks trash basket. The white seemed phosphorescent in the depths. He reached down and took it out again. Leave no evidence. She doesn't.

When the phone rang, he jumped. For a moment he really was a burglar, discovered in the act. He let it sound twice while he centered himself. It was his house. His phone. His life. He picked it up. Hello caught in his throat.

"Sorry," he said, clearing it.

"Sam?" said a woman's voice.

"Maggie's not at home," he said.

"There was no message, but I saw your number on Caller ID," she said. "I thought maybe . . ."

"Betty?" he said.

"Sorry to disturb you," she said. "I mean, I hope I didn't."

"Not a problem."

"Could you just ask her to give me a jingle after 4?"

"She's away for the weekend."

"Ah," she said.

"Bill and Anna get back from the game yet?" he said. "Megan still hasn't."

"Bill's away, too," Betty said. "College friends."

"Good weekend for it."

"He does this," she said.

"Well, enjoy the peace and quiet."

"You as well."

"I'll leave a note that you called."

"Don't do that," she said. "I mean, maybe I'll call her next week."

He kept the phone to his ear after she hung up, picturing her at the rink in a sweatshirt, a little too large for her jeans but with a round face that returned warmth. You could tell that she had been pretty once. The oaf had managed to keep the weight off and always had a different sweater and a fresh crease in his slacks. Don't visualize.

He shut down the computer and left the room, the paper in his hand smeared with snot and saltwater. When he reached the kitchen, he rinsed his face to get the red out of his eyes. Megan might burst in at any time, scraping her hockey bag against the wall, which always drew a comment from Maggie about the cost of painters. Megan would tell him the score and whether she had gotten any points. She would pound upstairs and shower, then come back down and turn on some music he couldn't fathom. Maybe it was still possible to make a proper life out of these little, daily things, a cocoon, at least until she was ready to break free of whatever it was that had become of her parents.

"I still need you, Maggie."

His voice startled him. It had come without his willing it, as if he had Tourette's. Needed her for the everyday things to hold.

Needed her so that he might be at home in his house. So that their daughter would have a family.

The doorbell rang. Megan was always forgetting her key. It rang again, then again before he turned into the hallway and saw through the door window the bulk of Dick Chase blocking the light. When Gunderman opened the door, Chase stepped in and took off his leather gloves.

"We have to talk," he said, removing his topcoat, which he threw on the back of the couch. He sat down in the chair where Gunderman liked to read the Sunday paper. Gunderman sat where Maggie used to when she still read the paper with him. Megan would sit on the floor back then with the comics and sports section. Sometimes she would read aloud to them.

"This is official," said Chase. "In your internal-audit capacity."

"We all know what we are," said Gunderman. "Would you like some coffee?"

He stood to get it.

"Don't fuck with me," said Chase. "You need to listen to what I came to say."

Gunderman sat down again. "I have to ask whether you are speaking to me in confidence," he said. "We can do it that way if you'd like, but whatever you tell me would have a lot more weight with others if they knew it came from someone of your stature."

A moment of uncertainty flattened Chase's expression. He shifted in the chair and tugged down his shirt, which was bowing open between the buttons. Gunderman hadn't meant to make a fat joke. Chase was finely tuned to such things, but fortunately, he seemed to have accepted stature as a euphemism for power.

"I'm not afraid to stand up," he said.

"You're here," said Gunderman.

Sitting down. In my chair.

"There has been suspicious activity on the system," Chase said. "Lots of it."

This was how it usually began with Chase. First a shock. Then silence. Then the attack.

"Have there been customer complaints?" said Gunderman.

Chase rearranged himself again, as gracefully as a man lifting a hundred-pound sack.

"Did I say anything about complaints?" said Chase.

Getting you off balance was also Chase's way, like a sumo wrestler. Take umbrage. Make it about you. Ordinarily, Gunderman avoided getting into the ring with him, not because he was afraid, just because it wasn't worth all the sweaty pushing and pulling. But this was different. If Chase knew of more intrusions, Gunderman needed to learn of them.

"Why don't you just tell me exactly what you're saying, Dick?" he said.

Chase paused for effect, but Gunderman was already racing ahead. A secret board meeting had been scheduled to get the approval to approach Gnomon. But if Chase had discovered another hacking, Joyce would have to decide whether to abort. He would demand details, the data.

"Greener has been seeing interventions under system administrator authority," Chase said. "Multiple interventions every day."

"That would be Lawton," said Gunderman.

"I know who has the authority," said Chase.

At one point he had raised a fuss that, as VP of Operations, he did not have it too.

"Lawton has been poking around," said Gunderman.

"Into individual files? What the fuck is he thinking?"

"He has a reason."

Chase leaned forward. His face seemed actually to inflate.

"You're blowing this off," he said.

"I've been working with him on it."

Chase fell back into his seat. He needed secrets the way other people need love.

"Can I speak to you now in confidence?" said Gunderman. "Strictest confidence."

"I'm a closed book," said Chase.

Gunderman knew that he should clear this with Rosten first, even Joyce, but Chase was already well on the way to figuring the thing out, and that could take everything into unpredictable orbits fast. The time to co-opt him was right now.

"Nobody is in on this beyond Joyce, Rosten, and Lawton," said Gunderman.

"I should have been told," Chase said. "Joyce and Lawton, OK. But Rosten? If somebody fucks the database, it's my ass, not some Finance geek's."

"It's all our asses," said Gunderman. "I'm going to the kitchen. You want anything?"

"I want more," said Chase.

"Of course," said Gunderman.

At the sink Gunderman drank cold tap water from a glass then filled it again. As he sat back down on the couch and pulled a coaster toward him across the tabletop, he said, "We had a little scare." Then he laid out for Chase exactly what had occurred when, the steps he and Lawton had taken, the algorithm, the null results.

"Lawton has kept checking," said Gunderman, "just to be sure."

"I need to be in," said Chase.

"Now you are."

"All the way in."

"There are others who will have to approve."

"You take care of it," said Chase. "I want Greener on the team that deals with this or anything like it."

"That will be up to Rosten and Joyce."

"Reason with them," said Chase.

He stood, put on his topcoat. He did not thank Gunderman, did not shake his hand. Gunderman stayed on the couch until the door had latched, the storm door had squeaked closed, and everything had fallen silent again. Dealing with Chase had jolted him out of the dead zone. The sun came bright through the windows. The house was warm around him. Any moment Megan would scrape into the hallway.

The club had a men's room of marble, polished in places to a shine as bright as the porcelain and brass. Even the partitions between the urinals were solid stone. Rosten stood before the mirror folding his tie and putting it into the pocket of his suit jacket. Behind him in the mirror was Bill Sebold.

"Tie on. Tie off," Sebold said.

Rosten rinsed his face and dried it on a towel that had the warm smell of having just been laundered. When he finished, he dropped it into a dented brass canister beneath the sinks.

"I'm glad Joyce finally brought you in," said Rosten.

Sebold pushed open the door of each stall. Joyce was obsessed with secrecy, hence the decision to convene the board at his club. And then there was the order that staff not put on ties until they arrived at the club and take them off again before leaving. This was supposed to be so that back at the Dome, nothing would seem out of the ordinary.

"Pinstriped worsted-wool suits and white, open-collared shirts," said Sebold. "What could be more inconspicuous?"

"Are you comfortable?" said Rosten.

"I'd rather be in khakis," said Sebold.

"About the direction we're heading."

Sebold gave him a lawyerly look.

"You're the man with the numbers," he said.

"I mean the other matter."

"We're here, aren't we?"

"I imagine he pushed you."

"It was an isolated incident. Documented. Nonrepeating. Nonmaterial," said Sebold.

"I tried to get him to talk to you right away."

"You're a pal," said Sebold.

"I mean, I wasn't comfortable."

Sebold had soaped up his hands. He met Rosten's eyes in the mirror. Water shushed from the faucet.

"You blessed the incident report," he said. "That's part of the documentation I looked at."

"Of course," said Rosten.

"And on that basis . . . ," said Sebold.

"That's all I was asking," said Rosten.

Sebold bent over and put his hands under the tap then dried them and took a comb from the Barbicide jar.

"I've got to run over to a meeting at Northern Trust on that indemnification issue," he said. "You have a car, right?"

"Run," said Rosten.

He was in no hurry himself. He walked up the grand staircase with its brass risers and banisters. At the top was the big, stately room where they held receptions. Portraits of the founders hung from the high walls. Huge, cut-stone fireplaces faced one another across a tennis court of oriental carpet. When Rosten stepped off it to reach the window, the polished old parquet floor squeaked.

At the board meeting the investment bankers had presented the pro formas, so Rosten's only speaking part had been to talk through a single page on the base-case projections of what earnings would look like in the absence of a deal. There had been no questions. Joyce had controlled the pace the way Michael Jordan in his prime had controlled a basketball game.

Joyce was just as masterful one on one. Simply by his tone of voice, he could bring Rosten in so close that it felt the way he imagined it would with a brother. At other times, one look could put Rosten back into a windowless room. When the security leak had threatened the deal, he had locked him there for weeks. When he let him out again, it was like the sun. Joyce had never been more intimate. He talked lovingly of the sea, said that come the summer he would like to introduce Rosten to the zen of the sail.

"Sounds relaxing," Rosten said. "I imagine you could use some relaxation about now."

Joyce pointed to a model of a destroyer on a shelf above the credenza.

"You get used to being on the bridge," he said.

10

He never expected to see her again. Then one day she summoned him.

"I'm in town," she said, "and I'll be requiring you at dinner."

Fisherman had gone on another one of his absences, so there was no question of informing him, nor any particular reason to. Ellen Bradley was just a single woman in London not wanting to dine alone.

He went home, showered, and put on a tweed jacket he had just bought, an extravagance that had left him a little short. He arrived early at the Indian restaurant in Chelsea that she had chosen. He did not want her to think him eager, but he went right in, which turned out not to be a problem, because when the appointed time came, she was still not there. He ordered a glass of wine, looked at the prices on the menu, which were within his range, but just. The waiter wore a button-down white shirt and a royal-blue vest with a turban to match. After a time he asked whether Rosten would like another glass of wine while he waited.

"A friend," Rosten said.

"Sometimes they require patience," said the waiter.

Just then Bradley flashed across the windows. It was a small place, so even if she hadn't been the way she was, everyone would have noticed her. The waiter caught Rosten's eye and gave a nod: Worth the wait. Then he approached and stood off just the right distance as Rosten pulled out the chair for her.

"Did you order?" she said.

"Wouldn't think of it without you," he said.

"Not even naan?" she said.

The waiter quickly made some appear.

"I don't have much time," she said.

"I'm sorry to hear that," he said.

"Nothing personal."

"Apparently," he said.

She unfurled her napkin and settled it in her lap.

"What's fast?" she asked the waiter. He told her and she said, "I'll have that, and he will, too."

Then her surprising eyes were on Rosten.

"I'm here for McWade," she said. "He needs you to keep watch on Fisherman."

"Looking for what, exactly?" said Rosten.

"Anything that seems strange."

"What doesn't?"

"Strangely strange then," she said.

"And why should I be willing to do this?"

"For me," she said.

She looked toward the waiter, who sprang into action, lifting a tray of food from the stand next to him.

"Maybe we should talk somewhere else," Rosten said.

At the closest table a man and his wife seemed to be hosting their two young-adult children. In the other direction were three couples, two of middle age, one who could have been on a college date.

"Where is Fisherman now?" she said.

"Forgive me," he said, "but no."

She took some from every dish then said, "Have you heard of a man called Kerzhentseff?" She bent down and lifted her fancy attaché case to her lap, hitting the combinations quickly and sliding out a file. "His photograph," she said, passing the folder across to him.

He held it between his body and the table.

"Well, open it," she said.

He leaned back and bent the cover of the folder until he could see inside. There wasn't much light, but it was enough for him to recognize the man in the suit he had seen in Leicester Square.

"This is him?" he whispered.

"Or was," she said. "They took him across in Berlin. He did not look like he was expecting a hero's welcome."

"You're saying he was ours?"

"Fisherman's," she said.

"And Nederlander knows this?" Rosten said.

"He shouldn't," she said. "At the Agency it's only the DCI. McWade was involved in the decision, so he knows, too. Nobody else."

"Except you."

"You would be surprised what I know," she said.

Rosten peeled back the corner of the folder again and looked more closely. The photo could have been from one of the dossiers—grainy, the contrast way too high, no way to know where it was taken. Anything with words had been dodged out by the lab tech's classified thumb, leaving only soot.

"We believe Fisherman gave him up," she said.

Rosten closed the file, returned it, and took a bite of food, which was galvanic in his mouth. He looked at the couple seated to their left—the man gap-toothed beneath his mustache, clearly British, the woman dark and fine-featured, maybe Sri Lankan. Neither of them looked back at him. They were well trained, just like the waiter.

"I'm leaving," he said. His words sparked.

"You have our numbers," she said.

Drizzle coated his face as he hurried to the South Kensington Tube station, where he watched at least a dozen people come down to the platform after him, looking for something about each of them that he could remember. The dash from the restaurant had made him clammy inside and out. He took the Piccadilly train and shared the pole with a trio of shop girls with translucent skin and eyes sunken in makeup. At Leicester Square he got out with them then popped back into the car as its doors closed. A painfully obvious move, but this wasn't tradecraft. It was giving whoever was following him the finger. At Holborn he left the Underground and went directly to his flat, where surely somebody was already in place.

On the table lay a pile of books from Fisherman's list of readings about the Persian Empire and the great Sunni caliphates that had preserved classical learning after Rome fell.

"Why these?" Rosten had asked him.

"For the same reasons the Muslims studied the Greeks and Romans," Fisherman said. "To understand the future. It won't be long before communism will look like just another European dynastic struggle. Professors will strain to explain how such obvious errors in the economic assumptions of *Das Kapital* could have led to the potential to destroy the world."

"Kerzhentseff must have believed at some point," said Rosten.

"He was worthy," said Fisherman.

Or had he used the present tense? Rosten couldn't be sure now. There had been nothing to lock in a memory. No galvanic taste in the mouth. Is, was. It had not mattered, until it did.

He saw no evidence that anyone had gotten into the flat, but they were skilled enough not to leave any. He smelled the breath of them. In the directory that he pulled from a desk drawer, he found the number of the restaurant and punched it into the phone. A message came on saying it was closed for the evening due to a private event. Reservations would be accepted starting at 10 a.m. tomorrow. It was not the waiter's voice.

Was it time to send Fisherman the signal by the *Telegraph*? She had not pledged him to secrecy. Maybe he had walked out before she'd had a chance. Or maybe McWade wanted him to go running to Fisherman. Rosten was in a room soured by others, talking to himself.

The next morning he woke up early, heated some water, and spilled the coffee crystals all over the counter. At the Embassy, he went directly to Fisherman's office, though he did not expect him to be there. As he stepped toward the inner door, it opened.

"Did you enjoy your dinner?" Fisherman said.

Positive met negative across Rosten's tongue.

"We need to talk," he said.

"I was just going to your office," Fisherman said, "but mine is a little cheerier. Better yet, let's take the sun."

Fisherman walked on stiff legs. Rosten found himself leading the way.

"Do you know where you're going?" said Fisherman.

Suddenly, Rosten did. When they got to the Ferris wheel in Hyde Park, he went to the booth and bought a long tail of tickets.

"You have been watching old movies," said Fisherman. "Hearing a zither, are you? You seemed shocked to see me. I hope you didn't think I was dead."

A pulpy-faced man with tattoos gone to blue opened a gate that reached no higher than his knees. He offered a hand to Fisherman. Rosten climbed·in after, and the man snapped the restraining bar in place. If it seemed strange to him that two men in dark suits and ties had decided to take a child's ride early in the morning, he did not show it. He engaged the gears, the machinery creaked, metal on metal, and they began to rise.

"So you had me followed last night," said Rosten.

The red-and-yellow paint around them was chipped, the bar they gripped worn to bare steel. They rose slowly to the top of the trees. Antennas on the Embassy roof spiked the sky above the highest branches. When the wheel carried Rosten and Fisherman to the apex and stopped, the car pulsed back and forth on its mooring. Rosten looked down through the mechanism. A woman and a little girl were getting aboard. They disappeared behind the center axle.

"They wanted me to spy on you," said Rosten.

"And are you?"

"I'm telling you."

"What exactly?" said Fisherman.

The wheel jerked, and they began to descend. On the way down, all they saw was girders and cables. A recording of a Wurlitzer through a tinny speaker grew louder, as festive as a busker with a monkey.

"McWade thinks you betrayed Kerzhentseff," said Rosten.

"I suppose he wanted to thank me," said Fisherman.

The car skimmed above the planks at the bottom, passed the pulpy-faced man, who was looking at some geese in the Serpentine. When they began to rise again, Fisherman said, "Kerzhentseff was less valuable than McWade may have been led to believe."

"Led by you," said Rosten.

"I had other sources," said Fisherman. "I thought it best that they be known to no one. Still, Kerzhentseff had his uses, as every human spark does if you know what to ignite with it."

"They showed me his photograph," Rosten said.

"I'm sure it did not do him justice," said Fisherman. "In his prime he was formidable. Then I found the lever to turn him. After that he declined, I'm afraid."

The wheel carried them over the top and into their descent.

"I saw him in Leicester Square the day you met with Nederlander," Rosten said.

"I imagine Peter's name came up last night, too," said Fisherman.

"She only talked about Kerzhentseff and you."

"McWade shares your view of Peter," said Fisherman. "He has not persuaded the Director of Central Intelligence."

"The people at the restaurant were Agency?"

"I think not," said Fisherman.

The conversation stopped until they had passed the bottom. As the little girl reached the top, she squealed loudly enough to take the operator's attention away from the geese.

"Quite a coincidence that you and Nederlander and Kerzhentseff were in such proximity," Rosten said.

"Somebody must have been turning the wheel," said Fisherman.

"They're running an operation against you."

"It has been tried."

"Is Kerzhentseff dead?" said Rosten.

"They're all in denial," said Fisherman. "The Soviet empire is falling. With our help, the mujahideen will drive the Russians out of Afghanistan, but we are doomed to a holy war with the victors. This means that we and the Russians will have a common enemy, the way we did in the Second War, though this time we are the ones who first made a pact with the devil. The Atlantic Ocean will not be enough to protect us, but it will be worse for the Russians. The zealots are hard upon their southern flank. Some at the Lubyanka recognize the new reality. At Langley they do not."

The wheel slowed. Fisherman fell silent. When they reached the bottom, the operator began to unhook the restraining bar. Rosten reached into his pocket and tore off two tickets, but Fisherman was already out of the car.

"Wait," said Rosten.

"Read the books," said Fisherman and turned and walked stiffly away.

The operator held the bar open. Rosten watched Fisherman go. The girl above them began to whine.

"Going or staying, mate?" said the operator.

Rosten handed him a ticket. The car rose. He watched Fisherman shuffle toward the cover of the trees. Rosten went over the top and down again. Up and over and down. After the second time around, Fisherman was no longer visible. Up and over and down. Eventually the girl and her mother left, and he was alone on the wheel. Then he reached the bottom, and the operator stopped the machine and set the brake.

"You all right, mate?" he said.

"Thinking," said Rosten.

"I got trouble with me dad, too," said the operator. "Left him in Australia and made a run for it."

"That work?" said Rosten.

"I'm still talking about him, ain't I?" said the operator.

11

When Rosten returned to his office, on the desk lay an old book. Fisherman must have left it, another history lesson. He picked it up and looked at the spine. *Personae* by Pound. When he lifted the worn cover, he saw that it was an original edition, signed by the poet himself in 1940. On the first blank page Fisherman had written:

> *For an old bitch gone in the teeth,*
> *For a botched civilization.*

Rosten sat down at the desk and read poem after poem. Troubadours, condottieri, jousting knights. Only one stanza really spoke to him:

> *For God, our God, is a gallant foe*
> *That playeth behind the veil.*

He set the book down, picked up the phone, and dialed. Schneider answered at the first ring.

"I need to talk," Rosten said. "Soon."

"That bad, laddie?" said Schneider. He did not pause for more than a second before he named a place. The Royal Albert Hall would have a crowd to hide in, he said. They were showing *Fantasia* with a live orchestra.

"*Fantasia*," said Rosten.

"When I saw the notice in the *Telegraph* the other day, I thought of you," said Schneider.

Rosten put *Personae* in the safe, splashed water on his face, and left the Embassy. Scores of kids were at the carnival in Kensington Gardens now, and on the paths through the green were mothers with prams, runners, old folks out for a hobble. He stayed to the edge, passing the Hyde Park Barracks and the Iranian Embassy, which was as heavily fortified as the American. Up ahead was the Royal Albert. Many times he had passed this great circle of red brick, Stonehenge of empire, but he had never been inside.

Within minutes Schneider appeared before him and conjured two tickets. A little girl stared, as if expecting a rabbit.

"This way," said Schneider, edging them into a spot near an entrance. Children and parents pressed uncomfortably close. "Kind of twitchy aren't you."

When the doors opened, the crowd swept them inside, Schneider in front. He turned into a stairway and was able to wait for Rosten to catch up. When they reached the second tier, they stepped into an alcove, which had just enough room for the two of them. The crowd surged on.

Rosten launched right into it—his dinner with Ellen Bradley, the file she had shown him, the inscription in the Ezra Pound book, Fisherman on the Ferris wheel.

"He was running Kerzhentseff," Rosten said.

"Stands to reason," said Schneider.

"Then what is this about?"

"That's too easy, laddie," said Schneider. "Revenge for a murder."

"The guy in the Charing Cross Tube station?" said Rosten. "You said Fisherman had nothing to do with that."

"Eventually McWade realized that he didn't," said Schneider. "It's the murder of another friend that he blames on Fisherman."

The throngs of children just kept coming.

Years after the Wheeler murder, Schneider said, Fisherman got on the trail of a man from the National Security Council called Michael Ross, who was working on a major nuclear arms-control deal with the Soviets. Fisherman learned that Ross was trading highly classified information with the other side, maybe to get a treaty done, maybe because the Russians owned him. "One Russian in particular," Schneider said, "the one whose picture the pretty girl showed you last night."

Eventually Fisherman proved that Ross had been doubled years before. He also discovered that Wheeler was onto Ross and Kerzhentseff and that they were the ones who'd had him murdered. When McWade found out, he lost it, demanded that Ross be arrested if not shot on the spot. But if Congress had learned there was a Soviet mole in the U.S. delegation, it would have put an end to the talks. Nobody wanted that, not even Defense. So a legend was written that attributed Ross's departure from the National Security Council to health issues, which did ensue shortly, by the way, ending his life. Thanks to the legend, the Soviets didn't realize that Kerzhentseff had been thoroughly compromised. To keep it that way, he needed Fisherman's protection, so he turned. Fisherman fed him information that reestablished him with his comrades. All the while, he kept Kerzhentseff's secret compartmented in a box with only three people inside—Fisherman, the DCI, and McWade.

"And the cat," said Rosten.

"The which?" said Schneider.

"You're in the box, too."

"Every man needs a pet," said Schneider. "Even Ernest."

He told Rosten how McWade ended up being promoted to replace Ross, on his way to even bigger things. "You would think he might have had a little gratitude," he said, "but then one of his own turned up dead, facedown in a canal in Berlin. McWade was sure Fisherman had put out the order. That's what this is about, laddie."

"You let me think Kerzhentseff was running Nederlander," said Rosten.

"There didn't seem any harm in it," said Schneider. "Nederlander is a shit."

The crowd was beginning to thin. Rosten lowered his voice.

"I saw Kerzhentseff in the park across from where Fisherman and Nederlander met," he said.

A bell began to chime. It was time to take their seats.

"Right here," said Schneider, pointing to the doorway directly across from them.

"It wasn't a coincidence."

"Not very likely."

"I don't think I was entirely wrong about Nederlander."

"In this business you're not usually entirely anything," said Schneider. "We'd better get moving or we'll miss the show."

The lady at the door sold Schneider an oversized souvenir book and directed them to their seats. The hall was so cavernous that even children could not fill it with noise. Schneider became immersed in the book, which had pictures of the Disney scenes and small blocks of large type.

Up front the orchestra prepared itself, a trumpet doing Stravinsky while an oboe played *The Nutcracker* and fiddlers scurried over a variety of phrases that, played simultaneously, produced a sound like a Cubist's Beethoven. At various places around the hall were huge movie screens. Beyond the closest one the pipes of an organ poked out the top. As the lights began to dim, the Disney logo appeared. The oboe struck a steady note, and the orchestra tightened itself down on it. Then the conductor appeared to polite applause and a scatter of little voices. Soon came the booming opening of Bach's D-minor Toccata and Fugue. The silhouettes of musicians appeared on the screen, slowly fading into clouds and then abstract patterns of light.

Next came a piece from *The Nutcracker*. When it concluded, a voice filled the hall, explaining that the story the next music told was almost two thousand years old, a tale of a sorcerer and his apprentice, a smart young fellow, too smart. Schneider pointed to the picture of the great magician in his book.

The first time Rosten saw *Fantasia* was when his mother and father took him to the Chicago Theater downtown, which had the biggest screen he had ever seen. He remembered the way he had found his mother's hand and held to it when he saw the enormous sorcerer, his face lit by glowing eyes. After being ordered to scrub the floors, poor Mickey managed a spell to command a mop to carry water for him then fell asleep to dreams of commanding galaxies. When he awakened, he realized he did not even have the power to command the mop to stop. He tried to destroy it with an ax, but this only managed to create more mops. Soon the place was a raging flood. When the sorcerer returned and fixed things, Mickey's only punishment was a smack on the rump.

Schneider's book still lay open to the image of the great sorcerer as the film moved on. When the word "Intermission" finally appeared on the screen, the children erupted. The lights came up.

"Why was Kerzhentseff in Leicester Square?" said Rosten.

"Ernest knows what he's doing, laddie," said Schneider.

Rosten stood. Schneider held the program book out to him. Rosten did not take it. He turned and followed the crowd into the corridor and then made his way to the first exit.

Outside, he walked quickly but without a destination. Saturday strollers idled in the park on the other side of the street. He turned into Kensington, proceeding through Knightsbridge, avoiding the Palace and the tourists, until he found himself in Westminster, which was mercifully empty on a Saturday. Up ahead was the Abbey. When he reached it, he saw a sign that gave the time for Evensong. He must have looked confused, because a small woman, probably in her fifties and dressed for High Mass, waved to him from a queue.

"You need a ticket." she said as he approached.

"I'm just here for the music," he said.

She reached into her enormous purse and pulled out a guidebook.

"Here," she said; finding the page and showing it to him. "Evensong is free, but it says that buying a ticket to tour the Abbey first helps you get a good seat. There, about halfway down the page."

He thanked her and went to the back of the queue. He was a tourist, just like her. He had been since the day he had left New Haven. Maybe he had been a tourist even there. Maybe that was why Hawthorne had selected him. A tourist is a pocket to be picked.

The sun was coming through a hole in the blanket of low clouds as Rosten approached the stone arch of the entry. A breeze off the Thames smelled of diesel and brine. The attendant handed him a map. Rosten followed it to the Poet's Corner, where Shakespeare presided, chin on fist, elbow on a stack of books, looking foppish, which was all wrong for one who knew the souls of those who have the power to hurt. Over there was Chaucer's canopy bed. Dickens was underfoot, lying with Kipling and Tennyson. But where was Wilfred Owen? No *dulce et decorum est pro patria mori* for him. That was for Kipling. But wait. There he was on a paving slate with Rupert Brooke, Robert Graves, Siegfried Sassoon, his words wreathing them: "My subject is War, and the pity of War. The Poetry is in the pity."

As Rosten stood with head bent, a man came through, announcing that the Abbey hours were ending. The woman's guidebook had said that to go to Evensong, you exited into the nave inside the Great West Door, where the map showed a stone in the floor for Winston Churchill near a memorial to FDR. One of these hallowed men had allowed Coventry to be bombed to protect a secret. The other had built the first nuclear weapon. The Abbey was a place fit for Fisherman—a small, forgotten stone in some anonymous corner, perhaps, but among his kind.

Rosten saw the woman again. She had placed herself near an iron gate. She waved.

"Was I right or was I right?" she said. "First in line."

When a man in a cassock came to open the gate, she and Rosten followed him into the shadows. The organist's lighted perch rose on their right, a candle in the dark. When they turned a corner, Rosten stopped. The Quire stretched out before him, pews facing pews across a wide center aisle, illuminated both from high above and by small reading lamps with bright red shades. Some of the seats bore plaques identifying them as belonging to the great dignitaries of the realm.

"Come on," she said. "You don't need a knighthood."

They filed in with the rest of the tourists and watched as the singers filled the empty sections, boys and men, all wearing white surplices over long red robes and carrying folders that matched the lampshades. Only the woman was between Rosten and the choristers. He felt as if he had let himself again be drawn into a place where he did not belong. Then the sweet birds sang. The anthem was old, its words Latin, a dead language on the lips of boys. He closed his eyes and let himself sink into a cavernous sense of mortality.

The service that followed was in English. The woman held out a book where it was written, but he did not recite. The choir sang again, this time in its native tongue. The preacher prayed. Then it was over, the choir filing out first, then the tourists. He hung back, breathing candle wax and old stone, the river and the must of graves, until the man in the cassock bade him out and clanked the gate shut behind him. A few people were praying in the nave, an elderly couple who seemed to be both together and alone, a scatter of singles, a woman dabbing tears. He found a place among them and sat.

Fisherman's game was too dark to divine. All Rosten could hope to do was to abide the plainest meanings. He reported to

Fisherman, but he had not signed an oath to a man. He served something larger. It was so easy to lose sight of this in his windowless cell, alone, *p* and *not p*. Maybe Fisherman recruited young, middling humanists like him simply because the study of poetry had talked them out of plain meanings.

The scuff of footsteps slowly died away behind him as the tourists left. Soon there was only the sound of the cathedral itself, which, like a seashell, whispered in the voice of something that wasn't there. He pulled out his wallet and found his AT&T credit card and McWade's number in Ellen Bradley's handwriting on a folded piece of paper. Then he stood and walked directly over Churchill's name and out the door.

It was easy to find a scarlet phone booth. When he closed the door, it smelled damp, but no worse than Edward the Confessor's resting place. The credit card would leave a trace, of course, but everybody seemed to know his every move anyway. When the call went through, McWade's secretary seemed to recognize his name. Cars hissed past as he held on the line. He pushed with his fingertips against the window, which did not yield the way they did in the States. When McWade finally came on, he did not let Rosten say a word.

"Get to the Embassy code room," he said. The phone clicked dead.

Rosten took a taxi. Kowalczyk wasn't on duty. The Marine guard at the entrance was new. He would not let Rosten through.

"Isn't my ID good anymore?" said Rosten.

"Sorry, sir," said the guard. "Somebody will be here to escort you."

"Is this Fisherman's doing?"

The Marine was as unresponsive as a guard at Buckingham.

It could not have taken more than a minute before the Chargé d'Affaires appeared, smiling and holding out his hand to be shaken. Rosten had seen him from time to time, but only in an official car coming or going. Technically, he was called the Deputy Chief of Mission, but Fisherman always used the French, which he said better fit the man. Even on a quiet Saturday, the Chargé wore a beautifully tailored gray suit and a school tie, knotted perfectly against the blue of his shirt front and the striking white of the collar.

"Let me take you up," he said.

When they reached the code room, the Chargé identified himself on a speaker and then punched in a combination on the keypad next to the code-room door, which swung open on a space that looked too ordinary to be secure—coffee pot half full, children's drawings pinned above a single Steelcase desk.

"I'll leave you with Jimmy. He'll take care of you," said the Chargé. "I hope we have a chance to meet properly someday soon."

"You'll be in there," said Jimmy, pointing to a door that opened onto a room not much bigger than a closet. "Don't fool with the phone until it rings. He'll call you."

Jimmy closed the door, leaving Rosten in a silence so deep that when he clapped his hands to break it, the room swallowed the sound. A phone, as gray-green as the river, sat on a device the size of a minirefrigerator. Rosten picked up on the first ring.

"I told Fisherman everything," he said.

"I expected no less," said McWade.

"But I see now that it is possible that Fisherman drew Kerzhentseff to Leicester Square to set him up," said Rosten. "For some reason Fisherman must have wanted Nederlander to get points with his KGB handlers."

"Did Fisherman tell you this?" said McWade.

"Of course not," said Rosten. "But he must have had a reason."

"He always does," said McWade.

Rosten talked him through the last conversation in detail, even mentioning Fisherman's reference to The Third Man.

"Orson Welles playing Fisherman," said McWade. "Gene Hackman would be closer."

"Why would Fisherman have sent me to Barcelona if he was working with Nederlander?"

"He wasn't yet," said McWade "He wanted a third opinion."

The voice on the scrambler phone came through with a slight gurgle, as if from deep underwater.

"Whose was the second?" Rosten said.

"He most certainly consulted Reg Schneider," said McWade. "He was on you the night you had dinner with the lovely Ellen. I assume you picked that up."

"I went to Reg for advice today."

"You're going to have to be more observant," said McWade.

"He told me you wanted revenge," said Rosten. "For somebody killed in Berlin."

"When Ernest goes down, revenge will be a collateral benefit," said McWade.

Then he went silent on the line, and the room closed in around Rosten. What little sound there was came from the phone mechanism itself—a diver's air, bubbling out.

"Did you tell Fisherman about my little exchange with Nederlander about the mujahideen?" McWade finally said.

"I told him everything."

"I imagine he perked up when you mentioned Afghanistan."

"Not that I noticed."

"You didn't notice Schneider either," said McWade. "Do you know where Fisherman is right now?"

"The last time I saw him was on the wheel," said Rosten.

"He's gone off our radar," said McWade. "Nederlander, too. Your friend Schneider got out of Royal Albert Hall clean. Looks like they may all have gone black."

"Black because of me?" said Rosten.

"Black is black," said McWade. "You can't see into it."

"I know how to reach him."

"I'll let you know when it's time," said McWade. With that, he was gone.

When Rosten emerged, he went directly to Fisherman's office. If he was there, it would mean that he hadn't gone black. Rosten could tell him of the conversation with McWade. This would make him a courier, nothing more. And if Fisherman was not there? Then Rosten would go to his windowless room and wait for someone to open the box.

He knocked on Fisherman's inner-office door, heavily the second time. Of course nobody answered.

When he returned to his flat that night, there were no calls on his machine. In the weeks that followed, he lived in almost perfect solitude. His world consisted of two men, and each had gone mute. The only voice that spoke came from within, and he barely recognized it. He went to the office every day, arriving early, staying late, going over files, revising his thoughts about believers and unbelievers then revising them again until he had a range of interpretation that even Empson would have admired. He bought Pound's Cantos and read and read. They spoke all languages at once. Now inscrutable, now hateful, now rambling, now insane.

And occasionally a moment of clarity.

there

are

no

righteous

wars

Maybe it took a traitor to see this.

As the days passed, he would have been no more surprised to learn at Bigsby's that Fisherman had turned up in Moscow with a medal on his chest than to hear on the BBC that he had been made the Director of Central Intelligence. Finally someone rapped briskly on the door of his cell, the way the cleaning ladies did at night. But it was daytime, wasn't it? He had lost track. The knock came again. Fisherman would not bother with such a nicety. Rosten went to the door.

It was the Chargé d'Affaires in a blazer and ascot.

"You have been summoned," he said. "Sorry to interrupt, but when the White House calls . . ."

"Did he say anything?" said Rosten.

"You have important friends," said the Chargé.

Jimmy showed Rosten into the padded room. The gray-green phone rang.

"How soon can you get to him?" McWade said.

Rosten told him about the notice in the Telegram, the book code.

"*Seven Types of Ambiguity*," said McWade. "Priceless."

"We have a prearranged location," said Rosten. "On the Strand. A moderate chophouse. I'll cross over from Waterloo Station to give him eyes on me."

There was nothing wrong with bringing McWade's people together with Fisherman. Rosten was like a secretary arranging a meeting. There had been some terrible misunderstanding. It needed to be talked through.

"This has to happen ASAP," said McWade.

Rosten went directly to the newspaper office to place the ad. It was mostly numbers.

The lady in drab flowers behind the counter winked at him.

"They'll catch you if you're running a lottery, luv," she said.

"It's just a little fun," he said, paying cash.

"No harm in that," she said.

Rosten set a date two days off to give Fisherman time to get back from wherever it was that he had gone. He returned to his office but left promptly at 5 to check his messages at home. If Fisherman needed to abort, he would call and simply ask for the Complaint Department. The message machine was empty. The phone remained silent.

The day of the meeting, he came home at noon, half-hoping the call would still come. When he finally left his flat, the air was clean from an afternoon rain. A transparent half-moon hung in the falling light over the city. He walked to Euston and took the Northern Line. Waterloo Station was still aswarm with commuters. He pushed his way in one direction and then another until he finally emerged on the busy street, which he crossed and took directly to the bridge.

He assumed that McWade's team was there watching. One could have been that girl coming toward him with colorless skin and raccoon eyes. Or the fellow standing against the wall just outside the human current, reading the Sun. If Fisherman had eyes on the situation, it would be old school like Schneider, maybe someone who had gone out in the purges.

As Rosten moved forward, he saw Fisherman up ahead, standing at the rail, looking up and down the bridge, then way out over the Thames past the Old Bailey and Fleet Street's Christopher Wren. He was risking exposure, which did not seem right. Then he saw Rosten and started to scan. Rosten had to fight the impulse to quicken his pace. Suddenly, Fisherman focused hard on someone on the opposite side of the bridge. Quickly he took something from his pocket, bent over, and jabbed at his lower leg. As Rosten approached him, Fisherman hauled himself over the rail, looking back from the parapet for a moment. His eyes may as well have already been dead. As he plunged into the river, something fell onto the walkway. He hit the water flat and went under.

"Oh, my God!" a woman cried.

"Someone help him!"

The crowd on the bridge knotted at the spot, with Rosten in the middle of it. He reached down and picked up a metal tube with its sharp, spring-loaded point. In one motion he rose, put his hand over the rail, and let the device drop. It was so small that he could not see the splash. He hoped it would be carried away along the bottom and never found.

12

The KGB's poison would have stopped his heart before he hit the water," said Rosten.

"My God, Tom," said Grace.

"He must have realized that I had set him up," said Rosten. "It would have been his last thought."

"He had been using you."

"And I failed him," he said.

In a matter of minutes Rosten was surrounded by police and spirited off to New Scotland Yard.

Had he seen anyone push Fisherman over the rail?

Rosten said the crowd had obscured him.

"Somebody with an umbrella?"

He said that it was a perfectly clear evening. Not a suggestion of rain.

"Then you would have noticed an umbrella, wouldn't you?"

All he saw was his boss going into the water. He wasn't looking at fashion accessories.

At some point the questions turned to Fisherman's state of

mind. Rosten told them that anybody who thought he could know that was an idiot.

"Was he despondent?"

"He made other people despondent."

"Including you?"

"Only those who deserved it."

"Could one of them have killed him?"

"If you don't know who he was, talk to MI6,' Rosten said. "They'll tell you that the world is full of people who would have killed Ernest Fisherman with pleasure."

After the police were finished with Rosten, the Agency questioned him.

"Why were you on the bridge?"

"I was meeting him for dinner."

"But he had vanished."

"We set the date before he left."

"Your idea or his?"

"Mine."

"Yours alone?"

"Of course."

"Why?"

"To catch up."

Then more questions about the poison, how it got into him and why, all going in the wrong direction—East rather than West.

McWade was radio silent, and when the questions finally stopped, Rosten dialed his private number from his flat. He didn't care that the call might be intercepted. He cared only about the way Fisherman had looked at him just before he jumped.

"Go to the Embassy," McWade said.

"I'm done with all that," said Rosten.

"The situation has not been resolved," McWade said and hung up.

This time the Chargé d'Affaires did not escort Rosten. Lance Corporal Kowalczyk made a call, and some functionary took him up and punched in the combination that let him through the code-room door. Jimmy dialed up McWade.

"What did you do to him?" Rosten said into the dirty green phone.

"Your boss was romancing the KGB. It was all about the mujahideen," said McWade. "He was offering the KGB information about our Afghan allies—names, precise locations—so the KGB could target them right under the noses of our guys on the ground. He believed the Soviet Empire will fall, and soon. He had become fanatically certain that when this happens, the greatest threat to the United States will the jihad. Strange for a man who read as much history as Fisherman did, he forgot that Islam isn't the only empire that can become more lethal as it declines."

McWade's spotters had seen the meeting at the tourist pub. They had photographed Kerzhentseff and Rosten in Leicester Square. The Cockney girl who called him a wanker and cadged a cigarette from the Russian was McWade's. Rosten had thought she was picking his pocket, but she was probably trying to plant a tracking device.

McWade said that Fisherman had Nederlander pegged as the mole, which was just the opportunity the old man had been looking for. But he needed to prove to the Soviets that his interest in making common cause was genuine. Kerzhentseff appeared in Leicester Square because Fisherman had summoned him. He wanted to demonstrate that Zapadnya was actually his Petrushka. This consigned Kerzhentseff to the Soviets' mercies and established Fisherman's bona fides.

When McWade's team saw Rosten in the square, they also spotted Schneider. The Cockney girl got a picture of him. Rosten had never noticed him. He might as well have been blind.

"You can't put this on yourself," Grace said.

"I have both Fisherman's and Kerzhentseff's blood on my hands," he said.

She took them in hers.

"McWade tried to tell me that Kerzhentseff had died for his sins," Rosten said. "I asked him what if Fisherman died for his virtues? 'Your man took himself over the edge,' he said. 'Yes,' I told him, 'I saw him hit the water.'"

Grace held his hands more tightly.

"I always thought that one day I would tell you everything," Rosten said. "I wanted to, but then the jets hit the Twin Towers. I don't know what I would have done if you had been hurt. Osama bin Laden was one of the men in the files Fisherman gave me. Everything turned out exactly the way he said it would. The Russians lost their empire and are a threat to nobody, but the fundamentalists are bloodying us up all over the world."

"Do you think he could have prevented it?" she said. "That you could have?"

"There are a lot of things I didn't think I could do," he said.

Within a week of Fisherman's death, they pulled Rosten out of the windowless room in the Embassy and reassigned him to London Station. The Agency came up with a narrative: Fisherman was onto the Soviet mole, and the KGB killed him; the type of poison they found in his system proved it. Rosten was expected to sing the ballad with conviction.

"Schneider never did surface," he told Grace. "People said he became disgusted, just up and left. Strange for someone so close to his pension. Sometimes I have a nightmare of finding him facedown in a Berlin canal."

"Tom," she said.

"They're capable of anything, Grace," he said. "Sometimes in the nightmare I put him there."

For more than a month they had Rosten on ice, like a deadly microbe. Nothing to do, not even little experiments. He realized that he had only two real options: to make his own game or to resign. Some people expected him to attempt the former. After all, he had been taught by the master. But on the Waterloo Bridge he had seen that he was not nearly good enough. He submitted the paperwork to leave the Agency.

Nobody in London tried to talk him out of it. He might as well have been submitting his taxes. His resignation letter went into the great machine, and a reply came back setting out in tedious detail the procedures, his continuing obligations of secrecy, the benefits he had coming, such as they were. It advised him to wait in place for his formal release. But before it came, he received an order to return to the States. He was to report to Isaac McWade at the White House.

When he got to D.C., the city was in the midst of a temperature inversion. The air smelled of exhaust and standing water. His flight arrived late, so he had to go directly to the White House with his bags. He was so anxious that he would have sweated through his suit even if it hadn't been 90 in the shade. He did not want to see this man. He wanted to forget and be forgotten. If the Agency had some experimental potion that did that, he would have volunteered to take it.

When he presented his credentials at the Pennsylvania Avenue gate, the security officer told him that because of the luggage, they wanted him to check in next door at the Old Executive Office Building. As he left the gate, a crowd of kids and their chaperones was walking down Pennsylvania. The kids kept bumping his suitcase and saying they were sorry.

"Are you somebody?" said a ginger-haired boy.

"Nobodaddy," Rosten said. The boy laughed.

Getting into the Old EOB was slow, but a young woman was waiting on the other side, and she led Rosten deep into the building. The last time he was there, he had been dazzled. Now it just seemed old. Wires ran along baseboards. Here and there the paint was peeling. The nameplates beside the tall doors were plastic, as if it were a Social Security office.

"We'll stop in here," the young woman said. "This is Mr. McWade's second office. I'll be bringing you to the one he has near the Oval Office. You can take a minute to freshen up if you'd like."

She let Rosten into McWade's private bathroom. There was a razor and Barbasol shaving cream on the counter, along with Mennen deodorant and a large bottle of aspirin. You might have thought he was a man like all men. When Rosten splashed water on his face, it got all over him. He waved his tie around to dry off the spots, but it became clear that he could do this for hours in the humidity and they would still be there. He must have looked like he was the one who had gone into the Thames.

"Don't worry about your bags, sir," the young woman said when he came out of the bathroom. "They'll be taken care of."

She walked him across to the West Wing entrance, checked him through security then pointed out the landmarks.

"The Situation Room is on the right," she said, "and there's the White House mess. We'll go up these stairs. Now this way."

Large photos of the President hung everywhere. The corridors were ridiculously narrow.

"Back behind us are the Cabinet Room and Oval Office," she said.

"Mighty close quarters," Rosten said.

"People choose proximity over legroom every time," she said. "Here we are."

She opened a door into a tiny room. A secretary was crammed into the corner.

"Tom Rosten for Mr. McWade," said the young woman.

"Go right in," said the secretary.

When she opened the inner door, Rosten found himself in another windowless room. McWade sat at a desk that was much too large. The credenza behind him pushed everything forward so far that when Rosten sat down, the back of his chair was touching the wall.

"You cannot resign," McWade said.

All Rosten could think of was: You can't stop me.

The paintings on the wall were oils of men in ruffled shirt fronts and waistcoats. Perhaps they were the first spies. A gray-green phone sat on the credenza.

"You have a future," McWade said.

"I have a past," said Rosten.

"My only question is how he did it."

"You know how."

"Not the toxin," said McWade. "I mean how he got it into his leg."

Rosten shrugged. But often it's harder to lie with a gesture than with words.

"You disposed of it, didn't you," McWade said.

"They didn't find anything on me."

"You must have made quick work of it," said McWade. "Even our spotters didn't see you do it. I'm guessing you pitched it over the side."

"Aren't you supposed to read me my rights?"

McWade leaned back in his chair as far as he could.

"Getting rid of the evidence was helpful," he said, "since we decided to make him a hero in the ghost wars."

"I don't suppose I have a need to know why."

"Congress smells weakness," said McWade, "and it doesn't even know about Nederlander yet. You can imagine what a mess it would be if we had to explain two moles. So Fisherman is honored, Nederlander is on the run, and there will be a change at the top at Langley. Fisherman's dalliance with Nederlander will be easy enough to explain: Your boss figured out that he was the mole and was about to take him down."

"P becomes not p," Rosten said.

McWade couldn't have known what that meant, but he obviously didn't care.

"I'm not sure who will get the DCI job," he said, "but I know

I'm going to need someone there with him. There's a future for you in that."

"What kind of future?" said Rosten.

"The DCI's special assistant," he said. "A lot more pay. Access. A room with a view. This is a great town for a young guy with power."

"Doing what?" Rosten said.

McWade smiled as if to say: Anything you want, kid.

"Whatever the organization chart might say, in reality there wouldn't be anyone between you and me," he said. "Look, Fisherman's getting a posthumous medal at Langley. He'll be up there on the wall of stars. You deserve something, too."

"I'd like to be at his ceremony," Rosten said.

"He might have seen the humor in that," McWade said.

"I wish I could tell you that I felt disgust," Rosten told Grace. "I wish I'd still had the clarity I did when Fisherman glared at me from the parapet. But as I left and looked over my shoulder at the White House, I felt the pull of enormous gravity."

"You don't have to go on," Grace said. He felt her weight shifting away from him. The darkness. The death. And he was not done yet.

"They'd checked me into the Hay Adams Hotel while I was with McWade," he said. "In the lobby I passed men with tailored suits and sheathed women. The window in my room caught a corner of the West Wing. I had a big, four-poster bed with the finest sheets I had ever run my fingers over. The sun was streaming in, but my internal clock was still somewhere over the Atlantic. I lay down. When the phone woke me, I thought

I was still in London. Then New Haven. I heard the voice as you."

"You were sleeping," the woman on the phone said.

"Who is this?" he said

"I have your ticket to the Fisherman event," she said.

"Bradley," he said.

"You might start calling me Ellen," she said. "Look, our last dinner was not exactly a pleasure. I owe you one. This time I'll be good. Shall we say tonight?"

"Have you already hired the actors?" Rosten said.

"I was thinking the restaurant at the hotel," she said. "Shall we make it 7:30? Barring a world crisis, of course."

"What exactly do you do?" Rosten said.

"Go back to sleep," she said.

"I had a dream of you," Rosten told Grace. "I never stopped having them."

"That's lovely, Tom," she said. She was obviously trying hard to find good in him. He could not leave it that way.

"You were bringing me alive with your lips," he said. "I reached down to touch your head. My eyes opened. It wasn't you. The hair was strawberry blonde."

"Let's stop," Grace said.

"I didn't stop," he said. "Because I wanted it, even though I knew it was compensation for delivering Fisherman, a down payment on the sale of whatever in me might somehow have remained unsoiled. It only ended because she eventually said I had to make a decision: this life or an ordinary one. 'It's time to decide,' she said.

"I fled. It wasn't that I had found the right path. I was afraid of the dark, a coward. I ran to you because I could not think of anyone else who would have the man I had become. The man I am."

"I need a taxi back to the hotel," she said.

"Of course," he said.

three

THE

SEVENTH

TYPE

1

Barbara Jean stood at the porch rail with the declining sun lighting her, a winter bird on a branch. Coming from the garage, Lawton said, "Tell me you haven't been standing here since I called." She spread the storm door like a great, transparent wing.

"It wasn't so long," she said.

"You are something," he said.

"I heard your car in the alley and the garage door going up."

He sloughed off his overcoat, which she hung on the brass rack then opened her arms to him.

"I told you it would be a good report," she said.

Words were jinxes. Dr. Dick, usually so guarded, this afternoon had used the phrase "full function." Lawton was afraid of it but asked when.

"You will know," said Dr. Dick.

It did not pay to let expectation run. So far he could not feel much. Oh, perhaps a little less vulnerability to changes in his environment, a bit more energy walking back to the Dome, but today that could simply have been the effect of good news metastasizing.

The security scare seemed to be abating, too. It would have been better if they had been able to figure out who had pulled the prank, but prank it had obviously been. Joyce and he had been the only victims, and it had not recurred. Gunderman was still fretting, but Lawton had stopped monitoring the database altogether, delegating this to Greener, who took to the tedious task as if it were the most important job in the company.

Joyce seemed to have put the incident entirely out of mind since the secret board meeting that wasn't a secret. His attention now focused on the deal, and that mercifully left Lawton on the margins. He would have plenty of work to do if it ever reached the stage of due diligence, but for now all he knew was that Joyce had spoken with Gnomon's CEO, a child king named Niko Nyström. Harms had found his picture on the web and pronounced him "a swarthy blond, with eyes as dark as an umlaut."

Word had it that the first conversation had been cordial, but that since then ice had come into the fjord. This did not seem to have daunted Joyce. He and the deal team had been in perpetual huddles with the bankers and legal advisors, so Lawton and a few operational peers were able to run D&D without the distraction of visionary leadership.

"It's a little early to think about dinner," said Barbara Jean.

"I kept my calendar free after the appointment," he said.

"And here we are."

She took his hand and pulled him in the direction of the stairs. She took a step upward. He followed. Then another.

"The report wasn't that good," he said, gravity asserting itself.

"Don't worry."

"I'm just not . . ."

"Of course not," she said.

He remembered when he had been, but he remembered without feeling, the same way he desired.

"I'm sorry," he said.

"Oh, for heaven's sake," she said, smiling down at him where he had balked.

"I wish . . . ," he said.

"I read somewhere that when your skin touches the skin of someone you care about, it sets off a cascade of chemicals in your brain that binds the two of you," she said.

"Even if . . ."

"Even then."

He let her levitate him up the stairs and into the bedroom.

"I don't want to be a disappointment," he said.

"Let me have your hands," she said.

He held them out. She put them on the buttons of her blouse.

"You can go right ahead," she said.

Underneath she was alabaster. The first time he had seen her like this, it had frightened him, the way standing on a high board did. From having gazed at her fully clothed, he had anticipated the shape of her breasts, but the pink of her nipples had startled him. They were small and looked painful, though when he touched them, they clearly were not.

"My turn," she said. "Now let's see you."

She worked on his belt after removing his shirt. Before, just her hand on the buckle would have raised him. Now the only sensation was a little tugging and the dull click of metal. When she had untethered him, he sat down on the bed and unceremoniously pulled himself out of his pants and socks.

"Let's take a shower the way we used to," she said. "Wash the doctor away."

"Why don't I just jump in?" he said, wishing he had his robe to cover the raw scar just above where his pubic hair was still growing in like a vacation beard. There was gray in it. Hers was tan, not as light as her hair, but he could see right through it.

"Shower alone? Not on your life," she said. "We're going to bathe in oxytocin."

She was enjoying this, but he was unteasable. Un-everything. He reached for the soap. She got there first.

"I showered when you called," she said. "This is all you."

She started at his neck, pressing her thumbs into the muscles where age had gathered.

"Let yourself relax," she said. "I'm not going to hurt you."

"It's just kind of difficult for me."

She worked the lather down his chest and then turned him around to do his back and buttocks, with special attention to Dr. Dick's province.

"Tell me if any of this is uncomfortable," she said and turned him back around. She ran her fingertips close to the scar. "This seems much better. Is there any tenderness?"

He shook his head. She shut off the tap.

"Out now," she said. When he complied, she swaddled him in a plush towel.

"Don't you get a chill," he said.

"I'm warm all over," she said. "You just get yourself into bed. I'll be there in a sec."

When he pulled back the covers, he saw the silk sheets they had bought on their first anniversary and had almost never used since.

Surely she had no expectation. And if she had, his inertness under the touch of her slippery, soapy hands should have dashed it.

"You look good," she said, emerging from the bathroom.

"Covered up," he said.

"We'll fix that."

"Can we just hold each other?"

"The very thing," she said, slipping beside him then covering his leg with hers so that he felt the tan hair against his thigh. Whenever he moved, she moved, as if he were leading.

"I would like to touch you," he said.

She seemed about to laugh.

"You are touching me," she said.

"I mean to make you feel good."

"You do."

"Really good," he said.

"I'm feeling really good now."

"For me then."

She rolled onto her back. He rose on his elbows and kissed her from above.

"That was nice," she said.

He drew back the sheet. Her breasts rose under his hand. Then he smoothed the tan hair below. It began to feel moist. He leaned down to kiss her belly and then shifted lower.

"I want you up here with me," she said.

"But you love . . . ," he said.

"Yes I do," she said, lifting his head with her two hands until they kissed.

Soon he felt movement under his hand as he dialed in to her need. He thought he felt something himself, only a kind of quickening, the first prickle of a limb that has fallen asleep. She made a sound. Then another. When she came, she touched him where he had been dead, and he heard a small sound of his own.

Nyström had agreed to meet with Joyce in New York, where both companies had appearances at the annual UBS All Things Data investor conference. This gave them cover, since everyone who mattered was there. They did not book the meeting into D&D's law firm. Joyce said that would be like asking a first date to meet you at a motel. They arranged a suite at the Michelangelo, where nobody from ATD ever went. The one-on-one was scheduled for an hour and a half after the end of Gnomon's presentation. Day and Domes would be on stage the following morning, and Harms worried about facing questions so soon after a tryst.

"Nobody will be able to read my thoughts in my face," said Joyce. "I mean, have you even once seen lust in my eyes?"

"Are we still talking about motels?" said Sebold.

"Easy, gentlemen," said Snow.

As they waited, Harms suggested they occupy themselves by rehearsing their Qs and As. She posed the obvious Q about third-quarter expectations and full-year revenue guidance, but Joyce responded with another Q: "Do we know what kind of water Niko prefers?" Harms tried to bring him back with a loaded question on potential strategic moves. "Strategy?" he said. "You ask about our strategy? Day and Domes laughs at the size of the ideas you call strategy."

He got up and poured himself a cup of coffee. Harms's hands squared her papers then squared them again.

"Don't worry," Rosten told her. "His irony was perfectly stable."

"English, please," said Harms.

"He's jerking you around," said Rosten.

To monitor Nyström's presentation, Rosten had sent Gunderman, because nobody knew him. He was not a man for nuance, so he made a tape and brought it back to the Michelangelo. On it Niko, of course, sounded brash. He was always all about buzz, a regular cicada. According to Gunderman, he went to the dais alone, no CFO, no revenue person. Bet on me, this said.

"Good thing we won't be talking price today," said Joyce, looking at his BlackBerry. "His just went up like a hot-air balloon."

"It's only seventy-five cents," said Harms, reading the quote on her phone.

"A one-point-three-eight percent increase," Gunderman said instantly.

"You're the kind of guy I hated in high school," said Joyce.

"Niko isn't exactly going to feel needy," said Sebold.

"At this stage, we want our date to feel like the most desirable at the ball," said Joyce.

Harms leaned close enough to Rosten that her hair brushed his neck.

"He doesn't understand women, does he," she said.

"Neither do I," said Rosten.

"Had me fooled," she said.

The team left Joyce at the Michelangelo to wait for Nyström and regathered in a salon at the site of All Things Data. There were great plates of sandwiches, salads, and the inevitable chocolate-chip cookies. Harms provided entertainment, imitating the child MBAs who would be doing most of the questioning the next day.

"What does the relationship look like between average kilowatt-hour rates and operating margins?" she asked, holding her BlackBerry like a notepad in her left hand and an imaginary pen in her right.

"Graphed on a typical Mercator projection, it perfectly describes the graceful rising curve of an extended middle finger," said Sebold.

"Easy," said Snow. "Crudeness is a form of harassment."

"So is humorlessness," said Sebold.

Eventually the fun in the salon faded. At about H hour plus ninety minutes with no word, things began to get tight. Finally Joyce appeared in the doorway.

"I see lust in his eyes," Harms whispered to Rosten.

"Easy," said Rosten.

Joyce hung his suit jacket on the back of a chair and sat down, obviously enjoying the suspense. After a couple of minutes of it, he said, "Niko gets it. He totally gets it."

"You've got the gift, boss," said Chase.

"He needs time to think, of course," said Joyce. "I told him that I'm a patient man."

"And he believed it?" said Harms. Chase could have learned a lot from her about how to flatter.

"I didn't want him to," said Joyce.

"Gesture of respect," said Harms.

"He ate it up," said Joyce.

"We need to think about next steps," said Rosten.

"Always keeping me on task," said Joyce. "But first we need to think about tomorrow."

They sat at the conference table and ran through the script and slides until it was time for dinner. Joyce had chosen a restaurant where you really had to be somebody. He'd had Marcia order in advance, and when the waiters brought the entrée, he collected compliments on his taste. Rosten would have preferred room service and CNN. He would not have called Grace, but he might have picked up the phone and hung it up a couple of times.

The haute cuisine was paired with the old wine of Joyce's other deals. The alcohol kept coming, inflating him. CEOs did not realize how much this exposed their vulnerable parts.

"You did your share of acquisitions, Tommy," Joyce said. "Was there ever one as big as this?"

Nobody had called Rosten Tommy since he'd asked his mother to stop.

"Not a one," he said, as he was meant to. "And I was only a number cruncher, never the principal."

"But you were there keeping the man honest," said Joyce over his veal.

"Trying," said Rosten.

"Tell us about Trinitrex and Global Dev so I can have a chance to devour this piece of art on my plate," said Joyce.

Rosten spoke of it as distantly as if he had followed the transaction on a Bloomberg machine. Trinitrex made this move. Global countered with that. The strategy. The structure. The financial engineering. The tax methodology. The cash piece. In his telling, it was all columns and rows.

"You're too modest," said Joyce. "Leverone told me that if it hadn't been for Tommy, Trinitrex would never have prevailed. He called him 'the rock.'"

The waiter poured him another glass.

"I don't think I have enough room even to look at desserts," Rosten said.

"Anybody else?" said Joyce. "Don't be shy."

"Tomorrow's a big day," said Rosten.

"Bright and early," said Harms.

"Don't worry about me," said Joyce.

"Some of us aren't such long-ball hitters," said Rosten.

"All right, all right," said Joyce. "The rock has spoken."

The check came, and Joyce signed it, but he still had wine in his glass.

"Do we dare start to leave?" Harms whispered, leaning soft into Rosten's shoulder.

"You first," Rosten said. And to his astonishment, she stood.

"Gentlemen, it's bedtime," she said.

"If only," said Sebold.

Harms silenced Snow with a look.

There were a few stagey complaints about the night being young, but chairs began to scrape and silver to rattle on china. Rosten stood, his arm still up against Harms's.

"Eight thirty sharp in the war room, right, Tommy?" Joyce said. "Everybody straight to bed. His own bed."

"Tight lines," said Chase.

"Isn't it loops?" said Sebold.

The team pushed back from the table but did not rise until Joyce did.

"When they're gone, we can sneak a nightcap," Harms said, locking Rosten behind the table as the others filed out.

"You know me," he said, "the dull, worker-bee type."

"It seems to be doing the job for you."

"Maybe we'd better let them clean the table."

"De facto chief operating officer," she said. "It's only a matter of time before he makes it official."

"Will I have a say?"

"You have a quiet authority," she said. "I didn't get your game at first. Not seeming to want it is why you'll get it."

"Sometimes not wanting something is not wanting it," he said.

"She lives in Manhattan, doesn't she?" Harms said. "The one who didn't want you."

He took a sip of water. The waiter saw this and offered more wine, which Rosten declined.

"You can do better," Harms said.

With that, she began to move. He followed her to the coat check, where she handled the tip. On the street she stepped forward and scored a taxi within a minute. She could have done it without even putting out her hand.

The team was on deck early the next morning. Harms had Gunderman calling in every fifteen minutes from the auditorium to report on the other firms' presentations. He made a special call when he spotted Nyström in the crowd.

"Listen up," Harms said over the clatter in the salon. When it was silent, she spoke into the BlackBerry so everybody could hear her.

"Where is he? No, I mean where in the room exactly?" she said. After a few seconds she held the BlackBerry off to the side and announced, "He's in the anteroom near the elevators." She put the BlackBerry back to her ear. "Can we slip into the Green Room without passing him? Great. If he moves, let me know."

She put the device down on the table in front of her.

"Time to call an audible, Brian," she said. "Do you want to notice Niko or not?"

Joyce showed no effects of the night before. His eyes were clear, his suit and tie crisp but not fussy, his bearing just what an investor would want it to be.

"Let's just play the bubble line past the hole," said Joyce.

For Rosten this might as well have been one of Ezra Pound's obscurities about the condottieri.

"Let's get moving," said Harms.

"We'll wait five minutes," said Joyce.

"That's cutting it close," said Rosten.

"A little suspense is good," said Harms, lowering herself back into her place, a flush growing above the V of her neckline. Rosten's eyes were drawn to it. He had to look away.

Finally Joyce stood, signaling that it was time. As it turned out, they did not encounter Nyström along the way. The first time Rosten saw him was from the dais after opening the Bible and buttoning his suit coat to keep from showing too much shirt. Nyström was not looking their way. He was talking with someone Rosten had never seen before.

The dais was small. Rosten always worried about falling off the back of the platform. The consensus was that the hosts arranged it that way to keep presenters on edge. They used to say that UBS stood for "You Be Shaky." In addition to Joyce, Rosten, and Sebold, Dirk Lowenstein of UBS squeezed in. He always wore the same thin tie to these events, the only time anyone ever saw him in a tie of any kind. His jacket looked as though he had bought it in high school. He was one of the highest-paid analysts in the sector.

In contrast with the dais, the auditorium seating gave people room to sprawl. Wide-bottomed, plush chairs surrendered to the varied angles and weights of the custodians of wealth who inhabited them. They rose, row after row, which assured perfect sight lines for all, regardless of total assets under management.

Day and Domes always drew a crowd. The biggest player in its primary market, D&D may have meant Dull and Duller to the high-flying hedge funds, but everyone knew that if it ever started to use its muscle, the earth would move.

Joyce kicked the presentation off with a tour d'horizon. The audience leaned forward to see what he saw, not next quarter or next year but five or six years out, by which time Joyce said the data sector would be barely recognizable.

"There will be enormous wealth creation," he said. "There will be disruption and consolidation. And Day and Domes will be at the center of the action."

Rosten's recitation of the numbers felt like a footnote. This is up a little from our previous guidance, that a little down. He moved through his slides quickly, flicking a page of the Bible from time to time but never looking at it.

The first question was always Lowenstein's.

"You sound like you have something in your sights, Brian," he said.

Rosten looked out into the crowd and found Nyström standing in the back.

"It won't be long before things start shaking loose, Dirk," Joyce said. "In the Navy we would have called it a target-rich environment." Rosten closed his eyes. When he opened them, Nyström had not reacted. "When it happens, it will happen fast, but anyone who tells you today that he knows what will move and what won't is just laying down a smokescreen."

While Joyce was speaking, Nyström nodded to the man next to

him, and they turned toward the exit. Some people in the audience watched them go, but that could have just been because of Nyström's attire—black T-shirt under a tailored gray suit, bright red handkerchief puffed up in his breast pocket. He wore his clothes the way he wore his umlaut.

The next several questions came to Rosten, who consulted the Bible for effect but handled them from memory.

"You need to be a tightrope walker who stumbles once every performance," Harms had told him once. "Wobbling tricks them into thinking you're for real."

When he was done, Harms caught his eye from her place in the middle of the audience. She raised her thumb at the V of her neckline and winked. Rosten brought his eyes up well over her head.

All around her the young geniuses were dressed as if they were slumming in the skyboxes at a Knicks game. They were not the real money, of course, nor even the money's keepers. They were money's scouts. They made what any normal person would think of as a bundle, but every one of them yearned to graduate to the Asset Class. In that socioeconomic category they would suffer no more tedious investor conferences, no more predictable, catered Chateaubriand lunches and tchotchkes from Tiffany, no more worries about whether the bonus would make it a six- or seven-figure Christmas.

The women in the crowd probably weren't wired any differently, but you would not guess that from looking at them. They all seemed to be wearing a substantial part of their income: Perfect suits. Cashmere. Silk. Dresses tight and short but never over the invisible line. Gold and gems cladding fingers and necks with sympathetic magic. Harms more than held her own.

The questions continued, focusing more and more tightly on the next quarter, which took Rosten back to a safer place. What was the guidance on revenue? Database growth? Full-time equivalents? The interest-rate assumption for pension expense calculations? When someone asked about the trend of costs in database security, Rosten was ready to dull it to death, but Joyce jumped in.

"They are not diverging from costs generally," he said, "but I assure you that Day and Domes does whatever it takes to guarantee the integrity of its data."

Sebold might have wanted a little less of a drumroll, but the questioner did not ask whether anything had happened, and Joyce did not say that nothing had.

Lowenstein finally called time.

"Stimulating, as always, gentlemen," he said, as he did to every group.

Four chairs moved back as one. Four men slid out sideways, like parishioners leaving the pews. A knot of people crowded up to the dais, some old familiars, some new faces.

"What's the margin of error around your Q3 revenue projections?"

Plus or minus your age.

"It's in the same range as the uncertainty around GDP growth projections," Rosten said.

"Which is? Ballpark, I mean."

The young man's badge said he was from Credit Suisse First Boston. "If I were you, I would use the number my bank uses," Rosten said.

"Can I call that an endorsement?"

Suddenly Harms was at Rosten's side, taking his arm. He started to pull back, but then he saw that she had Joyce's, too. Once she got them to the hallway reserved for presenters, she said, "Well done, men." Rosten felt a little squeeze of his biceps before she released him.

"What's the stock doing?" Joyce said.

She stopped to ping her BlackBerry, and Joyce kept striding ahead.

"Down a quarter," she said when she caught up.

"Not exactly a rave," said Rosten.

"Don't mind Tommy," Joyce said. "He is religiously opposed to exuberance. What's your take, Sandy?"

"We flashed the possibility of an acquisition, and the market held," she said. "All systems are go."

"You saw that Niko left during your answer to the first question," said Rosten. "He was talking away during the whole formal presentation."

"He already knew the numbers," said Joyce.

"Was I at least in good voice?" said Rosten.

"Your loop was so tight it would strangle a mayfly, Tommy," said Joyce.

"Didn't you see my thumbs-up?" said Harms.

"I did," said Rosten. "Yes, I certainly did."

2

A negotiation is about knowing more about the other party than the other party knows about you. With a publicly held company you can go to its Security and Exchange Commission filings, plug the information into the standard models, and make a good approximation of how your offer will look to your target. But beyond the numbers lies that vast fog that investment bankers call "the social issues." What does the CEO yearn for? What does he fear? These things Excel does not compute. No matter how exquisite the modeling, it could not simulate Niko Nyström. To do this required human intelligence, HUMINT, Fisherman's game.

What they had on Nyström was sketchy, but Rosten turned it into a story: The man had been only two years past his Wharton MBA when he had launched Gnomon as the market for dot-com stocks inflated. The press releases at the time called him twenty-five, but he had been on the Booz Allen roster for six years before Wharton. Nyström would have had a reason beyond vanity to lie about his age. When he launched, the media called him an old story. His business model was not pure digital. In Silicon Valley they were asking, "Does Niko even get it?" For a man with a dream, this kind of buzz must have been a dentist's drill.

But when the pretty, electric-blue, dot.com balloon burst, Niko's numbers stayed airborne. What saved him was the fact that his business served both the new economy and the old. Suddenly this made him a visionary. He had seen that you needed to build your castle with both bits and bricks. "The Perfect Hedge," Business Week called Gnomon. "Back to the Future" read the headline in *The Economist*.

Vindicated, Nyström did not have any obvious motivation to sell his company. On paper his net worth was advancing toward a billion. He was still young, whatever his real age, and he was already on the Davos list. He had Gunderman's mind and Harms's presence, and he carried himself like a lead singer—complete with a corps of groupies. As for intellectual challenge, the analytical tools Gnomon was pioneering offered plenty to engage his inner geek.

Rosten booked time with Joyce to talk him through all this, but Joyce had no patience for it. "If I wanted touchy-feely, I'd have called Alexa," he said. All he wanted from Rosten was one plus one. Day and Domes's data plus Gnomon's tools. That equaled at least three, didn't it? One and a half for Niko, one and a half for Joyce. If the total was five, two and three-quarters for Joyce and two and a quarter for Niko, which should be enough, even for a rock star, right?

Joyce had put together a subset of senior management to confer about the deal. The Admin News Network promptly dubbed this the Secret Committee. The group had already privately blessed the five. Rosten's team had pushed the numbers harder and eked out six, a fact that Joyce shared only with Sabby Chandrahari. He let two weeks pass after All Things Data before making a call to Nyström, who said it was time for another sit-down.

"How did he sound?" asked Sebold.

"Relaxed," said Joyce.

"He's up three points to less than a point for us," said Rosten. "I'd be relaxed, too." Because of the larger spread in the prices, now one plus one probably had to equal six and a half.

Joyce flew off to Palo Alto. When he returned, he reported to the Secret Committee that things had proceeded further and faster than he had anticipated.

"Let's talk social issues," Nyström had said straightaway.

"It might be a little early," Joyce had said. "A lot of social issues can be resolved with dollars."

"First we have to get past Go."

"What are you thinking?" said Joyce. "Socially, I mean."

You usually wanted to be the one to set initial conditions to put psychological anchoring to work for you. And yet Joyce had let Nyström make the first move.

"D&D is so much larger than Gnomon that I assume you will want to head up the combined company, at least for a time," said Nyström.

"He anchored way out beyond the harbor," Joyce told the Secret Committee.

"How many years?" said Rosten.

"It wasn't the moment to get down to details," said Joyce. "We spent the rest of the meeting filling in circles. Us. Them. We. Frankly, you all went into the Venn diagram, not that I have any intention of paying a premium price for Gnomon then putting its people in charge."

"How about body language?" said Sebold.

"He was a gymnast," said Joyce. "When he landed, he did not move."

"Next steps?" Rosten said.

"Schedule a conference call with the board," said Joyce.

The numbers endured another round of torture. New scenarios were developed, outside-the-box synergies imagined. Rosten began to have dreams. In one of them Sagrada Familia in Barcelona came alive, its stone botany choking off one of the spires like a strangler fig. In another the spreadsheets turned into Monet paintings of a haystack: different angles of vision, different characters of light, increasing opacity of the cataracts.

By the time of the board call, Rosten was back in the daylight world, and his team had tidied up the numbers and buffed all the assumptions. The haystack looked like spun gold.

"Nyström did not let me take the conversation to price," Joyce told the directors, who were represented at the table in Joyce's conference room by a gunmetal disk that spoke like some space alien. The Secret Committee members had assumed their accustomed seats, with the two satellite microphones pulled close to Joyce and Rosten.

"I am sure that you have considered the probability that Nyström led with social issues to discover your intentions," said Sabby Chandrahari. "When he told you what he thought you wanted to hear, it may have confirmed his fears. Perhaps he did not go to price because the last thing he wanted was an offer. My question is: How hostile are you prepared to be?"

"Before getting adverse to Nyström, I need to know the board's thoughts," Joyce said.

This provoked a cavernous clearing of throats over the speaker—a great hibernating animal starting to stir—followed by the rumble of elbows moving closer to speakers from coast to coast.

"Maybe we should talk about price ourselves," said one of the directors.

"Have you established your limit?" said another.

"It is to some degree situational," said Joyce.

"You mean it depends on how much steel rod Gnomon has up its ass," said Lou Leavitt.

Joyce's eyes flicked toward Rosten, who shrugged. You walked into the cul-de-sac, boss. Only you can walk out again.

"What I mean, of course," said Joyce, "is that our number will become clearer as we close in on how much will be stock and how much cash, among other deal points. We also need to get a look under their kimono."

"They won't open the kimono to a rapist," said Leavitt.

Unseen by the directors, Alexa Snow closed her eyes.

"We will have a deck out to you as soon as possible putting together all the intelligence we have gathered thus far," said Joyce. "Don't forget where our CFO used to work. He has ways."

Rosten looked deep into the grain of the tabletop.

"I would be asking myself a different question," said Sabby.

"You usually do," said Leavitt.

"A hostile takeover attempt would put us under an X-ray," Sabby said. "In fact it would be more like an MRI in three-millimeter slices. Are we prepared for that?"

"We should have a forensic audit done," said Teddy Diamond.

"Purely defensive, of course. I take it as a given that we have no reason to doubt our internal controls."

"I hope the Audit Committee chairman's confidence is duly noted in the minutes," said Leavitt.

It was too bad Gunderman wasn't here to witness Diamond going into a crouch, just as Rosten had said he would.

"I might think about it a little more broadly," said Sabby. "Opposition research on ourselves. A tough, outside view. At least as tough as what we could expect Gnomon to undertake."

"You mean A Team/B Team?" said Diamond.

"This has been a very useful discussion," said Joyce. "Thank you." It was lucky that facial expression did not register as sound. "To make sure we are all on the same page, let me sum up. I am hearing recommendations about preparing for a contentious acquisition, but I am not hearing opposition in principle." He did not pause to give anyone a chance to make him hear something different. "When we send you the deck, we will also give you a plan for testing our armor."

"You can't be too cautious," said Diamond.

"Actually you can," said Sabby, "but I don't see much risk of that here."

"May I suggest that we adjourn so that my team can get to work?" said Joyce.

Pages rustled. Good-byes were swallowed. Beeps signaled directors ringing off.

"Thank you for making a place in your schedule for this," Joyce said.

Someone on the line said, "It's our—" but Joyce punched out, cutting off the last words—perhaps "pleasure," perhaps "fiduciary duty."

The members of the Secret Committee tilted back in their chairs, so close to unison that an observer might have thought the conference room was accelerating. That went well, they said. Got the order. Look out, Niko!

It rarely hurt to ask, so Harms did: "How about you, Brian? Were you satisfied?"

Still sitting erect, Joyce stared down the table, his fingers bracketing its edge.

"One step at a time," he said.

Everyone acceded to the wisdom of that. Then Marcia came in and handed him a message slip.

"Teddy Diamond," he read aloud.

"Wimping out," said Sebold.

"Better come along, Tom," Joyce said. "He'll end up being your burden."

It was a short distance from the conference room to the round table in Joyce's office. The private hallway between was unlike any other corridor in the Dome. The walnut walls had a depth that suggested the wood had come from some ancient chamber where great lords once had walked. The ceiling was vaulted and carved in something that looked like ivory. It was said that the Founder had imagined the space as his burial chamber. The door to the office went all the way to the ceiling and appeared to be as heavy as stone, though Marcia was able to open it easily. She stayed on the sarcophagal side when she let it close.

Joyce dialed the call himself.

"Teddy," said Joyce into the speaker. "I was hoping you would still be there."

"It wasn't a suggestion, you understand," Diamond said.

"Of course," said Joyce.

"I believe I speak for the Audit Committee," said Diamond. "And anyway, we might as well get ahead of the heavy weather."

"Always good seamanship," said Joyce.

"I didn't mean to blindside you," said Diamond. "But you surprised us, too."

"I understand your concern and respect it, Teddy," said Joyce. "You've had experience."

"This is a different situation, of course," said Diamond. "Ours was just a bad apple. But take it from me—"

"I have to," Joyce said. "You're the audit chair."

"Good then," said Diamond.

"Are we done?" said Joyce.

"I've said what I needed to say," said Diamond.

"Calm seas and prosperous voyage," said Joyce.

He punched out and said, "Prick!" Then he pulled out his clippers.

"How do you want me to handle it?" said Rosten.

"Limit the inquiry to the financials," said Joyce. "We don't need any forensic auditor mucking around in the consumer database."

"And Gunderman?" said Rosten.

"He's the last person," said Joyce. "He wanted this shit."

"Foresaw it, I think is fairer," said Rosten.

"Don't put it to Poole that we're excluding Gunderman," said Joyce.

"This simply isn't relevant to his tasks," said Rosten.

"To the director of Internal Audit, anytime you say no, it's a red flag," said Joyce.

"Are we feeling urgency?"

"Not nearly as much as Teddy is," said Joyce.

How much less became apparent later that day when he called

Rosten to announce that despite the courtship of Gnomon, he was going to be taking some R&R. "You don't want the object of your desire to think you are too eager," he said.

Rosten immediately consulted Sebold and Poole on candidates for the forensic audit.

"What's wrong with Cooper-Jones? We've worked with them for years," said Poole.

"That's the problem," said Rosten. "Diamond won't see them as independent."

"How about Jake Theobald?" said Sebold. "He's of counsel at Winston & Strawn. I'm sure he's available."

"He's got to be pushing eighty," said Rosten.

He sent them away to come up with bolder names. The next morning Rosten told Joyce that they were still mulling. Joyce stood there in a shirt with epaulets and multiple pockets, even on the sleeves.

"I'll call with a short list within thirty-six hours," said Rosten. "I assume there is cell coverage where you're going."

"I kind of hope Niko tries to get in touch with me," said Joyce. "I'll have Marcia tell him I'm out of range on a freestone river. Make him Google to find out what that is."

He came out from behind the big desk that had been an antique when Thomas Woods Peterson had bought it at auction in London.

"Just in case of emergency," said Rosten.

"You'll man the bridge," said Joyce. "I've just sent out an e-mail to that effect. Pick the forensic auditor yourself. It won't hurt to be able to tell Teddy that I recused myself."

"Hope you catch a lot of fish," said Rosten.

"That's a jinx," said Joyce.

He had begun to fiddle with one of two large, leather duffels that looked as though they could hold him for a month.

"Doesn't it get awfully cold in the water at this time of year?" Rosten said.

"You've never had a steelhead on your rod."

"Always an acquisition," Rosten said.

He did not like the sound of being left alone on the bridge. As he returned to his office, a couple of lower-level people along the way congratulated him. Getting up from her desk, Gail said, "I'll have to remember to try to be nice to you."

"Not you, too," he said.

"Whatever happened to the happy face?" she said.

"Heavy is the crown," said Rosten.

"Don't let it mess up your head," she said.

Ordinarily auditors did not raise their voices. Taxonomy was the limit of their passion: Where should this number go in the columns and rows? Is it this or is it that? Though auditors were black-and-white, they did come in different sizes. Many were sharp pencils, drawing fine lines. Poole was a squat eraser in search of error. Auditors' nails were neatly pared, though they never used clippers in meetings or gave any other sign of boredom, even as half the room nodded off. But when an auditor let go, it was a thing to see, unless you could avoid it.

"Diamond is on the attack," Max Poole said. "It's war."

"He's just afraid," said Rosten.

"I think we should call in Morrie Berry," said Poole.

"Remind me never to use the word timid around you again," said Rosten.

"I'm that confident," said Poole.

"I'm glad to hear that, Max," said Rosten. "What do you think, Bill?"

"If you like tough guys," said Sebold.

"No harm in having him in for an interview," Rosten said.

Berry had been United States Attorney for the Northern District of Illinois, surviving two presidential transitions. He did not achieve this longevity by ingratiation. He did it by putting so many politicians from both parties in prison that firing him would have looked felonious. Eventually he left office "under my own power," as he put it. Ever since, it was said, his edge had only sharpened.

He arrived at the Dome with his former first assistant Lev Szilard, a distant relative of the great atomic scientist. The lawyers made an odd pair. In court Berry tended to run cool; Szilard was a reactor going critical. Berry was slight; Szilard overflowed his clothes. To the *Tribune*'s acerbic lead columnist, they were Little Boy and Fat Man.

After the two lawyers read and signed a nondisclosure agreement, Rosten explained that D&D wanted a hard frisk, but financial only—not operations, not HR. The confidential consumer database was strictly out of bounds.

"What do you suspect?" said Berry.

"We make a practice of kicking our own tires very hard," said Poole.

"Are you aware of my hourly rate?" said Berry.

"I can only imagine," said Sebold.

"My point is, you should be sure the job is worth it," said Berry. "I can't see how it would be unless you've either gotten a subpoena or you're girding for corporate battle."

"We are a punctilious organization," Rosten said.

"You obviously feel you need our reputation," said Berry.

"Your brains first," said Rosten. "Then your name."

"Refreshing if true," said Berry. "What kind of frisk would you like? Pat-down or strip? I have to warn you: We sometimes leave bruises."

Poole's shoulders were rising. Berry finally smiled.

"Don't worry. We aren't desperados," he said. "We ride for the brand."

Gunderman clicked out of the window where he kept his algorithm looping on endless sentry duty. All indicators showed the system running pure to six sigma—99.99966 percent error-free. When he got around to his e-mail, the first in the queue was from Sara Simons.

—How are the shirts?

—Very comfortable. Thanks again.

—If you ever need to talk, just ping.

—Likewise if you have any computer trouble.

—Good to know I can count on you, Sam.

He clicked that chain shut and went at his backlog. Junk. Delete. Routine. Delete. Routine. Delete. Routine. Delete. He cursed the man who had thought up the Reply All function. People wanted you to live their lives. Maybe one of them would like to lead his.

When Maggie had returned from her mystery trip, she had done nothing but complain. The spa was too crowded; you could barely get time in the sauna, let alone with a masseuse. The flight out was forty minutes late leaving; the one back was so bumpy she thought she would need the barf bag.

He told her he'd had an interesting conversation with Betty Cadwalader. She said that Betty was a piece of work. He asked if she had happened to cross paths with Bill Cadwalader lately.

"What does he have to do with anything?" she said.

"That's what I'm asking."

"'Welcome home, Maggie,'" she said. "'I really missed you.'"

"By coincidence it turns out that Bill was on a weekend with friends, too," he said. "Betty was worried about him. I told her that I didn't know what friends you were with either."

"Well, I hope he enjoyed it," she said.

They sat at opposing ends of the kitchen table without so much as a fabric runner between them.

"Turns out he's been going away a lot over weekends," he said.

"You have no right to question me," she said.

"I haven't gotten to a question," he said. "I don't quite know how to ask it."

"Good," she said and left him looking deep into the eyes of her empty chair.

Move on. Work to be done. Things he actually knew how to do. The next message was from one of the younger accountants.

—Did you give any thought to the proposed project plan I forwarded?

—Let me put it in the overnight processor and get back to you, OK?

Junk. Delete. Routine. Delete. Junk. Delete. No need even to open most of them, offers from every company he'd ever ordered from online, plus the spam and phishing expeditions. Hey, check out this great photo. Maybe he'd click on one of the links sometime, just to give his algorithm something to do.

The next message he did not delete, much as he would have liked to. The accounting firm that did D&D's annual routine audits provided monthly regulatory updates. It did not believe in executive summaries, so every member of the Internal Audit staff had to go through screen after screen: new Securities and Exchange Commission decisions, court cases millimetering their way through the system, IRS rulings. Almost never did any of this touch on computer issues, but he had to read the whole thing to be sure nobody had slipped something relevant into the middle, the way Maggie hid cash in books on the shelf. Excerpts from professional publications and learned journals. SEC advisory letters. Congressional committee actions. Suddenly he was caught by a barb.

Disclosure responsibilities in unauthorized database entries

The Commission has given guidance that all unauthorized third-party entry into financial systems must be considered material for purposes of quarterly disclosure under Section M, Topic 1 of the Staff Accounting Bulletin Series.

Gunderman was no lawyer, and he would certainly bring this to Sebold's attention, but it seemed to him pretty clear that this did not technically apply to D&D's incident, which did not involve the financial system and which he had determined, at least to his own satisfaction, did not involve a "third party."

He saved the document with a click, then opened it again and pasted the pertinent part into a new document so he could find it when he talked to Sebold. Then he went back to delete, delete, deleting, his wrist growing numb, until Chase came barging in, with Gail in pursuit. Her face said, "I could not stop him." Of course she couldn't. Nobody could.

"You fucked me," said Chase.

"I think I would remember that."

"Don't get smart."

"Basically you are or you aren't," said Gunderman. "It isn't something you get."

"You gave me your word that you would keep Greener in the loop."

"And so long as there was a loop, he was in it."

Chase tried to engage him in a battle of stares, but Gunderman would not play.

"Don't shit me," said Chase.

"Maybe you know something I don't," said Gunderman. "I suppose that goes without saying."

When Chase's face curled, it was like some weird topological simulation.

"They've brought in heat," Chase said. "Major heat. Morrie Berry."

"The federal guy?"

"A forensic audit. You'd better worry about whether he's auditing your ass."

"You want to sit down?" Gunderman said. "Gail, could you do me a big favor and bring Dick some coffee?"

"Is she still here?" Chase said, turning to look at her.

"Some people freeze and hope the lion won't notice them."

Chase lowered himself into a chair.

"Those must be some dumb fucking animals," he said. "By the way, this conversation never happened, Gail."

"I'm not only invisible," said Gail, "I'm deaf. Don't tell me I'm not, because I won't hear."

Chase watched her leave.

"She's got a mouth on her," he said.

"She knows what to say and what not to."

"You better keep your mouth shut, too."

"Smart? Not smart?" said Gunderman. "That's the question."

Chase was looking past him, as if there were something to see on the credenza other than the leaning towers of technical manuals, scatter of printouts, and the remains of lunch. Given all the things Gunderman had to worry about, being audited—even by Morrie Berry—was not material under Section M, Topic 1.

"You really don't know, do you?" Chase said.

"Smart," said Gunderman.

"And you don't care," said Chase.

"Not smart," said Gunderman. "But I doubt it's about me. Most things aren't."

"Then who?" said Chase.

"Somebody shaving nickels off bank deposits or giving contracts to relatives," said Gunderman. "It could be one of a thousand little hustles. But here's the thing. I actually have nothing to hide."

"You covered up the hacking," said Chase.

"No need to disclose," said Gunderman. "Look at the latest guidance from the SEC."

"I want Greener involved in the audit," said Chase. "Eyes and ears."

"Maybe it's about him," said Gunderman.

"Not smart," said Chase.

If it hadn't been for the recital, Donna would have gone north with Brian. He had told her to get him a ticket, but she had learned not to count on his presence until he was actually there. He had a very demanding job. He needed relief from the pressure, and she wasn't able to provide that so well anymore. She wished he had waited a day for her, but his schedule was so crowded. It wasn't that she wanted to fish. She really didn't understand the appeal, but it was worth the bugs and bats and smoky fireplaces just to be with him when he was relaxed. He would clomp into the mudroom in those chest-high boots that made him look like a sausage. If it was as cold as it was now, he would be wearing layer after layer that he had to molt. Hair a mess. Stubble on his face. Up in the woods he could have been a guy on a bus or a caveman in a diorama at the Field Museum, and she loved him that way.

In cold weather the dryness was hard on a viola, so she would bring the one she kept for students who broke a string. This made practicing less useful, because every instrument had its eccentricities. You got used to one, she told him, made accommodations to it if it was good enough.

"Like five-weight rods," he said.

"And the people waving them," she said.

.

When Sara encountered Sam in the halls, he always looked as though he had just turned the wrong corner. He would say hello but never risk eye contact. You often found the really brilliant ones somewhere along the autism spectrum. Forget about training them for sales. Maybe it had been a mistake to take him by the arm and bodily drag him out of himself, but he was just too good a person to be hurting so.

—Hey. You interested in lunch?

—Already ate.

—Another time.

She kept checking, but nothing came back.

"Morrie Berry!" Joyce said when Rosten reached him at the river.

"He'll satisfy Diamond," said Rosten.

"He's a shark," said Joyce.

"How is the fishing, by the way?" said Rosten.

"You hooked a Great White," said Joyce.

"Can you hear me?" said Rosten. "I'm getting a lot of static."

"I'm in the water," said Joyce. "It's snowing. Nothing is happening on the river. The phone rings. It's bad news."

"With Berry nobody can say we're not serious," said Rosten.

"Did you ever see him at one of his perp walks?" said Joyce. "Guys in perfect suits, Patek Philippes, and handcuffs."

"We're drafting the audit plan now," said Rosten. The river in his ear was like the sound of a fax machine sending.

"The document better be tight," said Joyce.

"Trust Poole," said Rosten. "You run a good ship. Trust me."

"What if he hears something . . . extraneous," Joyce said.

"He would come to us," Rosten said. "We would say, 'Thank you, but it is outside the scope of the audit.' This is a man of the world, Brian. He doesn't need to be young Lochinvar anymore. He gets paid to defend against Lochinvars."

"Do I know this Lochinvar?" said Joyce.

The engagement letter seemed fine, if fussy. Berry was good to go, but he sent it to Szilard for a look since he was the one who would be supervising the work.

"They're hiding something," Szilard said.

"Who isn't?" said Barry. "They don't own our reputations. They're only renting. We have the implicit right to do what we need to in order to get it back intact."

3

For Rosten's father, C. Northcote Parkinson's laws explained almost everything. Did Rosten's mother come up a little short before payday? "Expenditures rise to meet and surpass income." Too many high school papers due? "Work expands to fill the time available for its completion." An evening call from his boss over some niggling matter at the bank? "The time spent on a matter is inversely proportional to its importance."

His father's voice quoting the great man came back to Rosten as he got ready to leave the Red Carpet Club, stuffing files back into the accordion briefcase his father had given him. He was running late ("Work expands"), thanks to another long call from Poole, who rang at least twice a day to tell him that Szilard and company had turned up nothing, with not a hint of mission creep ("The time spent"). They did this today. They did that. Then they did this other thing.

As for the Gnomon deal, there was not an angle from which it had not been modeled. Rosten's analysts had created a four-dimensional picture all the way to the terminal valuation twenty years out. The public-record phase of due diligence on Gnomon had turned up no messes. Everything was proceeding smoothly, and yet Rosten's accordion briefcase was so bloated he worried it wouldn't fit under the airplane seat. Why? Ask C. Northcote Parkinson.

When he got to the gate, they were calling first class, and Sebold was in line. Rosten fumbled around, looking for his ticket.

"You go ahead," he said.

Joyce had taken the company jet the day before so he could attend a meeting of the Hoover Institution on the Stanford campus. The sit-down with Nyström was not until late tomorrow afternoon, but Joyce wanted Rosten and Sebold there well in advance for final preparations.

"What more preparation does he want?" Sebold said. "We're already the Navy SEALs of corporate acquisitions."

Rosten heard his father's voice and said, "The shorter the event, the more the training."

Parkinson had been in the British Army, which explained a lot. Rosten's father liked to tell the story of the troop ship to Korea. Every morning he got up and took a place in the chow line for breakfast. He wound from deck to deck until he could not tell where the line began or ended. When the KP finally ladled breakfast into his father's mess kit, it was time to go to the end of the line for lunch.

When Rosten came home from London, he tried to get his father past Parkinson to the darker parts of service. But there was so little time before his father died.

People on the jetway backed up around a corner, so Rosten could not see the door of the plane. By the time he entered the narrows of the cabin, the queue had reached the stage of physical intimacy. Purses slapped the shoulders of seated passengers. The man behind Rosten kept pressing up against him. Cradling his fat briefcase against his chest as if it were the Bible, Rosten stepped over Sebold's knees and bounced into 5A. Eventually the commotion subsided, replaced by a whir like a garage-door opener's as the little TV screens appeared. Then came the safety briefing. The voice said, "Note that the nearest exit may be behind you."

C. Northcote Parkinson couldn't have put it better.

Immediately after his father's funeral Rosten had raced to the airport to catch a flight to Tokyo. He had fallen asleep in first class and had not woken up until they were off the clock and calendar on the other side of the planet. Today, as they raced toward a deal that could change everything, he felt that way again. He wished his father were still alive, even though he wasn't sure what he could have asked.

"You may now use approved personal electronic devices," said the voice from above.

He put on his Bose earphones but did not plug them in. It was an expressionless silence he wanted, the kind he had shared with his father. He slept.

Turbulence over the mountains startled him awake. Sebold was deep in his laptop, working on a red-lined document that probably would have been dull in ten colors. Rosten closed his eyes again, but the plane kept shaking him back to himself, so eventually he surrendered and pulled out one of the copies of *The Economist* that had piled up.

"You'll regret it," said Sebold.

"Knowing what is going on outside D&D?" said Rosten.

"Screwing up your circadian rhythm," said Sebold. "Taking

that nap means you're not going to be at 100 percent for the big game tomorrow."

Later, in the hotel bed that night, Rosten finished all the magazines he had brought, including the *New Yorkers*, in which he read every article, even the reviews of dance. When he finally did doze, he woke at 3 a.m., 5 o'clock Chicago, as if by the alarm in his apartment bedroom that he always set but did not need. He wondered if he had turned it off before leaving. It beeped in his head until the time came for breakfast.

The three men read the morning papers over omelets then arranged to regroup in fifteen minutes in Joyce's suite. It had a grand piano in the living room and on a sideboard carafes of coffee and plates of sweet rolls. Marcia hovered almost unnoticed, as an executive assistant should, near where she had set up a laptop and printer in case her boss needed it.

Sebold stood above the piano keyboard and struck a credible chord. "Donna here?" he said.

"Of course not," said Joyce.

Sebold closed the fallboard softly.

The preparation session quickly became a monologue. I'll make these initial points. If Niko says this, I'll say that. Permutation upon permutation. Occasionally, Sebold or Rosten would interject, then Joyce would go on as if nobody had.

"Worst case I'll use this," he said, handing each of them a document of a single page.

"The opening bit about a spirit of candor sounds suspiciously like Hardy Twine," said Sebold. Joyce did not bother to respond.

The letter was a formal offer, mostly stock for stock. Gnomon shareholders would have the option of getting cash, so long as the stock piece was at least 70 percent of the total.

Joyce stood and went to the sideboard, where he surveyed the pastry as if it were jewelry. He picked up a Danish and held it up. Sebold nodded; Rosten did not.

"You don't mention the social issues," Rosten said.

Joyce took another look at the roll with a lapidary's eye and rejected it.

"Don't worry," he said. "You're safe."

That was uncalled-for. Rosten had never once voiced any concern about job security.

"My point is that for Nyström the social issues are probably the heart of it," he said.

"This isn't written for Niko," said Joyce. "It's meant to show the board how serious we are. If shareholders were to hear the sound of our money, they wouldn't give a shit whether the Gnomon name survives, much less Niko's. What the hell is a gnomon anyway?"

"It is a rectangle that, added to another, makes a rectangle of the same proportions as the original," said Rosten. He had once tried to use the figure in a poem for Grace about love, of all things.

"I have to point out for the record," said Sebold, "that this letter goes beyond what our board is expecting."

"I talked it through with Sabby," said Joyce.

"He liked the letter?" said Sebold.

"He didn't say no."

They spent the next hour fidgeting over details such as whether the letter should carry today's date or tomorrow's to give Niko a little time. Then there were the incantatory issues that lawyers loved: a conditional tense here, a missing "thus" there. Wine to blood. Words to money.

When they were finished, the letter had barely changed. Joyce had Marcia print it out on heavy bond. He held it up in the light and admired the watermark. Then he signed it in a bold hand.

"Do we each get a pen?" said Sebold.

"When the deal gets signed," said Joyce.

"The sooner resolved the better," said Rosten.

"That's the stuff," said Joyce.

They rode in a black Lincoln Navigator to the meeting place, a neutral site in a new, lightly occupied office park some distance from Palo Alto. The developer had clearly built it for start-ups. First an idea in a dorm room. Then a round of funding from a venture-capital firm. Then a move to a small office in a place like this. For the fortunate few, someday there would be a campus with dorms of its own, concierge services, squash courts, all-night cafeterias, and wide expanses of grass beneath a sky wafting with Frisbees.

The Navigator pulled up to a low-slung building that was as plain as geometry. They got out into a desert sun. In their dark suits and ties they would have appeared—to anyone who bothered to look—as though they had gotten lost. But nobody would bother, because they were utterly unknown here. Not so with Niko, of course, but his presence would only provoke chatter about what start-up he had his platinum eye on now.

Marcia was prepared, as always, and led them to an unmarked door that opened onto a conference room with forgettable art on the wall, furniture of a neutral color, and soft lights above. Rosten wondered how much it had cost D&D to set up here and how much Marcia had paid the attractive receptionist to welcome them and confide that they were the first to arrive.

They bided their time by looking at the view of the arid western landscape, reading the letter over silently, and catching up on their BlackBerries, which had four bars despite the isolated location. Nyström was fifteen minutes late, verging on insult.

Sebold broke the silence.

"He's making a statement," he said.

Some very smart people had no sense of what true things not to say.

"I have a few statements to make myself," said Joyce, slipping the folded letter into its envelope, which was so fine it could have taken a wax seal.

They took more turns at the window. Silence bore down on them again; remarkable how much it could thrum.

Then the receptionist's eager face appeared in the doorway. "Mr. Nyström is pulling up," she said.

"Well, at least she's excited," said Sebold.

Nyström's entrance was operatic, one of those modern ones with almost no scenery. The tenor wore chinos and a muscle T-shirt. Except for the tattoos, he could have been a high school wrestling coach. His ink did not blare, barely peeking out from beneath the strained fabric around his biceps. One figure seemed to be a pair of ideograms. The other was a logarithmic spiral.

Nyström took two steps inside and let the starched shirts come to him. It wasn't easy to read the body language of one so obviously sculpted. *We are not natural human beings.* He accepted Joyce's hand with an intensity that could have been either sincerity or a demonstration of his grip.

"Niko," said Joyce, "this is Bill Sebold, our general counsel, and my right-hand man, Tom Rosten, the CFO."

"I didn't realize you would be bringing staff," said Nyström.

"If you would be more comfortable . . . ," said Joyce.

"No, no," said Nyström. "It was a long way to come is all."

Joyce waved it off, but then Nyström added, "We can get this over quickly."

Joyce stood straighter.

"I have discussed our interaction with my board," said Nyström, "and the response was strong and unanimous. We have absolutely no interest. None."

"Well, I'm sorry to hear that, Niko," said Joyce. This must have been what he had looked like when he had commanded a ship in hostile waters. "I'm disappointed," he said, "but undeterred."

"I assure you that there is no reason to persist," said Niko.

"I don't believe in abstraction," said Joyce, reaching into his pocket. "This is concrete."

Nyström turned away from the envelope.

"You have an obligation to the board to bring this to them," said Joyce. "Isn't that right, Bill?"

"I don't need advice from your general counsel," said Nyström. The ideograms beneath the fabric had emerged almost completely as he flexed and left the room.

Joyce stood silently. Rosten went to close the door. Sebold looked as though he thought he would be held responsible.

"It is only one step in the dance, gentlemen," said Joyce, slipping the envelope into his breast pocket and patting it in waltz time. Or was it the beat of a heart? "Just a step in the dance."

Marcia was prepared to have the letter messengered immediately. Joyce pulled the trigger before they left the office.

Not long after the D&D team returned to the Dome, Joyce called Rosten to his office to show him a press release that would announce his appointment as Chief Operating Officer. He would also retain the CFO title.

"I'll do the dancing," Joyce said. "You keep the music playing."

4

A solitary Sunday. Maggie on her travels. Megan off with friends, supposedly to do homework. Very little paper in his briefcase. Gunderman sat in the living room, staring at the cold fireplace as if it were a television. From time to time he pulled out a document. There was a sound at the front door. He put down his papers. When he reached the hall, he saw that it was Betty Cadwalader, holding her coat collar to protect her face, though it was not so very cold.

"Come in, come in," he said. "Please come in."

She took the step and dropped her arms but did not raise her eyes.

"I assumed that Maggie was away," she said.

"Yes," Sam said.

"May I show you something?"

"Here, let me take your coat."

He hung it on an open hook where Maggie kept hers when she was at home.

Betty followed him into the living room, where she opened her purse and took out a piece of paper worried into a scroll.

"I've made a list of the dates Bill was away," she said. "Do you mind if I sit?"

She lowered herself onto the couch and began trying to flatten the paper on the glass of the coffee table.

"Maybe you have a list, too," she said.

She gave up trying to uncurl the scroll and handed it to him.

"You're shivering," he said. "Can I get you some coffee or tea?"

"The dates I've listed should correspond to days when Maggie was out of town," she said. "It isn't fair to involve you, Sam, but let's face it, you are involved. Nothing about this is fair."

He reached for a box of Kleenex that Maggie kept on the shelf for colds. Betty waved it off. He put it between them on the coffee table.

"I'm sorry we've done this to you," he said.

"You didn't do it. It's just who Bill is, who I've let him be. I don't want to be that person anymore."

He pushed the tissues toward her. She took one and blotted an eye.

"She'll come back to you, you know," she said. "He'll tire of her. That's nothing against her. He always tires. I hope you'll be able to put things back together."

"I can't see that far."

He turned his gold ring. It moved smoothly in the groove between the calluses it had made over the years.

"I'll look at your list," he said, raising the scroll.

"I don't think it will end up public," she said. "My lawyer says having the proof will make him come to terms."

"They'll say coincidence."

"I guess we could split the cost of an investigator."

"I wasn't thinking anything like that," he said.

Only of things the Wise Man told him not to.

"I haven't even confronted him yet," she said. "I'll warn you before I do. Anna and Megan are so close. But it can't be helped. I assume Maggie denies everything."

"She hasn't given me the chance to give her anything to deny."

"My lawyer says that he always advises cheaters to go on the offense," she said.

He unrolled the paper. The list was written in a steady hand, the dates lined up as perfectly as if on a spreadsheet.

"The sooner we do this, the better," she said. "I'm assuming you'll need proof, too."

What he needed was proof of what would become of Megan. But that was beyond the accumulation point—where everything was chaos, blind and without form.

"We have to be hard-nosed," she said. "I know that isn't you. But . . . Look at me, Sam." Before him was a woman at least as hard as Maggie had become. "It isn't what either of us wants."

After she left he found himself dithering. He could not focus on the work he had brought home. He was drawn to the data on the glass table, memory on silicon. He picked up the scroll and carried it to his office, where he kept the shredder that Maggie had probably used to get rid of incriminating cell-phone records and credit-card bills. He had never used it for anything but work.

He switched on the computer, which whirred and ticked for a few moments then settled into a steady hum. The screen on his desk drew a lovely Nautilus-shell spiral. He clicked the mouse, bringing up his calendar, which was shaded with meetings and hockey games. From the toolbar he started a new, blank calendar, gave it the name "Correlates," then toggled to the original.

His Sundays were almost always empty, just as the house was now. No events to navigate by. Fridays were different. That was when Maggie usually left. He toggled back to Correlates and put an asterisk and ampersand in the boxes for this Friday, Saturday, and Sunday. Asterisk for Maggie, ampersand for Bill. Then he went to the scroll and found the next-most-recent entry. Toggling to his work calendar, he saw that it, too, was a Friday, when he himself had been traveling, doing a spot check on one of the data warehouses. His travel had caused a complication because Maggie was leaving on a weekend excursion, and he could not be certain he would get home, the airlines being the way they were. Megan said she would just sleep over at the Cadwaladers, but Maggie wasn't happy with that. They had imposed on the Cadwaladers too much, she said, suggesting another friend. Megan had no problem with that, but Sam started thinking what he wasn't supposed to think. Now he put an asterisk and an ampersand in the boxes for that weekend.

Where did they go? He slid out the shredder receptacle and exposed the paper snakes. Do not imagine.

The next dates Sam checked, Maggie had been home. They had gone to a game together. Megan had scored. Bill and Betty had been in the stands. The weekend before this, he'd had a miserable meeting with Chase and his team about audit procedures for database sampling. Greener had been the only reasonable one in the bunch, in his backing-in way. Sam had arrived home exhausted. Dinner wasn't ready, despite his having called before he'd left the Dome. Maggie had turned him right around to go out for a bucket of Kentucky Fried. Sure enough, on Betty's list,

Bill was home that weekend, probably making life miserable for his wife.

Back and back Sam went: Check calendar, check memory, check Betty's list. Place asterisk and/or ampersand. Repeat. He lost himself in the task. The pain eased as betrayal became data.

Then the correlations wobbled. One weekend Bill was marked absent, but Gunderman was sure Maggie had been home because they'd had to endure a dinner with some of her friends. This had probably been before she had presented her bill of particulars against him and said she was tired of keeping her life on hold, and certainly before he had offered to find some three-day weekends and she had told him not to bother. She might have already been with Cadwalader but not yet in the heavy traveling phase. Don't imagine. Just record an ampersand but no asterisk.

As Gunderman went further back, there were more of those and only a few ampersand/asterisk weekends. Bill must have been cheating on Betty with someone else in addition to Maggie. Gunderman wondered whether number four was some other girl's mother. It would have been helpful to know the rate of decay of his relationships, but the asterisks and ampersands did not establish this. He made one last click-through of the Correlates calendar and then put it into a folder that he protected with the password 1dbtthc2t. ("I don't believe that things have come to this.") If Maggie had developed the chops it would take to break this, he should hire her. Then they would finally have something in common.

He returned to dithering, knowing and not knowing, things coming briefly into focus and then vanishing. SEC filings always stated that past results do not necessarily indicate future performance, but D&D's business was built on the belief that in at least rough approximation they did. If someone failed to pay his debts once, he'll do it again. A cheater cheats because it is who she is.

Gunderman went back to the documents from his briefcase but quickly gave up, got himself a beer, and pulled down some photo albums from the shelves beside the fireplace. They took him to play groups, picnics, birthday piñatas, Christmas presents, and block parties. Megan's cradle and crib were in the pictures, too. They'd probably been dangerous as hell, given what the papers were reporting these days, but she had survived. There were so many dangers that you don't see, even when you are looking right at them.

He heard the key in the lock and quickly shut the album. He wished he had skipped the beer. It was too early. Bad example. Megan was at the age when she noticed. She wouldn't guess why he had taken the albums down. Just Dad's sappy sentimentality, not a crazy hope that past experience would *be* the future, that they would fill more albums together, the three of them. High school graduation. College. Wedding. Grandkids.

He stood and wiped his eyes. But it was not Megan. It was Maggie. She was dropping her luggage in the hallway and laying her coat across the bags, though the rack had plenty of room for it. She did not have to speak. He knew.

Sales for the quarter had come in even stronger than Sara had expected. A late burst of activity, probably just orders pushed early, which would make the comparisons tougher next quarter. But you took it when you could get it and worried about tomorrow tomorrow.

Joyce called her.

"Just saw the numbers, Sara. Impressive," he said.

"Thank you."

"No," he said. "Thank *you*."

"My team," she said. "Especially Margery Strand."

"Of course."

She passed the compliment on, exaggerating its intensity a little, because salespeople need intensity in order to face down rejection. They cheered when she told them. And again when she said, "The future begins today." You learned to get yourself up for battle this way. During the bad streaks when you didn't seem able to close so much as a door, you talked to yourself in the mirror. *You can do this. You look great. You'll blow them away. It's your turn.*

She gave herself permission to bail out early. Let the future begin tomorrow. Today she would just wander down Oak Street and maybe pay too much for something out of the money she'd be getting for her team's performance. You had to look like a million to sell a million. She might just get a pair of spike heels. Stretch a little. Make herself taller. Feeling fine. Successful. Not thinking of what it cost.

She turned toward the elevators just as Sam appeared from the opposite direction. He didn't see her at first, and when he did, he actually seemed to shrink.

"You look terrible," she said.

"I guess I should have worn your shirt and sweater," he said.

He was trying, poor man. She put out her hand to touch his forehead with the back of it. He recoiled.

"Sorry about that," she said. "To my dad everything was a fever and Vicks the cure."

"Placebo effect," he said.

"It seemed to work," she said. "It's like a positive mental attitude, I guess. But you guys in tech and finance don't do that, do you. You have to be hard-core realists. Where's the fun in that?"

"I'm just tired is all."

"What you need is a drink."

"Got to get home," he said. "Megan."

"I heard about Maggie," she said. "I'm sorry."

"Thanks."

"Maybe some other time."

He turned back toward his office. "Forgot something," he mumbled.

He was obviously afraid to ride in the elevator with her. She knew that feeling. She had seen it in her own face in the mirror on days when she did not think she could sell a soda in Death Valley.

5

Data Firms Gird for Proxy Fight

"What do you know about this?" said Rosten, holding out the second section of the *Wall Street Journal*.

"Stock's down," said Harms, as if she were telling him the time.

"There was no warning?"

"We got a call late," she said. "We no-commented."

"And you figured I could read it over my Special K?"

"I told Brian," she said, "and he said not to bother you. He wasn't at all rattled. You noticed that Gnomon shares are majorly up."

"So is the price of the deal," Rosten said.

The day's trading had barely begun, but millions of shares had already moved. The market had factored the *Journal*'s information into the stock price the instant the news broke, if not before. The prices told you that the smart money believed Day and Domes wanted the deal too much and would overpay for it.

"Now Nyström's shareholders know how much it will cost them to keep Niko in his job," she said.

"Just how calm was Joyce?"

"Don't go there," she said. "He's too smart."

"I've encountered smart people before," he said.

As they talked, she glided around the edge of the desk until she was close enough that he smelled her morning shower.

"I wasn't accusing him," Rosten said.

"Thank you," she said.

"Who then?" he said.

"Well, there's you," she said.

Lots of people inside D&D knew about the financials, but only Joyce, Harms, Sebold, Rosten, and of course Marcia knew what was in the letter. Sabby did, too, as lead outside director. Then there was the great merger-and-acquisition sage Hardy Twine, but he did not make his money by being indiscreet; that was the investment bankers' business model, and they had been kept in the dark.

She took the *Journal* from him, close enough that they almost touched. It felt as if the air was electric and newsprint an imperfect insulator.

"Did you tell your lady friend?" said Harms.

"She's out of the picture."

"Really."

A meeting, of course, was called. Twine attended by speakerphone but did not say a word. For an hour the Secret Committee debated what to say publicly. This was what they ended up with: "Day and Domes does not comment on speculative stories." C. Northcote Parkinson would have smiled.

By the time it ended, Rosten was way behind. Gail had managed to bend and squeeze the calendar, but while he was in the middle of a delayed session with a group of bond-issue underwriters, she slipped him a message.

"Sorry," it said. "The boss says now."

When Rosten entered Joyce's office, everyone else was already there, and Marcia was passing out a piece of paper. Rosten sped through it. From the language, neither Sebold nor Joyce had written it. Twine had earned some of his fee.

"I want to get this to Niko's board ASAP," said Joyce.

"We would send it to the board members directly?" said Rosten.

"You'd better read it before objecting," said Joyce.

The letter began with assurances that the *Journal* article did not reflect Day and Domes's position. "We approached Gnomon in good faith and with utmost respect," it said, "in the belief that together we could seize a dominant competitive advantage unavailable to each of us separately."

"Dominant?" said Sebold. "I'm surprised at you, Hardy."

The speakerphone did not speak.

"It's my word," said Joyce.

"I strongly advise . . . ," said Sebold.

"Strike it," said Joyce.

"Strong or unique or even leading, if you must," said Sebold.

Joyce took his pen and drew three lines through dominant. It was so easy that he must have put it in to be taken out.

The rest of the letter repeated the proposal from the letter Nyström had refused to look at. One difference in the new version: Joyce had increased the offer.

"This is awfully rich," said Rosten.

"We simply applied the original premium percentage to Gnomon's current price," Joyce said.

"A price that now, thanks to the leak, already has some of the original premium we offered built in," Rosten said.

"That's our math," said Joyce. "It wouldn't be theirs. Anyway, the new offer is only a few ticks up."

"May I remind everyone that a tick is twenty-five million dollars?" said Rosten. "I think it would be a good idea to hit the pause button."

"The bankers have run the numbers if you'd like to review them later," said Joyce.

Rosten looked to Sebold and Harms for support but got none.

"The market obviously doesn't like the deal," said Rosten.

"The market doesn't appreciate the synergies," said Joyce.

"It believes we will lose our financial discipline," said Rosten. He tried to get Harms's eye; she was looking at Joyce.

"I'll cc Niko on the letter," said Joyce. "As a courtesy."

Then he stood and thanked everyone. The speakerphone beeped as Hardy Twine left the line.

Lawton's energy was returning. Sweet homeostasis steadied his soul. When he laughed, his little sphincter held. Soon he would have the confidence to get out of Depends. And then maybe someday . . . Still, he could not keep himself from checking for warning signs. No blood on the absorbency pad. No chill, even as he passed out of the revolving brass door into the cold.

No more than a general wariness about things going so well led him to sign in as System Administrator when he learned that a board call had been arranged. As he waited for the screen to load, he shifted his swaddled groin in his chair. Why did they call it navel-gazing? That was definitely not where men focused.

As soon as he saw his own data field, he felt a bloom of moisture. Anyone might have peed himself. From what the computer showed, Lawton should have been on a street corner with a hand-lettered sign and an empty paper cup. Foreclosed mortgage. Eviction notice. Revoked credit cards. IRS liens. Cell service suspended. Car repossessed. He clicked over to Joyce's file. Same story. The two of them huddled around an empty oil drum, burning trash to stay warm. Rosten's records were even worse. They included arrest warrants. Sebold's file showed him disbarred. Snow's. Chase's. Harms's. Everyone's was a wreck but Sara Simons's.

A chill went through him, followed by a wave of vertigo. He had never thought to spot-check the members of the board, so he punched in Sabby's name and waited seven lives for the file to come up. Praise whoever's God was responsible, the data was as fastidious as the man. Teddy Diamond, same story. Tobin. Horst. Leavitt. Robinson. Sullivan. Fusilli. He moved to the customer-complaint dashboard. Nothing out of the ordinary there.

He needed to get himself dry, but first he hit speed-dial and said it was urgent. After pulling on a fresh pad, he collected Gunderman, and they went together to Rosten's office. Rosten marched them straight to Joyce.

"This can't get beyond the four of us," said Joyce.

"Chase will want—" said Gunderman.

"Screw Chase," said Joyce.

"We'd be better off bringing him into the tent," said Rosten.

"If he comes inside, Greener does, too," said Gunderman.

"Is it a tent or a clown car?" said Joyce.

"We need to think about what we tell the board," said Gunderman.

"I'll worry about the board," said Joyce. "You find the terrorist who is doing this to me."

"He did it to all of us," said Gunderman.

Lawton knew what Joyce was feeling. Fifteen percent of men are diagnosed with the disease, but in all the world there is only one case.

"Morrie Berry has handled shit storms," said Rosten.

"He's caused them, too," said Joyce. "Keep him away."

With that, they left him and went to Rosten's new office next door.

"How confident are you that this really is somebody inside?" said Rosten.

"Until today I was at about 85 percent," said Gunderman.

"And now?"

"I'd say more on the order of 60 percent, which could grow when we have time to put the algorithm back to work."

"What does the fact that Sara Simons's file wasn't touched tell us?" said Rosten.

"Somebody is trying to put this on her," Gunderman said.

"We'd better look at Sales and Marketing first," said Rosten. "Somebody with a grudge. Maybe somebody who needs money."

"Sara doesn't even know how to do control-alt-delete," said Gunderman. "She calls me when her machine won't boot. I go and plug it in."

"We'll need to bring HR into the loop," said Lawton.

"You heard Joyce," said Rosten.

"No way around it," said Lawton.

"I'll talk to him," said Rosten. "You go ahead."

"There will be privacy issues," said Gunderman. "Sara will be sensitive about that."

"Somebody is in our knickers," said Rosten. "You bet there are privacy issues."

"Knickers?" said Gunderman.

"It's a technical term," said Rosten.

After the board call Rosten had to get out of the Dome so he could breathe. Through the window it was one of those days when the air carries no moisture and the winds off the lake blow away any hint of haze, making every edge a blade.

"You going to tell me where you're going?" Gail said as he passed.

"Nowhere," said Rosten.

She looked at her screen.

"That's not on the schedule," she said.

The call had gone smoothly. The conciliatory letter with its increased offer was sent. But Joyce flatly rejected Rosten's advice to let the directors in on the hacking.

"It's graffiti," Joyce said. "Guy with spray paint hanging over the edge of a bridge. It's the only way a creep can make a mark. Just find him and fire him."

"It's a crime," said Rosten.

"Package him out of here," said Joyce. "I'm counting on you."

"What does Sebold say?"

"He's in," said Joyce. "Are you?"

This was never a question. Just as he had turned to finance because it clarified things, now he looked to the org chart to keep him from falling again into the bottomless pit of self. He was responsible to Joyce, and it was Joyce who was responsible to the board. This was the plain order of things.

When he left the Dome, he looked up Michigan Avenue to the Wrigley Building, its terra-cotta lace visible even from a half-mile away. Ahead was the old library, which had been stripped of its books and turned into a visitor center. On the Randolph Street side, he mounted a short flight of steps that led to the doorway he had entered so many times when he was growing up. There hadn't been a coffee bar inside then. There had been no tables where people could eat a muffin or just stay warm. In those days the homeless were called bums.

Rosten took the steps of the grand staircase slowly, not bounding up them the way he had in junior high when he had taken the train downtown on Saturdays on the excuse of study. He remembered the exotic, pigeony smell of the streets, the crowds full of people you would never see at home. And the books, some of them on open shelves in the great rotunda inlaid with quotations. Goethe. Voltaire. Strange names. Strange languages. The whole world was here, all the way down to the men in tattered coats insulated with newspapers who sat at the wooden tables with open books before them and yellow eyes that did not read, the woman with the bluebird on her hat of straw, the man whose face was so dirty Rosten was not sure whether he was white or black.

At the top of the stairs he paused and looked up at the names in gold: Emerson, Longfellow. The Tiffany rotunda was set with tables and flowers. At the front stood a lattice arch for a wedding. Spenser. Bacon. Maybe the bride's and groom's parents had come here when they were kids to call for microfilm rolls of old *Tribune*s with accounts of Pearl Harbor and the St. Valentine's Day Massacre. Shakespeare. *Sweetest things turn sourest by their deeds*.

"We're talking about getting into position to ride the wave," Joyce had told the board on the conference call. "If we do, we could be the next Cisco Systems, the next Oracle. If we don't, we'll become a mom-and-pop credit bureau without enough resources to keep the brass polished in the lobby."

Rosten looked again at Shakespeare's golden name. Then he turned away. He could not hope to hold the opposites of the universe inside him, all the p's and *not* p's. If it can't have the clarity of numbers, then at least let it be about knowing your place. "Are you in?" All the way.

As he returned to the Dome, he checked his BlackBerry. Having nothing to say about the *Journal* report was not viable. D&D's price continued to drop. It was as if Rosten's doubts had suddenly appeared on the screen of every Bloomberg terminal. But if he had learned anything, it was that at the bottom line, you had to believe in the leader more than you believed in yourself.

"Joyce is looking for you," Gail said. "Really looking."

Rosten found him in a state.

"Out for a constitutional?" Joyce said.

"Trying to clear my head," said Rosten.

"It better have worked."

He turned and laid his hand on the Bloomberg on the credenza. Its graphs had become a horror movie. The Something of the Apocalypse.

"We need to work the phones," Joyce said.

"Selective disclosure?" Rosten said.

Joyce punched a button on his console. The phone at Marcia's desk rang.

"Get Sebold," he said. "Harms, too . . . No. If I wanted anybody else, I would have told you."

He dialed Twine, but the guru was not immediately available. Instead, Twine's right-hand man came on the speakerphone.

He advised that they could safely say there had been very pre-
liminary discussions but that the report of a proxy fight was
false. This needed to go out on the wire before any telephone
calls were made to investors. An open conference call would be
a very good idea.

Harms came in on the tail end of this.

"They'll ask if you would consider going hostile if discussions
break down," she said as Sebold appeared.

"It would be best if we could simply rule out the possibility,"
Sebold said.

"No present plans," said Joyce.

"That's limp," said Sebold.

"Niko knew we'd be pushed in this direction," said Joyce. "He
counted on it when he leaked."

"We don't know that," said Sebold.

"What exactly do we know, counselor," said Joyce, "other than
fifty ways to cover our ass?"

It wasn't hard to shut a man down. There were a lot more than
fifty ways to do it.

To Rosten's surprise, Harms spoke up.

"The market wants visibility going forward," she said. "You
need to come out strong."

"I will say that the only people talking about a proxy fight are at
the *Wall Street Journal*," said Joyce.

"Works for me," said Sebold.

"Nyström might leak the letter you just sent," said Rosten.

"It doesn't say a word about going hostile," said Joyce. He
pulled out the text and read it aloud.

"People can read between the lines," said Rosten.

"OK. Sure," said Joyce. "But this is all beside the point. Niko won't dare leak a document. Somebody could tie it right to him, and he'd be looking at prison time. How do you think pretty boy would do on that market?"

"I think we should get a straw-man press release working," said Harms.

"Write fast," said Joyce. "We reconvene in thirty minutes."

In his prime Rosten could have knocked something out in a third of that. But that was when he was spending his days imagining the stories of unnatural men.

When they gathered in Joyce's office again, they tortured Harms's wording the way the analysts had been torturing the numbers in the acquisition models. Twine had become available again and blessed the final version. He only said about thirty words, most of one or two syllables.

The Q and A on the open conference call was rambunctious. After it ended, the Secret Committee scattered to throw together a few things and race to Midway for wheels-up at 8 p.m., destination Teterboro. They had back-to-back sessions scheduled with leading buy-side firms starting at 8 a.m. Eastern. That meant snaking their way back and forth across town all day to be snarled at. The more of D&D a firm owned, the angrier it would be.

When they arrived at the Plaza, the lobby was still alive. Rosten was not. He went straight to his room but did not even have a chance to pee before the phone rang. It was Harms, saying they had better talk. He met her in the bar.

"It was just you and me today," she said. "Sebold folded."

"It was you," Rosten said. "You were the rock."

"But you are obviously the only one who has the clout to keep Brian out of trouble tomorrow," she said.

"He knows the script."

"I don't know where we would be without you."

"You would be in the Oak Bar with someone else."

"Who would you be with?" she said.

"Nobody," he said. "Nobody at all."

"That's just a waste."

She clearly enjoyed whatever his face was showing.

"We'd better focus on the stock price," he said.

"Or we could think of harm well done."

"There's something to fall asleep thinking about," he said.

Grace heard the slam of the bathroom door, the sibilance of the shower. Luisa was finally astir. It was a late start for both of them. Some kind of teachers' meeting delayed the morning bell. Fortunately, Grace had nothing until a conference call at 10, but she ended up rising at the usual hour anyway and using the time to put out breakfast properly for a change—place mats, napkins, two vitamins for Luisa, four for herself.

The *Wall Street Journal* lay centered on the doormat, as always. Otherwise, the hall was carpeted with copies of the *Times*. In this building they thought in terms of second acts, not second derivatives. Increasingly, Grace did, too. Response to loss, she supposed, the flash of recognition that brought down the curtain.

She carried the *Journal* to the table and turned to the market agate, hoping numbers would take her mind. Bond spreads were widening. She heard the bathroom door open. Thirty-year treasuries up, currencies adjusting to one another like riders crowding onto the subway. Once Luisa began to move, it was like compound interest, excruciatingly slow at first but accelerating until she exploded into the kitchen with blemishes all covered, hair just so. Without a word to Grace, she wolfed down her cereal, left the vitamins, and raced for the bus.

Grace went to the sink with the dishes, which Mrs. Cruz would take care of. The place mats and napkins she left in place for dinner, just in case Luisa deigned to appear. After a quick check of her face in the bathroom mirror, Grace picked up the *Journal* and turned on the light at her desk.

The front page always comforted her—its old-fashioned etched portraits, its snippets on the left, the gray orderliness of it all. As always, she started with "What's News," just in case she didn't have a chance to get through the whole paper. Ordinarily she worked her way from top to bottom, but when she noticed the words "Day and Domes," she jumped to them. It was the Gnomon deal. She turned to the second section. She hadn't heard a word at the bank, but since she had asked off the team, she wouldn't have. Off meant off. That had suited her just fine until now.

She read the article twice. A proxy fight made no sense. They were almost never good for the acquiring company. Before she left Chicago, Tom had already squeezed the numbers until they cried out. He had qualms at a lower price than Gnomon was selling at today. One night, he had talked through some of his thoughts with her, saying, "Where do we go from here?"

At the time, she had not imagined that it could also be a relationship question. She had not thought that where she would go was back to New York alone. She had been stupidly confident that everything would work out if he just opened up, but when he did, he did not even seem to need to draw breath, and she needed to escape.

She had never assumed he had been faithful to her after he had left her in New Haven. Oh, maybe at first, but not once he disappeared and Jim sprang up in his place, though even then she had struggled with guilt about sleeping with Jim in the room where she had slept with Tom. She could not put a date on when she had stopped feeling disloyal. It was not a discrete point in time. It was more like a downward-sweeping curve, growing steeper as it approached the x axis, as if guilt were a wasting asset. And then Jim became one, too.

She folded the *Journal* and pulled herself upright. No need to blow her nose or fix her eyes. That phase was over. She had to get going. The conference call wasn't going to be that important, her part in it even less, but she hated when someone dialed in from a cab, always losing the cell signal, beeping on and off the line like a smoke alarm with a low battery.

The doorman blew his whistle, and a taxi pulled right over. She gave the address and opened the paper as they pulled into traffic. She tried to attend to the Fed on the front page but gave up and returned to the second section. After rereading the article, she pulled out her BlackBerry and pinged D&D's stock price. The market had just opened, and it was down significantly. A few minutes later she pinged again. Down further. They would be trying to talk the price back up, because if they didn't, it might reach the red zone where somebody might try to put the company in play.

She opened a blank e-mail and typed enough characters to pop Tom's name into the address field. In a foolish moment she had erased his private address from her contacts, so if she sent him something, it would have to go through Gail. This made her queasy as she began to thumb the keys. First the heading: WSJ Article. Then the message.

—I just saw the WSJ. You OK?

She looked at those words and began deleting from the end. Then she zapped the whole message. He had enough trouble today without her inserting herself into it. She had already intruded once on whatever hard-won sense of order he had managed to achieve. The townhouse without books. The rooms without signs of life. When the taxi pulled up, she was ready with the fare, though she almost left her laptop on the seat.

She reached her desk and dialed the conference number before taking off her coat. Things were still at the beeps and mumble stage. She cradled the phone against her shoulder—always a painful mistake—so that she could snap her laptop into the docking station. She and the call settled down together. As it rambled on, she Googled D&D and read the traffic stacking up behind the leak. She turned in her chair and checked the Bloomberg. Analysts were quoted with nothing good to say. Eventually, the conference call went the way of all conference calls. The client's guy thanked everyone with formality covering irritation. It ended early, leaving her with ten minutes of found money before the next thing on her calendar. She called her boss.

"I can't talk about it, as you know," he said.

"I'm not asking you if the *Journal* was right," she said.

"What else is there to ask?"

"I don't know."

"That isn't like you."

"Is everything all right, I guess," she said. "That's what I'm asking."

"I guess the Chinese wall doesn't keep me from saying it's a Chinese fire drill," he said.

She went about her business as well as she could, doing the

meetings, doing the e-mail, doing lunch with a representative of a client of the bank. On the walk back she went to her Black Berry. Nothing there but junk. D&D finally holding, but in the sub-basement. Something led her to go to her Sent queue to make sure she had succeeded in passing on to a client the information he had asked for. That was when she saw it, the cut-off message to Tom that she thought she had deleted.

—I just

Somehow she had managed to push Send. She stopped dead on the sidewalk. Someone stepped on her heel.

Why couldn't you call an e-mail back? Why couldn't questions answered be unasked?

Donna could gauge how upset Brian was by his timbre. Dynamics were not the measure. *Pianissimo* could be a whisper across the pillow or a warning hiss. When he had called last night to say that he would miss the children's choir concert, she could barely hear him. She did not dare reveal her disappointment. His voice . . . she had never produced such a *pianissimo* on her fiddle. It was not a sound she wanted to make or hear.

When he called from the plane the next day on his way home from New York, he was sounding right again. Sometimes his resilience astonished her. If she so much as hit a ringer in rehearsal, she was a wreck for weeks. Over the noise of the plane he asked how the boys had done, and she told him they had blended in nicely. She asked him how his meetings had gone. He simply said, "OK." She knew he had to be careful because the plane was full of people who tuned to his 440 Hz A. Suddenly the line went flat, the connection broken. She waited, but he did not call again.

On her BlackBerry she checked D&D's stock price, the way Brian had shown her to do. It had gone back up, but just a little. She could only imagine how much she and Brian had lost, let alone the whole company. The voice inside him must have been shrieking, a string bowed behind the bridge.

The volume of messages pouring into Rosten's queue after the leak was so great that he told Gail to do triage on them. Any that came from addresses in the financial community she was to forward to Harms's office, where a nonresponse was being prepared. She did see Grace Bondurant's name and recognized it, but it was from the bank's address and referred in the subject line to the newspaper article, so she did what she had been told and dispatched it unopened to Investor Relations.

6

"You are still wearing the ring."

"Megan is hurting. She wants everything back the way it was. Last night I smelled alcohol on her breath."

"This was a shock?"

"She was in her room when I got home. I knocked and asked for a hug. She took a while, but eventually she opened the door, smelling of Listerine and gin."

"Did you get the hug?"

"I told her I wanted to teach her the right way. We could have a glass of wine at dinner, like they do in France. She started to cry. Tell me how I could have kept all this from happening."

"Could-haves get in the way."

"I feel like I'm about to fly into pieces."

"Is that what you need the ring for? To hold yourself together?"

Gunderman had to pull and twist to get it past the callus it had built up. The skin beneath was fishy white.

"Here. Take it."

"Being a depository for people's bad memories is not one of the services I provide. Tell me how you feel without it on."

"I suppose you want me to say free."

"Just say what comes."

"Loss then."

"Part of yourself?"

"Something that's me and not me."

"Dispose of the ring whenever you feel it is right. Or put it back on. It may be protecting you from other people."

"Who?"

"Don't you want to find out?"

Gunderman looked at his watch.

"Time's up."

"Maybe we should think of double sessions for a while."

"Because I'm in such bad shape."

"To hasten the progress."

Gunderman stepped into a hallway that, thankfully, was empty, but when he reached the lobby, everyone seemed to be looking at his left hand. He put it in his pocket, and there was the ring, feeling large. He lifted it on the end of his finger, stirred it around, then took his hand out again. A nicely turned-out woman strode toward him on the sidewalk. He felt blood rising into his face and looked at his feet. Don't be a fool. The woman didn't so much as glance—at finger, feet, or face.

Inside the Dome he left his naked hand exposed and imagined the talk on the Admin News Network. Did you see his ring finger? I didn't take off my wedding band until I left the courtroom. Do you think he's saying he's available? Sam Gunderman? You've got to be kidding.

"Morning, Mr. Gunderman," said Maurice at the security desk.

"When did you start calling me mister?"

"Well, I've worked here twenty-five years."

Gunderman stepped into an empty elevator and pulled out the ring. Then the elevator slowed, and he quickly dropped it back into his pocket. The door opened on Sara Simons.

"Well, hello," she said. "You're looking better today."

His hand went to his pocket, where it made contact with the changeless gold.

"And you?" he said.

"A glitch in the United Airlines billing," she said. "Your guys were quick off the mark."

"They aren't mine anymore."

"To me they are," she said as the elevator reached her floor. "Well, I guess I'd better go tell the customer the good news. When you fix a problem, it is usually better than never having had one."

"There's a thought," he said.

"Win-win."

"The best most games get is zero-sum."

"You lost me there, Sam," she said and got off.

He continued up and found Alexa Snow waiting for him in his office. He had forgotten that they had a meeting. She looked at him as if she were going to wrap him.

"Sorry," he said.

"I always think of you as punctual," she said.

She had covered his round table with files in neat little stacks. Even before he could take off his coat and sit down, she was reciting the details of her pursuit of the hacker, step by tiny step. From time to time she opened a file and passed it to him. It was incredibly tedious. Was this how qualitative people compensated?

"I'm with you," he said. "You can skip ahead."

"I thought auditors were supposed to obsess about methodology," she said then went right on, pencil to yellow legal pad, checking off each item on her list.

Gunderman struggled to pay attention. Preemployment test results from the shamans at the industrial psychology firm, records of annual evaluations, salary and benefits history (including medical), individual assessments by supervisors for succession planning, telephone records, e-mail—and, of course, credit records.

"The e-mail review," he said. "I assume it was Boolean?"

"Excuse me?" she said, as if he had belched.

"A keyword search," he said. "What were the parameters?"

"I'll have to get back to you on that," she said then went on again with the pad, the pencil, the list, the files.

He sank into torpor until he heard her say, "Long story short, I think we found her."

"Her?"

"The hacker."

"Who?"

"You are going to be surprised."

"It's not Sara Simons," he said.

"Stay with me," she said.

Her evidence began with the database itself. Nobody in the Sales and Marketing hierarchy had been tampered with.

"Sara is not stupid," said Gunderman.

"Her preemployment intel test showed her to be well above average," said Snow. "Not in your league or mine, of course. The database did show some late payments in earlier years."

"It's highly probable that most people have missed a payment or two," said Gunderman.

"Sixty-four percent in the past five years," said Snow, "though only 40 percent of D&D's managers and directors."

Finally some numbers, and they were irrelevant.

"Simons has received an average of 4.7 out of 5 on her performance reviews," said Snow, "and this has been remarkably consistent over the past decade. It puts her in the 93rd percentile of managers and directors companywide, and 87th percentile among directors and their direct reports."

Why did HR people even try? The trouble with performance ratings is that there was no constant. Gunderman had tried to make this point when Snow had first started reporting numeric comparisons among the divisions. The ratings were as much about the rater as about the ratee. Gunderman had not given up until the room began to groan.

"Who are we talking about here?" said Gunderman.

"A name would bias you," said Snow. "We are talking about evidence."

"We've been talking about Sara Simons."

"You're the one who put her on the table."

His eyes went to it.

"There is evidence of personal usage of company landlines and cellular phones," said Snow. "I'm sure that when we're able to pull the numbers, we will find the same pattern in nonbusiness Internet usage during business hours."

"How many people reimburse the company when they call their bank or make a dinner reservation?" he said.

"I don't have that figure," said Snow. "But it doesn't matter, because it turns out that the medical history tells the story. The suspect is deep in analysis and has been for years. It turns out that the visits increased in the period before the first database breach was discovered. One of the diagnostic criteria on the insurance claims suggested anger-management issues."

"You get this kind of information?" Gunderman said.

"We're self-insured," she said, as if that were an answer. "Unfortunately our e-mail scan proved disappointing. There were no inappropriate references to Sara Simons or anyone in senior management, not even to colleagues or subordinates. Frankly, we were expecting to find expressions of racial hostility."

"Racial?" said Gunderman.

"She's African American," said Snow.

"You're not talking about Margery Strand," he said.

"There have been complaints over the years," she said. "None has risen to a level that required a formal inquiry, but from time to time I have had to ask Simons to counsel her."

"What have people complained about?"

"An attitude," she said. "Strike that. Make it an edge."

"These are all white people, right?"

"Let's not go there."

"Where else is there?" said Gunderman.

"Next step is to get hold of her laptop," she said. "We'll need to think up some reason. You can help."

"Saying we need the laptop to search for viruses will certainly fool somebody who managed to get into our database and make a mess."

"Let's not get sarcastic."

"Do I have an edge?"

"I assume that's one of the things you are working on with your coach," said Snow.

"I can't let you do this," he said.

"We don't need a warrant," she said. "Check your employee handbook."

"You have a better idea?" said Rosten.

Gunderman and Poole stood before his desk like truants. He had called them in as soon as Snow had launched a preemptive strike against interference with her investigation. The fact was, Rosten didn't much like Snow's choice of a target either, but if Margery Strand did turn out to be the hacker, the case would close neatly. Not only had the incident not been material; it had been purely personal.

"I'll bet when we look at her laptop, we'll find that she doesn't even know how to block the history on her browser," said Gunderman.

"Just let it play out," said Rosten. "Get Greener to help Snow if you don't want to be party to it. He's got the chops, doesn't he?"

"I trust him," said Poole.

"Then we're all in agreement," said Rosten.

When Simons heard the Admin News Network rumors about Margery Strand being in some kind of trouble with the internal auditors, she closed her office door against the world. She had been fool enough to think Gunderman had been shy of her, when in fact he was one of those who waited until your back was turned. She should have seen it all in that Mitteleuropa face of his. It was a map of the geography her father had fled, pursued by such faces.

She went into the bathroom and ran water over her wrists, something her father had taught her was an antitoxin to rage. Cool, the water; cool and cunning, the mind. Don't take them head-on. There are too many of them. Closing her eyes, she let the numbing current spread from her fingertips toward her center. When she opened them again, she was looking in the mirror. You are strong. You can do this.

Gunderman's closed door did not stop her. His startled expression did not stop her, nor did the sweater she had picked out for him, the pathetic, frayed collar of one of his old shirts curling out from under it.

"What the hell do you think you're doing?" she said.

As she drew closer to Gunderman, she saw perspiration beading on his forehead. She hoped it was not only the cashmere.

"I just learned about it myself," he said.

He was not a customer that D&D had wronged. He had not purchased her deference with a big, multiyear contract. Do not soften, woman.

"You did this, you *momzer*," she said. "It's all over the fucking Dome."

"I've been trying to think," he said.

"You're all think."

"Is she in her office right now?"

"No, thank God," she said. "She's off with a customer."

"Good," he said. "Trust me."

He sprang from his chair with more force than she had ever seen in him. As he swept past her, there was not much she could do but follow. Keeping up with him as he bounded up the stairs was a challenge in heels. Trust him? She had never met this man.

"Which office is it?" he said as they approached the Sales and Marketing area. "We're lucky everybody's on lunch break."

She followed him in, hearing her father's voice: Be cunning, Sarale. Bear witness.

Gunderman went straight to Margery's desk. The computer screen was dark. He booted it up.

"Stop that," she said. "I'll call security."

"Security is not Margery's friend," he said. "I am."

"You barely know her."

"I know you," he said.

When the time came for her password, he got by it somehow and moved quickly from screen to screen, tapping the keys until something made the machine sit there churning. Then he looked up.

"This will work if she doesn't do anything stupid," he said.

"What's this all about?" she said.

"Someone will come and ask for her computer," he said. "He will give a reason. Something lame. She has to let him."

She looked at the screen, which was like a riffling deck of cards.

"She'll refuse," she said.

He turned away from her and sat watching the screen until it came to rest back at the opening icons.

"There," he said. "Send Margery a message to come see you immediately when she gets back to the Dome. Tell her this: Do not look right or left. Do not listen to anyone. When she is face-to-face with you, tell her what is happening. Settle her down. Tell her I have taken measures."

"Measures," she said.

He spoke the way her father said they had spoken to him just before he fled.

7

Poole, who ordinarily hovered over Berry's troops at the Dome, had suddenly become elusive. He is behind closed doors. Out of the building. On a conference call. He'll get back to you. The man's underlings would not even respond to a simple document request. This kind of thing happened all the time when you were dealing with an adversary, God bless the subpoena. But at Day and Domes it made no sense. Berry's team had been playing nice, even Szilard.

The *Wall Street Journal* article might have been an explanation, but the story had nothing to do with Internal Audit—unless D&D was thinking about mounting a leak investigation. Berry would strongly discourage this, if asked. Don't put a question you don't want to know the answer to. This was just basic.

Thanks to attorney-client privilege, the answers you got from a client very rarely hurt you. The danger there was something you weren't told. So when D&D froze up, Berry liberated Szilard to be Szilard. The time for putting the greatest pressure on a client was when the other pressures had already taken him to his limit. Someone in that deep, with creatures that did not have names brushing up against him in the dark, was ready to do anything to get back to the surface.

Fortuitously, Berry's calendar had a big hole in it. A large agricultural company had canceled. It had become lax about his counsel as its antitrust disaster faded into the past. But it would come back. Eventually they all did.

Gunderman took Szilard's call. The lawyer asked to meet. Gunderman put him off then notified Poole.

"Your involvement was not contemplated in the audit plan," Poole said.

"Why?" said Gunderman.

"Exactly," said Poole. When he used his audit voice, he could be holding a handful of nothing or evidence of fraud and you would not be able to tell.

"I'm off limits?"

"Precisely," said Poole.

"Szilard said he couldn't get through to you."

"There's a reason for that."

"Well somebody had better deal with him," said Gunderman, "because he sounded like he's ready to drop a bomb."

Poole was silent—no paper rattling, no finger taps on a keyboard.

"There is a concern about your objectivity," he finally said. "Hold the line. I have to make a call."

The phone went mute. Gunderman clicked on a new folder

and applied a strong password to it: 0m,wawg014? Oh my, what are we getting ourselves in for? He dragged a very large file into it and watched the hourglass spin.

Poole came back.

"Talk to Szilard," he said.

"But I'm out of the loop," Gunderman said.

"Exactly," said Poole. "Fill him in on Sarbanes-Oxley compliance. Take him through the technical aspects of our financial systems controls. Talk to him only about what you are responsible for."

"I feel responsible for all of it."

"Within your current job description then," said Poole. "The rest is off the reservation. Are we on the same page?"

Not five minutes later the audit admin buzzed and announced, "Mr. Lizards is on the way up."

"Szilard," said Gunderman.

"Oh, God, I wonder if I said it to him that way," she said. "I just can't get it out of my head."

Rosten had started the Lizards/Szilard thing. He liked to play with letters the way Gunderman liked to play with numbers. Gunderman's default was binary. One zero zero one one. One one zero zero one. Able was I ere I saw Elba.

When the admin showed the lawyer in, Gunderman rose and said, "Has something come up regarding financial system controls?"

"From what I hear, you're a lot bigger than that," said Szilard.

"A little fish, I'm afraid."

"You're too modest."

"It's only financial forensics you are doing for us, as I understand it."

"These things tend to go where they want," said Szilard. It was clearly not easy for him to produce a smile.

"Have you ever worked at a large corporation, Mr. Szilard?"

"This isn't about me," said Szilard. "It's about Day and Domes. Why isn't anyone willing to talk to me?"

"An antinomy, right?" Gunderman said. "It's not about you, but it is about you."

"You're a clever one."

"Small fish, small pond," said Gunderman. If he was even in the pond anymore. Zero zero zero zero was the same any way you looked at it.

When the crisis team met, Greener reported that he had secured Margery Strand's laptop without incident. The loop had bellied way out since back when Joyce had stumbled on the first breach. There was Greener, there was Chase, and there was Snow, who had somehow become the project manager, even though when they had done the last upgrade of the HR system, she couldn't even get the hang of signing on. There was Harms, and finally there was Poole, rubbing his hands with antibacterial.

The way Lawton saw it, the only one they really needed wasn't there. He had pushed for Gunderman, but Chase had stood in the way. The man was not reliable, Chase said. Look at the way he had tried to deflect the investigation away from Sales and Marketing. He obviously had a thing with Simons.

"So we've got the laptop," said Rosten. "What else?"

"I talked with Strand," said Snow, as if she thought this could possibly have been helpful.

"Greener has already begun the analytics," said Chase.

"Wait one," said Poole. "That's an audit function."

"I believe the Gunderman issue is closed," said Chase.

"But there are procedures we must follow," said Poole.

"Tom can detail Rob to your team," said Sebold. "Simple fix. I'll paper the file."

Lawton did not understand lawyers and accountants any better than they understood him.

Rosten asked Greener to outline his work plan and timeline, which he did at some length. Sebold proposed to do the documentation, an arrangement that Poole approved. Lawton wished he could get hold of Strand's machine.

"Perhaps we should have a second opinion," said Lawton. "What do you think, Bill?"

"Condom and diaphragm," said Sebold.

"Careful," said Snow.

"Is that what they call thinking like a lawyer?" said Harms.

Greener did not laugh.

"I'll get it right," he said.

"Nobody is questioning that, Rob," said Lawton, who had had this kind of conversation with his former subordinate many times before.

"The responsibility is yours," Rosten said to Greener.

Then he tapped the edge of the table three times.

"I think we're done," he said.

After talking to Margery, Sara was desolate. What could she have said to her? What could anyone say to Sara? The thing was too ugly for words.

That night she could not sleep. She dusted the blinds then took down every keepsake from her shelves and dusted it, too. She vacuumed the carpet, scrubbed the kitchen and bathroom floors. She bathed the orchids. She ran vinegar through the coffeemaker and oiled the dining room table. Then she started doing things over again. In the morning the doorman called to say that he had a strange man in the lobby who said his name was Gunderman.

Sara was as silent as a phone recording the message.

"I'll do whatever you want with him," the doorman said.

"Be careful what you offer," she said. "But I guess you'd better let him in."

When the knock came, she opened the door. He was looking at the carpet.

"The living room," she said. "Let's get this over with."

He laid his ratty overcoat over the back of the couch.

"I need to tell you something that I shouldn't," he said.

"If you shouldn't do something, then don't."

"How proficient is Margery with computers?"

"That's not telling me a damn thing," she said, which set him to examining his knees.

"I'm not doing very well," he said.

"Either tell me or don't."

"There's been a series of hostile incursions into the credit database," he said.

"God in heaven," she said.

"They think it was her."

"Ridiculous," she said. "She makes me look like you."

"They've cut me out," he said. "I think it's because they believe I'm too close to you."

"What would make anybody think that?" she said.

He began racing, talking about algorithms, wormholes, "The Sorcerer's Apprentice."

"Slow down," she said. "Begin at the beginning. How long have you known?"

"The first incident was before Christmas," he said. "But it was small."

"We need to notify our customers," she said.

"That's what they are trying to avoid. We haven't even told the Audit Committee."

"What were you thinking?" she said.

Gunderman did not know what he had been thinking. Or rather, the problem wasn't what he had been thinking. He had seen it the way she did all along. The trouble was that he had not acted, not forced the issue. He never did.

"So far as we know," he told her, "nobody outside the company has been affected."

"So far as you know," she said.

"I am 95 percent sure the hacker is inside D&D," he said. Where had he pulled that number from?

"I'm 95 percent sure this is a goddamned mess."

"They don't want to tank the Gnomon deal," he said.

"And what will happen when it gets out that for months we've known that we have a cyberterrorist and have covered it up?"

"That may be a little exaggerated," he said, though once you started splitting mops in two, the increase could become explosive, like nuclear fission.

"Exaggerated by how many percent?"

"If we catch the guy, everything will be fine."

"And so you're ganging up on somebody who doesn't even know how to download a PDF file," she said.

"I have a different person in mind," he said.

"I need to start making calls to customers."

"Give me just a little time," he said. "Please."

The next day Rosten was in his office having a sandwich and skimming a skeptical a newspaper article about Vladimir Putin's increasingly autocratic ways. He was one of the few people from Fisherman's Soviet dossiers that was still heard of. Rosten had written one of his narratives about him. The last thing he would ever have predicted then was that a man Fisherman considered a narcissist with nothing worth looking at would end up leading all of Russia.

Suddenly Simons burst in, saying she knew all about the hacking and what she called a cover-up. She said it was all over the Dome, but Rosten knew that was a lie. Gunderman must have told her.

She went on and on. Her responsibility to her customers. Her reputation for candor. Her integrity. Hers. That told you all you needed to know about motivation. He told her that her loyalty to her subordinate was admirable, but there was a greater loyalty she needed to remember. It was then that she threatened that if the company did not do the right thing, she would tell the world. He warned her of the consequences, first for D&D, but most pointedly for her. She walked out.

Rosten told Joyce, and he ignited. She had been the one who had leaked to the newspaper, he said. She and that idiot Gunderman. You saved that man. Jesus, Mary, and Joseph, what a pair of demons. Rosten tried to remind him that neither was involved enough in the deal to have known the details that had appeared in the paper. "Get them out! Both of them!" Joyce shouted.

Rosten responded in a voice barely more than a whisper. "If we move on her right now, she will be more likely to make good her threat," he said. "Let's button down the facts first."

"Get it fucking done!" said Joyce.

"Greener found the smoking gun," Chase announced at the team meeting late that afternoon.

"Outstanding," said Snow.

"Thank God," said Harms.

Rosten wanted details. Greener walked him through the way Strand had done it. The code she had put into the system had allowed her to trigger the second attack the moment the story appeared.

"So she was the leaker, too," said Snow.

"I'm afraid I can't prove that yet," said Greener.

"Has to be," said Snow.

As everyone went way past the data, Rosten intervened to note that it was only necessary to prove that she was responsible for the hacking.

"Kiss," said Harms.

"Pardon me?" said Snow.

"Keep it simple, stupid," said Harms.

"I'll shoot Strand as soon as we're done here," said Snow.

"Let's be sure we've pulled everything together first," said Rosten. "Let me know when it's tight."

"We need to document the chain of custody," said Sebold.

"Strand's machine has never been out of Greener's control since he took it from her office," said Chase. He lifted his chin toward Greener, who took the cue and, with both hands, raised the laptop above his head as if it were the Stanley Cup.

"Never let it out of my sight," said Greener. "Even when I went to the men's room."

"To paper the record?" said Sebold.

Lawton assumed the thing was all wrapped up when Rosten called him into the office, closing the door behind him.

"I want Greener's work checked," he said. "Do it yourself. I don't want Gunderman anywhere near it."

"Chase will go ballistic," said Lawton, "not to mention Joyce."

"I had Greener make a copy of Strand's hard drive for safe-keeping," said Rosten. "Sebold has it. I've told him to give it to you. Chase won't know."

"Until he does," said Lawton. "What is it I'm looking for?"

"Anything that could come back and bite us."

"Gunderman is the one I'd trust."

"He's a talker," said Rosten.

"Is he in trouble?" said Lawton.

"One thing at a time," said Rosten.

"I never do this sort of thing. I shouldn't have told her, and I knew it."

"But there was a reason you did."

"And now she's threatening to tell the world."

"Some people say that our intuition gives us our purest moral knowledge."

"I am not into Zen. I'm all logic."

"Fortunately, you aren't."

"I believed that she was right."

"Good."

"But that's all tied up with how I feel when I'm with her. You can see what a mess it is."

"I think we are doing very well here."

When Donna saw that the call was from him, she put on a face to protect the children. She need not have. His voice was song. They couldn't hear him, but when they saw her smile, they brightened. Everything had modulated, minor to major.

He said he had gotten some good news. He did not say what.

"Let's celebrate," she said.

"Why don't we just relax at home?" he said. "Give Mrs. Yu the night. We'll order pizza."

"Pizza," she laughed.

The boys clapped.

"We'll watch some TV," he said.

"Celebration," she said. "That's what I meant."

8

Double-parked beer trucks as big as semis made a lacquered wall along Clark Street. The Cubs were in Arizona, so the diner had plenty of tables. Two police officers in Kevlar vests sat in one booth. A big guy covered with tattoos and a sixty-something gentleman in a burgundy sweater and white shirt were in another. Someone in a shabby jacket hunched over a plate of eggs at the counter. This was not a D&D kind of place, which was probably why Lawton had chosen it.

Poole had ordered Gunderman to take some time off. Poole said it was his idea, but Gunderman knew Rosten was behind it. They wanted him out of the way while they took down Margery Strand. He had no idea why Lawton had called him for lunch, let alone at such an odd place, but it was a relief to get out of the empty house. Anything was better than sitting there with nothing to do but think.

The sun flashed off the tin cladding behind a grill that reminded him of Hal's Burgers next to his high school. He used to sit at the counter with the guy from the Music Mart, the TV repairman from Ekhard Electric, the gentleman from the jewelry store with a lens on a cord around his neck and dandruff on the shoulders of his black suit jacket. They would all be old men now; he had heard that Hal had died.

A skinny waitress came quickly with a cup in one hand, a pot in the other, and a menu tucked under her arm.

"Coffee do you, honey?" she said.

"I'm meeting somebody," he said.

"Always pays to be awake," she said, pouring, "so they can't sneak up on you."

Gunderman turned the heavy beige mug by its rim. At Hal's he would sometimes order hot chocolate just to be able to contemplate the steam the way the others did. The coffee was strong and just short of scalding. The waitress reappeared.

"See anything you like, honey?" she said.

She was a two-variable equation of the first degree, all angles and no curves, with tetrahedrons under her T-shirt.

"Think I'll wait until the other party arrives," he said.

"Wink when the party starts."

He could not remember ever winking at a woman. He could not even imagine one winking back.

"Traveling on a beam of light?" said Lawton, sliding into the booth. "You were looking straight at me, but I couldn't get your attention. Where in the universe were you?"

"Trying to figure that out, I guess," Gunderman said. He squared one of the menus on the rounded rectangle of Formica then slid it across. "How about you? You all right?"

"With you out on waivers and the Strand thing, what do you think?"

"I mean physically," said Gunderman.

Lawton put the laminated menu off to the side near the window. The light showed the greasy smudges.

"I have a copy of Strand's hard drive with the bad code on it," he said. "Rosten told me to keep you away from it. So I've been fooling with it and accomplishing nothing." He bent to his briefcase and took the device out.

"I hope you've thought about your medical insurance," Gunderman said.

"If you don't find anything, I never gave it to you," said Lawton. "If you do, well, we'll just have to figure what to do then."

Gunderman picked the external hard drive off the Formica.

"I do know what to do with this," Gunderman said.

"I knew you would," said Lawton.

Rosten had just come back from another difficult conversation with Joyce. Lawton wanted more time, but Joyce wasn't having any of that. He ordered Rosten to move against Strand. Now. As Rosten stood staring out his office window, he heard something behind him. Harms was so close that he turned right into her. Anyone seeing them might have thought the hug she gave him was innocent. But her hair against his cheek was a skein of nerve cells entangling his. He drew back.

"What's this about?" he said.

"It's hello," she said, still so close he could taste her breath.

Let it be business. Problem and resolution. He put the table between them and sat.

Instead of sitting down herself, she passed behind him and slid her hand across his shoulders. He was sure she could feel the tremor under the cloth.

"I'm worried Sara will go public," he said.

"Then position yourself," she said. "The board sees you as Joyce's natural successor."

"I stand with him," he said.

"Play it right and you can stand wherever you want," she said. "And I can stand with you."

"In a room with a view?" he said.

"A room at the top."

"I just told him we had to come clean with the board," he said.

"What did he say?"

"That I was out of my depth."

She put her hand on his shoulder.

"You placed yourself on record advocating the prudent path," she said. "I assume you'll memorialize it."

"It wasn't positioning," he said.

The pressure of her hand lifted.

"Sometimes I don't think you even want what you could have," she said.

"You have to be as worried as I am."

"I don't see much risk in this for me."

"The institution, I mean, a hundred years of history."

"History is after I'm gone," she said.

They only notified Simons after they had pulled Strand in and formally accused her. Simons got a call from Snow's admin, Taleisha, summoning her. When she got to Snow's office, the admin greeted her with a recorded smile.

"You can't be comfortable with what's happening," Simons said. "I mean the racial aspect."

"I call people to meetings," Taleisha said. "They come and they go."

Snow was not interested in listening to Sara's objections. This was just some kind of Inhuman Resources formality, the reading of the verdict.

"You can't protect her this time," Snow said. "You'll only hurt yourself."

"She's my responsibility."

"You'd better pray that she's not."

After Harms left, Rosten pulled down the Cantos and found the passage he was looking for:

in war time we want men of ability
in peace we want also character

In wartime, character caused you to hesitate, second-guess the man in command. It could get people killed. There were seven times seven types of ambiguity, but at times like this, one plus one equaled one. That is what loyalty meant.

He left his desk, walked down the hall, and asked Marcia if Joyce was still free.

"For you," Marcia said.

He stuck his head in the door. Silence was as close to permission as he could expect. He centered himself in front of the desk.

"I'm with you," he said.

"Good to know," said Joyce.

"I mean about disclosure," said Rosten. "Everything stays inside the Dome."

"I assumed you had gotten the message," said Joyce.

From Snow's office Simons went to her own and punched out a short letter to the Union League Club. She printed it and put a stamp from her personal stock on the envelope. On the way out of the Dome she dropped the letter in the slot by the elevators. When she reached the Standard Club, she recognized the man standing at the desk in the lobby, but he did not recognize her. She had not been back since her father had died.

"May I help you?" he said.

"I need to talk to somebody about becoming a member," she said.

When Gnomon failed to respond to Joyce's conciliatory letter after the *Wall Street Journal* article, Rosten had come to believe the deal was dead. So had everyone else on the Secret Committee, though Joyce had clearly not given up. Then suddenly one morning a very encouraging message arrived from Gnomon's chairman. Nominally it was also on Nyström's behalf, but nobody believed that. Joyce acted as though he had expected this turn of events all along.

"We think it would be useful to get Day and Domes's perspective on what symbiosis would be possible in a potential relationship," the letter said.

Joyce shook his head. "Business isn't about bees and flowers helping one another," he said. "It's about the physics of very large, heavy things in motion." Nonetheless, when Rosten and Harms drafted a presentation to make to the Gnomon board, they used the word symbiosis more than once, and Joyce did not remove it.

Things moved very quickly. It was wheels-up at midnight for an early-morning meeting in Silicon Valley. Gnomon's chairman greeted the D&D team at the door of a splendid conference room in the offices of Gnomon's outside counsel. It had an onyx conference table and earth-tone walls. The dress code was bespoke casual. The chairman's French cuffs were linkless, press-folded and loose.

He introduced two other board members, not mentioning that they constituted a committee that had taken control. He did not have to. He concluded by expressing apologies for the inconvenience of the trip, the drop-everything urgency.

"We like urgency," said Joyce.

The chairman turned the floor over to Nyström, who presented an overview of Gnomon so brief that somebody had obviously truncated it. Then the chairman invited Joyce to take as much time as he needed.

A future was sketched. Like all serious acts of business imagination, it was plausible, even compelling, and most certainly in its details wrong. The Gnomon group had the social grace not to make a point of this. The presentation moved on to the symbiosis that could develop between vast and growing stores of data and compelling, innovative, and rapidly evolving analytic tools that would permit customers to mine and refine it. Rosten thought Joyce overstated the importance of Gnomon's contribution, but this was the stage for flattery. The hard truth about what things are worth comes only at the end of negotiations. Examples of symbiosis were given. Questions were asked and answered, the responses as spotless as the crystal glasses clustered around the stylish bottles of water that sat at intervals along the table.

"Symbiosis can be achieved by contract, of course," Nyström

interjected at one point. "After all, the butterfly is not the flower it pollinates."

"Very poetic, Niko," Joyce said.

"Contractual relationships avoid the inherent challenges of full integration, difficulties that lead most mergers to fail to achieve their financial goals," said Nyström.

"They forgot to tell that to Jack Welch at General Electric," said Joyce. "But I take your point. It is our view, however, that the distinction between data and analytics will soon be entirely artificial. Enterprises structured along it will be built on a fault line."

Rosten might have suggested another metaphor, as they sat along the San Andreas, but happily, nobody on the Gnomon side seemed shaken.

Joyce went on: Transaction costs—the time and money spent getting two sovereign entities to yes—are the enemy of urgency. You pay them just once in a merger. In a joint venture, you pay them every day.

Nyström had taken his MBA at the University of Chicago, home of the laureate of transaction costs, and so he was able to fight back with erudition. The members of his board must have heard all this before, but that was not the only reason they looked bored. They were obviously not thinking about costs; their minds were on price.

As the meeting proceeded, it became clearer and clearer that the deal was going to happen. When Gnomon's stock had shot up after the *Wall Street Journal* article, the pressure had started to build. Now getting to yes had become seismic.

9

Gunderman returned to the Dome as soon as he had the proof. He went directly to Simons's office, but she was not there, and the temp outside had no idea where she had gone.

"Look on her calendar," he said.

"I don't think I'm supposed to do that," she said.

He took out his BlackBerry and walked down the corridor until he had enough bars. Simons's line rang twice and went to voicemail. Next he looked for Lawton, who was not in either. Charlene said that Chase had called him to a meeting.

"Pull him out," said Gunderman.

"Chase won't like that," said Charlene and smiled as she dialed.

Just then Lawton rounded the corner. Gunderman rushed toward him at such a speed that Lawton stopped and put up his hands against a collision.

"You aren't supposed to be here," Lawton said.

"We've got him," said Gunderman.

All the admins inclined themselves to hear.

"Not the place for this, Sam," said Lawton, turning him and walking him through the office door, closing it behind them.

It was only a status call, but Berry revived whenever he breathed advocates' air. He needed it the way an asthmatic needs an inhaler. He told his colleagues he was making this routine appearance to put the government on notice. Just his presence in place of a young associate might prompt the favorable plea deal he was looking for. The young assistant U.S. Attorney watched him enter the courtroom. Berry nodded: You against me, son.

After the next court date had been set and the assistant had called him aside to suggest a telephone conversation, Berry left through the lobby of glass and granite, breathing easily. The first time he had been inside the Federal Building, he had been a summer associate at Kirkland & Ellis. In those days you could walk right in, get on the elevator, and go straight into a courtroom with not so much as a glance from the bailiff. No metal detectors. No pat-downs if your artificial hip set it off. The only people who couldn't come and go were in handcuffs.

When he was U.S. Attorney, he had arrived by car driven by a marshal. Though you would not have known from looking at it, the black Lincoln was hardened against 7.62-mm tungsten rounds. There had been credible threats. Danger justified luxury and smoothed his commute. Now he lived within walking distance and could buy whatever luxury he required; it was the danger that he missed.

The firm was in an office building near the Federal Building. He displayed his ID to the rent-a-cop at the security desk and was ticking along the stone floor toward the elevator bank when he heard the echo of his name.

"You're gonna love this," Szilard said, coming to his side.

"Who am I going to love?" he said.

"In the elevator," said Szilard.

A security camera's red eye blinked above them, but there was no microphone unless you pushed the emergency button. Szilard turned his back to the eye.

"D&D is in a hurt," he said. "Their credit-history database has been jacked. They've fingered a very unlikely suspect. They've known about the problem for months and not disclosed it, even to their Audit Committee. Seems our mission just crept."

There was nothing quite so satisfying as knowing someone's secret when he doesn't know that you do. Berry only wished that, in this state of grace, he were on trial.

When she wanted to, Marcia was able to pull a Masque of the Red Death face that could stop a party. The Gnomon meeting had just ended, and everybody was shaking everybody else's hand when she pressed a note into Joyce's palm. He looked at it and handed it to Rosten.

"See what he wants," he said.

Marcia led Rosten to an empty office that she had prearranged for just this sort of eventuality.

"You'll get four bars," she said as he unholstered his BlackBerry.

Rosten had no idea what Berry could have said to give her the face. If he had found so much as a phony taxi receipt, Rosten would be shocked.

"What does he want?" he asked.

She whispered, "He said it was regarding the hacking."

Rosten stared at her.

"Well, you asked," she said.

When he told Berry's secretary that he was from D&D return-ing the call, she told him to wait. Not "Please hold a moment for Mr. Berry." Not "May he call you back?" Just "Hold" and then a shallow silence. There wasn't even any music.

Marcia tipped her frosted hair toward the door, and Rosten nodded. Many minutes passed.

"I'll connect you now," the woman finally said, as if she were doing him a favor.

"Brian?" said Berry.

"Tom Rosten. He's in the middle of something."

"Yes he is," said Berry.

"As long as I have you on the phone, I want to tell you that we are feeling a lot of urgency about completing the forensic audit," said Rosten.

"Actually I have you on the phone," said Berry. "And you are not my first choice."

"In any event."

"Let's get to your real problem."

"The audit plan you signed off on makes abundantly clear the limit of your involvement," Rosten said.

"You haven't thought it through," said Berry. "Even if you have the black woman dead to rights, you still have trouble."

"That is none of your concern."

"I did not give my children expensive educations by handling clients' first mistakes," said Berry. "I did it by handling the prob-lems they created by thinking they could handle their first mistake by themselves. What happened was a crime. An undisclosed major corporate crime."

"It was of no consequence," said Rosten.

"Oh, it had consequences," said Berry. "It caused you to cover it up. That's going to help me educate my grandchildren."

"Let me be sure what you are saying," said Rosten.

"I want you to understand that this isn't a threat," Berry said. "It would be easier for you if it were. It is a prediction. Share it with your boss. Tell him that next time, he needs to take my call."

"So this is the way you get business," said Rosten.

"I have more business than I need," said Berry. "This is fun."

Gunderman was waiting at Simons's office door when she returned from lunch.

"What are you doing here?" she said, blowing past him.

"Just listen. Please," he said, following her to the closet door. "When you and I went into Margery's office, I made a copy of her hard drive. Now I've been able to compare it with the one Greener used to implicate her. The bad code wasn't there before Greener got hold of her laptop. That proves that she is not the hacker."

"You let her be humiliated," she said.

"It wasn't until Dell snuck me back into the loop that I could prove her innocence," Gunderman said. "Please understand that."

"I don't understand anything," she said so the whole floor could hear.

"We should close the door."

She did, loudly.

"It was Greener," Gunderman whispered. "He put the evidence on her computer then accused her."

"They treated her like a criminal," she said.

"I'm sorry, Sara," he said. "I did the best I could."

She looked at him looking down. What kind of name was Gunderman? You couldn't tell any more from it than you could from Simons.

"Will you help me off with my coat?" she said.

He was clumsy, but he managed.

When Rosten emerged from the little office, the Gnomon people were still mingling with the D&D team in the lobby, basking in possibility and taking one another's measure. He went outside to wait in the parching sun. Soon the limos pulled up. He let Sebold and Harms get in with Joyce. This always seemed important to them. Before Joyce ducked into the car, Rosten whispered, "A word with you at the terminal."

Rosten rode with Sebold's deputy and the director of financial analysis. How did you think it went, Tom? Don't you think we could have left out that third slide? Rosten mumbled something and retreated into his BlackBerry. There he saw that during the meeting, a call had come in from Gunderman, of all people. He disregarded the voice mail; one hundred seventy-nine e-mails had priority. But he could not concentrate. The limo sped down a freeway lined with new money. He opened a piece of spam and rested his eyes on it.

When they reached the Signature FBO at the airport, he went directly to the counter and spoke to the woman with wings on her chest. She said that if they needed privacy, they could use the office of the assistant manager, who was on vacation. She had the kind of smile he remembered receiving from stewardesses in the old days. The office was two doors down on the right. Rosten had to peel Joyce away from Harms.

"We need a minute," he said.

"Boy talk," she said.

"He's a man of secrets, as you know," said Joyce.

On the walls of the assistant manager's office were photos of airplanes soaring in the blue. The window looked out onto the tarmac, where the D&D pilots stood talking on their cell phones near the nose of the company plane. Joyce went to a plastic model of a Falcon 20, which was just like the one outside except for the color of the striping and tail. He picked up the model as if he owned it.

"We'll probably have to get another, with all the back-and-forth," he said. "Maybe a 50 for range. Before you know it, we'll be global."

"I talked to Berry," Rosten said. "He knows about the breach in the database."

Joyce banked the plane this way, then that.

"That's old business," said Joyce, bringing the model in for a smooth landing.

"He also knows about Strand," said Rosten.

"You were supposed to make the limits of his role clear."

"He thinks we don't fully appreciate the risks."

"Which he would be happy to talk us through slowly at his exorbitant rate," said Joyce.

"He called the way we've handled this a cover-up."

"Put the whole thing in the deep freeze and close the door," said Joyce. "Pay Berry to follow you in." With that, he turned his back, left the office, and soon was striding across the tarmac as if he commanded an air force.

Rosten was last into the plane. The seat facing Joyce had been left open for him. Location made it coveted, even though it meant flying backward. He buckled up tightly. The pilots liked to catapult off the runway as if it were a carrier deck. As the Falcon went into the third derivative, the force bent Rosten over his seat belt, the rate of acceleration accelerating like something at the far edge of control. Soon the thrust eased. The seat belt loosened across Rosten's belly. As the plane settled into a steady cruising speed, mountains came into view, then the whiteout of the clouds.

Joyce's seat had a console that let him control the temperature, raise and lower the lighting, and select the music. One year the senior team had bought Joyce a captain's hat for his birthday. He had worn it once during the weekly staff meeting. No one ever saw it again.

He was reading the newspaper, paying no attention to Rosten, which had become pretty much the rule. Ever since being named chief operating officer, Rosten had been trying to figure out who that meant he was supposed to be. There was no space at the top that Joyce did not already fill. He gave Rosten only tasks that he despised, and it was not long before the work started to become the man. Joyce seemed to look upon him as an infirm part of himself—a crack in the voice, an eyelid that twitched, a tired muscle that would not lift. Rosten would stare into the mirror in a men's room and see there a photo in a trade journal, a man a step behind Joyce or in his shadow at a reception, with a drink in hand. The caption recorded his name, an empty line of letters. He could not remember the time when Joyce had actually sought and accepted his advice on a matter of consequence. If someone had asked him what a COO did all day, he would have had to point at a mirror where the face in the trade journal lived and say, "Better ask him."

Joyce seemed about to come up out of his newspaper, so Rosten took cover in his BlackBerry. The pilots did not believe in the FAA rules, so most people left the antenna on, pinging away into the ether as if to call, "I'm here. I'm here." Rosten's had no bars now, but before takeoff his message queue had grown to more than two hundred. It contained the usual mix of spam and gruel. Focused now, he deleted item after item, opening only a few to make sure they did not say anything. As he purged from the top, new items rolled in from the bottom. One had the heading "Old Flame." It came from Harms.

From the time stamp she must have sent it in the middle of the deal meeting. He scrolled down until he was on it then looked over at her in the seat directly across the aisle from Joyce, the next-best position after Rosten's. She kept brushing her hair away from her eyes as she leaned over her laptop.

He opened the message, which forwarded another. Harms had obviously given it a new heading and added her own introduction:

—This got intercepted after the leak. Somebody finally realized it was personal and was thoughtful enough to give me a look. Good luck.

Beneath this, Grace's message was short—cut off, in fact. His first thought was to reply. He tapped with his thumbs, erased, tapped again, but the words were either too cold or too close. After erasing everything, he hit Send. It was a ping into the void— "I'm here"—two vessels running silent in the dark.

The plane bounced and dipped as it passed over the crest of the Rockies. The seat belt sign was on, but people were up in the aisles on sea legs. Rosten tightened his belt a pull and continued through his queue. A little before Harms had forwarded Grace's message,

Gunderman had sent him one under the subject line "The Real Hacker." Something had gone a little off in that man. They said his marriage was collapsing. Keeping him on after he had made a fool of himself in front of the board had been a bigger mistake than bringing Berry in. At least Berry might come in handy.

—We got it wrong. I know who the real hacker is. And I can prove it. Call me ASAP.

Rosten deleted the message immediately, as if words could be made to disappear despite all the servers that backed up servers that backed up other servers. He needed the airphone, which was in the console under Joyce's arm.

"Sorry to disturb you," he said. "I have to make a call."

Joyce said nothing as he opened the compartment, pulled on the retractable cord, and handed the device across.

Whatever it was that a COO was supposed to do, certainly among the duties was to contain trouble and protect the CEO from unpleasant surprises. He punched Snow's number into the back of the handset.

"I'm sorry," said Taleisha. "May I say who called?"

"Find Ms. Snow and tell her Mr. Rosten needs to talk to her from forty thousand feet in the air. Right now," said Rosten.

"I'm sorry, sir," she said. "I didn't recognize your voice."

To avoid looking at Joyce, Rosten turned to the window as he waited. The clouds below were a featherbed, but he was anything but comfortable.

"Tom?" Snow shouted.

"I can hear you at a normal tone of voice," he said.

"I guess you know," she said.

"I guess I don't," he said, the words poised between her on the ground and Joyce in the air across from him.

"Does Joyce know?" she said.

"Better start with me."

A hiss enveloped him. He looked at the little screen on the back of the phone to see if he was still connected.

"Tom!" she shouted so loudly that even Joyce heard it. He made a question mark with his face. Rosten just closed his eyes and shook his head.

"I'm right here, Alexa," he said. "Better talk fast and not shout."

"Long story short, Greener has done a number on us," she said.

"How?"

"He's the cybercriminal," she said. "And Strand is not happy."

"Can you manage it?" he said. Contain. Protect.

"It would help if Simons was on our side."

"Elaborate, please," he said, glancing at Joyce again.

"She is even unhappier than Strand, if that's possible."

"Should I call her?" he said.

"She's ready to blow."

Rosten beeped off the call. Now Joyce was watching him. He reached his hand out for the phone.

"I have another to make," Rosten said, "unless you need it."

"Something happening?" he said.

Rosten forced a laugh.

"When isn't there?" he said.

"Everything under control?" said Joyce.

"The center is holding," said Rosten.

Joyce opened up a *Forbes*, and Rosten punched Simons's number into the handset. There was a rush of white noise in his ear. Fortunately, she picked up herself, so he did not need to say her name. The interference made it seem as if they were speaking in a gale.

"Sam?" she said.

"Tom Rosten," he said.

"Oh," she said.

"Can you hear me?" he said.

"If I decide to listen," she said.

"We're in the air," he said.

"Lucky you," she said. "Down here we're all in the mud."

"Don't do anything until we get back to the Dome," he said. "I'll come to your office."

"To shut me up," she said.

"Obviously we need to talk," he said.

10

ndrea from Goldman had it all arranged: a quick dinner then the show. Grace went along because Luisa had a sleepover. Since getting half in touch with Tom again, being alone in the apartment without Luisa didn't work for her.

The taxi stopped at a dingy block of buildings with razor wire on the window ledges. Only a poster next to a dinged-up metal door indicated that the place was a theater. The performance got started very late, but half the seats were still empty when the house lights finally dimmed.

Two women entered from opposite sides of the stage and wandered about, talking, sometimes to one another, sometimes to themselves. Did they know one another? Were they lovers? A third character arrived, a man in sweats. Whenever one moved, the others shifted position. It wasn't drama; it was planetary motion.

Grace tried to get into it the way she used to with the obscurities of the Yale Rep back when she was majoring in impossible texts. The glow from the screens of BlackBerries around the audience suggested that she wasn't the only one bored. She glanced at Andrea, who actually seemed fascinated, then angled herself toward the aisle and fired up her own device, scrambling to disable the ringtone just in case Luisa decided for once to check-in.

When she got to her e-mail queue, she saw Tom's name. God, the message must have been sitting there for hours as she raced home to change and then sat through dinner listening to Andrea's complaints about compensation. It had been days and days since she had fumbled and hit Send, thinking it was Delete. He must have thought she was losing it, leaving the sentence hanging without even an ellipsis.

She looked at the subject line: "RE: Old Flame." Her finger touched the key that would open it but then pulled back. Touched and pulled back again. Why would he use those words? He wouldn't be tormenting her again with that one in Washington, would he? And why the RE:? She pushed the key.

The first thing she saw was a message from Harms to Tom:

—Good luck.

She scrolled down further and found her own broken thought:

—I just

Just was confused. Just sorry. Just sitting here losing it. She read the chain from top to bottom. There was nothing at all from Tom. He had forwarded Harms's without comment. Harms had forwarded Grace's message to him, which was the first he had seen it, because somebody in Tom's office had apparently sent it to someone in Harms's office the very day Grace had sent it to Tom. *Good luck.*

She turned the BlackBerry facedown on her lap, smothering the light, and made an attempt to catch a thread from the stage that she could use as a lifeline. Woman Number Two approached very close to the Man, back onstage now in a tight T-shirt and jeans. It must have taken some minimal sense of the dance for the two of them to move around one another as they did, mirror reflecting mirror, never touching, as if to do so would be to vanish. She turned the BlackBerry back over and looked again.

—I just

Her thumb on the little wheel rolled up and down. Up and down.

The intermission came and dragged on. When everyone was seated, there was another delay. She took out her BlackBerry and went to RE: Old Flame. She hit Reply. Then Send.

She had turned her back on his shame when he had confessed it. She had confirmed this with her silence since. Now he had sent silence to her. And she had reciprocated. Silence to silence, conversing.

But she could not leave it at that. She hit Reply again. Though she worried her words, the message she sent him was brief.

Eventually the room went black. Applause pattered here and there. The house lights came up.

"What do you think?" said Andrea.

"I don't," said Grace.

"Perfect," said Andrea.

Even with the convenience of the company plane, it was past business hours when Rosten met with Berry and Szilard. The conversation did not go well.

"You do understand that someone is going to pay," Berry said. "If it isn't Greener right now, it will be all the rest of you later."

"We need to keep him on ice," said Rosten.

The known traitor in place had value.

"The price of inaction goes up quickly with time," said Berry. "I don't think you appreciate just how critical a moment this is."

Contain. Contain the memory. Contain the fear.

"The deal needs to get done," said Rosten.

"Everything will eventually be known," said Berry. "If it becomes known too late, there will be six kinds of trouble with the law."

"What Greener did wasn't material," said Rosten. "We have received guidance about that."

"Did the miraculous Hardy Twine give it to you in writing?"

"It was not required."

"Ask him for a formal opinion letter and see what you get," said Berry.

"I guess you and I will have to agree to disagree," said Rosten.

"I don't agree to anything," said Berry. "You will get my opinion letter tomorrow. It will be very explicit."

By the time Rosten got home, he had been up for more than thirty-six hours with no more than a short, troubled nap on the plane to California. Still, he was unable to sleep. He sat on the couch in his living room, something by Philip Glass on the speakers, repeating and repeating, with variations so tiny they might as well have been subliminal. He looked at his BlackBerry again. He had no right to expect her to respond. Respond to what? He had said nothing, which was exactly what he could offer her.

The music bored into him, turning and returning. You think you have learned your lesson. But what if it doesn't matter? What if the man ends up on the parapet anyway, with you standing there watching him die?

He closed his eyes and tried to breathe out everything, pattern, variation, everything. His BlackBerry vibrated, pulling him back. He looked. It was from her. It was blank.

He dropped the device on the table and closed his eyes again.

—I just

Perfectly just. The music turned and turned, elliptically, held by an unseen mass. The BlackBerry on the glass tabletop vibrated again. He picked it up. She had changed the subject line to "More."

—I understand. I don't understand.

Of course.

Work with me and you will be safe. Berry could not count the number of times he had threatened someone with safety, but this Rosten was a hard case. What kind of safety was he looking for?

In order to get around him, Berry accepted, belatedly, an invitation to buy a table at the Symphony Gala, which had been delayed because of the illness of the maestro. Berry had no trouble filling the table. He simply posted a notice, open to everyone in the firm, first come first served. They were all grabbed by admins and paralegals within an hour.

He rose by escalator through the Palmer House's ornate lobby. When he used to think about running for office, he dreamed of holding a victory celebration here. Two more escalators and he reached the Grand Ballroom, where he checked the seating and placed himself a reasonable distance from Joyce's table so he could wait and observe and at the right time appear as if by chance. Within a few minutes he saw the target working the crowd.

"Brian Joyce," he said, walking up to him, hand presented and, after a pause, taken. "You are a hard man to work for."

"Donna Joyce," said the woman, presenting her hand.

"Morrie Berry," he said, taking it.

"Morrie has been handling some matters for us," Joyce said.

"Do you have a minute?" Berry said.

"It's Donna's evening," Joyce said.

"I should say hello to some people," she said, smiling and moving off.

When she was gone, Berry said, "She's well trained."

"This encounter is unwelcome," said Joyce.

"Understood," said Berry. "But if I'm making a mistake, it will only mean losing one relatively minor client. You, on the other hand, have everything at risk if you make the mistake of not hearing me out."

"What are you saying?"

"Your man Rosten is fucking up."

"He's my right hand."

"It is paralyzed," said Berry. "He's of no use."

"But you are, I suppose."

"Work with me," said Berry, "and you will be safe."

Gunderman smelled it as soon as he entered the house.

"Megan!" he called.

The scent was pungent. He would have thought that an animal had gotten inside if he hadn't smelled this same odor once before, while walking along the lake with Megan on a summer afternoon.

"It's not a skunk, Daddy," she had said, laughing. "It's skunk. Just skunk."

"Translate to Dadspeak."

"Bud," she said. "Marijuana. If it smells sweeter, it's hashish."

"How do you know these things?"

"They're in the air," she said.

He could not deny that, but he had always been certain that she would never take any of them into her lungs.

He pounded up the stairs, the smell growing stronger. When he opened the door, a blast of cold wind from the wide-open windows met his face.

"Megan," he said.

"It's a kind of incense," she said. "They sell it."

"Megan," he said.

The red in her eyes may have been from the smoke, but the tears were for her name.

"What in the world have we done to you?" he said.

When Donna returned to the table, the lawyer was gone. She had recognized him from the news. There were a lot like that at the Symphony Ball.

"Business done?" she said.

"As done as it gets," he said. "Sorry about the interruption. Tell me who you saw."

She did, and he paid attention.

"Let's dance tonight," Brian said.

"He must be quite an attorney."

"We shall see," he said.

All the signals pointed to final negotiations over the weekend, which would let them take advantage of the dead time between the market close on Friday afternoon and Monday morning's open. For several weeks now, intense discussions had been taking place at all levels, though Nyström had barely been heard from. The business media's choice as the Next Big Thing had become the Man Who Never Was. Meanwhile, the chairman and Joyce were talking nearly every day. The lawyers had completed nondisclosure agreements in record time. Due diligence was a sprint, but Rosten was confident they were going to be ready.

"The world is data," Joyce said.

"The empire of the empirical," said Rosten.

"Something like that," said Joyce.

"Do you think she had never tried it before?"

"She has always been so responsible."

"And now she isn't?"

"I was ready for the alcohol."

"You were never young yourself, of course."

"I was older, much older the first time I smoked. It was with Maggie. They say the drug is so much stronger now that it might as well be heroin."

"It is not heroin, of course."

"I can't believe you want me to look the other way."

"What does Maggie want to do?"

"She accused me of leaving Megan unsupervised. I said that until Bill Cadwalader starts sending me child-support payments, I have to earn a living."

"It didn't take long before the conversation moved away from your daughter."

"I'm not proud of that."

"I could have told you how it was going to go."

"You're saying that divorce is a predictable linear function, but to me it feels like we're operating way beyond the accumulation point."

"Do you see how you just hid in language?"

"I'm using the language I know. My language isn't the problem. What Maggie said is the problem."

"Tell me."

"She said that maybe we had made a mistake to separate."

"What did you say?"

"Nothing. I said nothing, and she went right back to blame."

"Which was safer for both of you. What went through your mind?"

"It made me angry. What she had done to Megan, and now never mind?"

"Done to Megan?"

"I mean, Megan has always refused to put anything into her body unless it's organic."

"And marijuana isn't?"

"Not funny."

"What do you suppose was the meaning of what she did?"

"She's in pain."

"There are a lot of places to smoke other than in her room, knowing that you are on the way home from work."

"She wanted to hurt me?"

"Or to tell you that she is human, too, that she is capable of letting you down. A time will come when you are going to have to decide what is really best."

"How to discipline her."

"Whether divorce will be a mistake or a favor to all concerned."

Through the window, Rosten watched the red taillights pulsing, outbound on Lake Shore Drive. He had already let the admins leave. The last e-mails were arriving with their attachments, comfortably ahead of the deadline he had set. This was his finance group at its best, driving forward, getting it done. The Gnomon team, led by the chairman, was going to arrive in Chicago Friday. The fuse was short. But the attachments needed no revision, so it was just a matter of putting the pieces together and sending them west.

He thought he heard something, but he did not look up. Then he felt a presence, and there was Harms, framed by the doorway. The gold pendant at her throat was askew. Her perfect hair was mussed. He thought he could even see a spot on her starched blouse. Rosten rose up out of the numbers. He had never seen her disordered this way.

"Come on in," he said, waving her to the chair on the other side of the desk.

"Has Szilard talked to you?" she said.

"Berry did," said Rosten. "I think they've given up on me."

Her fingers twisted her hair.

"He was talking crime," she said.

She pulled the pendant tight in front of her and then let it drop into the darkness.

"I thought you didn't see any risk to yourself," he said.

She stood.

"Nobody was talking about prison then," she said.

"Look," he said, "the boss is the boss. He has solid, independent sources of advice."

"Hardy Twine doesn't have skin in the game."

"Szilard dared you to try to get an opinion letter from him, right?"

"You'll go down with Joyce, you know, the way you've decided to play it," she said.

"You're worried about me?"

"We can all be ruined," she said. "But yes, I am concerned about you."

"I can live with the consequences."

"You have a duty beyond Joyce, you know," she said. "You have a responsibility to tell the board."

"Szilard has gotten you to do a lot of thinking."

"We could do our best thinking together," she said then leaned forward. The pendant flashed in the depths, like something dropped into the water.

Lawton had not even wanted to see Greener's face, except perhaps to spit in it. Joyce had agreed with Rosten to string the man along and see what they could learn, but Lawton didn't like it.

Snow had persuaded Strand to go off on an all-expenses-paid vacation. Greener didn't know that, and the Admin News Network didn't either. As far as everyone but the crisis team was concerned, she had been packaged out and had disappeared. As per the plan, Snow let word slip that Strand may not have been working alone.

The first thing Greener did when he arrived at the team meeting was to report that Chase's nose was out of joint as a result of not being included.

"What does such a nose actually look like?" Lawton said. "I mean, is it cocked to one side? Twisted up like a screw?"

"Gentlemen," said Snow. She turned to Greener. "Strictly speaking, you should not have been talking to him about our work."

"So he's a suspect," said Greener.

"Nobody thinks that," said Gunderman. "We just have to be extremely careful. There is every reason to believe that a very smart individual is behind what Strand did."

"Who brought you back?" Greener said.

"If at any point you have reason to suspect me or any one of us," said Gunderman, "you need to take it straight to Rosten."

"That would be the proper procedure," said Snow.

Greener took out his BlackBerry and began playing it with his thumbs.

"Rules of the road," he said. "Let's get them down in writing. For everyone's protection."

Lawton wanted to tell him the only protection anyone needed was to wear a hazmat suit around him.

"Good idea, Rob," Gunderman said. "I should have thought of it myself."

Greener finished his message and it popped into everyone's queue. Lawton saw Rosten's name in the address line and shot him a message of his own.

—Disregard Greener's last. All part of the game.

As Snow reviewed the bidding, Greener took to his thumbs again.

"I would rather you didn't do that," she said.

"I'm sure you would," Greener said.

They went through the motions of laying out a plan of attack. Greener deflected it at a few points, and Gunderman agreed with him. The meeting ended. Greener left quickly. Snow held Lawton and Gunderman back.

"Do you think he bought it?" she said.

"I made him the smartest man in the room," said Gunderman, smiling. "Who wouldn't buy that?"

"Only a fool would," said Lawton.

"He needs to thinks we're all the fools, especially me," said Gunderman. "I'm the one who got him displaced."

"How long do we have to string the little shit along?" said Lawton.

"There are certain turning points in the life of a corporation," Joyce said to Rosten the evening before the final negotiations. "The founding. The completion of the Dome. The day they rang the bell at the stock exchange to mark the initial public offering of shares. Next Monday will be another."

There would be long banks of phones ready to connect with the key stakeholders the instant the announcement went out on the wire. There would be a conference call before the start of trading. Harms would preside over the preliminaries, waiting as the operator reported the number of people who had dialed in. The number would grow very large. When the time came, Harms would welcome everyone and give the usual boilerplate disclaimers. Then she would introduce Brian Brady Joyce, the man who just redrew the map.

"I have a very good feeling about this," Joyce said.

11

Shouldn't you be rehearsing?" Sam stood in his doorway, which opened onto a messy hall and a flight of muddy stairs, at the top of which Megan brooded in her room.

"Corporate is running the show," Sara said. "It's all about Joyce."

"I'm sorry everything is such a clutter," he said. "It's a teacher training day at the high school. I stayed home to spend time with Megan, which isn't working. I should have tidied up. You'll have to forgive me."

"Sorry is my territory today," she said.

"Let me at least clear off the sofa."

"Do stop."

"May I take your coat?"

"I won't be long," she said, sitting down, but barely. "I came to apologize."

"Look, all you really knew about me is that I could fix your computer," he said.

"And your shirt size. Don't forget that," she said.

"Can I get you a glass of water or something?"

"I've been with D&D for twenty years," she said. "I made my-self fit in. Some of its ways I didn't like so much, but you get used to them, and eventually its ways aren't things apart from you any-more." Her fingers touched her face. "They're like blemishes you cover up with makeup. On good days you don't even think about them. You never notice what's become of you, because it happens so gradually. All you feel is that you are bigger in the world. But then all of a sudden everything turns. When they accused Mar-gery, I realized I wasn't part of the large thing at all. I was an outsider, like Margery, and I didn't recognize myself anymore."

He did not know what to do about his left hand. Hide it in his pocket? He started to fold his arms, hands under, but somebody had told him that put people off.

"I swept you into my problem, Sam," she said. "I made you into Day and Domes, but you're an outsider, too. Maybe we all are. Do you know what I thought to myself when I was feeling betrayed? 'Gunderman is a German name.' That's what I thought."

"Dutch," he said. "My family thought Gurman sounded too much like German. So of all things they came up with Gunder-man."

"I am so sorry for what I thought about you," she said. "I really don't know how to say more."

She stood. He was terrible at things like this.

"I have some whiskey," he said. "I don't think it's very good."

"I will if you will."

"I take mine straight, like medicine."

"Perfect."

The bottle had been untouched for so long that the cap felt ce-mented on. She watched as he poured quite a lot into her glass, not wanting to seem stingy. Then he poured the same amount into his.

"Well," she said, looking through the lens of clear, dark liquid, "you must think I need quite a dose."

"Or I do."

"We really don't know each other at all, do we," she said. "My father taught me that you can never get information about a customer when you need it, and you can never get a relationship when you need it. You have to do it before. You have to figure out what each person needs, really needs, no matter what they may say or do. Needs for herself: To be liked. To be admired. To be feared. You don't suppose Chase had anything to do with this, do you?"

"He did push Greener," said Sam. "But no. I don't think so."

"Doing things in secret isn't his way," she said. "He needs to be seen."

"What did your father say about people like him?"

"On Maxwell Street the technical term was schmuck." Her ease with the word surprised him, her ease with him.

She told him her father's story, how he had never thought of himself as anything more than a peddler, how he had worked himself into a state when he was trying to become a member of the Standard Club.

"But it's open, isn't it?" he said. "I mean to Jewish people."

"I've applied for membership," she said, "if they'll have me."

Their glasses sat empty on the coasters she had slipped under them. He raised the bottle. She raised her eyebrows. Then she used her finger to show him how much to pour. He took the same amount, even though he was feeling numb around the nose.

"And what about you, Sam Gunderman?"

"I'm kind of a mess," he said and took the medicine for it.

"Can I help?"

He heard Megan thumping down the stairs and realized that they were sitting in the dark. It took two attempts before he managed to switch on the floor lamp, which oscillated dizzily when he let it go.

"Have you met my daughter?" he said, trying to rise but dropping back into the cushions.

"Megan," said Sara.

"This is Ms. Simons," he said. "From the office. We were talking about work. Forgot to turn on the light, we were so deep into it."

Megan was not looking at either of them. Her eyes were on the bottle. What kind of example?

"We just resolved something," he said. "Decided to toast."

"It's OK, Daddy," Megan said. "You both have IDs."

"Won't you sit down with us?" said Sara. "I want to hear about your hockey."

"Mine is the same as everybody else's."

"Let's start with your plus/minus," said Sara. "You're a forward, aren't you?"

Megan finally looked at her and gave her the statistic.

"What line?" said Sara.

"First," said Megan. "And the power play."

"A real shooter then," said Sara.

"Do you play?" said Megan.

"God, no," she said. "No agility, no balance. But I'm good on my butt in the stands. My father used to take me to the old Stadium, the original Madhouse on Madison. That was before your time. It was so loud that he put cotton in my ears."

Sam had not dared to touch his drink since Megan had appeared, but Sara sipped hers as she asked about college, Division 1 scholarship prospects, and then even boys. They agreed that girls grew up faster.

"And stay ahead," said Sara.

"Not in everything," said Megan. "We could still beat them as freshmen. Not anymore."

"That's just bulk," said Sara. "Luckily, in business there isn't any checking, at least not the physical kind. Look, I've intruded too much on your time together." She rose, her glass empty on the table. "I only came to thank your father for helping me with something. He is a very strong man. But you know that." Sam felt Megan's eyes on him as he stood. He wasn't sure whether he was moving or the floor was. "It was great meeting you, Megan. I've wanted to ever since I heard about your skill on the ice. Get your dad to take you to a Hawks game sometime. I know somebody who can get you tickets right behind the glass."

Megan stood and put out her hand. Sara stepped forward and gave her a hug, which Sam was afraid was too much. Then he saw that Megan was hugging back.

He walked Sara to the door.

"Thanks for everything," she said, leaning in as she did. Maybe it was no more than always, but he found himself leaning away. She smiled. Then she was gone.

Back in the living room Megan was still sitting on the couch. He picked up the glasses, choked the bottle, and took the mess to the kitchen. When he returned, she had not moved.

"Do you like her?" she said.

"She's very good at what she does."

"I like her."

"I'll tell her that."

"I think she likes you."

"She's grateful."

"Yeah, that, too."

Joyce had decided to hold an early dinner for Gnomon at the law firm's deal facility, which would be both sides' prison until something either happened or didn't. It was located a few blocks from the firm's regular offices, heavily secured, extremely well appointed, complete with a dedicated kitchen and wait staff, all of whom had been vetted for discretion. Its executive chef had earned a Michelin star before going into semiretirement. They said that some companies decided to merge just because it was the only way to get a table.

Rosten did not fully trust the arrangements. Nothing prevented the Admin News Network from drawing a conclusion from the mass senior-level absence. It would not take much stealth for some newspaper reporter to follow one of the executive assistants as she carried documents from the Dome to the office listed on the building directory as HLC Trading Co., which did not show up in Dun and Bradstreet. But at least time was a friend. The damage a leak would do was greatest before the week's market close, only a few minutes from now. After that they had sixty-five and a half hours to get to yes before the market opened again.

If not Agency-grade in its security, the facility did provide what Gnomon's chairman might have called an ecosystem: banks of phones; conference rooms with long, long tables to accommodate the throng of lawyers who would go over endless documents line by clotted line; two smaller, more elegant spaces stocked with food, soft drinks, and coffee, where the senior teams could meet separately; a grand dining room, down one floor, guarded by a large deltoid in a suit.

The menu for the opening dinner was going to feature PowerPoint with pear salad, lamb, and chocolate mousse with Q and A. Rosten would handle most of the presentation. He'd had to do some selling to get Joyce to agree to Simons doing the incremental revenue opportunities.

"Can't trust her," Joyce had said.

"She was right about Strand," said Rosten.

"And wrong about everything else," said Joyce.

When Simons finally arrived, Rosten thought he smelled whiskey behind the perfume, but she showed no signs of impairment. The team went to the dining room as a group. They passed the security man, his eyes as empty as a Greek statue's, shook the hand of the executive chef, who responded with the hauteur of a royal and then disappeared back into his realm. Every member of the team but Joyce paused upon seeing the sparkle of the crystal, the deep white of the linen, the perfect arrangements of low flowers that would block no one's view. Rosten walked everyone through the agenda, then Sebold briefed on the logistics. After each course, the wait staff would vanish, to reappear only when Joyce summoned them by pushing a button on the underside of the table at the captain's place, which was at the precise center of the long side.

It turned out that they could not even begin the final run-through until someone solved the inevitable problem with the computer–video screen interface. The techie, of course, was not in the room. This caused a delay, but even after having to wait for Simons, they had plenty of cushion.

"This kind of glitch must not happen at H hour," said Joyce.

"Nothing will go wrong," said the techie.

"Be there when it does," Rosten said.

The run-through was reasonably smooth, other than a little issue with salad. Should it be on the table when the guests arrived or, more elegantly, delivered as soon as everyone was seated? This drew in the executive chef, who feared for the vitality of the lettuce.

"It's not about another Michelin star," Joyce said.

Rosten would have preferred not to spatter the chef's whites, but there it was. Hauteur a bit diminished, the great man withdrew.

Joyce's summary of his opening remarks was perfunctory. This caused looks among the members of the team, but Rosten was confident the boss was saving it for H hour. As the time neared and the waiters brought out the salad under the concerned eye of the executive chef, Gail appeared in the doorway. People turned, even the waiters. She was not in the script. Rosten went to her.

"This had better be important," he said.

"Trust me," she said.

"Can't it wait?" he said.

"The hacker is back," she said.

Rosten quickened her into the hall.

"We just got a call from Gnomon's IT Department," she said.

"Gnomon's," he said.

"And its law firm. And its investment bank," she said. "They did not like what they found when they checked their names in our database."

"What does Gunderman say?" he said.

"He's on his way to the Dome now."

"Someone needs to check the data on every person coming to dinner tonight."

"I believe that's being done."

Joyce was clipping his nails when Rosten returned and whispered into his ear.

"Jesus, Mary, and Joseph!" Joyce said. Every face in the room looked as if he had stricken them with a curse.

"We have a problem," Rosten announced. "The hacker has struck at Gnomon."

"Their system?" said Lawton.

"Their personal files in our database," said Rosten.

"I thought we caught the bastard," said Joyce.

Lawton took out his BlackBerry to make a call. Rosten turned to Joyce.

"You need to get on the phone with the chairman," Rosten said.

"Niko did this," said Joyce. "It's been that little prick all along."

Snow did not tell him to be careful. Careful was not an option. Careful was the executive chef in his kitchen.

"Right now this is about us, not them," said Rosten.

"What exactly do we know?" Joyce said.

"Not much," said Rosten. "The data on Gnomon personnel has been altered. Gnomon informed us. Apparently they got an e-mail."

"Who the hell from?"

From Jesus, Mary, and Joseph. From the gremlin in the interface. From places unseen where hides a man without a shadow.

"We can only guess," said Rosten.

Joyce told Lawton to get his team on a conference call ASAP.

"Make sure Gunderman is there," Joyce said. "He seems to be the only one around here who knows anything."

He took Rosten by the elbow and led him into the hallway. The security man was there near the elevator, watching the opposite wall.

Joyce dialed. Rosten stood, as he often did, an audience of one.

"Yes," Joyce said. "I have just been informed,"

Rosten would not be able to testify to what the Gnomon chairman had to say, if it came to that. All he could swear to was that it was a lot.

"We think we're on top of it," said Joyce. "We believe we know who is responsible. And needless to say—"

The chairman did not give him the opportunity to say what he did not need to. Joyce stood silent in the onslaught.

"Give me a half hour," he was finally able to interject. He looked past Rosten toward the kitchen door, which emitted the scent of lamb.

"That is fair, yes," said Joyce. "Is this the best number for you? OK, then."

Joyce took the BlackBerry from his ear and looked at it for a long moment before killing it with his thumb.

"He's inclined to abort," he said. "But he says he can be persuaded. We have twenty minutes."

"The call to the Dome should be ready," Rosten said.

The techie had rigged up a speakerphone on the linen in the center of the table. Rosten brought the team to order and asked Gunderman to report. The attack had neatly coincided with the arrival of Niko and the others at O'Hare, Gunderman said. The corruption of data seemed to have been confined to the Gnomon board, senior management, and close affiliates involved in the deal. They had all been transformed into deadbeats. In order to make sure Gnomon discovered this before the deal discussions began, the attacker had made the system send messages to each of the victims. The Gnomon deal team had probably learned of the attack by airphone somewhere over the Great Plains. This meant they had known before Joyce did. The chairman must have been counting the minutes until Joyce called.

"Do you believe Niko could have done this?" said Joyce.

"Low probability," said Gunderman.

"On what basis?"

"Occam's razor. The simplest explanation is usually the right one," said Gunderman. "We know who attacked the system before. It is highly likely that he's the one who did it this time, too."

"I thought you people were supposed to be guarding the straits," said Joyce.

"I'm guessing he had put the code into the system quite a while ago, before we got onto him, and armed it to lie dormant until he was ready," said Gunderman.

"Where is the motherfucker now?"

Nearly everyone looked away.

"I have him working the problem," said Gunderman.

"That's nuts," said Joyce.

"He's in a dummy system, and we're tracking every keystroke," said Gunderman.

"You're a little late," said Joyce.

"Let's not go too far into hindsight," said Rosten. "Nobody will look very good."

So far, Gunderman reported, there had been no unusual customer or consumer complaint levels.

"This was not a bomber," he said. "It was a sniper."

"Niko will beat us with a leak unless we hustle," said Harms.

But Joyce did not hear, did not see. He was face into the gale somewhere, longitude and latitude unknown. Lawton slipped into the silence and asked for detail on next steps. Snow wanted to talk about process. What exactly was Greener's status, and how should it be documented? Sebold joined in. After a few minutes, Joyce returned to shore, pushing aside the crystal goblets and pulling the speakerphone toward him.

"Can we restore the original, undamaged files?" he said.

"It's already been done," said Gunderman.

"Keep everyone on deck," Joyce said. Then he punched out of the call and led Rosten back into the hallway, where he began to dial the chairman.

"Remember," Rosten said as he did, "they will all be in the room there listening to you. Including Nyström."

Joyce turned to the elevator before completing the phone number. They passed the security man and rode up one floor to the private office set aside for the CEO. Joyce put the call on the speakerphone. Rosten closed the door. The line hollowed out as it reached toward whatever room at the Ritz Carlton in which the Gnomon team had gathered. The ring came. It came again. And again. The chairman was making them wait.

"Yes," he finally said.

"I am happy to report that we have completely repaired the damage," said Joyce. "We truly regret this act of sabotage and trust that it will not be permitted to accomplish its obvious objective."

Rosten heard this as an accusation of Nyström. He hoped the audience in the Ritz Carlton did not.

"If I did not mistake you," said the chairman, "you said earlier that you had identified the attacker."

"We believe we have," said Joyce.

"My people tell me that this would have been impossible in so short a time," the chairman said.

Rosten wrote quickly on a notepad and turned it to Joyce: "Careful."

"We have advanced methods," said Joyce.

Rosten tore the note into small pieces and put them in his pocket.

"Yes, well," said the chairman. "We think you knew about your problem long before you called me."

"I called the moment I learned that your files had been tampered with," said Joyce.

"But this was not the first incident," said the chairman.

"Who said that?" said Joyce.

"I assure you that our people know all the advanced methods, as you call them," said the chairman.

"I resent the implication—" said Joyce.

"We are returning home, Brian," said the chairman. "Need I say with shaken confidence?"

"You are being precipitous," said Joyce to a speaker that had shrunk to a single dimension. Rosten knew that it would have made no difference to the outcome if Joyce had used the correct word.

The first bulletin broke on the Bloomberg wire as the senior team's cars pulled up to the Dome. Lawton was in the backseat with Rosten, getting ready to exit as the limo slowed to the curb. When they heard what Harms was saying, their hands came off the door handles.

"Read it to me. . . . Shit!" she said. "Who's the source? . . . Read it again."

As soon as she told them the gist of the story, Lawton knew where it had come from. It reported a conversation described as "angry" between the chairman and Joyce. It quoted a source saying the deal was dead: "Gnomon is not about to pour itself into a black hole." That had to be Nyström.

"He didn't leave anything to chance," said Lawton.

"We need to get out a statement," said Harms.

"We'd better get to Morrie Berry," said Lawton. "This is more than public relations."

"But what the hell do we say?" said Harms.

"We can't very well deny any of it," said Rosten.

"Help me," said Harms.

Rosten dictated: "Day and Domes has determined that the attack was confined to a small group of files, apparently chosen purposefully to sabotage ongoing talks with Gnomon Co. All affected individuals have been notified and their files restored to an uncorrupted state. Day and Domes's database is accurate and secure. Period."

"Don't we need a sentence that says that Day and Domes has taken steps to lock down the system against any further attack?" said Lawton.

"Should it be a small group of files or small number?" said Harms.

"You decide. Just write it," said Rosten. "We'll need to run the draft past Joyce. Run being the operative word."

"He had everything riding on this," said Lawton.

"He can take us all down with him," said Harms.

"Let's try to get everyone into the life raft, OK?" said Rosten, opening his door into traffic.

As Lawton got out on the passenger side, he saw a TV van

flashing its headlights as it closed in. Run is the operative word. That he could even do it surprised him. When he reached the revolving door, out of breath, he looked back and saw Harms, still in the limo, speaking into her BlackBerry. He rushed back and knocked on the window, which hummed down as she continued to speak.

"Unless you want to do dictation to the cameras, you'd better take it inside," he said.

She was remarkably quick in heels.

When Simons got the word, she was still at the deal facility conferring about contingency plans. They hadn't even gotten to the worst scenario when suddenly they were in it. She immediately began calling the top ten customers to brief them on what had happened and reassure them that it had not in any way affected them. Some said thank you. Others affirmed their confidence, not always persuasively. A few tried to negotiate a lower price.

When she finally reached the lobby of the Dome, she saw that awful lawyer getting into the elevator. With him were two men in suits who should have been in sunglasses scanning a crowd and speaking into their thumbs. She let the elevator door slide shut. Lawyers and security were in somebody else's silo. What she needed was a plan for reaching out to all of D&D's clients, face-to-face eventually. It would also be necessary to communicate quickly to the millions of people whose credit history resided on D&D's computers. This could have been orderly had they gotten ahead of it, but now they had lost that option. She called Margery Strand's cell phone, wherever in the world she had gone.

"We have a mess," Simons said.

"I heard," said Strand. Behind her was the sound of the Klaxon of an emergency vehicle speaking a foreign tongue. "I also heard about all you did for me. Sam Gunderman called."

"He's the hero," Simons said.

"He was all about you."

"We both owe him a very expensive dinner."

"I think he would rather have it with you alone," said Strand.

"How soon can you get back?" Simons said. "I need your help."

The news popped onto Grace's BlackBerry as she arrived at a meeting.

Day and Domes hacked. Gnomon deal dead.

She took her place at the table, but the BlackBerry never left her palm. News items arrived in rapid succession. Dow Jones. Reuters. Associated Press. Bloomberg. She did not care whether her colleagues around the table thought she was inattentive. In this business, people were never fully anywhere. She punched up D&D's stock price every few minutes. Down, down, down. At one point she looked at Gnomon. It had dropped, too, all the acquisition air pffffting out of it. Based on the fundamentals, D&D's price should have been held up some by the elimination of the risk that it would overpay for Gnomon, but at a moment like this, financial theory gave way to mob psychology.

It was no use sending Tom another e-mail. D&D would be in flood-control mode, and her message would be diverted to a reservoir, probably controlled by Sandra Harms. RE: Old Flame. She wished she'd had enough imagination to get a personal BlackBerry and her own e-mail account. Then if she sent something to him, the algorithms would not treat it as coming from the bank. As if he would look at it even if it went straight to his queue. As if he gave a thought to her.

"Grace."

The voice couldn't have come from the BlackBerry. She looked up. The meeting had ended. The conference room had cleared, except for her boss.

"Sorry," she said.

"You weren't in attendance," he said.

"Did I miss anything?" she said.

"Turn that around," he said. "Is there something I should know about?"

"Day and Domes."

"Oh, that," he said. "Turns out you were smart to walk away. Looks like they screwed the pooch."

"I think the pooch did it to them," she said.

"Usually takes two to get this badly fucked."

When she returned to her cubicle, she used her BlackBerry to dial Tom.

Gail answered on the first ring.

"This is Grace Bondurant."

"Well," said Gail.

"I know it's a bad time," Grace said.

"He is being awfully selective," said Gail, "but can you hold a moment?"

Before Grace could tell her simply to give him a message, she found herself locked in a small room with a harpsichord playing. She could not break free, because what if he actually entered the room and she was gone?

Then the music stopped.

"Grace?" Tom said.

"I really only wanted to get a message to you," she said, "but then I was on hold, and I didn't want you to think I'd hung up."

"It's good to hear a voice that isn't furious," he said. "You aren't furious, are you?"

"I've been thinking of you, with all this," she said.

"I've seen worse," he said.

"I know," she said.

"I'm afraid I have to go," he said. "A million fires. Thank you for thinking of me."

"I wish I could do something."

"Do you still pray?"

"When I'm scared," she said.

"Do that," he said.

Then he was gone and she breathed in his voice, which was incense.

The next complication was a man identifying himself as Special Agent Harold Jansen of the FBI. He said he was inquiring about a potential violation of the Computer Fraud and Abuse Act.

"I assume the news reports are substantially accurate," he said. The words did not seem shaped by his own mouth.

"I think you had better speak with our general counsel," said Rosten.

"I am officially notifying you, as chief operating officer, that you must retain any and all information, documents, and records in any form, including digital, regarding this matter," said the Special Agent.

Rosten flashed on the games of hide-and-seek with the Sisters on the night streets of Washington, how dogged and predictable they were, but how close they came to catching him.

"Again, Sebold is the one," he said.

"No, you are the one," said the Special Agent. "As of this moment, you and Day and Domes are on notice. Any destruction of evidence will be deemed an obstruction of justice."

When Rosten arrived at Sebold's office, he heard the agent on the speakerphone, same words. Sebold seemed to be reading scripted responses to the scripted message, but there was nothing on the desk between his flattened, tightly stretched hands.

"We will, of course, cooperate to the fullest appropriate extent required by law," he said. "We want the person who did this brought to justice."

When he hung up, the two men drafted an all-hands message to go out under Rosten's name calling a halt to all file destruction until further notice.

"Should we run this by Berry?"

"He's with the boss," said Sebold. "I'll have Szilard eyeball it."

"You'd better keep control."

"You, too, chief," said Sebold.

Rosten himself did not have much evidence to preserve. He did not believe in memos to file. He tried to avoid saying anything of importance in e-mails. Long ago he had given up confessional poetry. What he did retain was capacitance in his brain. He could not erase any of that, no matter how much he might want to.

A few minutes after 7 p.m. Sebold informed him that the Securities and Exchange Commission had just gotten into the act. Same message, different statute.

"I thought they went home at 5 p.m. sharp in Washington," Sebold said. "But you would know about that."

"My agency didn't keep regular hours," said Rosten.

"Berry has arranged for Greener to be arrested," said Sebold. "Media has been notified so they can broadcast the perp walk out the front door live on the last news show. Harms is coordinating. Why weren't you at the meeting?"

"What meeting?" Rosten said.

The harpsichord took the Fugue much too fast. Donna did not recognize who it was. Ordinarily, Marcia would call back when Brian was ready. But today Donna said she would rather go on hold. She wanted to ask Marcia how he was holding up, but there was not much point. Even Marcia could not penetrate what Brian called the mask of command. "This mask," she had asked him once, "is it you?" "It's shaped to my skull," he had said, "otherwise people wouldn't be able to recognize me. But it's also shaped by my will. In that sense the mask is more mine than the face I was born with." Sometimes she wondered how often he wore a mask with her.

He came on the line.

"Only have a second," he said.

"I was worried about you."

"We'll be fine."

"Can you still complete the deal?"

"Right now that's way down the to-do list."

"I hate not being there with you right now," she said. "Just know that I love you always."

She did not know at what point he had rung off.

"Harms is about to make a statement to the cameras. It's all over the Admin News Network," Gail said as Rosten came out of his office.

"Nobody's here," he said, looking down the corridor.

"They're all down in the lobby," she said. "Take a look out your window."

On the street below he saw a tangle of cameras, cables, and reporters. There was a single mic stand and a scrimmage line in a ragged semicircle around it. Harms was not there yet. When he reached the lobby, he pushed through to Au Bon Pain, which had stayed open and was doing quite a business. From its windows he got a good look at the situation, which he soon realized also gave the situation a good look at him. He returned to the lobby, where he positioned himself near the revolving doors, barely visible to the street. Maurice came to stand next to him.

"Never thought I'd see something like this," he said. "It'll damp down though, won't it?"

"You won't need your umbrella for quite a while, I'm afraid," said Rosten.

The crowd turned and hushed. Rosten looked toward the elevators. It was Greener, armless, supported by faceless men. Somebody shouted, "You!" Rosten saw that Greener's hands were bound by a plastic band, like something cinched for shipping. Not as smart as he thought; nobody was.

They took him out the handicapped door under the mosaic of Jean Baptiste Point du Sable at the mouth of the Chicago River. The crowd began to rustle and talk again as soon as he was gone. Whenever an elevator door opened, heads turned, but Harms did not appear.

Rosten had been working all evening in a bubble with his team of analysts, preparing a presentation that he and Joyce could take on the road to try to talk the stock price back up. At one point he put a call to Joyce. It made sense for them to be operating on separate tracks, of course. So much to be done. Joyce was concentrating on the public stuff and legal issues, so there was no need for Rosten to. He must have been in touch with Sabby Chandrahari and Teddy Diamond. But there would have to be a full and formal communication with the board as soon as possible, so Rosten wanted to touch base before getting started on the preparations. Joyce never called back.

The noise level quieted again. Rosten looked toward the elevators and saw Harms, dressed in a jacket and skirt the color of her eyes. Her hair looked as though she had just had it done. As he drew close to the revolving door, she spotted him and looked away.

Lawton stayed in his office and listened to it live on news radio. Harms handled herself just right until she said, "Day and Domes guards its numbers with its life."

The first question was "Then why did the guard abandon his post?"

She probably should have seen that coming, but it was easy to get a little funny in the head when the stakes are mortal.

The media people vanished as quickly as they had gathered, and after a certain period of recapitulation among the crowd in the lobby, the Dome finally began to empty into the night. Rosten returned to his office and had barely sat down when Gail buzzed to say that Joyce wanted to talk with him before he went home.

"Tell Marcia I'll be right up."

"It was Mr. Joyce himself who called."

"Since when is he mister?"

"Since things got scary, Mr. Rosten," she said.

Joyce was standing as Rosten entered. His shirt was fresh, his chin shaved, and there was a memory of familiar perfume in the air. He led Rosten to the table. Marcia offered a tray with a pot of coffee, two cups, and four cookies on a china plate.

"It's decaf," she said then left.

"Quite a day," said Joyce.

"Not the one we prepared for," said Rosten.

"Von Moltke says no plan survives the first contact with the enemy," said Joyce. "I don't suppose at the Central Intelligence Agency you studied the great Prussian strategists."

"If the enemy got even a whiff of contact, we failed," Rosten said.

"I want you to know that I appreciate your pursuit of our mole," said Joyce.

"Gunderman deserves the credit."

"The man on the bridge is responsible for what his subordinates do, good or bad," said Joyce. "Gunderman flowered under your command. I was this close to letting him go, more than once."

"I want to make sure I'm playing the role you need me to," Rosten said.

"Getting the public piece right was critical today, but that's not your added value," said Joyce. "Harms was all over it. She had a draft of the first release written even before she left the limo. She was very protective of you, by the way. She had to remind me a number of times not to pull you away from the operational side."

"I'd expect nothing less," said Rosten.

"My point is that I needed you to do exactly what you've been doing," said Joyce. "Getting people to battle stations. Trimming the ballast."

"The team in Finance pulled together a draft PowerPoint that we can take to the Street," said Rosten. "I want some guidance from you about what we should prepare for the board. But first I should tell you that Lawton is implementing steps to totally lock down the database. It may slow response times, but not materially, and we need to be sure all the doors are closed tight before we can even think about a long-term security strategy. Gunderman already has some good ideas about that."

"Lawton has been behind the curve, hasn't he," said Joyce.

"We all have been."

"Greener was his guy."

"Actually, he was Chase's," said Rosten.

"Lawton trained him," said Joyce.

"I'm sorry to say that he started in Finance," said Rosten.

"I'm not saying complicity, Tom," said Joyce. "It obviously humiliated Dell to have this happen. I think Greener wanted that. Dell was the first man he attacked."

Actually, Joyce had fallen prey before Lawton, but only by a matter of seconds. There was no point in correcting him.

"I don't imagine all those medications Dell is taking make it any easier to stay on top of things," said Joyce.

"He's done with chemo," said Rosten. "He's cancer-free."

"They never are," said Joyce. "But I'm glad to hear things have looked up. It makes it a little easier to think clearly about him."

"What I'm saying is that the fact that he was sick has become irrelevant," said Rosten.

"Then you agree," said Joyce.

"He's solid."

"We are going to have to move on him," said Joyce. "He was the man on the bridge when we hit the iceberg."

"Chase was the one who pushed Greener," said Rosten. "If anybody has anything to answer for—"

"Forget about Chase," said Joyce. "He's a server farmer. He doesn't signify to the Street and even less to the government."

Whose voice was Rosten hearing?

"Have you discussed this with Morrie Berry?" said Rosten.

"He has given me his insights," said Joyce, "just as you are giving me yours."

"What does he say the government wants?" said Rosten.

"Somebody a lot bigger than Greener," said Joyce.

"We've got to assume they want the right person," said Rosten.

"Talk to Snow," said Joyce. "Work out a fair package, but run it by Szilard before you lay it on Dell. We do have to be careful that we don't appear to be buying silence."

12

For years Berry and Szilard had ordered the same lunch: Union League Club black-bean soup and a half Cobb salad, mixed. If someone had put them in the witness box and demanded to know who had been first, each would have been able to swear that he had no present recollection.

They did not share every habit. Berry liked to arrive at work before 6; Szilard left well after Berry had gone home. Szilard read mysteries for pleasure, Berry biographies. Once Berry realized that his personality was not suited to winning elective office, he stopped going to church. Szilard still kept attending, out of habit, just as Berry kept ordering the half Cobb salad long after Szilard began opting for animal flesh.

"Is Rosten prepared?" Berry said.

"Best coaching we sell," said Szilard.

"Lawton certainly stood tall," said Berry.

"You were right about him," said Szilard. "He was the safest to terminate. Will that do it, do you think?"

He had finished his roast turkey and looked like a man feeling the tryptophan, but it was Berry who yawned.

"If Rosten doesn't fuck up," he said, "I think our government problem will be over. Then we'll see."

"They haven't questioned Simons," said Szilard.

"They aren't thinking," said Berry.

"Let's hope," said Szilard.

"You know, we used to see her in here a lot at lunch," said Berry.

"I thought she was a member," said Szilard.

"Maybe she's avoiding us," said Berry.

The thought lifted him, like a sugary dessert.

Q: When you first learned that the credit-history database had been tampered with, didn't it occur to you that the government needed to be informed?

A: It was not material.

Q: We may have a different view of that, Mr. Rosten

A: It only affected two executives of the company.

Q: And one of them was only the CEO.

A: It was a malicious prank. But it was isolated. And not material.

Q: It was a violation of a number of federal criminal statutes.

A: I'm not a lawyer, but in the real world it was not meaningful.

Q: To the law, the statutes are the real world, Mr. Rosten. Did anyone at Day and Domes inform Gnomon Co. of the security breaches?

A: We were prepared to discuss any and all subjects, including data security, but as you know, Gnomon canceled the meeting.

Q: You were planning to inform them the day the attacker struck Gnomon?

A: We were prepared to discuss any and all subjects.

Q: Was it in your formal presentation?

A: We anticipated questions. In fact, this was indicated on the first slide, which laid out an agenda for the evening.

Q: For the record, the agenda says Q and A, nothing more. Let's move to the second attack. It went beyond your CEO, did it not?

A: The first one did, too. It targeted Dell Lawton.

Q: The man with cancer you fired.

A: The second attack was very similar to the first, affecting only a slightly larger group of very senior executives of D&D.

Q: Including you?

A: Yes.

Q: You must have felt the materiality of that.

A: Actually the second incident reinforced our view that the activity was a strictly limited internal personnel issue. I'm sure Dell Lawton was able to explain why better than I can.

Q: Confine yourself to what you know, not what you assume others have told us. Or have you discussed with Mr. Lawton his testimony?

A: We did not speak.

Q: Not since you threw him under the bus?

A: Not since he left the company.

Q: Why did you decide you needed him out?

A: Database security had been his responsibility. I believe he understood.

Q: You chose the man who was expendable.

A: The decision concerning Dell Lawton was made in light of all the facts and circumstances.

Q: Facts and circumstances. If I didn't know better, I would

think you were a lawyer, or had been taught to speak like
one.

Counsel: I must object to the insults. The Assistant United
States Attorney did not even ask a question.

Q: You think it is insulting to tell someone he sounds like an attorney at law?

Counsel: I am not here to be questioned.

Q: Let's turn to the issue of disclosure. Mr. Rosten, did you ever
talk with Mr. Joyce about whether to report the crime?

A: We discussed operational matters regularly.

Q: Did you recommend disclosure?

A: My role is to identify options. Pluses and minuses. Disclosure
at various levels was among the options.

Q: And did you favor it?

A: I tried to keep an open mind.

Q: Didn't the CEO want your view?

A: He got advice from many people, including distinguished
outside counsel.

Q: Are you talking about the man sitting next to you?

A: I am talking about his firm and about Hardy Twine.

Q: You certainly bought a Lexus and a Lotus.

Counsel: It is not for you to comment on the company's legal
team.

Q: You're just unhappy that I didn't call you a Porsche.

Counsel: I am advising my client that the interview is obviously
over and he is free to leave.

Q: Struck a real nerve there, didn't I. Stay where you are, Mr.
Rosten. I want a direct answer to whether you favored disclosure.

A: The CEO and I concurred in the decision.

Q: Didn't you advise him to at least notify the Audit Committee?

A: We discussed it. We agreed that there was nothing material to notify the Audit Committee about.

Q: Given all the multifarious facts and circumstances.

Counsel: You do not have to respond to that.

Q: So you did not notify your Audit Committee or board. You did not notify the firm you sought to acquire. You most certainly did not notify law enforcement authorities. You wanted to acquire Gnomon without its shareholders and yours being any the wiser about the failure of your security systems and the felon in your midst.

A: We were prepared to deal with all issues pertaining to security if the discussions reached that point. But of course they did not take place.

Q: So if they were smart enough to ask exactly the right question during a frantic weekend, you might have given them a straight answer.

Counsel: I am not hearing a question.

A: I cannot say what would have happened. The negotiations were aborted. I can only say that we were prepared.

Q: Just as you have been so very well prepared today.

Counsel: Will that be all?

Q: For the moment.

The prosecutor stood abruptly. She was first out of the room.

Joyce could not hide from Rosten his strained relations with the board. The directors had hired their own lawyer. There were long executive sessions with Joyce out of the room. Decisions were held in abeyance. Pending what? The Admin News Network provided nonstop rumors. One had it that Sabby Chandrahari had been asked to become CEO but that he preferred to continue running money. Another was that the board retained Joyce only on condition that he identify and groom a successor. But in the end nothing happened, except that the executive sessions abated and the company settled back into itself.

Joyce seemed firmly in command as the spring board meeting approached. Rosten had a group working up a list of new acquisition targets. If it had been up to him, D&D would not have plunged back into the hunt so quickly. Drive operational results. Let employees catch their breath. Give the stock price a chance to rise. He was pretty sure that the board was not feeling a need for speed. In fact, on a conference call Sabby had observed that relationships on the rebound did not usually last. Afterward, Joyce told Rosten that if he ever wanted a marriage counselor he would get one without a turban.

The board meeting went well—with Joyce magisterial and Rosten doing the numbers with his hand on the Bible. The directors' questions showed that they were engaged, but not dangerously so. There was a bit of discussion about next steps, but Joyce suggested they hold it until staff left the room.

After being dismissed, the members of the senior team waited in the Green Room. Eventually they heard a door open. Two directors sped past, heading for the urinals. Rosten left the antechamber and came face-to-face with Sabby. "First-rate, as always," Sabby said. "Thank you." He turned to the elevators before Rosten had a chance to thank him back. All the directors seemed more eager than usual to be on their way. After they cleared, Rosten went to Joyce's office.

"Thought I'd debrief," he said.

Joyce nodded.

"They seemed satisfied," Rosten said, "though they weren't too talkative after. Sabby was complimentary."

Joyce continued nodding, the way he did when he wasn't listening.

"It's been a good run, you and me," Joyce said. "But nothing is forever."

It took a moment for this to register with Rosten.

"They can't do this to you," he said.

"It isn't a marathon," said Joyce, "one man going the distance. It's a relay. A runner goes as hard as he can, then he puts the baton in the next man's hand."

"If you leave, I'm leaving, too," said Rosten. "I hope they realize that."

"I'm staying on," said Joyce. "It is time for you to step off the track."

When Lawton walked away with the package Snow offered him, friends told him he should have hired a lawyer. He could claim age discrimination and a violation of the Americans with Disabilities Act for starters. He told them that if he had known how good things would be, he would have gotten himself fired years ago. That day to this, he'd had little contact with D&D save a few short e-mails from folks in his old department checking in. Life is good, he always replied. Very good. Then came the news that Rosten had been let go and soon after that a call from Gunderman asking to get together.

Gunderman was already seated when Lawton arrived at the diner. His fingers were turning a large, sweating soft drink on the table.

"Don't get up," Lawton said.

"You look well," said Gunderman. "Really . . . Well, really well."

"I feel great," said Lawton.

"I mean, you would never know . . . ," said Gunderman.

"Relax, Sam," said Lawton. "I survived. Rosten will, too."

The waitress came and took their order. When she left, Gunderman had his glass spinning like the icon on a frozen computer.

"It should have been me," he said.

"Is that why you came all the way up here?" said Lawton. "Or were you just envious?"

"I was responsible for system security," said Gunderman.

"Not when the trouble started," said Lawton.

"I left you a mess," said Gunderman.

"That was some other universe," said Lawton. "Say, how about that daughter of yours? Didn't I see her name in the *Tribune*?"

"I never said one bad word about you," said Gunderman. "They tried to get me to. Alexa Snow. The investigators. But I didn't."

"You don't have to answer to me for anything," said Lawton.

"The prosecutor was all about the people above me," said Gunderman. "Who put Greener on the investigation team? I told her I did. But somebody approved, she said. Was it Rosten? Joyce himself? And why did we fail to notify the Audit Committee? I'm just a computer nerd, I said. But did you agree? I don't have opinions about anything but code, I said."

"Sounds well played," said Lawton.

"The whole thing," said Gunderman, "I can't get it to sit right. She was pushing, pushing, and finally she got me to admit that I had warned Rosten. Ever since, I haven't felt good in my skin. I failed the test."

"It was that old nightmare, Sam. We've all had it," Lawton said, "the one where you never took the class."

Bureaucratic rules are supposed to hold everything together. A server farm in Iowa must look exactly the same as one in Colorado. A cubicle in a newly constructed building in North Carolina should have precisely the same dimensions as one on the sixth floor of the landmarked Dome. This was why it had taken an age for Sara to get the full-length mirror in which she was now examining herself for flaws. There simply were no corporate specs for "mirrors, door mounted, individual." The one they finally installed was so heavy that whenever she closed the door and watched herself disappear, it felt as if she were locking herself in a vault.

She stood sideways before it, talking to the image the way she did before a cold call. You've made the most of what you were given, old girl. No, not so very old. Younger than the man you're dining with, though he seemed to live outside of time. When she finished and closed the vault, he was standing there.

"Am I way too early?" Sam said. "I always do that. I don't know why. Can't seem to help it. I'm sorry."

"Goodness," she said, "I don't believe I have ever seen you in a suit and tie."

"I wanted to be sure they let me into that club of yours," he said.

"Not even at a board meeting," she said. "Ratty sport coats, yes, but jacket and pants that match?"

The suit had lapels as wide as wings.

"Wedding," he said.

"Vintage."

"My wedding, actually."

"Ah," she said.

She maneuvered him toward the closet then swung the door back open until the two of them were in the same frame. For a moment she leaned out of it to lift a hanger from the bar. When she came back into the picture, she held a sharp new sport jacket against his chest.

"Thank goodness it works with your pants," she said, though they were almost as floppy at the cuffs as bell-bottoms.

"I wouldn't feel right," he said.

"Yes, you will," she said. "Exactly right. I had it tailored from the measurements the salesman made when we were at Brooks. We do need to bring you in for final alterations. Would tomorrow work for you?"

"I can't accept it, Sara."

"And I can't return it," she said. "Anyway, it isn't only me. Margery went in on it. We both owe you."

She went behind him and slipped off his suit jacket smoothly, the way she had learned working retail, so that he felt no more than a breeze whispering across his shoulders. It had been a long time since she had taken a jacket off a man.

"Isn't there a policy about gifts?" Sam said as she put the new one on him.

"It looks great," she said. "You look great. Look at yourself."

Her line of sight was over his shoulder, which made it appear that they were much closer than she dared. She moved a little to the left so that their cheeks seemed to touch.

"You will be the envy of all the gentlemen at the Standard Club," she said.

"Because of who I'm with."

She caught him looking at the reflection of her eyes, but then he looked down. She circled slowly, keeping her face to him like an old and stately dance from Masterpiece Theater. When she was back in front of him, she settled his lapels and swept his shoulders.

"Shall we?" she said.

It had taken a lot to get him to agree to dinner. He had obsessed about being spotted by the Admin News Network. Maybe they should leave the Dome separately. The only way she was leaving the Dome, she had told him, was on his arm. Now, in the lobby together under the mosaics—he in his sharp new jacket, she having made the very best of what God gave her—she slid her hand into the crook of his elbow, and he did not pull away. Nor did he stammer an explanation to the guard. And after they did a quadrille through the brass revolving door, he actually opened a space for her hand between his elbow and his side and took a long, deep breath of the cool June air.

She led him with gentle pressure and the shifting of her center of balance. He seemed comfortable enough following as she turned him at the corner and then again at a light. They did not walk fast. It was a lovely evening, he said. Yes, she said, the kind she had hoped for.

She had not been at her new club often since it had granted her membership. She had been taking clients to restaurants. The club was still her father, not her. When they entered the lobby, she balked. Sam wasn't expecting it and continued forward a step. She did not know the entry protocol. Fortunately, the man at the desk looked up, smiled, and nodded. She turned Sam toward the stairs.

"Do you mind walking up?" she said.

"How many floors?"

"Just three."

"Just," he said.

The walls were clad in travertine. "It's only a kind of lime-stone," her father had told her the first time he brought her here to dinner.

"Fine marble is limestone, too, Daddy," she said. "It's just been under more pressure."

"Then it won't be long before they can chisel a statue out of me," her father said.

Sam lagged on the stairs. She could hear him breathing. When he reached the top, she took his arm again and led him into the dining room. A large abstract painting dominated the far wall.

"I don't belong here," he said. "Even with the jacket."

"You sound just like my father," she said, letting go of his elbow and taking him by the hand as the maître d' showed them to their table.

When the man left, she said, "Some people are skittish about being in a Jewish club."

"My mother's father was Jewish," he said.

"That doesn't count."

He opened the menu carefully.

"It's OK," she said. "It's kosher."

They started with a cocktail, which loosened him. His parents were Protestant, he said, but not churchy. They kept a Bible somewhere, but it was old and stuffed with obituaries, birth announcements, and programs from weddings and graduations. He had never seen anyone actually reading it. His father was a quiet man, a bookkeeper. At home he read *National Geographic* and Russian novels. He loved *Scientific American*, always saving the "Mathematical Games" for last.

"Sometimes he would take me through a solution," Sam said. "Of course, I couldn't really follow it."

"Smart father," she said. "He made you want to. That's how you got so bright."

When the waiter returned, he delivered a dramatic reading of the specials. She ordered the salmon. Sam did, too. The salad came with merciful speed.

"Good dressing," he said.

"Thank you," she heard herself say.

The entrées offered a wide range of conversation topics: the freshness of the fish, the interesting texture of the lentils, the fineness of the china.

"Have some dessert," she said as the plates were removed from the table.

"Not for me, thanks," he said.

"You don't have to worry about calories," she said. "Look at how fit you are."

The busser swept the cloth. Sam took his napkin from his lap and spread it before him, covering up spots of salmon juice.

"Why are you doing all this?" he said.

"Dinner is not so much of a thing to do," she said.

"Dressing me up, telling me I look trim, how bright I am," he said.

"You have no idea how uncommon you are," she said.

"Out of step," he said.

"Uncommonly unassuming, considering your brain," she said. "Uncommonly considerate. Courageous. Pretty good-looking, too, when you don't hide in dumpy old things. You are a catch, Mr. Gunderman."

He looked past her.

"Your wife made you feel worthless," she said. "That's what people do to the one they're betraying."

"Can you excuse me?" he said.

He got up from the table and turned, as if to hide his face. She had not wanted this. She had thought she needed to sell him on himself before she could hope to sell him on her. She was selling, and it was driving him away.

"Are you all right?" she said when he returned. "I'm so sorry I brought her up. I had no business."

"I should get home," he said.

"To Megan," she said.

"I just should."

"Well then."

She did not take his arm as they left the dining room. They passed through the lobby in silence until the man at the desk said, "Have a good evening, Ms. Simons." Maybe he had looked her up, but no matter. He recognized her existence. You can do this, girl.

Outside, the slight chill gave her an excuse to take his arm again and hold it tightly.

"I should have brought a wrap," she said.

"Take the jacket."

"Not a chance."

They reached the corner of Jackson but did not step out from the wall of the building because of the wind.

"Do you need a cab or something?" he said.

"Usually the man offers to take the lady to her door," she said. "Then the woman, if she is so inclined, asks the man up for a nightcap or a cup of coffee."

"This late?"

"It's not about caffeine," she said. "The man usually accepts."

"Is that what we are?" he said. "A man and a woman?"

"I would very much like to find out," she said.

Berry wasn't sure that even he could have broken Rosten. Under questioning, the man had not had to eat a single piece of bad paper. Not an e-mail. Not a memo to file. Not a handwritten note that turned up in somebody else's drawer. Though Berry knew that Rosten had pushed Joyce to disclose, the man avoided saying so under intense interrogation, even as Joyce was preparing him a shroud.

Being unafraid protects a man better than any lawyer can. There were times when Berry wished he could have had Rosten as his client rather than Joyce, but Berry had his partners to consider, and if anyone was going to survive to do more business with the firm, it was obviously not going to be Rosten.

Of course, at the outset there had been a fair chance that the board would call Joyce to account. The directors had probably balked because they had reasoned, badly, that firing him would be an admission that the security problem had been material. If things had been different and the directors had hired Berry as their separate counsel, he would have advised them that changing out a CEO after a company soiled itself was a fiduciary's safest move. He would have warned them that if they let Joyce stay, he would not necessarily be chastened. When a bullet brushes past a big man's temple, it often makes him feel both invincible and fixated on vindication, as if do-overs eradicated mistakes. In Berry's firm they referred to this as the corporate mulligan, and it kept many attorneys' families in luxury cars.

As the investigation played out, there had been no doubt that the prosecutor felt she needed to break Rosten. She had him back for questioning four times. The last two sessions, Berry himself represented him. She was relentless. It was for just this quality that Berry had hired her when he had been U.S. Attorney. He wasn't surprised that she stepped over the line and asked whether Rosten had been trained by the CIA to lie.

"I did not have that kind of assignment," Rosten had said.

"What exactly was your assignment?" she said.

"If you are cleared to know," he said, "you will be able to find that out for yourself."

He was simply masterful. He never told a single plain lie, as far as Berry knew. Evasions, yes. Deflections. Incompletions. But never a contradiction of provable fact that she could use to pry him open. This reduced her to insult.

"You were terrified that you would be fired if people found out about the hacking, weren't you," she said.

"I'm afraid I'm not the frightened person you want me to be," he said.

Berry regretted having to sacrifice such a man, but the directors made it clear to Joyce that somebody had to go down if he didn't. Berry assured them that there was very little chance of Rosten flipping, even if they severed him. The man seemed to want nothing for himself.

"A man to be envied," said the Sikh, who was the only director who spoke up for Rosten's retention.

"It must have been hard for you," Donna said.

"He let me down," Brian said, picking up the pile of mail she had put at his place at the table.

The troubles at the Dome had closed him up. When she said so, he told her it was her imagination.

"Is it the boys', too, then?" she said.

"I'll come to the school play or whatever it is, if that's what they want," he said.

"I don't think it's that," she said.

She had thought that when the board finally embraced him again, it would bring him some peace. Instead, it launched him on a mad search for a major deal that he could complete and that would complete him. It was as if he had not lost a business opportunity when he lost Gnomon, but rather one of his limbs.

"We'll blow Gnomon out of the water," he said.

"It isn't a North Korean warship," she said.

"Data is going to be huge," he said. "Cash-register receipts tagged by loyalty programs, official records opened up by the Freedom of Information Act, click-throughs on web sites. One day those BlackBerries everyone is carrying will reveal in real time what their owners are doing—GPS location, imagery from built-in cameras, actual voices. Algorithms will sift through the vast stream of e-mails. We will know every person in the market, really know him."

He did not seem to care about the fleshy versions. They were simply emitters of information, like antennae, like stars, like violas, like Donna.

He did not notice, but she doubled the hours she practiced—scales, exercises, études. It was not that she had designs on moving up a chair. She practiced in search of her own voice, what was left of it after all the years of trying to meld with his. The viola spoke things she could not say. Dissonant double stops. Cries at the top of the instrument. Anyone who had heard it might have feared for her. But he did not hear. When he was there, she was silent. And he was not much there.

One day, after she got the boys off to school, she repaired to the music room and found, atop the piano on a cloth of wine-dark velvet, a precious baroque viola. Next to it lay an ivory card impressed with a description of the instrument's provenance. She ran her finger over the indentation of the letters but did not read the words. Instead, she slid her two hands under the cloth and instrument and carried them to his office at the opposite corner of the house. There she laid them on his desk and wrote on the back of the card, "Thank you, Brian. But this is not me."

The courtroom ceiling was so low that it seemed to bear down on the raised bench. For some reason Grace had expected a cavernous space, a theater of justice, but this one had just two short rows of pews behind the railing and but a few steps between the lawyers' tables and the judge. There was only one person in the room when she poked her head in, an elderly fellow in a worn plaid jacket, striped vest, and denim shirt. A colorless tie dribbled down his front. He was asleep.

She had managed to get to the courthouse more than an hour early, prodded by the fear that something awful would happen and she would not get there at all. She had checked and rechecked her alarm before going to bed and risen an hour before it rang. In the taxi, she had compulsively pulled at the sleeve of her dress to get to her watch until the jersey knit sagged.

She wished they could have concluded the divorce without appearing in open court, but her lawyer wanted to get Jim under oath that his financial disclosures were accurate. This had infuriated him. She had assured her lawyer that the numbers were right; she was the one who had kept the books. Money wasn't what Jim lied about, she said. "When they lie," her lawyer said, "they lie."

Rather than fretting in the courtroom, she decided to take advantage of the weather. She wandered up Centre Street to Broome. When she and Jim were new to the city, they had come here often and pretended it was the other side of the globe. The smell of ginger in hot oil. Ideograms stacked up on the signs like mah-jongg tiles. The gold on vermilion that you never saw anywhere else. She and Jim would make their way through the crowds, past old people in faded black, until they found an authentic-looking place to eat. The menus were always stained with sauce, the translations delightfully approximate.

The other side of the globe and together had both been illusions. Apart forever was what she wanted now. In the courtroom on Centre she and Jim would stand on either side of the aisle, his lawyer his best man, her lawyer her father taking her back. Then it would be over. Grace felt a fullness in her eyes.

Tom had wanted to be with her, which was sweet of him, but she had said no. She was glad of it now. If he had come and they had wandered in Chinatown and the tears had gathered, he might have thought they were regret rather than fear that it would all happen again, that one day he would look at her as if he saw a stranger looking back.

She took a different route returning to the courthouse, passing only official buildings, which gave off no scent. Once Jim arrived, late and annoyed, the proceedings went quickly. Grace fixed her eyes on the official seal on the front of the elevated bench. She could not bear to look at anyone, not even the small woman in robes.

"Are you satisfied that you are being fairly treated in this settlement?" the judge asked. "I'm speaking to you, ma'am."

Grace forced her eyes upward.

"Yes," she said, her voice so fragile that she sounded even to herself like a woman who needed protection.

The judge then pronounced the words.

Jim was quick out the door. She waited to let him clear. Outside, she hailed a taxi, which sped up the West Side Highway. Tom would probably be deep in a book when she got home. These days he spent hours and hours reading. There were times when she looked at the volumes piled on each side of the chair and wondered how long he would be satisfied moving them from one side to the other.

Maybe a job, though neither of them needed the money, what with his net worth and her settlement. It frightened her to see him idle. He was drawn to intensity, and she was its opposite.

"Perhaps going back for a Ph.D.," she said.

"Do I look like a professor to you?" he said.

In his chinos and open-collar dress shirt, sitting between his Doric columns of words, in fact he did.

"Maybe an MFA," she said.

"I've become a citizen of a nation of actuaries," he said. "I have nothing to say."

Secrets of state, dead men, and wicked women. Corporate scandal. There was a reason danger marked his past. Nothing to say? He did not see the pattern. Maybe only others could. She was afraid that someone like Harms would walk into his boredom. Or that woman in Washington. An intensity so raw that it would capture him again.

Stop. He was not at all like Jim. He was the anti-Jim. He had never lied to her. The worst he had ever done was to be brutally honest. Now he told her that he was feeling a contentment he had never known. "Believe me," he said. But when they made love, he seemed to hold back. She wanted to scream for him to crack her open and let everything she held in pour out. But she never did. Afterward he touched her back lightly with his fingertips as she lay atop him, a generous energy passing between them over a completed circuit, alternating current, back and forth. If only this could be enough.

She had asked him once if it was. He had said she could not begin to know how much it was. But he knew how to speak shadows the way poets did. What he said was that she could not begin to know. Those were his words. She could not know.

The taxi dropped her at the corner. The doorman said her name. She opened the door of the flat, and there he was, still showing the glow of a run. He put down his book. It was Browning. He rose, and she folded into him.

Even with the labor of breath and the acid gathering in the muscles of his legs, the river enchanted Rosten. It was a moving sheet of coated glass reflecting the sky, or the sky the water, both pure surface and infinitely deep. It did not seem right to feel so peaceful while Grace was in a courtroom living out the end of a great sorrow.

Not long after moving to Manhattan with her, Tom had taken up jogging—if you could dignify his shuffle with such a word. He had been too long sedentary. Too much had pooled inside. He needed to sweat it out. And never more than today, when things were beginning and coming to an end.

Grace had bought him athlete's clothes, praised him every day that he ran. She was so patient with him. No, she had been patient the first time, when he had shown up out of nowhere, lost, and rung her apartment buzzer. This was much more than patience. This time she had come to him.

By the time she did, he had become an urban hermit. Plastic forks and knives lay in the sink by the dozen. Greasy cartons of fried rice moldered in the trash. He had not breathed open air since leaving the Dome. Before Berry's rent-a-cops escorted him out of his office, he had centered his company BlackBerry on his desk, gotten his suit jacket from the closet, and asked Gail to box up his personal things. If anybody questioned any of the items, let them have them, he said. All except one book of poems that he pulled down and handed her. Gail suggested that he take it along, but he said he wasn't ready.

Weeks later he still wasn't. His things sat unopened on his living room floor. From time to time, lines of verse came back to him as if spoken from inside one of the boxes. One from Browning haunted him with hope, as it must have haunted Pound: "Why is it that, disgraced, they seem to relish life the more?"

Then came a knock on his door. He wasn't going to respond, for the same reason that he had unplugged his telephones and stayed off e-mail, but it was so tentative that it had to be just some child soliciting for a cause. He pulled a fifty-dollar bill from his wallet to make the problem go away.

If he had looked through the fish-eye, he might have snuck back to the living room, but he did not look. And when the sticky outside air rushed in at him, there she was, the summer sun behind her, a roller bag on the doorstep at her side.

"You shouldn't be here," he said.

"There was no other way to reach you," she said.

"There's a reason for that."

"May I come in?"

He looked at her roller bag.

"I came straight from O'Hare," she said, "with no strategy."

He stepped aside, leaving his arm outstretched to hold the door. Once she was inside, he watched her take in the pizza disk congealed on the table, the smudged glasses with amber residue, the unopened boxes.

"What happened?" she said.

"I stayed loyal this time," he said.

"It isn't a repetition."

"Except the part with the man on the Wall of Stars and me running to you."

"I seem to have run to you," she said. "And nobody died."

He cleared the couch for himself and let her stay that night. The next day she gathered up the garbage and put it in the Dumpster. Then she picked up a rag and began to wipe down surfaces. He began to vacuum.

When he was ready to listen, she told him his story her way. Introducing him to himself, she called it: He had resisted the deal as too expensive. He had urged Joyce to disclose their security problem. He had been steady when things had started to unravel. If he'd had his way, Day and Domes would have been a lot better off right now.

They began walking together every day along the lake. Finally she led him back to his bed. Then he opened the boxes and eventually got many more so that he could load the other things in the apartment and go to New York with her.

Now here he was on the Upper West Side, taking the air on the greensward along Riverside Drive, marking his days by a calendar of books that moved from one side of his chair to the other. Occasionally he allowed himself a regret that he had come to this place so indirectly instead of straight from New Haven a long time ago. It had apparently required disgrace.

When she returned from court, she wept. He held her.

"Why am I so sad?" she said. "I wanted this."

"I guess what a person wants sometimes comes with loss inside," he said.

"I'm afraid," she said.

"So am I," he said.

"Even now, after everything?" she said.

"Yes," he said. "That's why."